MARK ROBSON

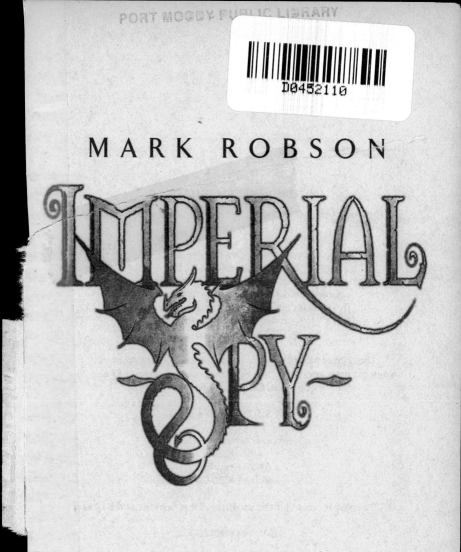

SIMON AND SCHUSTER

SIMON AND SCHUSTER

First published in Great Britain by Simon & Schuster UK Ltd, 2006
A Viacom company

1 3 5 7 9 10 8 6 4 2

Simon & Schuster UK Ltd
Africa House
64-78 Kingsway
London WC2B 6AH

A CIP catalogue record for this book is available from the British Library

ISBN 1-416-90185-X

Typeset by Rowland Phototypesetting Ltd, Bury St Edmunds, Suffolk
Printed and bound in Great Britain by
Cox & Wyman Ltd, Reading, Berks

For Ruth (Senior),
Mother, Grandmother, Great Grandmother,
Wise Woman, Word Wizard and Friend.
All this and still only 35 ... plus a bit of VAT!

DRAMATIS PERSONAE

In Shandrim, Capital City of Shandar

FEMKE – Talented young spy for the Emperor of Shandar. Mistress of disguise.

SURABAR – Military General of the Shandese Legions. Becomes Emperor after the death of the imposter Emperor, Lord Vallaine.

SHALIDAR – Member of the Guild of Assassins and long time adversary of Femke.

LORD VALLAINE – Sorceror Lord of the Inner Eye. Known for his cunning and evil. Is using his powers of sorcery to pose as Emperor after using Shalidar to kill the real one.

VAMMUS – Commander of a Shandese Legion. An overweight soldier with ideas above his station.

LORD FERRAND – Master Spy. Mentor of Femke. Missing, presumed dead for two years.

LADY ALYSSA – A phantom. That is, an alias of Femke. A spoilt young woman known to be the daughter of a rich Merchant Lord from a coastal city. The true Lady Alyssa – An unattractive young lady. Reclusive daughter of a Merchant Lord from the coastal city of Channa.

VERSANDE MATTHIASON – Proprietor of the Silver Chalice, a high class inn located in the centre of Shandrim.

RIKALA – Dressmaker and friend of Versande Matthiason.

REYNIK – Newly qualified Legionnaire of the General's Elite Legion. One of only two such elite Legionnaires yet to reach their eighteenth birthdays.

LORD DANAR – A handsome young playboy of the Imperial Court. Only son of Lord Tremarle, a powerful old-school Lord. Renowned as a philanderer in the Shandese Court, he is smitten with Lady Alyssa, an alter ego of Femke.

LORD TREMARLE – Powerful old-school Lord of Shandar. Father of Lord Danar.

LORD KEMPTEN – Old-school Lord of Shandar. Regent of the Shandese Empire in Emperor Surabar's absence.

SIDIS – File Leader from the General's Elite Legion. Companion to Femke during her journey to Thrandor.

KALHEEN – Overweight servant from the Imperial Palace in Shandrim. Prone to exaggeration and an incessant storyteller. Travelling companion to Femke during her journey to Thrandor.

PHAGEN – Servant from the Imperial Palace in Shandrim. Slim and introvert travelling companion to Femke during her journey to Thrandor.

LADY KEMPTEN – Gracious Lady wife of Lord Kempten. Known affectionately as Izzie by her husband.

In Mantor, Capital City of Thrandor

MALO – King of Thrandor. A kind old man, used to reigning over a peaceful kingdom, but who has recently faced hostile invasions of his country from both North and South.

KRIDER – Head of the Royal household staff of the King of Thrandor.

VELDAN – Chief Butler at the Royal Palace in Mantor.

LORD SHANIER – Acolyte of Lord Vallaine who outwitted his master by deliberately leading a Shandese army to their destruction in southern Thrandor.

BARON ANTON – Long time close friend of King Malo. Potential heir to the throne before his murder.

COUNT DREBAN – Unsavoury Nobleman of the Royal Court of Thrandor.

ENNAS – A name assumed by one of Femke's fellow Imperial spies. Sent by Emperor Surabar to help Femke.

LORD BRENDEN – Thrandorian Nobleman. Speaker for the prosecution at Femke's trial.

COMMANDER SATERIS – Commander of the Shandese First Legion. Speaker for the defence at Femke's trial.

PENNOLD – Alchemist called as a witness at Femke's trial.

PROLOGUE

'Seize that man! He's to be held on charges of treason.'

For the slightest instant, Shalidar was off balance. He was expecting to meet the Emperor. Instead, General Surabar was standing inside the Emperor's study, pointing at him with an accusing finger. The two guards who had entered the room with Shalidar were slow to react to the order. Survival instinct and a wealth of experience gave him the edge he needed. In the blink of an eye, Shalidar spun, hands flashing blows that felled both guards before they had a chance to move. Without pause, he drew a knife and hurled it at the General.

Time seemed to slow as he released the blade. As it left his hand, he saw the spy girl, Femke, draw a blade from her boot. Her face held a strange combination of pain and determination and her grey-blue eyes chilled him with their intensity. General Surabar swayed aside, avoiding the thrown blade in an astonishing display of agility for one so old. Almost simultaneously Femke threw her knife as

Shalidar launched into a dive out through the open door.

The knife sliced past him so close that he felt it go by. It rammed home into the wooden door-frame with a juddering thud, leaving the assassin in no doubt that it had been thrown with deadly force. Nobody had come that close to killing him for many years. Worse, the blade had been thrown by a young woman who had barely crossed the threshold into adulthood.

Assassins were normally the unseen killers – unknown and unexpected. Hits were planned meticulously to avoid any chance of the assassin being caught. There were always random factors that defied the best planning, but Shalidar had a flair for improvisation. He was the best in the business and only the richest could afford to call on his services. No hit was planned today, but somehow, Femke had turned the tables on him. The young woman had set him up, for which he would exact a painful retribution in due course. For now, his focus was on a clean escape from the Palace.

Like a shadow fleeing from the light, Shalidar raced down the corridor. His footfalls made no sound and he ran so smoothly that he appeared to flow along the passage-ways. After a few turns the assassin paused to glance behind him and listen. There was no sign of pursuit, but he refused to take unnecessary chances.

Shalidar was known around the Palace, though few knew his profession. Most thought him a bodyguard or an advisor to the Emperor. The secrecy was essential, for if the truth of his role in the Palace became known, he would become useless as a weapon.

Thoughts flashed through Shalidar's mind as he reviewed

his situation. The complexities of his web of deceit and his history of meddling in Imperial affairs were now in tatters. It was most infuriating. Anger burned in his gut, but he clamped down on the emotion and concentrated.

It appeared that General Surabar was assuming power in Shandar, which was extremely bad news for all assassins. The General was well known for his dislike of hired killers. He believed that killing was what soldiers did out of necessity in battle, not a trade for those who looked to gain wealth at the expense of the lives of others. It made sense for Shalidar to get out of the capital as swiftly as possible. Maybe he should even consider leaving Shandar altogether.

Shalidar had always had an aloof disdain for what he saw as the oafish and obvious ways of the military, but he did respect General Surabar's reputation for efficiency and thoroughness. With the huge numbers of troops in the city maintaining public order in the wake of the recent unrest, General Surabar had the power to make life difficult for Shalidar.

'Time to move on,' he whispered, unconsciously twisting a silver wristlet part hidden by his sleeve. 'But first, one loose end to tidy up.'

Proceeding at a brisk walk, Shalidar slipped along the corridors towards the nearest exit. Within minutes he was outside of the Palace building and heading for the nearest of the gates out into the city. The guard at the gate barely glanced in Shalidar's direction as the killer left the Palace grounds – his remit was to keep undesirables out of the Palace, not to keep people in.

Once out into the streets, Shalidar slowed his pace to a

stroll, blending his passage into the normal bustle of the city. Lots of soldiers were abroad, mainly in small groups of six to ten, patrolling for signs of trouble. Shalidar chose his route to avoid areas of the city where disturbances were likely. None of the soldiers gave him a second glance as he ambled past their patrols. Street by street, he moved purposely from the central area of the city towards the heart of the military district.

Normally, Shalidar would spend days planning a hit, but now he did not have that luxury. He knew the layout of his next victim's residence intimately, otherwise he would have been forced to abandon the kill. As it was, the risk involved was considerable, but that could not be helped. His current employer, Commander Vammus, knew too much about his recent activities. If the General leaned on him, Shalidar knew the Commander would bleat. Vammus had done nothing wrong, but to Shalidar, he was redundant – a dangerous source of information to be disposed of before General Surabar had a chance to reach him. There was no question of conscience, or regret. This was business. There was one small problem. The Commander was staying with the other top commanders in the General's residence.

There would be one fleeting opportunity for the hit. The audaciousness of what he was about to attempt brought a wolfish smile to his lips as he imagined how his fellow assassins would view it: a hit with all the hallmarks of a legend. He pulled back his right sleeve and gazed at the stylised image of the dragon on his silver wristlet. Yes, he thought. It would be a kill worthy of the dragon.

Shalidar knew no other assassin who would brave General Surabar's house in broad daylight without prior planning, kill one of his commanders, and expect to get away with it. Yet Commander Vammus had made this both possible, and almost straightforward. The Commander had arranged to occupy the room that offered the easiest concealed access to the house. He had done so to facilitate secret meetings with Shalidar in a place that no one would expect conspirators to meet. If all went well, the Commander's duplicity would now prove his undoing.

Shalidar approached the house along the alleyway that ran between the General's residence and the adjacent house. There was no one in sight and the assassin quickly scaled the high garden wall, being careful to peep over and confirm that the garden was empty before pulling himself onto the top. There was one small window on this side of the house and Shalidar knew that the chance of someone looking out and seeing him during these few seconds were slim.

From the top of the garden wall, a narrow ledge that ran right around the house was one large step away, and in daylight the short jump was easy to judge. Shalidar jumped across without hesitation, conscious that success now depended upon speed, silence and a moderate amount of good fortune.

As swiftly as he could, the assassin shimmied along the ledge and around one difficult corner to the back face of the house. Once there, Shalidar reached up and felt for the ledge below the Commander's window. His fingers found purchase and with a heave he pulled himself up, soundlessly transferring his weight onto the flat of one forearm once high enough.

Commander Vammus was alone, scratching away intently at a parchment with his quill. He was so absorbed in his work he did not notice Shalidar until the assassin quietly opened the window.

The Commander's eyes went wide with surprise.

'Sha . . .' he started, rising from his chair.

Shalidar's stare caused his name to die on Vammus's lips. Leaping down from the window ledge to land silently inside, Shalidar placed a finger to his lips and then pointed at the door. Just as he expected, Vammus unconsciously turned his head to look where Shalidar was pointing. The assassin used that moment to step up close and, with an expert grab and twist motion, snapped the hapless Commander's neck in one swift movement.

Shalidar staggered as he prevented Vammus from falling to the floor, cursing under his breath that the dead Commander had not kept in shape. Shalidar's former employer was so overweight that he would have struggled to lead men in an infantry campaign. It was amazing to Shalidar that a renowned General like Surabar would tolerate an officer like Vammus under his command. Fat and incompetent, Shalidar thought with a grimace. If it weren't for the information you held, Surabar might have thanked me for killing you.

Careful not to make any unnecessary noise, Shalidar heaved the dead Commander's body to the door and opened it a crack. There was no one on the upper landing, but Shalidar could hear voices in conversation emanating from one of the rooms to his left and further voices down-stairs. For a moment, Shalidar wondered if he needed to make the Commander's death look accidental. The General was unlikely to be fooled, so why do it? He could slip out of the window now and no one would be any the wiser, but the top of the stairwell was so near and Shalidar hated a sloppy job. The body falling down the stairs would provide an excellent diversion, masking any sounds of his escape.

His resolve hardened. He opened the door and dragged Vammus swiftly to the top of the stairs. One powerful heave and the Commander's body tumbled down the staircase with a series of loud thumps and thuds, bringing exclamations and the sound of running feet.

Shalidar was fast. In a flash he was back through the door and had silently closed it behind him. Seconds later he was outside the window and lowering himself back down to the ledge beneath.

No one except Surabar would suspect that Vammus had done anything other than trip and fall down the stairs, but Surabar was still at the Palace. The commotion inside made Shalidar smile. The hit had worked like a dream. The dragon had struck again.

CHAPTER ONE

'. . . Very well, I'll take the Mantle of Emperor, but I want it known that I'm only acting as Regent until a more suitable candidate presents himself.'

'Your Imperial Majesty,' Femke said, curtsying deeply and bowing her head, 'might I suggest you would be better not to announce your future intentions, or you'll be inundated with Noblemen, major and minor, all claiming to be suitable candidates for the Mantle. Why don't you take the title, then bestow it on the most suitable candidate in your own time? If no one knows your intent, you'll be more likely to see them as they really are.'

'Good, Femke! Your logic is sound. There are commanders I've worked with who could do with a dose of your powers of reasoning. So be it. Go. Spread the word that Emperor Surabar is in control and things are going to change.'

'Yes, your Majesty. With pleasure.'

Before leaving, Femke walked around the desk to recover

her first dagger from the shoulder of the dead Sorcerer Lord, Vallaine. Even in death, Vallaine's eyes emanated a disturbing evil. Femke considered leaving the dagger where it was, but did not want to display her discomfort to the new Emperor. She bent and jerked the blade forcibly from the Sorcerer's shoulder.

Blood pooled in the wound, but did not flow out; the final proof that Vallaine's heart had stopped. The Sorcerer had shown surprising resilience to her poison during their struggle. The thought had occurred to Femke that he might be using sorcery to fool her again, but there was no faking this. The Sorcerer was dead.

In the past, killing had always produced a profound guilt in Femke. The taking of another's life was a terrible deed, and the young spy had often been haunted in dreams by those whose lives she had taken. The list of her victims was not long, but there had been times when killing had been necessary. Femke had never ducked responsibility. Taking the life of Lord Vallaine, however, brought no guilt. Looking at the twisted features of the Sorcerer, Femke judged that if evil could manifest itself as a person, then Vallaine's was a fitting guise.

Vallaine's devious plot to win ultimate power in Shandar had been clever. He and Shalidar had fooled the entire Palace staff with their deception. Shalidar had killed the real Emperor of Shandar for Vallaine. The Sorcerer had then used his powers to alter his own wizened features so that he could replace the Emperor with no one the wiser. Where they had hidden the real Emperor's body was still not known. It had taken Femke months to piece together the puzzle and see through Lord Vallaine's disguise, but today she had ended the Sorcerer's evil machinations and sent Shalidar running. With General Surabar taking the Imperial Mantle, the Shandese Empire could look forward to a brighter future. If anyone could tame the wild plotting of the Shandese Court, it was the General, Femke mused.

As Femke left the Emperor's study, Surabar was helping the conscious guard to his feet and telling him to mobilise the Palace guard force into a search for Shalidar.

'Femke, could you send a medic to attend to this fellow?' Surabar asked over his shoulder, indicating the unconscious guard. 'He should be all right, but someone should look him over.'

'Certainly, your Majesty,' Femke replied. With a sharp tug, she pulled her second blade from the wooden doorframe and secreted it back up her sleeve. 'I'm on my way.'

It was a very tired young woman who wearily pulled the blankets over her body that night. After the tense action of the morning, there followed an afternoon and evening of dashing around the inner city, spreading the news of Vallaine's deception and Surabar's rise to power to the most effective gossips and rumour-mongers in Shandrim, Shandar's capital. As Femke's eyes closed, her lips turned up in a gentle smile of satisfaction as she contemplated her day's work. Everyone would believe the General had unmasked Vallaine's evil deception. Her anonymity remained intact and once again she would fade quietly into the background – the perfect place for a spy. Femke hoped that Emperor Surabar would employ her skills as the last true Emperor had. She enjoyed her work.

The streets of Shandrim were buzzing with the news the next morning. There was just one topic of conversation, and Femke was pleased to note that few voices aired negative views of Surabar as the new Emperor. Femke spent an hour wandering the streets, listening to the run of conversation before returning to the Palace.

The General was in the study where Femke had last seen him the day before, though the room was barely recognisable. The drinks cabinet had gone, and the recess in the wall used by previous Emperors to conceal spies was now shelved and loaded with neat lines of books and scrolls. The desk had been moved so that it faced the door, forming an instant barrier to the person entering. All other chairs had been removed, and previous pictures and decorations replaced with a selection of gleaming weapons, all mounted with exacting military precision. There was no doubting the background of the room's owner.

As Femke entered, she bowed, sparing a quick look around to absorb the changes before returning her attention to the General's welcoming smile.

'Well? What do you think of it?' he asked with a sly smile.

'To be honest, your Majesty, I feel like I've just walked into a Court Martial, and that I'm the one on trial,' Femke replied with an apologetic shrug.

'Perfect!' he said firmly. 'That is the general idea. It's

good to see you're brave enough to be honest. I hope you'll stay that way.'

Surabar's eyes caught hers with a piercing look. The expression was easy to read – anyone close to him must be loyal to the last breath. Femke had started her relationship with the new Emperor well, but she did not know how Surabar viewed spies. His dislike for assassins was common knowledge. If he had a similar view of spies, then Femke was out of a job.

'Tell me, Femke, have you heard anything of Shalidar since yesterday?'

'No, your Majesty. I've been too busy to worry about following up on him. I take it your men haven't found him?'

Surabar scowled and tapped at his chin with a forefinger in irritation. He looked at her appraisingly for a second, his eyes taking in her slim build, straight stance and bright, intelligent eyes. His own eyes narrowed as he wondered if the blonde, shoulder-length hair was real, or a very convincing wig. Probably the latter, he decided.

The girl was perfect spy material. She was clever, deft of hand and deadly in a fight. She was neither tall, nor short. Her nose was straight and unremarkable. Her cheekbones were not distinct like a classic beauty, yet there was something of beauty in the symmetry of her features. This evenness made her features incredibly adaptable. A very useful tool, he realised.

'Apparently he was seen strolling out of the Palace after his abrupt departure from our little meeting yesterday,' the General said eventually. 'Nobody has seen him since. It appears he called on Commander Vammus in the early afternoon to pay his respects.'

'I assume the Commander didn't personally inform you of the visit,' Femke observed, giving a slight wince.

'Vammus suffered a nasty accident. Witnesses heard him fall down the stairs, but nobody heard him cry out. His neck was broken when he reached the bottom. I strongly suspect he was dead before his body rolled down the stairs.'

'I'm sure you're right, your Majesty. Shalidar is renowned in certain circles for his abilities. He wouldn't want loose ends. If Vammus had information about Shalidar's activities within the Palace, Shalidar would be sure to silence him. It looks a clear case of murder.'

Femke's thoughts settled for a moment on her mentor. Lord Ferrand had hated Shalidar. The assassin had once been a colleague and close friend of his, but Shalidar had betrayed his espionage training. He had traded his honourable status as a trusted spy for the gold that evil men were willing to pay for the hire of a professional killer. This had earned Ferrand's eternal enmity. Femke felt similarly betrayed. The mere thought of taking lives for money turned Femke's stomach.

'I thought you should be aware of this, as Shalidar might also consider you to be a loose end,' the General added, watching her reaction closely. 'The assassin appears to have been party to Vallaine's deception, though his choice to work with Commander Vammus was a strange one. Shalidar was clearly manipulating events here in the Palace to his own ends. You ruined his plans so you'll need to be very careful. I'll have my men searching for him at every opportunity, but given the ease with which he penetrated my residence in the military district, and his intimate knowledge of the Palace, you must remain alert.'

Femke was momentarily shocked. Becoming a target of the assassin had not occurred to her. They'd crossed one another several times over the last few years. Shalidar seemed to have fingers in every pie. Femke had a strong suspicion he had killed one of her few true friends in the Palace a year ago. He had also dropped hints that he knew something about her mentor's mysterious disappearance the year before. Femke had expressed her distaste for him over time by annoying him whenever possible. This had brought little satisfaction, but had given momentary pleasure on occasion.

Annoying an assassin was dangerous, but there was a certain protection offered by the Assassins' Creed. All members of the Assassins' Guild swore an oath never to kill for pleasure. Killing was business. Now the situation was different, though. Femke had crossed the line from being a simple annoyance to interfering with Shalidar's real business. He would not forget how close her knife had come to hitting him, and he was unlikely to forgive her for ruining his chances of a prosperous future in the Palace. If Vammus had gained the Emperor's Mantle, the rewards for Shalidar would have been great. Femke developed a sudden, uncomfortable feeling between her shoulder blades as her mind came to grips with her vulnerability. It was difficult to prevent the unconscious urge to roll her shoulders and relax the muscles, but she was determined not to let the General see her discomfort.

Once she had digested Surabar's theory, her sense of reasoning began to assert a new hypothesis and the uncomfortable feeling subsided.

'I'll be safe enough for the time being,' Femke said thoughtfully. 'If Shalidar wanted to take his revenge then he would have struck quickly, as he did with Vammus. With your troops scouring the city for him, Shalidar will make himself scarce for a while. If I were he, I would lie low for a few weeks until the hunt had diminished. Then I'd return and make my hit.'

General Surabar considered Femke's logic for a moment and shrugged.

'You may be right,' he admitted. 'Still, it won't hurt to take a few extra precautions. I don't want you staying in the Palace. Go to whichever safe house in the city you consider to be most secure. Report to me each day this week, but at a different time every day. I'll write you a schedule, which should be kept between you and me. Do not enter or exit the Palace through predictable gates. Keep your movements around the city random – I'm sure you know the drill.'

'Thank you, your Majesty. I'll be sure to be careful.'

'I have it in mind to give you a special mission that should put you out of Shalidar's reach for a while,' the General added, his eyes going automatically to an immaculately stacked pile of documents on his desk. 'But I'll explain that after my official crowning ceremony tomorrow.'

'Tomorrow!' Femke exclaimed. 'That will take the Nobles by surprise. They won't anticipate a ceremony that soon.'

'First rule of combat,' Surabar grinned. 'Keep the enemy

16

on the back foot. If you can keep enemies off balance and unable to anticipate your next move, they're always going to be on the defensive. The ceremony will not only be tomorrow, but as a General of the Legions, I'll ensure that the whole coronation is swamped by a heavy military presence. The Nobles won't be able to move without tripping over soldiers. I doubt that they'll try anything stupid whilst I'm surrounded by hundreds of loyal troops.'

Femke laughed aloud. There were going to be some frustrated and flustered Noblemen at the ceremony tomorrow. There would not be an assassin in the Empire crazy enough to attempt a hit with this lack of notice, in the presence of so many soldiers. The General's tactics looked excellent, though he too would need to be careful for a while – at least until the more troublesome Nobles were identified and either convinced of the soundness of his rule, or brought under control.

'You appear to have everything in hand here, your Majesty,' Femke said, mirth still evident in her voice. 'You should know that the feeling on the streets of Shandrim about your rise to power is very positive. You're naturally being attributed with single-handedly foiling the plans of Lord Vallaine. I'm sure you'd find some of the wilder versions of how you engineered his downfall amusing. More importantly, you have little to worry about from the general populace. There are many speculations as to what you'll do about the recent plans for city folk to be drafted into the Legions. And after our military defeat in Thrandor, people are curious to see how you will deal with the resulting diplomatic situation. After all, we were the invaders.

The people know that we cannot sit idly by hoping the King of Thrandor will forget our incursion. There will inevitably be reprisals unless something is done swiftly. Citizens seem curious, rather than worried. It appears the people already have a certain degree of trust in your judgement.'

Surabar nodded, his eyes distant, as he considered the implications of her information. He drummed the fingers of one hand on the surface of the desk for a moment, but did not linger long on his thoughts.

'Anything else that I should know?' he asked.

'Nothing of particular interest, your Majesty. Do you have a mission for me today? Any rumours you would like me to start, or information that you'd like me to obtain?'

'Nothing specific, Femke. Please continue to listen carefully to current rumours. I don't think you need add to the speculation at the moment. I'll start feeding information to the people after tomorrow's coronation. Rumour of the event will spread fast enough when the Nobles get their invitations this afternoon. Just be careful and lie low for now. I'd like you to be at the ceremony tomorrow. Do you have suitable clothing to pass as a Noblewoman?'

Femke raised one eyebrow slightly and smiled. 'Is the moon silver?' she asked. 'I'll blend in, your Majesty. I've mixed with the Nobility before. I'm well known to be the daughter of a country Lord from one of the coastal cities. There'll be no problem with my attending.'

'And are you the daughter of a Lord?' Surabar asked with a smile. 'I'm beginning to think nothing would surprise me about you, Femke.'

'Not at all, your Majesty,' Femke laughed. 'But I enjoy playing the part.'

'Good.'

The General pulled a piece of parchment from the desk drawer, dipped his quill into the inkpot and wrote down a list of times in a neat, bold hand. He passed it over the table to Femke. 'Here you are. Commit it to memory and destroy it. Tomorrow's meeting is in the evening to give you a chance to report on information from the ceremony. Try to get a feel for who amongst the aristocracy will support my rule, and how fully.'

'What time will the ceremony start, your Majesty?'

'The coronation will begin at the second bell past midday. There are invitations for all the local Nobles. I got the list from one of Vallaine's records. His paranoia has served me well – apparently he was having most of them watched to some degree. Here's an invitation for you as well. Who should I make it out to?'

'I'll be there as Lady Alyssa, your Majesty,' Femke replied, smiling brightly with anticipation.

Surabar wrote the name onto the invitation and handed it to her. He watched her curtsy, turn and leave the room. He smiled as he considered the task he had in mind for her. Yes, he thought. Femke will be perfect for the role. She's younger than I'd like, but she's more than sharp enough.

Femke spent that night in luxury. It made sense to be close to the Palace and she wanted to re-establish her identity as the spoilt daughter of a rich Nobleman, so she booked into

19

the Silver Chalice, one of the most expensive guesthouses in Shandrim. Before she did so, Femke made a quick side trip to change into appropriate clothing and to arrange delivery of some luggage to the guesthouse later in the day.

Shandrim was an old city. It had been the capital of Shandar since before the great expansion of the Empire. The city centre had a few buildings that dated back centuries, but large areas had been demolished and rebuilt when the present Imperial Palace was commissioned. The builders had used the opportunity to widen main streets, reducing the density of buildings and making the city centre a lighter place. In contrast, the outer quarters of Shandrim had close-packed housing with dark, narrow streets. Criminal organisations flourished and competed, making the poorer sectors dangerous to the unwary.

Femke knew every street and back alley intimately. Her network of informants and agents was extensive. Other contacts supplied her with safe houses and storage for her stashes of equipment and disguises. The nearest of these held all she needed for her role as a Noblewoman.

A wig of dark hair, intricately curled and braided in an elaborate style, combined with careful make-up and exquisitely crafted clothing, changed Femke's appearance so drastically that none but those who knew her well would have recognised her. A carefully rehearsed haughty expression and a dismissive manner completed the disguise. Femke could not help but smirk as she surveyed the results in the mirror.

Lady Alyssa was one of her favourite alter egos. Quite why Femke enjoyed playing the part of the attractive but obnoxious young Noblewoman so much, she could not say. The fact that Alyssa always lived in luxury was part of the reason, though by itself this did not explain the attraction. Femke had often posed as other wealthy characters and enjoyed similar comforts. Perhaps it was the secret enjoyment of seeing the outrage on others' faces at Alyssa's utter selfishness. There was something deliciously naughty about insisting that the owner of the Silver Chalice, Versande Matthiason, bring Alyssa's bags up to her personally, and demanding that Versande's daughter serve as her personal maid for the duration of her stay.

The Silver Chalice was one of the oldest buildings in Shandrim, giving it character that was lacking in other expensive inns in the city centre. Her room was beautifully decorated and Femke luxuriated in walking barefoot on the soft, thickly piled carpet. Everything about the room had been designed tastefully. The pictures of Nobles and horses blended with the rich, dark wood furniture and the deep reds and greens of the carpets and curtains. The bedcovers were of a creamy white with beautifully embroidered flowers, giving the bed a fresh, inviting look. The sheets had been perfectly pressed and folded with precision around the ample mattress.

It was hard to find things to complain about, but in her role as Lady Alyssa, Femke knew that it was both necessary and expected. Femke had Versande remove one of the pictures from the wall, declaring that she found one of the gentlemen in it offensive, as he appeared to be smirking at her wherever she went. She also had him remove a vase of flowers that she described as vulgar. In fact it was one of the

21

most beautiful displays that she had ever seen, but Alyssa was renowned for her irritating nature and Femke was determined not to disappoint.

Versande did as he was asked without question, for he knew of Lady Alyssa's reputation both for being a difficult guest, and for having a very deep purse. He was always willing to overlook the nuisance factors and eccentricities of his guests when they paid well.

Femke relaxed in the luxury of her room and waited until the rest of the Nobility were sure to have received their invitations to the coronation. With a mischievous heart she kept up a string of impetuous demands throughout the afternoon. It was easy to justify as character maintenance, but it was also deliciously enjoyable.

First she enjoyed a steaming hot bath, which naturally had to be at exactly the right temperature, requiring several adjustments with first hot, then cold and then hot water. After this she dried herself with soft towels, which she insisted were pre-warmed. Then she ordered dahl and was delighted to receive a wonderfully aromatic brew served with warmed cakes and a generous helping of whipped cream. Even Alyssa would have difficulty finding complaint with this, Femke decided, as she allowed the hot liquid of the dahl to dissolve the light cake on her tongue.

A gentle knock at the door sounded not long after she had finished, and the serving girl who had brought the dahl entered.

'Was that to your satisfaction, my Lady?' she asked shyly, her head down as she recovered the tray.

'It was adequate, thank you,' Femke replied haughtily.

'Tell me, girl, do you have a dressmaker on the premises? I believe I'm going to need a new outfit for tomorrow, so I shall require someone to make one for me tonight.'

'A dress by tomorrow?' the girl squeaked, a mixture of incredulity and horror in her voice. 'I'm not sure there's anyone here who could do that, my Lady. But I'll ask Father. Perhaps he will know of someone.'

'Oh, I'm sure he will,' Femke declared confidently. 'He seems like a competent enough fellow. After all, there must have been others who have needed the services of a dressmaker. I'm hardly unique in needing new clothes every now and again.'

'Yes, my Lady. I'll go and ask at once, my Lady.'

Versande's young daughter left with a flustered curtsy. The man was clearly resourceful, for within the hour a dressmaker was knocking at Lady Alyssa's door.

The dressmaker, a small, stout woman with a face that expressed little emotion, worked swiftly and with virtually no deference to Lady Alyssa's rank or station. The moment Alyssa raised her voice in complaint at the woman's brusque voice and no-nonsense manner, the little dressmaker stopped what she was doing and fixed her with a firm stare.

'Do you want a new dress by tomorrow, or not?' she asked.

'Well, of course I do—'

'Very well,' the dressmaker interrupted abruptly, 'if you're serious, then do as I tell you and give me no grief, or I'll walk out of here right now. I can guarantee that you'll find no other willing to make you a dress in less than a day, and if they did, they would not have my skill. So, what will it be?'

Femke was genuinely taken aback by the little woman's manner and realised that she had met her match. There was little to be gained by playing the stuck-up Noblewoman, so she acquiesced with a demure nod and allowed herself to be pulled and pushed around without a murmur as the dressmaker took a myriad of measurements. There were no others in the room to see her so humbled, and Femke somehow doubted the dressmaker would speak of it. She did not seem the sort to gossip.

The woman acclaimed herself the best dressmaker in Shandrim and refused to be told what to make.

'I'll make you a dress and you'll like it, or you'll not. It will matter little to me. I can always sell my wares,' she stated, her head held high. With Femke's measurements all noted on a piece of slate, the woman whisked out of the room, leaving Femke to wonder what manner of garment she would be brought the next day.

Femke need not have worried; the woman had not been bragging. The dress was stunning. It was made with a deep red silk and was perfectly complemented by superbly detailed silver thread-work. The subtle cut of the neck-line, the beautifully stitched bodice and the delicate trim around neck and cuffs were all exquisite. It was incredible that something so beautiful could be created in less than a day.

'Oh, wow!' she breathed in awe. 'That's incredible. May I try it on, please?'

'With that manner, you may,' the dressmaker responded, clearly pleased by the effect of her work.

'How is it that I've never heard of you before?' Femke asked, unconsciously slipping out of character for a moment.

'Well, I don't just work for anyone, young Lady. Friends earn my work, and Versande has been a good friend over the years.'

'Please, I have been terribly rude to you, for which I apologise. May I ask your name, for I would very much like to order clothes from you again in the future. You're a genius.'

'You may ask, Lady Alyssa, and I'll not turn down such an honest request. My name is Rikala, but giving you my name does not automatically grant you the right to my services.'

Rikala helped Femke into the dress, carefully fastening the long double row of tiny buttons up the full length of the back. It fitted perfectly, and Femke admired herself in the mirror.

'It's beautiful, Rikala. Thank you – thank you so much. How much do I owe you? Whatever the price it will be worth the result.'

'Treat my work well, Lady Alyssa,' Rikala replied. 'I will know if you have not. You may pay Versande my fee. I'm sure that he will exact a fair price. Good day now.'

Incredible, she thought, twirling again in front of the glass. No matter how much I learn about Shandrim, there are always more surprises around the corner.

To prove herself worthy of Rikala's trust, Femke ordered

a carriage to take her the short distance to the Palace that afternoon. Though it was no more than a minute's walk to the gates, Femke felt that Alyssa should arrive in a style befitting her new outfit. Besides, the Emperor's treasury was paying for her to be a rich young Lady, so she felt duty bound to play the role properly.

When she climbed out of the carriage at the Imperial Palace gates, there was no shortage of volunteers to help her down the steps. Lords and Ladies aplenty were arriving for the coronation ceremony. All were dressed in their finest for the occasion, but none failed to notice the stunningly elegant figure of Lady Alyssa. It felt wrong that eyes should be on her, as she spent most of her life being inconspicuous, yet here she was – centre stage, and loving every second of it. By being so noticeable, Femke had made herself invisible. Nobody would fail to notice her presence, but all they would see was a beautiful Noblewoman.

'Ceremonial guard duty,' grumbled Nelek from the other side of the tent. He was sitting cross-legged on his pile of blankets with a piece of armour in one hand and a cloth in the other. 'Five years in the General's Elite Legion and I'm reduced to ceremonial guard duty! What's wrong with the regulars? Why can't they polish their buckles and stand in a line?'

Reynik smiled to himself. Some people were never satisfied. The idea of standing on display for all the Nobility of Shandrim to see appealed to his pride in being a part of the General's special force. To be chosen for this Legion was an honour. Those taken straight from basic infantry training were a select few, and competition was fierce for the handful of places available each year. Reynik was one of only two members in the entire Legion who had not yet celebrated his eighteenth birthday, so the achievement felt all the more special.

The young man stared for a moment at his reflection in the shining breastplate that he was polishing. Even distorted as it was by the curving surface of the metal, Reynik was pleased to see that the face looking back at him was no longer that of a boy. The intense training programme that he had undergone had matured him both physically and mentally. Only when he grinned did the boyish exuberance still shine through in his features.

Nobody deigned to answer Nelek's grumbling. Instead, the men concentrated on getting their ceremonial armour as immaculately polished as they could. The file leader would be quick to chastise if he found so much as the slightest of blemishes in their uniform. No one with any sense upset the file leader. As far as the soldiers were concerned the file leader was a god. It followed that the file second was a demi-god, and therefore also to be obeyed without question.

Commanders, generals and those Noblemen who involved themselves with military matters were largely viewed by the men as strutting peacocks, full of their own importance but out of touch with the tough realities of front-line military life. Reynik, however, had a unique perspective on the officer ranks. Both Reynik's father and his uncle had been Commanders in the Legions. Now that he had completed both basic infantry training and advanced training for his current post, Reynik appreciated just how extensive the officers' knowledge had to be. He viewed neither his father nor his uncle as anything but the most professional soldiers he knew, and his ultimate goal was to emulate them by progressing through the ranks to the top levels. He desperately wanted to make his father proud.

Reynik had been subtly trained from the moment he took his first steps. His father had shown him first how to walk in step and then how to swing his arms like a marching soldier, making the whole process a child's game which Reynik had loved playing. As he had grown, so had the games. The father and son rough-and-tumble games that he had enjoyed had not been like those of most children. Where some dads simply rolled around on the floor in fun, Reynik's father gently introduced the techniques of unarmed combat, subtly training his son in skills that many grown men struggled to master.

As a boy, Reynik had loved to listen to his father and uncle debating tactics and military strategy. Looking back now at those discussions, it was easy to see how an officer's perspective had to differ from that of the average soldier. If his uncle had not been killed a little over two years ago, Reynik would have enjoyed listening to those debates even more now.

The memory of his uncle's murder caused a momentary knot of anger to spasm in Reynik's gut. He had been there when it happened. His uncle had not stood a chance. There had been no warning, no discernible motive, no provocation that could excuse the cold-blooded killing. One moment Reynik, his cousin and his uncle had been playing a game together in the street. The next moment a stranger had appeared as if from nowhere, stabbed Reynik's uncle in the chest and run off into a nearby alley.

Reynik had gained a fleeting glimpse of the killer's face. He knew he would never forget it. He had chased the man into the alley, but had stopped after a few paces. His cousin's cry for help had halted him in his tracks, torn with indecision. Looking back now, it was plain to see that his choice to comfort his distraught cousin was the correct one. If he had followed the killer, it was unlikely that Reynik would have survived an encounter with him.

According to his father, the killer was most likely an assassin. It was, therefore, not surprising that the authorities had never caught him. Even now Reynik always scanned faces in public places on the off chance that he could spot the killer with the idea of bringing him to justice.

'Right, men! Look lively.'

The powerful voice of the file second disrupted Reynik's reverie. Everyone scrambled to their feet and stood to attention at the end of their beds.

'Ceremonial dress. Inspection. Outside. NOW! We march to the Palace at the next call, men. Look lively now. We don't have all day.'

CHAPTER TWO

'Who is *that*?' Lord Danar breathed, his voice low and conspiratorial.

The small group of young Noblemen around him followed Danar's eyes with subtle glances and noted the progress of an attractive young woman in a regal, deep-red dress. One of the men coughed slightly.

'A fascinating match for you, Danar. Lady Alyssa has an interesting reputation.'

'Interesting? In what way, Sharyll? Speak up, man – I've never heard of Lady Alyssa before, nor seen her in Court.'

'Perhaps she has deliberately avoided you, Danar. You do have something of a predatory reputation when it comes to the ladies,' laughed one of the others in a low voice.

'No, I doubt that,' Sharyll said with a slight shake of his head. 'Lady Alyssa is a random element in Shandrim. There are times when she will attend formal functions and private parties for a week or two, and then she is not seen for months. When she next shows up, it's as if she has never been away. Where she goes and how she keeps herself so well abreast of the tattle of Court, nobody knows. She is something of an enigma.'

'Ah, I do love a challenge,' Danar muttered, his eyes still following Alyssa through the Great Hall.

'Well, you could have fooled me, after some of the young ladies you have chosen to share your affections with recently! You can hardly say your last conquest was a challenge now, can you? She was all over you like a rash the moment you showed the first sign of interest in her.' Sharyll's eyes danced with amusement as he observed Danar's intense gaze. 'Lady Alyssa is very different to your usual fare. One might say her lack of relationships is what makes her unique – she's the impossible catch. It's said she's the only daughter of a wealthy Merchant Lord from one of the coastal cities, though which city I've never heard confirmed. Money drips from her fingers, but her moods are capricious and she shuns the slightest hint of any romantic advance. You may as well try to catch the dawn mist in a jar, Danar – you'll get nowhere.'

The young Lord tore his gaze away from Lady Alyssa and fixed his eyes on his friend's grinning face. An expression of amusement lit his roguishly handsome features and he ran his fingers unconsciously through his jet-black hair. With a grin that accentuated his boyish dimples and set a light in his bright blue eyes, Danar gave a chuckle.

'That's a gauntlet I can't resist. Ten gold sen says that I'll have her walking by my side within a week,' he announced.

'Done,' accepted Sharyll without hesitation. 'I can feel the extra weight of your gold in my purse already. You're throwing your money away, my friend. The old Danar charm will work no wonders on Lady Alyssa. She'll see through you in an instant. You're setting yourself up for a fall, Danar, and we'll all have a laugh at your expense and a keg of ale when you pay up.'

The other young Noblemen sniggered, but Danar ignored them, choosing instead to scan the crowd for Alyssa again, his mind whirling with ideas on how he should approach her.

The gathering in the Great Hall of the Imperial Palace included Shandrim's entire high-society clique. Everyone who was anyone milled amongst the towering pillars of the Hall, but far from being civilised and light-hearted, the buzz of conversation harboured a potentially explosive mixture of emotion. Pockets of anger and outrage were interspersed with excitement and jubilation. Facial expressions ranged from sober to virtually ecstatic; from eager anticipation to foreboding frowns. Femke was glad that Surabar had decided on a heavy military presence. Her senses were screaming warnings that the event was a disaster waiting to happen.

Maintaining a serene visage, Femke breezed through the crowd, turning heads wherever she went. It was easy to play the Lady looking as she did. She silently blessed Rikala again. With subtle curtsies to the more senior Lords and nods to the junior ones, Femke walked the length of the Great Hall identifying groups that looked to be brewing trouble. Several looked hostile to the forthcoming coronation, but her knowledge of those characters gave her confidence that they would not do anything foolish. Despite the fact that enough bile flowed amongst the Nobility to spawn a thousand assassination attempts, Femke started to relax.

'Maybe I'll get to enjoy the occasion after all,' she muttered.

It was the old-school Noblemen who worried Femke most; those Lords who believed nobility came from one's bloodline. They would never welcome an Emperor born out of the military – even if he were a General. Surabar had no Noble lineage and no 'House' to back his claim to the Emperor's Mantle. The old school did not care about Surabar's fitness to rule. To them he was a pretender to the Mantle, and they were unlikely to rest until one of true Noble blood held it in his stead.

Despite the pockets of bad feeling, Femke felt no air of imminent action within the Hall. The announcement of the coronation had been too sudden and surprising for any attempts at plotting. Surabar's plan of keeping the Nobles off balance was starting well.

When Femke spotted Lord Danar moving through the crowd towards her she groaned inwardly. There was nowhere to escape to and he was homing in on her like a moth drawn to light. 'Of all the venues for him to single me out at!' she cursed silently. There could be no quick excuse here, followed by a swift exit. Femke would have to politely negotiate his inevitable advances as diplomatically as possible. Danar was a notorious womaniser. He was also the eldest son of Lord Tremarle, one of the most powerful Lords in Shandrim. Therefore, despite an insane urge to kick him between the legs, she curtsied and met his sparkling blue eyes with appropriate respect for his rank. His sweeping approach and ridiculously low bow for one of such seniority set her teeth on edge before he had even opened his mouth to speak.

'Well met, my Lady,' he said, flashing a smile that was clearly reserved for the ladies.

'Indeed, Lord Danar, it is an auspicious day for meetings, is it not?'

'You have me at a disadvantage, my Lady. Whilst you obviously know my name, I do not yet have the pleasure of knowing yours.'

'Come now, Lord Danar, you're not trying to tell me that amongst the notable group of young Lords you were with as I entered the Hall, not one could tell you my name? I find that hard to believe,' she said, with a tone of gentle reproof. 'I would have thought Lord Sharyll at least would have remembered me, for we had a lengthy conversation not six months ago.'

'Unmasked as a rascal from the start,' he admitted with a shrug, employing the boyish grin that he knew to be devastating. 'Alas, I merely wanted to hear the name from your own lips, my Lady, for I did wonder if they were setting me up. It's not uncommon for my friends to play practical jokes, and I'm sure that if you look at the group you mentioned, you'll see eyes that follow us closely.'

Femke looked. Sure enough heads turned away rapidly, causing her to laugh aloud. She also used the moment to sweep the crowd with her eyes again, but there was no sign of imminent trouble. Femke returned her focus to

Lord Danar, and despite her irritation at his interruption to her task she felt a flutter of attraction. Under other circumstances, Femke knew she would have enjoyed being courted by Danar – even though she knew him to be a philanderer. But Femke would not risk her cover identity to pursue a frivolous flirtation on this occasion.

'I am Alyssa,' Femke said, deliberately dropping the 'Lady' title as was appropriate when speaking to a more senior Lord.

'Lady Alyssa,' Danar acknowledged with another polite bow. 'Curious. It seems that Sharyll not only remembers you, but he chose to tell me your real name. Do you think he was double-bluffing me? Or maybe . . . oh, whatever! The connivances and games of the young men of the Court are unlikely to interest a beautiful young Lady like you.'

'"A beautiful young Lady like you?" And what exactly does that mean, Lord Danar?' Femke asked with raised eyebrows, her focus slipping over his shoulder for a second to observe the groups of Noblemen behind him before meeting his gaze again.

'Oh, nothing sinister, I assure you,' he replied easily, not noticing her split attention. 'I merely observed that you didn't seek out those of your own kind on entering the Hall. Indeed, seldom have I seen someone so at home with her own company.'

'Very perceptive, my Lord, but why then did you choose to invade my comfort space? I'm not known for my love of male company, so you must have a reason other than your own loneliness. A bet, maybe? A wager with those conniving friends?'

Danar was thrown by her keen insight, but was careful not to let his discomfort show. Alyssa was sharper than the women he usually courted and that would make an interesting change. To spend time with a woman who was both attractive and quick-witted would be a rare pleasure, he decided.

'Not at all, Lady Alyssa! I'll not deny the others told me of your lack of interest in courtiers, and that this did pique my interest. But it was not the challenge of a potential conquest that drew me to you. It was my eternal quest to find a soul mate. My perfect partner, if you will. I've been searching most of my life, but alas, I have not yet been successful . . . unless . . .'

For a second, Femke was tempted to ram a finger down her throat to display what she thought of that line. Then her instinct was to lash out verbally, but she controlled it and kept her reply deceptively mild.

'Ah, the perfect woman for Lord Danar! From what I've heard, that lady would be a find indeed,' she said, taking the opportunity to circle around him, as if inspecting an animal in the marketplace, but actually creating the opportunity to scan the crowd again. Danar was making her assignment far more difficult than it needed to be. 'Somehow, I doubt I would fit the mould for that particular role,' she added, completing her circuit.

'Really? On what do you base that opinion?' Danar asked, his voice brimming with curiosity.

'Extrapolation. You have been notably particular in your choice of young women in the past, my Lord. I could point out that many of them possess considerable physical assets, which I lack. Also, most have a similar outlook on their status in society – to marry well and to procreate. I can say with all honesty that I have little in common with those ladies.'

Danar laughed aloud at her honesty and pointed observations. 'Granted, you're different. But different is not necessarily a bad thing. Who's to say that I've not been searching amongst *completely* the wrong sort of women? You're attractive, single, and have your wits about you – why shouldn't I want to get to know you better?'

About a dozen sharp retorts sprang to Femke's mind, but at the precise moment she opened her mouth to give her chosen riposte, she spotted something out of the corner of her eye that made her blood run cold.

'I'm sorry, Lord Danar, I don't wish to be rude, but much as I would love to continue this conversation I've just noted that Lord Kempten is here. If you would please excuse me, I have urgent business to discuss with him that cannot wait. Maybe we could meet up some time and continue our chat?'

Femke instantly wished she could swallow those words. Why had she opened the way for Danar to call on her? What was she thinking of?

'Well . . . certainly. If you wish,' Danar replied, virtually lost for words. He had thought he was making good progress with her, yet suddenly she was brushing him off. What had he said? Their conversation had been harmless, and Lady Alyssa had appeared warm in comparison with the picture painted by his friends. Now she couldn't wait to get away. 'You intend to conduct business now, my Lady?

The ceremony is about to start. Couldn't you just . . .'

But Femke was already moving and did not stop to hear him out. Lord Danar's parting observation about the ceremony was correct. Trumpets blared out a triumphal fanfare, announcing the arrival of Surabar. It also heralded the arrival of his armed guard. A great column of soldiers swept through the doors ahead of the General, marching straight up the middle of the Great Hall towards the dais at the far end, clearing a central path through the crowds as it went. The column split smoothly as the soldiers marched. One man after another peeled away from the front of the column to take up a predetermined position. With slick, inch-perfect precision, two tight, inward-facing ranks were formed in a mesmerising display of parade drill. This created a clear walkway about three paces wide for the General to proceed along.

'Not now, my Lord – hold that thought until we next meet,' Femke said firmly over her shoulder, and she swept away with the barest of curtsies. Her eyes were firmly fixed on Lord Kempten and she silently prayed she could reach him in time without creating a disturbance that attracted his attention. It was not certain that he would make an attempt on Surabar's life, but the brief glimpse Femke had caught of his face had filled her with foreboding. She had long since learned to trust such instincts.

Femke was the wrong side of the forming ranks of soldiers to intercept her quarry. If she did not get to the other side of the Great Hall before the human walkway blocked her path, then she would be powerless to inter-vene in whatever Lord Kempten attempted. Ducking and weaving through the crowds of Nobles, Femke apologised and excused herself at virtually every breath, but did not pause in her progress. For a moment it looked as if she would be cut off by the line of soldiers, but with a final ducking manoeuvre past a group of ladies, seemingly mesmerised by the precision of the military men and their gleaming armour, Femke managed to slip ahead of the column and cross to the other side of the Hall.

'Damn! Where's he gone?' Femke muttered. During the final part of her eel-like progress through the crowd, she had been forced to concentrate on getting across the Hall rather than tracking Lord Kempten. 'He can't be far away.'

Stretching up on tiptoes, Femke scanned the crowd for any sign of him – without success. What she did see, though, was General Surabar entering the Hall and moving along the still-forming human walkway of soldiers at a regal pace.

Femke's mind raced through possibilities. What would I do in Kempten's place? she thought, trying to calm her heart. It was thumping so loudly in her chest that she would not have been surprised if those around her started commenting on the noise. He hasn't had time to plan anything elaborate, and by the expression on his face earlier he's both nervous and determined. Come on, Femke – think! He's a traditionalist with a reputation for being honourable in all his dealings with others. Whatever he's doing, he's acting alone – he's not the type for conspiracy. It's possible that others are involved, but I'd give long odds on that. If I were going to try to kill Surabar, and if I were a man like Kempten, how would I do it?

There were too many soldiers present. Lord Kempten had few options unless he was willing to martyr himself. Bells suddenly rang in her head.

'Oh, the fool!' she exclaimed softly, and she started to weave her way through the crowds to get as close as she could to where Surabar would pass. That's it, she thought frantically. He's going to martyr himself. A dagger attack most likely, and he'll have poisoned it to make sure. No wonder he looked nervous!

What to do? The question burned in her mind. If Lord Kempten was going to attempt a suicidal attack on General Surabar, how could she prevent it from happening? Femke could hardly justify killing him on the basis of intuition. She did not want to kill him at all. Yet if she failed to act and Lord Kempten did make a successful attack on Surabar, then she would be responsible. It was a tough dilemma made worse by her having lost sight of him.

Suddenly that part of the problem was solved. Femke spotted Lord Kempten nearby. Sure enough, he was at the front of the crowd. His face was a waxy pale grey with tiny beads of sweat just visible at his temples. The instant she saw him, Femke knew her instincts were well founded.

Surabar was not far away. There was no more thinking time. Femke had to do something – and it had to be now. At that instant she realised killing Lord Kempten was not an option. Even if she managed it undetected by those around her in the crowd, she had foolishly told Lord Danar she was going to talk to Kempten and he was likely to be still watching her. Danar might be an irritating flirt, but he was not stupid. He would put two and two together if Kempten dropped dead in the crowd.

Without pausing to consider her next move, Femke removed a comb from her hair and wormed her way quickly through the crowd until she was directly behind Lord Kempten. She pressed one end of the comb lightly against the kidney region of his lower back and whispered quietly into his ear. 'Don't move, my Lord, or I'll kill you where you stand. Concealed within the comb at your back is a spike tipped with deadly poison. Please don't make me use it. If I do, then your death will have served no purpose at all.'

'What . . . ? How . . . ? Lady Alyssa?' he spluttered.

'Shhh!' Femke hushed, her whispered admonition in his ear barely audible. 'Stand still until Surabar has passed. Then we'll take a little walk.'

They did not have long to wait, for the General was approaching. As Surabar stepped past them at a measured, stately pace, Femke grinned as she realised that the General had taken the bold step of accepting the Mantle in his full military regalia, including the armour. A wise precaution, she mused. It would infuriate the old-school Lords by rubbing their noses in his background, but that could not be helped.

'All right, my Lord,' Femke whispered, leaning close on Lord Kempten's shoulder. 'Let's go now. Make all your movements as smooth as you can, please. I don't want to jab you with this by accident; poisoning you here would prove embarrassing. Neither of us want that to happen, do we?'

Lord Kempten shook his head slightly. Guided by Femke's hand at his back, he eased away from the line of soldiers and into the crowd. The two of them moved slowly through the mass of lords and ladies, taking care to do nothing that would distract from General Surabar's progress.

As Femke directed Lord Kempten towards the side of the Great Hall her mind was racing. She had him in her power, but what should she do with him now? It occurred to her that she could lock him in a holding room until she could hand him over to Surabar. That was the most logical solution, but Femke knew that if Lord Kempten subsequently confessed, then Surabar would show no mercy. Lord Kempten would die as surely as if she had poisoned him. Surabar was fair, but Kempten had planned to assassinate the Emperor-to-be. That was a capital offence. Femke did not want another life on her conscience. Was there a way to resolve this situation without more bloodshed?

It was less crowded near the side wall of the Great Hall, and as the sonorous voice of the High Cleric of Shandar boomed out the initial phrases of the coronation ceremony, the vast majority of the gathered Nobility edged forwards to watch and listen. With the focus of the people on the front of the Hall, it was easy to edge Lord Kempten with quietly whispered promptings slowly back towards the nearest exit. The door was locked. Femke would have been surprised if it had not been secure. General Surabar was unlikely to allow any obvious security breaches today. The only way out of the Hall was through the main entrance, which was currently surrounded by dozens of soldiers.

There was nothing for it. Leaving before the end of the ceremony was out of the question.

'My Lord, we are going to position ourselves as close to the main exit as possible. We will leave as soon as the new Emperor makes his exit. Be assured I wish you no harm. Quite the opposite actually, but we need to have a quiet talk before I can let you leave the Palace.'

'You're going to let me leave, Alyssa? That makes no sense. I thought you would hand me over to the guards. You're certainly full of surprises, young lady. How did you know what I was going to do?' Lord Kempten asked in a startled whisper that could have been a lot quieter.

Femke gave a quiet hushing sound without moving her lips and then nodded subtly at the raised dais at the far end of the Hall. 'Concentrate on the ceremony, my Lord. We're being watched, and I don't want to raise suspicions. Let's say for now that I have eyes in my head and I use them. You were obvious. I didn't want you to throw your life away unnecessarily. Shandar needs you, and others like you. We'll talk more later.'

The final flattering comments were calculated to make Lord Kempten relax. They had the desired effect. As they had moved towards the back of the Hall, Femke had spotted Lord Danar pushing through the crowds to follow their progress. Femke inwardly cursed the inconvenience of the encounter. Danar was easy to pick out, both because he was taller than most and because he was the only person in the Hall who kept obviously looking away from the dais. She needed a clean getaway without interference and unnecessary complications from her would-be suitor.

As the High Cleric droned through the stately formalities of the ceremony, every minute stretched out in Femke's mind until she felt the event would never end. Then, with sudden finality, his voice fell silent. He reached down, silently lifted the Emperor's simple circlet of gold and placed it on Surabar's head, to a muffled applause. Next he placed the regal Mantle that was the true symbol of power in Shandar across Surabar's shoulders and fastened the ornate clasp at the front. The applause this time was more general, though hardly rapturous.

Bestowed with the symbols of office as Emperor, Surabar made a short speech giving an abridged account of the deceptions and treachery of the Sorcerer Lord, Vallaine. The previous Emperor had foolishly listened to Vallaine's advice and given him control of several Legions. The Sorcerer Lord had sent this large army into Thrandor having claimed foreknowledge of the future through a prescient vision. He guaranteed the army would take the capital city, Mantor, provided that a certain Lord Shanier led the Shandese forces. Vallaine hoped to win power in Thrandor for his own purposes, but his interpretation of the vision proved incorrect. Lord Shanier duped him. The result was the slaughter of the Shandese army and Lord Vallaine's fall from grace.

Surabar then told how Vallaine had secretly murdered the real Emperor and how he had changed his appearance using sorcery to replace the Emperor, thus covertly seizing ultimate power in Shandar. The Sorcerer's abuses of power and his twisted ambitions were quickly outlined, followed by some general statements on how Surabar intended to heal some of the wounds that Vallaine had opened with their neighbours, the Thrandorians.

'Peace,' he stated firmly, 'is always preferable to war. War should always be the last option, to be used only when all other means of negotiation have failed. As a soldier of many years' experience, I can say with authority that whilst war will sometimes gain the Empire new territory and subjugate peoples, the pain and loss involved in achieving those gains are seldom worth the price paid in human lives. I hope that my reign as Emperor will reflect these views and that Shandar will prosper as a peaceful Empire under my rule.'

Polite applause followed the speech. Femke sensed that there were a few amongst the Nobles who were responding more warmly to his words than they would like to admit. But though Surabar had struck a positive first note, it would take more than a few words to stave off the inevitable attempts to remove the Mantle from his shoulders.

The trumpets blared as Surabar withdrew down the aisle of soldiers, who in turn peeled inwards in a precision display of formation marching to reform the column and march out of the Hall behind him. As the last soldiers left the Great Hall, Femke steered Lord Kempten to follow on behind them. Instead of heading for the main corridor towards the official exit, Femke diverted Kempten off into a side passage and led him into the heart of the Palace. Once clear of the crowds, Femke tried the door to one of the Palace administrators' offices. It opened. Given that all eyes would follow the progress of the new Emperor, the chances of being disturbed here were slim.

Once inside, Femke invited Lord Kempten to take a seat

whilst she sat on the edge of the desk. The height of the desk meant she was looking down at him. It was a small advantage, but it gave the illusion of authority. There had been some time during the ceremony for her to formulate a plan, so Femke cut straight to the chase. The truth – or at least some of it – would make her task here easier.

'Now, Lord Kempten, let's place any unpleasant thoughts of harming one another aside for a moment, shall we?' Femke asked, casually pressuring the final tooth on her comb with a thumb. A needle sharp spike suddenly appeared out of the other end with a metallic ringing tone. It was good for him to see she had not been bluffing. She placed it on the desk beside her and crossed her legs in a relaxed pose. 'I'm sure you're aware what would happen if I branded you a traitor. If I called for the guards and had you searched right now, they would find a weapon. If my supposition is correct, then tests would prove that weapon to be poisoned, as is my comb.'

'How do you know this? I told no one – not even my wife!'

'How is irrelevant. Listen; I'm currently in the fortunate position of having the new Emperor's ear, and there's a lot about him you don't know. You were a fool today. A brave fool, but a fool nonetheless. Throwing your life away in an effort to prevent Surabar becoming Emperor would have been a pointless waste. Your eldest son is growing up fast, but he isn't ready to fill your shoes yet, my Lord. Please don't rush into any self-sacrificial nonsense again. The truth is, Surabar doesn't want to be Emperor. He doesn't intend to keep the Mantle long.'

'What? Then why in Shand's name has he taken the Mantle at all?' Kempten asked in disbelief.

'Try to look at it from this perspective, my Lord – who would you expect to see take the Mantle if not Surabar?' Femke replied.

'Well, I don't know exactly. There are several Houses that have legitimate claims to the Mantle—'

'Exactly!' Femke interrupted. 'To be more precise, my Lord, there are several Noble Houses that would cut each other to pieces in order to place the Mantle on the shoulders of one of their Lords. It would be a blood bath. What Shandar needs now is peace, not more killing. We suffered drastic losses during the ill-advised invasion of Thrandor. The last thing we need now is to decimate our Noble Houses by entering a bloody succession feud. When General Surabar unmasked the traitor, Vallaine, he decided, for the good of Shandar, to take power for long enough to re-establish order. He will then decide which of the Houses has the strongest claim to the Mantle. My understanding is that once he's established who among the Noble families has the most deserving and able candidate, he intends to abdicate his position to this chosen person. You must agree, my Lord, that there are Nobles who, though they have a claim to the Mantle, would make terrible leaders for Shandar.'

'Yes, that's true,' Kempten admitted. 'I follow the logic, but do you honestly believe that Surabar will give up the Mantle? Power can be an addictive drug.'

'Surabar has been a General for some years now, my Lord. He is used to wielding power over large numbers of

47

people. To my knowledge he has never abused that responsibility, and he's well known to be a man of his word. I believe that he'll follow through his intentions. He took the Mantle under duress. I can say no more of the circumstances, but I want you to think *very* carefully about what I've said. Please – no more assassination attempts. I must also advise you that the Emperor's intentions are to remain secret. Surabar will be watching for the strongest candidate to emerge. Tampering with this process by leaking his intentions will have dire consequences both for you, your family, and the Empire. You're to tell no one. If it is discovered that his plans have spread further than your lips, then you, and your entire House, will die swiftly. You have been warned, Lord Kempten. I'll lead you back out to one of the Palace side exits now. I suggest you support Emperor Surabar and encourage others to do so as well. Those who listen to you stand to benefit greatly, particularly if they belong to one of the major Houses.'

As Femke watched a thoughtful Lord Kempten leave through one of the servant gates a few minutes later, she felt satisfied that he had taken on enough of her speech to make him cautious. He would doubtless feel great relief at his reprieve from a traitor's death. This would remain at the forefront of his mind for some time. Femke had read his responses. She was convinced he would sit back and watch Surabar for a while before moving against him again. Femke would have to inform the Emperor of the risk Lord Kempten posed, but Femke felt sure she could make Surabar see the benefits of her solution. If Lord Kempten took her speech to heart, then intercepting him today could prove more important to Emperor Surabar's life in power than the coronation ceremony.

Lord Danar watched with frustration as Lady Alyssa slipped out of the Great Hall ahead of him. He wanted to try to pick up his conversation with her, but the press of people was making it impossible to catch up. Sliding in and out of the crowds as politely as he could, he kept pausing and standing tall as he was forced to slow by the mass of bodies funnelling into the narrow corridor. Stretching on tiptoes he tried to see over the heads of the people ahead. Lady Alyssa was nowhere to be seen, and Lord Kempten had disappeared with her.

A commotion involving the clashing of many weapons drew him to push forward. Ignoring the complaints and protests, he squeezed his way through to find out what was happening. To his amazement there was a fully-fledged battle being fought in the Palace forecourts. The newly invested Emperor and his soldiers had been forced back against the front wall of the Palace. They were surrounded and outnumbered, but appeared to be holding firm as a great mass of men in nondescript clothing swarmed around them.

None of the Noblemen were openly armed and none appeared ready to reveal weapons if they were hiding them about their persons. Much as in the Great Hall, the response of the Nobles to the situation was mixed. There were those who looked genuinely shocked, those who seemed openly pleased and those who were trying to dis-associate themselves from the instant rebellion. Notably, there were none who threw themselves into the fight on behalf of the new Emperor.

The fate of Emperor Surabar was of little consequence to Danar. The man could live or die. There would be plenty of Noblemen ready to don the Mantle in his place. Judging by unfolding events, one or more of them already had it in mind to take over. Danar did not care. His thoughts were elsewhere and he was completely uninterested by the politics of the moment.

What did Alyssa want with Kempten, Danar wondered, his eyes searching for them amongst the masses of people still spilling out from the large doors at the front of the Palace. Surely she isn't fostering a romantic relationship with the man . . . ? He shook himself. Don't be ridiculous, he told himself firmly. Kempten isn't the type. He's the most loyal family man around. He's always the first to con-demn any infidelity amongst the rest of us. So why were they walking so closely? Alyssa seemed to have her arm around him much of the time. Could it be that she prefers the company of older men?

Danar scoured the surging mass of people for any sign of her distinctive red dress whilst remaining careful not to get dragged into the fighting. The dress was nowhere to be seen. For today, it seemed, his pursuit of Alyssa would have to wait. However, he resolved that he would win his wager – not for the wager's sake, but because he was attracted to this mysterious young woman. As Sharyll had promised, she was an enigma. Danar had never been so intrigued by a woman before. His friends had named her the impossible catch; but assuming she had not been killed in this ridiculous mêlée, his instincts told him he still had a chance.

'You may have given me the slip today, Alyssa, but I'll find you,' he promised himself in a muttered whisper. 'I'll find you.'

CHAPTER THREE

By chance, Reynik was standing right next to the Emperor when the attack came. A large crowd of men, all dressed innocuously as servants and footmen, were loitering by the Palace gates, apparently waiting for their respective Lords and Ladies to exit the main building. Nobody noted until afterwards that none of them were wearing any distinguishing livery.

The timing of the attack was precise. The Emperor was too far from the main entrance doors to get back inside. The instant the first weapon was drawn, the men of the General's Elite Legion responded.

'FORM WEDGE ON ME!' The commander's bellowed order rang clear as the totally unexpected charge by the disguised enemies closed the distance between them quickly. There was no hesitation. If the soldiers were surprised, they displayed none of it. With the same precision they had shown during the ceremony, Reynik and the others sprang into a V-formation, with the reinforced point of the V aimed directly at the oncoming enemy charge. The Emperor and the High Cleric were safely encased between the two protective lines.

It was an excellent choice, as the main charge was split the moment it struck. The major thrust of the enemy simply divided and glanced off the front of the wedge. Within seconds they were spreading out along the lines of troops, without any forward momentum, into the defending group.

Reynik's position was on the inside of the left arm of the wedge, which extended back to the outside wall of the main Palace building. As such, all he could do was to hold his position, watch and wait as the charging mass of men crashed against the outer edges of the wedge. His palms felt sweaty and his heart pounded in his chest as the clashing of weapons, the yelling battle cries, and the screams of the early wounded and dying filled the air with confusion. Of all the places to gain his first real battle experience, he had never anticipated it being inside the Imperial Palace grounds.

Reynik was not sure if he should hope to cross swords with the enemy, or if they would be routed without the need to bloody his weapon. There was lots of jostling and pushing for position as the full weight of the enemy pressed home their attack, but the wedge formation held firm with the Emperor safely positioned in the middle.

On instinct, Reynik glanced over his shoulder at the Emperor to see how he was reacting to this violent beginning to his reign. Despite the Imperial Mantle, Surabar looked every inch the General. His face was calm as he surveyed the scene and his sword was drawn, ready for use.

There was no sense of shock or surprise in his expression. Reynik could see only a detached, professional interest.

In contrast, the High Cleric looked both outraged and terrified. His knuckles were pinched white as he clutched his golden ceremonial staff against his body for comfort. Reynik began to smile at the sight of the frightened Cleric, but the corners of his mouth had barely begun to twitch upwards when his face froze. From around the corner of the building, not far from the thinly defended right flank, another group of men appeared, sprinting forwards in an all out charge. The group were tightly packed and looked far from friendly.

'Your Majesty!' Reynik yelled, pointing at the incoming enemies. His shout was loud enough to catch Surabar's attention, and the Emperor's head turned to look where Reynik was pointing. There was no time for a change of formation. Reynik knew he was disobeying a direct order by moving from his position in the wedge, but the right flank needed support and the left flank was holding firm without him.

The new mass of fighters smashed into the right flank, instantly buckling the line inwards and breeching it briefly. A small group of enemy men penetrated the defenders and charged at the Emperor. Before they could reach him Reynik intercepted them in a maniacal charge of his own. A spontaneous battle cry burst from his throat as, with a slashing stroke of his sword, Reynik turned aside the blade of the leading fighter. Without losing any momentum, he dropped his shoulder and hurled himself into the group, sending bodies flying like skittles.

The unorthodox counterattack ripped any sense of cohesion amongst the enemy group to tatters. Before they had a chance to recover, Surabar had killed two of them. There was no sign of his age in his fluid sword strokes and swift movements.

Reynik had collided with the leading fighter so hard that he had lost hold of his sword. As he scrambled to his feet, there was no sign of it anywhere. This left him facing several swordsmen with nothing but a belt knife and his ceremonial armour to protect him. For a split second he wondered if his was to be the shortest career in his family's long history of military service. Then, survival instincts took over.

In one swift motion, Reynik drew and threw his belt knife at his nearest adversary. Fast as he was, his target was faster. The man swayed out of the path of the flashing blade, but Reynik did not care. The throw had served its purpose as a momentary diversion. Reynik followed the throw by launching into another rolling dive through the small gap between enemies that his thrown knife had created. He heard the swoosh of air and felt the glancing impact of a blade as he passed between the two men. No pain accompanied the hit. The blade was turned aside by his armour. Reynik did not give it another thought as he rolled to his feet next to the High Cleric.

With a wrenching grab, Reynik tore the Cleric's ceremonial staff from his grasp and spun to meet his opponents with the golden-coloured length of wood already a blur in his hands. The staff was lighter and longer than Reynik preferred, but suited his need perfectly. If the attackers had been surprised by Reynik's first suicidal charge, they were astonished by his second. However, for the first time during the short fight, the young soldier was confident with the odds.

Reynik had first been given a cut-down staff at the age of five and had been an expert in fighting with such a weapon for some years. His father had always maintained that at close quarters, particularly against multiple opponents, the staff was a more effective weapon than the sword. Reynik trusted his father's judgement and set about proving him right.

This was no place for fancy twirls. With a brutal efficiency, Reynik downed one after another of the enemy fighters, sweeping aside sword blades as if he were walking through a forest and they were merely branches in his way. The men were totally unprepared for the versatility of the double-ended weapon as Reynik struck again and again at vulnerable body parts, inflicting pain and unconsciousness on several fighters in quick succession. As each opponent went down, Surabar was quick to step in and take advantage. He gave no quarter. They made a formidable pair.

Two more of Reynik's fellow soldiers from the left flank, finally aware of the breach, joined the Emperor in finishing off the last two remaining enemy fighters. The right flank of the wedge had recovered its integrity quickly after the initial impact of the charge. The superior fighting skill of the elite soldiers was taking a heavy toll on their adversaries. Despite their superior numbers, the heart went out of the attacking force when it became apparent their surprise tactics had failed. The fight did not last much longer. The attackers were swift to realise they were not going to prevail against the expertly trained soldiers. A few minutes later, they were in full retreat.

'Nice staff, your Eminence. Sorry about the paintwork,' Reynik commented with a straight face as he casually handed the battered ceremonial icon back to the High Cleric.

The holy man was still in too much of a state of shock to do anything but take the staff with a dazed expression on his face.

'What's your name, soldier?' Emperor Surabar asked, unable to totally hide his amusement at Reynik's irreverence.

'Reynik, your Majesty.'

'Thank you, Reynik. You fought well.'

Femke completed her report to Emperor Surabar. The Emperor was not convinced that letting Lord Kempten walk free was wise, but he had heard her out without comment. After thinking the matter over, he decided to support Femke's plan. Awareness of the potential threat Lord Kempten posed made monitoring his activities far easier. It remained to be seen if he had been instrumental in organising the attack after the ceremony, but with the number of men they had captured, the Emperor was sure any involvement would soon become apparent.

'Time will tell whether you made the right choice,' he said, then he moved swiftly on to new business. Femke said nothing of Lord Danar's advances in her report, as it had little bearing on the subject of the Emperor's security. Some things were best kept private.

'Your next mission is in Thrandor, Femke. You're to go with full Ambassadorial status to the Royal Palace in Mantor and instigate a peace process with King Malo. I don't need to tell you how important this mission is. It is vital to the future of the Empire.'

'Thrandor! Me?' Femke exclaimed. 'Why me, your Majesty? I know virtually nothing about Thrandor. I have no experience as a diplomat. Surely you've many people at your disposal who are far better suited to the role of Ambassador.'

The Emperor smiled and shook his head slightly.

'You have more experience than you credit yourself with,' he replied. 'It's true there are some who know more about Thrandor. There are also people more experienced at international diplomacy, but you possess specialist skills that none of those people have. Your powers of observation and your reading of people's character are excellent, you're good at covertly digging out information, and you're highly discreet. What's more, you're a survivor. I saw that the first time we met. You bested Shalidar, a top assassin, with guile and cunning. There are few who could claim as much. I'm confident I can trust you with this mission, Femke. Don't let me down.'

'I'll do my best, your Majesty.'

'That's all I can ask. I'm sure that your best will be good enough. Whilst you're in Thrandor I'd like you to do more than extend a hand of peace and reconciliation. I want you to gather information about the King of Thrandor and his close advisors. Any insights into the way Thrandor's King runs his country will be useful in future negotiations. Information on how they defeated our armies so decisively is to be top of your list of objectives, but any Palace intrigue and rumour will also prove useful.'

'I understand completely, your Majesty. I have a few practical questions, if I may?' she asked, trying to sound confident, but feeling anxious about the daunting task ahead.

'Of course, go ahead.'

'The first question is simple – when do I leave?'

'The day after tomorrow – at first light. The sooner you leave, the better,' he answered. 'You need a little time to organise the journey, but you must go quickly. I want you there before the Thrandorians think about retaliatory strikes. They might have initiated a counterstroke already, but I feel it unlikely. You must ensure they understand Vallaine is gone and that I don't intend to follow his aggressive example. Stress my background. It will make them think twice about counterattacks. I want them to know Shandar remains strong, but with the change of rule, the Empire's stance has altered to one of defending its borders whilst offering the chance of friendship and increased trade.'

Femke nodded. The message was one she would be glad to deliver.

'Am I to go alone, your Majesty, or will I be travelling as part of a delegation?'

'Not alone, no, but I don't think a full delegation will be necessary. I'll appoint two of the Palace staff to accompany you as servants, and two soldiers to ensure your safety. A bigger party would attract attention and would move too slowly. Five of you will be able to travel swiftly and won't be perceived as a threat.'

'Very good, your Majesty. I have one last question. You mentioned I should present his Majesty, the King of Thrandor, with gifts. Do you have anything particular in mind, or should I organise this?' Femke asked.

Surabar laughed.

'Don't worry,' he assured her. 'I'll arrange appropriate gifts. They will need to be substantial if we're to show the Empire is serious about peace. I'll arrange for the treasury to supply you with all you'll need.'

'Thank you, your Majesty, I'll go and begin my preparations. There is a lot to do. I'll need to make sure Lady Alyssa makes a suitable exit from Shandrim before I become the Ambassador.'

'It's a complicated life that you lead,' Surabar acknowledged with a smile. 'Still, this trip will take you out of Shalidar's sight for a while. By the time you return I hope to have apprehended him, or given him sufficient time to dull his need for revenge.'

Privately, Femke felt it unlikely Shalidar would drop the idea of avenging her interference with his plans, but the assassin was a strange character. Anything was possible. One thing was certain, however – Femke was determined her guard would still be up if Shalidar made a move.

With her orders clear, Femke left the Emperor's study and returned to the Silver Chalice. Lady Alyssa was hardly suitable to be a Shandese Ambassador. This task would require Femke to play a different persona entirely. 'A shame really,' she mused. The last couple of days as the petulant young Lady had been fun.

Versande Matthiason was in the small reception area of the inn when she arrived. Femke could not resist the opportunity to indulge herself in a few last antics, and she ran the innkeeper and his staff ragged after trivialities before announcing her imminent departure. Versande managed to maintain his composure at Alyssa's declaration that she would be leaving soon, but Femke could see by the relaxation in the lines of the man's face that he was relieved. Copious amounts of gold would no longer be pouring into his coffers, but Versande clearly felt he had endured enough for one visit.

There was no point in Alyssa staying at the Silver Chalice any longer, and Femke did not want to tie Alyssa's leaving Shandrim to the same day as the Ambassador departing for Thrandor. Even a day apart was too close, but she had little choice. As the Ambassador would not look like Alyssa, it was perhaps unlikely that anyone would make connection. To leave this evening would be suspicious, though, for although Alyssa was capricious by nature she rarely travelled any distance on impulse. Therefore, Femke enjoyed one more night of luxury as Lady Alyssa.

There was a lot to do. Alyssa had to be seen to leave the city and, ideally, the Ambassador should be seen arriving. With that in mind, Femke did not annoy Versande and his staff for long before she changed into less distinctive clothing and slipped out unnoticed to visit some of her contacts in central Shandrim. It took her several hours to arrange everything to her satisfaction. Femke returned to the Silver Chalice in the early evening, content that everything was ready.

'A young man called for you, my Lady. He left these and he asked me to pass on his compliments, together with a request that you dine with him this evening,' Versande informed her as she entered the reception hall of the inn. He handed her a small but exquisitely arranged bouquet of flowers. With the flowers came a note.

> Dear Alyssa,
>   Sorry we did not get the chance to finish our chat earlier. Maybe we could resume over dinner? I'll meet you in the Chalice dining room at the eighth hour.
> Yours,
> Danar

Femke groaned softly. 'As if life isn't complicated enough,' she muttered.

'Is something wrong, my Lady?' Versande asked. 'Is there anything I can do to help?'

'Yes, Versande, there is. I'm sure you noted who left these. Lord Danar will arrive here shortly. He has indicated his wish to dine with me and expects to meet me in the dining room at the eighth hour. When he arrives, kindly inform Lord Danar that I'm indisposed. I'll take a light snack in my room later.'

'Yes, of course, my Lady,' Versande agreed, bowing slightly. 'I understand completely.'

Femke rather doubted he did, but did not elaborate. It

was enough that Versande would keep Lord Danar at bay.

'One last thing, Versande.'

'Yes, my Lady?'

'On no account tell Lord Danar that I'm leaving in the morning. If you do, he may insist on seeing me – and I will not countenance any disturbance tonight. Do you understand?'

'Yes, my Lady. A sensible precaution, my Lady. I'll send Soffi up in a little while to see what you would like to eat. I trust you will sleep well.'

The next morning, Femke rose early and packed her things. It was barely light when she descended the stairs to the reception desk to settle the bill. Femke was not surprised to find Versande there already. She wondered if the man ever slept at all.

'Good morning, Versande, I trust there was no unpleasantness last night?' Femke asked, looking as imperious as possible.

'Nothing that couldn't be dealt with quietly, my Lady,' Versande assured her. 'Lord Danar was a little . . . upset that you were not available to dine with him, but he did not cause undue disturbance. You wish to settle your bill, I assume?'

Femke nodded with a glint of mischief in her eye as she wondered what 'a little upset' had looked like.

'Well, my Lady, I've prepared your account. I hope that you enjoyed your stay.'

'Yes, thank you, Versande. The room was most adequate. You and your staff have been very kind,' she responded, struggling against the urge to tell him that the room was excellent and the service could not have been better. Still, 'most adequate' and 'kind' were high praise indeed from Lady Alyssa. Versande would take no offence, particularly given the rates that he was charging.

Femke looked at the total and, without batting an eyelid at the exorbitant amount, proceeded to count out the appropriate number of gold and silver coins. Inside she was outraged at the amount Versande had charged her for a change of sheets, the use of a suite for a couple of nights, and some light food and drinks. Rikala's bill for the dress was included, but Femke was sure the amount on Versande's bill was hugely inflated from that which Rikala would receive. Femke sent Versande upstairs to fetch her bags personally, partly as Alyssa's parting shot and partly as a token personal protest at the astronomical bill. She was determined to get every last ounce of work out of him for the money.

Femke had arranged for two footmen to accompany her from the inn. Precisely on the call of the sixth hour, they arrived with her horses. Without a word they loaded Lady Alyssa's bags and held her horse whilst she mounted. Without a backward glance, Femke rode off along the street, leaving Versande standing on the doorstep of the inn, apparently already forgotten.

The switch was flawless. Femke rode through the city along the main eastbound streets and out into the country-side. At a rendezvous point she met with another of her contacts, who had brought the clothes, wig and make-up items she had specified, together with a fresh horse. It was easy to change her appearance sufficiently to be unrecognisable as Alyssa, and to ride off-road in a wide arc around the city.

Femke re-entered Shandrim through the southern quarter and went swiftly to the Palace. Her final briefing was held in the Emperor's study. Little was added to the instructions of the previous day other than a quick account of the gifts that Surabar had selected for the King of Thrandor and the names of those who would be travelling with her. In the event, the information did not prove totally accurate, for when they came to leave the next morning one of the two servants was too sick to travel and had to be replaced. The servant chosen to go in his stead looked bewildered by the whole affair, but managed to get ready so quickly that there was minimal delay.

As this assignment was a long one, Femke decided that she would travel under her real name. The soldiers and servants were unlikely to know there was no real Shandese Ambassador named Femke, so she felt sure they would not inadvertently unmask her as a fraud. Also, it removed the problem of keeping a fictitious name at the forefront of her mind. Once the replacement servant had loaded his bags onto his packhorse, there was a quick round of introductions before Femke led them out onto the city streets.

'We can do proper introductions as we ride,' she said with a tone of authority. 'There'll be plenty of time to get to know one another before we reach Mantor.'

After two weeks of travelling, Femke reflected on those departing words with a grimace. The spy had never been comfortable on a horse. Although she was a competent horsewoman, she had never derived pleasure from riding and did not ride often. Within five days of leaving Shandrim, Femke's bottom was so sore that the rest of the journey became a physical torment, made worse by her four companions.

The two soldiers, Sidis and Reynik, were cold and professional. Sidis held the rank of File Leader, whilst Reynik was a humble Legionnaire. Femke quickly formed the impression Reynik was shielding a pleasant personality under his cold exterior, but would not allow anything except the professional soldier to show in front of Sidis. The older soldier was a cold fish who had no time for civilians. Sidis clearly did not want to be on this mission. To him it was a babysitting job, unfitting for a soldier of his experience and rank. It was not long before Femke wished she could grant his obvious desire to be back with his Legion.

As if the remoteness of the two soldiers were not enough, Femke also had to live with the eccentricities of the two servants, Kalheen and Phagen. The servant who had joined them at the last moment, Phagen, was so quiet that he could have been mute. Femke eventually gave up trying to engage the slim young man in conversation. At best she could draw only one- or two-word answers. He appeared intelligent and capable enough, but was so introverted that Femke's best efforts to include him in conversation fell flat.

The one occasion when Phagen did come forward during the journey was when he realised that Femke was suffering with acute saddle-sores. He approached Femke discreetly at the campsite on the evening of the fifth day and gave her a salve for her aching posterior. The numbing effect of the cool salve gave such relief that it brought tears of thankfulness. Afterwards, Femke was far more willing to forgive his reticent nature.

Kalheen was the antithesis of Phagen. He always had something to say. Stopping his incessant flow of monologues and reminiscences proved as impossible as getting Phagen to say more than 'Yes, my Lady' and 'No, my Lady'. To begin with this was fine. Some of Kalheen's stories were amusing – obviously hugely exaggerated, but they helped the miles roll past. His deep voice was expressive, and his pace and story construction showed qualities many bards lacked. However, each story would prompt another and then another in an endless stream. This became tiresome within a day.

Where Phagen was thin as a pole, Kalheen tended towards fatness. At the campsites Kalheen always seemed to find the least physical tasks to do. This was not a problem, for the other three men and Femke were all fit, and happy to do the work, but after a few days it began to irk Femke that he shamelessly shirked physical effort whenever possible.

Two days out of Shandrim, Femke was ready to throttle all her companions for one reason or another. If they had not been crucial to maintaining her façade as an ambassador, Femke would have dismissed them all. However, her party had been chosen for her and there was no time to exchange them, so Femke gritted her teeth and endured their idiosyncrasies.

'Thank Shand!' Femke sighed when they crested the

67

ridge to the north of Mantor and saw the city for the first time. 'Hold for a moment,' she announced, deliberately interrupting Kalheen's latest story mid-flow. 'Let's go over our plan again before we enter the city.'

Everyone halted their horses and looked at her. Sidis wore an expression of bored disinterest, Kalheen looked irritated at having his story interrupted and Reynik appeared distracted. The young soldier kept looking towards Sidis as if seeking guidance on whether to listen to her, or ignore her. The only one who appeared to be attentive was Phagen. He looked embarrassed at the rudeness of the others. Though he said nothing, there was a flash of anger in his eyes as he glanced around at them.

'All right men, I'll keep this brief. When we enter the city we'll head straight for the Palace. Ask for directions if necessary, but don't be drawn into conversation. Keep heads and eyes straight ahead as much as you can. We must give the impression of discipline and focus. I hardly need remind you we're here on behalf of the Emperor to speak to the King of this land. I'm not the only Ambassador here. Each of us is on display to the people of Thrandor today, so let's show them we've come to do business. Sidis, Kalheen and Phagen will accompany me to the audience with the King. Reynik, if you can get leave to go out into the city, I want you to go and do the shopping we discussed. Please, all of you keep your eyes and ears open. Anything we can learn about these people and their customs will be useful information to report to the Emperor. We're not here on a cloak and dagger mission so don't do anything foolish. Is everyone clear on what they have to do?'

The men all nodded and Femke met each set of eyes in turn as she swept her gaze around. They all returned her stare with enough confidence to satisfy her.

'Very well, men, let's go visit the King of Thrandor.'

The two soldiers wheeled their horses and took the lead, with Reynik holding the white truce flag so that it fluttered above his head in the breeze. Femke took up position directly behind them and the two servants followed along at the rear, leading the short train of packhorses.

The Thrandorians were curious to see Shandese folk visiting their capital under the white flag. All eyes followed them from the moment they arrived. The guards at the city gates were unwilling to let Femke and the others proceed inside the city without an escort. They insisted that Sidis and Reynik give up their weapons before entering, but Femke had anticipated this. The two soldiers handed their swords and bows over without argument. Then there followed a short delay while the Thrandorian soldiers raced to get four men mounted on horseback so they could accompany the Shandese group.

The final ride through the city to the Palace took some time. The horses walked at a steady pace, but the city covered the entire hillside and the King's Palace was at the summit. Femke kept her head forward the entire way, but her eyes were roving and her mind accumulating information about the city structure.

Mantor's hilltop construction was different from Shandrim's. The relationship between wealth and position on the hillside made class distinction easy. As they climbed through the city, the houses became progressively more luxurious. Femke wondered how the darker elements of the city found this. Thieves would know which houses held the most potential loot, but one would also assume that if a militia patrol found someone in the higher levels of the city who did not belong there, then blame for any crime in the area would be automatically assigned. This was nothing like Shandrim, where there were rich and poor in every quarter of the city. The poorer elements could often be seen travelling through the streets of the wealthy in the Shandese capital. The structure of Mantor had advantages for maintaining order, though Femke found the arrangement alien and disturbing.

Towards the top of the hill, Femke spotted three men walking into one of the larger dwellings. For an instant she could have sworn that the middle one of the three was Shalidar. A shiver went through her before common sense began to reassert itself. The chances of Shalidar being here in Mantor and walking within sight of Femke were preposterously slim. The resemblance was remarkable, but had to be coincidence. As the man and his associates slipped inside the building, Femke berated herself for being skittish.

'Focus, Femke,' she ordered herself sternly. 'You haven't time for foolishness.'

When they reached the Palace there were the normal bureaucratic delays. Firstly, at the main gate the Royal Guards insisted on fetching the Captain before escorting them inside the Palace walls. When they walked up the great steps Femke marvelled at the grand, columned front-age. The stone steps climbed between two rows of shaped ornamental shrubs, before passing under a line of huge Royal banners that hung from horizontal flagpoles sticking out from the high rooftop.

Before climbing the steps between the two central columns to the main doors, a backward glance rewarded her with an amazing view of the city spread below. Her wonder at this sight was interrupted by an odiously formal, immaculately-dressed man named Krider, who met them at the doors. He quizzed Femke on the nature of her visit, before insisting the three small chests of gifts from Emperor Surabar be emptied and thoroughly searched. These were then refilled and returned. Krider watched over every detail of this with hawk-like precision before directing other less senior members of the Royal household staff to take Femke and her companions to suitable waiting rooms. Femke and the others took the opportunity to get cleaned up and to change from their travel clothing into more formal wear for their audience with the King.

The Shandese Ambassadorial party were not left alone for a second. At every step of the way from their entry into Mantor until they finally walked into the King's audience chamber, someone maintained a watch over them. Afterwards, Femke realised it was not the constant monitoring that bothered her, but that not one of the faces was smiling, or pleased to see her. The first time Femke felt a hint of warmth was when she entered the King's presence. But even then, the feeling was guarded.

The Chief Butler, Veldan, escorted Femke and her three chosen gift-bearers to the King's audience chamber. Veldan was cool in manner, but not hostile. To Veldan, Femke was simply another person to introduce to his Majesty, the King.

'May I present Lady Femke, Ambassador of Shandar, your Majesty,' Veldan announced. The waiting was over and her stomach churned with nervous anticipation.

I should not be nervous she told herself silently. I walk into Emperor Surabar's study without a second thought. This is no different.

It *was* different, of course, but Femke controlled her nerves and smiled with every ounce of friendliness that she could muster as she entered the King's chamber. To her relief the King smiled back with what looked to be a measure of genuine pleasure. King Malo was not alone and Femke took the opportunity to do a lightning scan of the room as she curtsied.

'Welcome, Lady Femke. It's always a pleasure to receive a *peaceful* emissary from our nearest neighbours. What brings you to my humble Kingdom?' the King asked. His tone was friendly, holding warmth blended with a tinge of irony.

Femke studied his face, which looked benevolent and wise. King Malo wore his age well. His silver hair complemented his simple gold crown. He sat straight, his eyes bright with intelligence. There was no place for unnecessary lies here, Femke realised.

One close aide, two armed guards at the door and a young man who could be the King's son sitting to one side, she noted. And Veldan, she added, completing her mental list by accounting for the footsteps behind her.

'Your Majesty, his Imperial Majesty, Surabar, the *new*

Emperor of Shandar, sends greetings and offers gifts of compensation for the recent unwarranted invasion of your Sovereign territory. He wishes to convey his apologies on behalf of the Empire and to seek a way of initiating a new era of trade and cooperation with Thrandor,' she announced, pleased that she managed to inject both confidence and warmth into her tone. With a wave of her hand, Sidis, Kalheen and Phagen stepped forward and opened the boxes of treasure they bore.

Femke was gratified to see the slight raise of the King's eyebrows, indicating genuine surprise at the contents of the small chests. Surely Krider, or one of his other servants, would have briefed him on the contents of the chests, she thought. But apparently not, she concluded. *Unless the King is a better actor than I am a judge of expression.*

She noticed the King glance across at the young man with fair hair who sat to one side of the chamber. The slightest of nods from him brought a smile to the King's face. *I wonder what that was all about?* Femke's mind raced with possibilities. *From that look, the young man seems in too superior a position here to be the King's son. Could the youth be Lord Shanier, the Sorcerer who outwitted Lord Vallaine and destroyed the Shandese invasion force? He looks younger than I am!* Femke knew she looked younger than her twenty years unless she deliberately disguised her age. Perhaps this man was the same. *He appears too young to be a threat, making him all the more dangerous,* she mused to herself. Youth had often proved a useful deceptive tool when hiding her abilities, so she found a certain empathy with the young Sorcerer – if Sorcerer he was.

As a mistress of disguise herself, Femke could appreciate the benefits of Shanier's apparent youthfulness, but she knew it was possible she was not seeing Shanier's true appearance. Lord Vallaine had fooled everyone, Femke included, into thinking he was the Emperor of Shandar for months. If the rumours were true, Shanier wielded powers of sorcery even greater than Vallaine. Who could say what he was capable of?

'Lady Femke, I gladly accept these tokens from Emperor Surabar and I shall in due course provide you with a suitable response to his overture of peace. These last few months have been difficult times for us all, but Thrandor has always tried to court peace with its neighbours. I would do my subjects a great disservice if I were to turn aside such a proposal now. Be welcome in my Palace. Veldan will find you suitable quarters. I'm sure you're tired after your journey and I understand you've had no time to rest since reaching the city. Go and rest now. We'll talk again tomorrow. I would like to hear more of Emperor Surabar, and would value the chance to learn of his plans for peace and increased trade.'

'Certainly, your Majesty,' Femke answered, still smiling. 'Thank you for your kind welcome. It is most generous, given the wrongs inflicted on you by my people recently. I place myself at your service for as long as I remain here, your Majesty, though I fear my stay will be brief on this occasion. His Imperial Majesty, Emperor Surabar, is keen to hear your reply to his offer of peace, and I am bound to his call.'

74

King Malo inclined his head in acknowledgement, pursing his lips a little before replying.

'I understand, Ambassador. I would wish the same given his position. For now, though, be welcome. You may wander the Palace and its grounds at will, for none will harm you within the walls. However, if you or your men wish to venture out into the city, then I insist you take an escort – for your own safety, you understand? There are those amongst my people who have lost loved ones recently. Blood still runs hot with thoughts of vengeance. Let's not give unnecessary chances to those who might do something foolish in the heat of the moment.'

'That sounds a most wise precaution, your Majesty. Until tomorrow,' Femke replied, once again dipping in a deep curtsy before turning and walking out through the door that Veldan was quick to open for her.

The Chief Butler led her to the West Wing of the Palace and showed her to a suite of rooms on the first floor that boasted luxury greater than any Femke had ever enjoyed. Even when playing the role of Lady Alyssa, Femke had never inhabited an apartment like this.

The living area was huge, with beautiful chairs and tables arranged in a casual fashion around the room. Rich hangings and exquisite paintings adorned the walls, whilst a soft, thickly piled and intricately patterned carpet covered the floor from wall to wall. There were two bookcases laden with many leather-bound volumes, a writing bureau and a large open fireplace. The grate was set with kindling and a good supply of logs was stacked in a special recess in the wall nearby. Oil lamps, both in corner stands and on available surfaces, promised plenty of light in the evening and generous vases of flowers and bowls of fruit, together with other small snacks, were evident around the room. The bedroom and the bathing rooms were yet more sumptuous. Femke was hard pressed not to laugh when Veldan asked if the rooms were to her liking.

'They are most comfortable, thank you, Veldan,' she replied, careful to keep her voice composed and her face perfectly straight. 'I would like to take a bath, if that would be possible? Could you arrange for someone to bring hot water for me please?'

'No need to have it brought by hand, Lady Femke. We have some clever people in Mantor. One of them earned a knighthood some years ago when he developed a system of pumping hot water through pipes directly to the baths. I'll send in someone to operate the pump for you and your bath should be full in a few minutes.'

'Thank you, Veldan, I will watch the procedure with interest. If this pump proves as efficient as you say, I would like to meet this knight. Do you think he would consider a commission to fit the Imperial Palace in Shandrim? I'm sure his Imperial Majesty would love to stop all the staff traipsing around his Palace with pails of water.'

'Who knows, my Lady, who knows?' Veldan said with a wry smile. 'If you desire anything else, then please pull the bell rope in the corner.'

'One last thing, Veldan,' Femke called hastily as the butler started to leave. 'Where are the rest of my party quartered, please?'

'They're in the South Annex, my Lady. The guest quarters there are not quite fitted to the same standard as these, but I can assure you they will not find their accommodation wanting,' Veldan replied. Looking around her room, Femke did not doubt his word.

'I'm sure you'll look after them admirably, Veldan. I was merely thinking I would like to talk with them occasionally. I will have instructions for them during our stay, concerning preparations for our return,' she said, her expression warm. Then she dropped her voice into a mock conspiratorial whisper. 'Mainly in the form of a shopping list of souvenirs.'

'Of course,' Veldan said, clearly amused at her confession. 'Simply ring the bell. Your room servant will lead you there at your request.'

'Thank you kindly, Veldan, you've been most helpful.'

'My pleasure, Lady Femke.'

Veldan departed and Femke marvelled again at the size of the huge sunken marble tub in the bathing room. It would afford her more of a swim than a bath, she decided with a shiver of anticipation. It amazed her that something so heavy would be fitted in an upper-storey room, but it certainly fitted the surroundings. The entire Palace had been decorated on a grand scale.

Force of habit made her check the rooms for signs of concealed entrances, spy-holes and escape routes. To her surprise, Femke found no sign of surveillance points. Either the King did not see fit to monitor his guests, or the spy points were so well disguised that Femke could not locate them. After her second sweep of the suite, Femke dismissed the second option and concluded that the King's spy network, if indeed he had one, was not operating on the same scale as the one in Shandrim. Intrigue and plotting were a way of life to the Shandese.

Femke was delighted with the results of her search. It would make her job here easier. With no organised spy network to contend with, the Thrandorians had effectively handed her the keys to the Palace and said, 'Go ahead, take whatever you need.'

Reynik was disappointed not to meet the King of Thrandor. To ride all this way and then be excluded from the main event was galling. He was still not sure that coming to the attention of Emperor Surabar during the fight after the coronation ceremony had been a good thing. He had worked so hard to get into the General's Elite Legion. Now, before he had even begun to settle in, he had been yanked from the ranks to play travel guard for a Lady Ambassador.

Ambassador Femke was pleasant enough. Reynik knew it was not her fault he was here, but he was frustrated that his time in the General's Legion had started with such a duty. Some of his fellow soldiers had been jealous of his opportunity to see Mantor. This would inevitably create friction upon his return, which was never a good thing as the new boy. All he could hope was that he would gain experience from this trip that would prove useful to his career.

Sidis had been a miserable travelling companion. The sour-faced old File Leader had stifled any prospect of fun. Reynik suspected that had Sidis been more genial, the Ambassador would have made pleasant company. As it was, the entire two weeks had felt like slow torture. And what was more, Sidis had not wanted to engage in weapons practice, so Reynik felt sadly stiff and unfulfilled.

Servants led Reynik through the Palace to his quarters. The place was a maze. He would get lost here for sure, he thought grimly. However, when they opened the door to his room, Reynik could not help but smile. It was more luxurious than anything he'd known in Shandar. Perhaps the trip would not be so bad after all, he mused.

CHAPTER FOUR

'Gone? Gone where?'

Lord Danar was infuriated by the placid face of Versande Matthiason. The innkeeper appeared imperturbable in the face of Danar's anger. Like a rock on a stormy seashore, he let the waves of emotion wash over him, and if there was any wear from the pounding action of that crashing surf, then it merely served to make his surface smoother.

'I'm not sure where Lady Alyssa went, my Lord. It's not my place to question guests on their movements, but I did notice her saddlebags were full. If I were to hazard a guess, then I would say she has left the city and is riding home,' Versande answered in a calm voice.

'Left the city!' Danar exclaimed. His eyebrows rose so high they were nearly lost in his hairline and every crease of his expressive face showed disbelief. 'When did she leave?'

'This morning. Early. I'm sorry, Lord Danar.'

Alyssa had eluded him again. First she had evaded his

efforts to see her after the coronation. Now she had made him look a fool in front of Versande. As an added insult, the humiliation would cost him ten gold sen when his friends discovered she had left. 'Have you any idea when she'll be back?' he asked, with little hope in his voice.

Versande shook his head. 'I'm afraid not, my Lord. When Lady Alyssa left, she gave no indication of when she might return.'

'That seems to be one of Alyssa's more consistent tendencies,' Danar muttered. 'She left this morning, you say? Well maybe I can catch up with her,' he added, more to himself than the innkeeper. 'Thank you, Versande. If you hear anything more from Lady Alyssa, I'll be grateful for news of her.'

'I understand, my Lord. If I hear anything of the Lady's whereabouts, I'll send word. If it helps, Alyssa and her servants turned down the Eastern Avenue.'

Danar nodded, then turned and walked slowly out of the inn, his face thoughtful. Was he deluding himself? Had he really made a connection with Alyssa, or was it his imagination? He was used to women falling in a swoon at his feet the moment he showed interest in them. It was irritating yet strangely refreshing that Alyssa was not so easily won. Should he follow her? He did not even know her home city, but surely there could be few women who fitted Alyssa's description and status in the coastal cities. He could try to follow her trail. If he lost it he could enquire at the next coastal city. Would Alyssa be impressed by his persistence if he followed her, or would he brand himself a nuisance to be avoided? It was a difficult dilemma. Danar did not yet know Alyssa well enough to make a balanced assessment.

'Whatever I do, I must decide now. If I leave it any longer, her trail will go cold,' he muttered. He stopped and stared silently into space for a moment. 'It's no use. I must do something. If I let her go, then I may never see her again. I don't want to spend the rest of my life wondering. Right or wrong, I must go after her.'

The streets were busy. It was nearly time for the midday bell. Soon it would get busier as folk took time out from their jobs to seek food during the lunchtime period. People strode along with an air of purpose. There was no time for chatting, and those who did engage in conversation spoke in brief staccato sentences. Everyone was in a hurry to do something. With his mind made up, Danar launched into the bustling crowd and set to work.

He left messages for his friends and family that he would be out of the city for a while, and then gathered some travelling gear. Danar was not well travelled and had never been on the road alone. He had no real experience of camping, or knowledge of the roads he intended to take. When he set off from his father's residence along the Eastern Avenue later that afternoon, he did so with poorly-packed saddlebags, ill-chosen equipment and the flimsiest of plans. He was blinkered – unaware of his shortcomings and totally focused on his goal.

The weather was fine as he left Shandrim, adding to his illusion that the journey would be a wonderful adventure. He had a good horse from his father's stable, a fine sword, and plenty of money. He felt prepared to face anything. It was ironic that as he left the city heading east, Femke re-entered the city from the south.

Femke had been at the Thrandorian Palace for two days before the luxuriant spell was rudely broken.

'My Lady, my Lady,' panted Kalheen as he burst into her suite without warning.

'Manners, Kalheen!' Femke snapped, her voice hard with reprimand. 'You've been in service long enough to know you never enter a room without knocking – especially the room of a lady.'

Femke was amazed Kalheen had broken such basic protocol. If the servant thought he could be familiar with her because they had travelled together for three weeks, then Femke was ready to stamp on him hard to eliminate such misconceptions immediately.

'I'm sorry, my Lady,' he gasped, quite obviously struggling to recover from having run to her room. It was difficult for Femke to imagine how far Kalheen had run, as she did not yet know the full layout of the Palace. He was not fit, so she suspected he had not run far. 'I promise I'll observe due manners in future, but this is too important to wait on politeness. There's been a murder, my Lady – here in the Palace.'

'A murder, Kalheen? Who?' Femke asked. Hairs prickled at the back of her neck. Instinct told her she would not like Kalheen's news.

'Baron Anton, my Lady. He was found dead in his room this morning, but that isn't the worst of it . . .'

'Spit it out, Kalheen, what is it?'

83

'Everyone thinks *you* killed him,' Kalheen wheezed. 'Well – when I say "everyone", I exclude myself, of course. Phagen, Sidis and Reynik won't believe it either, but the Thrandorians believe you killed him. There's a party of guards on their way here to arrest you. That's why I ran. You have to get away, my Lady. Now. You have to run. If they catch you, who knows what they'll do?'

The words came tumbling in a panicked rush, made less intelligible by his thick chest heaving from recent exertions.

Femke did not panic. She took a deep breath and counted slowly to five in her mind. The discipline worked. 'Thank you, Kalheen, but I'm not ready to run yet,' she said calmly. 'I've committed no crime, and certainly not murder. I've been here in my room all night, so why do they think I'm responsible?'

'They found your brooch clutched in the Baron's dead hand and a Shandese-style knife in his chest. It was the brooch you wore yesterday on your green dress.'

'Did they indeed,' she stated more than asked. 'Let's see about that, shall we?'

Femke strode through to her bedroom and over to the large, walk-in wardrobe where she had hung her clothes. The green dress was on the front hanger where she had put it the night before, but there was no sign of the brooch and the dress was ripped slightly where the piece of decorative jewellery had been pinned through the material. Someone had torn the brooch from the dress, but Femke doubted it was Baron Anton. Whoever had stolen the brooch was out to frame her. Worse, when she checked her knife belt, a blade was missing. The matching hilts had a distinctive

84

Shandese styling that would be hard to mistake. A few moments before the idea of running away had seemed foolish – suddenly it appeared to be a much better idea.

Femke knew she could never prove her innocence from the inside of a dungeon, or worse, dangling from a gibbet. Running would make her appear guilty, but at least it would give her the freedom to seek out her unknown adversary and try to discover his motive. Femke had little knowledge of the Thrandorian justice system, and less of how they would deal with a foreign diplomat charged with killing an eminent Nobleman and friend of the King. With a shudder at the wave of possibilities that assailed her, Femke decided not to wait around to find out.

'Bar the door, Kalheen,' she ordered. 'I've been set up. You're right – I have to get out of here, and I don't think I'll get far through the corridors.'

Femke ran into the living room and over to the window. Throwing the larger section open, she leaned outside for a moment and studied the escape route she had in mind. It was a dangerous one. She had not expected to have to leave the Thrandorian Palace in a hurry, yet force of habit had led her to search out all exit options. This was the best shot she had. It was not the first time her preplanning had proved useful.

Rather than climb straight out of the window, Femke ran back to the bedroom and rifled quickly through her things. Grabbing a small knapsack she threw a variety of items into it. Thrandorian money, a couple of changes of clothes, her small collection of knives and lock-picks, along with the small wooden jewellery box containing her store of poisons in tightly-corked tiny metal phials concealed under the false bottom. A loud knock at the door to the living room made Femke's heart leap in her chest. Time was up. She had to leave.

Femke slung the knapsack over her shoulders, swapped her court shoes for short slip-on boots and ran to the open window. A dress was hardly suitable clothing for this sort of activity, but there was no help for it now. As she climbed out onto the ledge, Kalheen helped her maintain her balance. Femke turned back for a moment. She noted the burly servant had already thrown the bolts on the door.

'Try to delay them as long as you can. I'll be grateful for any time you can buy me,' she whispered.

'I'll do my best. Good luck, my Lady,' he replied.

The ledge was narrow. The knapsack sticking out from Femke's back prevented her from facing out from the wall, so she was forced to sidestep along, face to the wall and almost blind. The hem of her dress flapped around her thighs, an added distraction as the breeze plucked at the material with invisible fingers. There were four large window ledges to traverse before she reached her path to the ground. Femke was concerned about being spotted from within as she crossed these, but luck was with her. The rooms she passed were all empty, and as she reached her descent point there was no sign that whoever had knocked at her door was looking outside for her yet.

Femke craned her neck to look over her shoulder. The nearby tree had seemed much closer to the wall when she had viewed it from the window of her suite. Now the distance between her ledge and the nearest branch made her feel as if she needed to grow wings to successfully negotiate the gulf of air between them.

Femke paused to consider her options, but they were limited. Although she was only one storey up, the West Wing had been constructed on a grand scale, with all the rooms having high ceilings. If she were to lower herself until she was hanging by her fingertips from the ledge, Femke would still have to drop some twenty feet to the ground below. Dropping that far would risk breaking limbs. At best it would result in bruising and pain that she could ill afford.

There was the option of continuing around the ledge, breaking in through a window and hoping to avoid discovery within the corridors of the Palace for long enough to get down a stairwell to the ground floor. But with people actively looking for her the risks involved in this were unacceptable.

Femke was left once more to face the leap into the nearby tree. Her mind baulked at the thought of it. Could she jump that far? If she missed the catch, would the lower branches give her a second chance, or would she have too much momentum to arrest her fall?

Femke had never feared death and on occasion her bravery tended towards recklessness. This was one of those occasions. Closing her eyes she drew in her focus. For one heart-stopping moment, time appeared to slow and her heart threatened to climb up into her throat as Femke bunched her legs into a crouch. Adrenalin coursed through her veins as her body overbalanced, committing her to the jump. As her body began to topple, Femke exploded out of her crouch and propelled herself backwards into space with every ounce of strength she possessed. Twisting mid-flight, Femke stretched out like a trapeze artist, reaching for the rapidly approaching bar.

The jump was perfect; Femke's hands finding the branch that she had aimed for – but to her horror the branch was too thick for her fingers to grip properly. As her body swung past the vertical under the branch, her grip failed and she flipped feet first into the tree. Twisting a second time mid-flight, like a cat righting itself before impact, Femke managed to turn face down in time for her body to smash into a lower branch. The branch caught her full across the stomach with an abruptness that drove the wind from her lungs. Her eyes watered as the initial wave of pain blasted through her body.

Draped over the branch, Femke did not have time to find her balance. Before she could recover from the impact, she started to tip over, feet first. A frantic scrabble of hands and feet followed before she managed to secure footholds and restore her equilibrium. Temporary safety was restored, but if she remained exposed in the leafless tree for long, someone would spot her. Femke had to get over the outer Palace wall and into the city if she were to stay free long enough to prove her innocence.

The muscles in Femke's bruised stomach protested as she climbed limb by limb down the tree, but there was to be no respite. As she dropped from the lowest branch a shout sounded out from the first-floor window of her suite. The chase was on. She launched into a run towards the outer wall, vaguely aware of answering shouts coming from the grounds somewhere to her right.

The wall towered above her as she reached its base. At first glance the entire face of it looked smooth, but from a previous walk in the grounds of the Palace, Femke knew that this was not universally the case. There were many places along the wall with enough cracks in the stone-work to allow an agile climber sufficient holds to scale it with ease. She simply had to find one of those points, and quickly.

A new sound brought another lurch of fear that gripped her insides and twisted them mercilessly. Femke turned and for an instant she froze. Royal Guards were running towards her, still some distance away, but closing fast. The sound that chilled her did not come from the guards, though, but from the huge, brutish-looking dogs that loped alongside them.

'Stay where you are,' she heard one of the guards call. 'Stop, or we release the dogs.'

Femke did not hesitate. She exploded back into action, running away from the approaching guards at a full sprint. It was impossible to ignore them, but she concentrated her focus on finding a section of the wall that she could climb. Her first instinct was that the guards were bluffing. They were unlikely to release the dogs on an Ambassador. Surely her diplomatic status would make them think twice? Unfortunately, considerations of diplomatic immunity did not seem to be a part of the guards' thought processes.

The pain from her fall into the tree was forgotten and Femke raced alongside the wall, mentally blessing the architect and gardeners for doing such a good job of levelling the lawns. Femke found just the spot she was looking for. She leaped up, jammed her fingers into the first crack and then pulled herself as far above the ground as she could.

Femke had just found her first good toehold and was pushing higher up the wall when two things happened simultaneously to distract her. First there was a snarling snap as a dog raked her leg with its teeth. A tight fiery pain erupted above her ankle, but the momentum of the dog had denied it a firm hold and carried its body on past her. It took a moment for the animal to land and turn for another attack, during which time a newfound desperation drove Femke to pull her body even higher from the ground. At the same time as the dog made its attack, a crossbow quarrel smashed into the wall to her right, showering her with splinters of wood and stone.

'Don't shoot her, you idiot!' someone shouted. 'The King wants to question her. It's hard to do that if she's dead! Quick. Catch her before she gets over the wall.'

Femke would have grinned if she had not been gritting her teeth against the strain of the climb. Her ankle and stomach were painful. Her right eye was in spasm and watering profusely from a flying stone chip that had struck it when the crossbow bolt shattered against the wall. However, nobody was going to catch her this side of the wall now and a fierce exultation gripped her as she neared temporary safety.

With a last heave, Femke mounted the top of the wall and glanced back down at the guards who were now at the base of the wall.

'Come down, Ambassador. If you leave the grounds of the Palace, I won't be able to protect you any longer,' shouted up the guard whom Femke identified as having ordered the others to stop shooting. Femke reasoned he must be the senior man present.

'Protect me? You call a dog attack and being shot at protecting me?' Femke laughed. 'I'll take my chances outside, thanks.'

'The King only wants to talk with you,' the guard insisted. 'Please come down from the wall. I promise I'll escort you personally to his audience chamber.'

'And I suppose you will then escort me from the audience chamber to your dungeon as well? I don't think so,' Femke added sarcastically. 'I've been framed for murder. I'm not about to stay around to see this scenario through to its logical conclusion. Give your King my regards. Tell him I intend to find out who killed the Baron. When I have that information then I'll come and talk to him.'

'Don't do it, Ambassador,' the guard warned in a 'Don't push me' singsong tone.

Femke ignored him. Lowering herself down the other side of the wall until she was hanging by her fingertips, she let go. Despite landing lightly and allowing her body to collapse, converting her inertia into a rolling motion, the shock of hitting a stone pavement rattled through her body. More pain coursed from head to toe, but Femke knew there was no time to nurse her wounds.

Hobbling away, she could feel the trickle of blood running down her leg into her low-cut boot as she scouted the nearby streets for hide-outs. She could not remain in the open for long. The Royal Guards would soon be out in large numbers and would purge the upper city streets in quick time. One thing in her favour was the guards did not know she was hurt, so they would expect her to run much further than she intended.

There were fewer streets in the vicinity of the Palace in comparison with the lower reaches of Mantor, but Femke's instincts told her the guards would expect her to run like a frightened rabbit. They would not search the upper city with any great care. Eventually Femke wanted to blend into the masses in the lower city, but for now she would happily settle for a hidey-hole in which to evade the initial searchers.

There were few residences to choose from, as they were all large and widely spaced. The houses were set in enormous gardens, which could work to her advantage. The deserted streets helped. And so far Femke had not seen a soul, which meant no one to tell of her passing.

It was strange to think that the lower city would be busy now. Stallholders would already be hawking their wares on the flea markets that abounded on the streets, shouting and waving to attract attention to their stalls. Upper city life progressed at a more sedate pace. The residents who lived nearest the Palace had secure incomes or family fortunes that did not depend on rushing around to make ends meet. The busiest time of day here was evening, when the rich gathered to entertain one another with parties and other social gatherings. Mornings were for recovering and clearing up, but this did not mean the rich were ignorant of what was happening around them. Femke knew that care was needed wherever she went in this city.

Breaking into a house would be fraught with more danger. Normally Femke would stake out a house for some time, preferably days, before breaking in. Patterns of behaviour of the occupants were vital information if she were to get in and out undetected, but there was no time for such preparation now. The only option left was to hide in an outbuilding. A stable or a workshop, a shed or a summerhouse – any would do, providing it offered a quick, easy, effective place to hide.

By instinct, Femke paused and looked around. Something prickled at her senses like watching eyes, and though she judged it to be her body's senses working at a hyperactive rate, still intuition sparked the feeling that more danger lurked nearby.

Whatever had triggered the sensation, Femke dismissed it for now. All danger was relative. Her priority was to stay ahead of the Royal Guards and, hobbling as she was, this would not be easy. Anything else would have to be dealt with on the run. Risks were inevitable; this was but the first of them.

Femke found what she was looking for a few hundred yards from the Palace wall. An impressive house boasting neatly kept gardens had a small outbuilding, little more than a dozen feet long by about eight feet wide, alongside the main house. With another swift look round to see if anyone was watching, Femke hopped over the waist-high garden wall and limped to the door of the small building.

The door was locked, but this presented no great obstacle. It was a simple matter to pick the lock and get inside. With a silently mouthed expression of pain she slipped her knapsack from her shoulders and rummaged until she found an appropriate lock pick. The clatter of hooves approaching from the direction of the Palace gave Femke added incentive. Time was running out fast. The Royal Guards had mobilised more quickly than she had anticipated. The combination of time pressure and the pain of her injuries made what should have been a simple operation take an apparent eternity.

Femke felt trickles of sweat run down her forehead as she worked the pick inside the mechanism of the lock. She knew she was applying pressure in the right place, but the lock was reluctant to yield. The young spy suffered an agonising moment of doubt as the horses approached at pace, then the stiff mechanism of the lock finally turned with a soft grating noise. Femke swiftly drew the door open and stepped inside. Fortunately, the hinges had been better oiled than the lock, and the door swung smoothly and silently both ways. Moments later, Femke had relocked the door from within and she heaved a pained sigh of relief. The searchers were unlikely to open locked doors in their initial search.

'There's nothing worse than a dry lock to ruin your day if you're under pressure,' she quoted, thinking back fondly to lessons with her mentor. How right he had been! What would Ferrand say if he could see her now? This assignment had always promised to be unusual, but Femke could not help wondering how it had gone from being straightforward to a complete disaster so quickly. There had been no hints that anything was awry. The Thrandorians had not exactly welcomed her with open arms, but they had been civil. From what little Femke had seen of life in the Palace there was no suggestion that murder was the norm in Thrandorian politics. Ferrand would have known what to do. He had always appeared in control, regardless of circumstance. Was that what had caused his downfall? Femke still had no idea what had happened to her mentor. It was one of the most widely speculated mysteries in Shandar. Even the Emperor of Shandar had not known the fate of the spymaster, but Femke felt sure her old friend must have breathed his last.

Ferrand had always been an oddball in the intelligence community. Most spies made their living by remaining grey and anonymous, silently gathering information in the background. Ferrand was rarely out of the limelight. Being a powerful lord, he was a leading figure in Shandese high society, though few knew he was also a master of disguise. For many years he had been the Emperor's top spy and Femke had been lucky to be his apprentice.

She sighed aloud at her melancholy thoughts. There would be time for such reminiscence once the present danger was past. Her current hiding place represented a huge gamble. If the Royal Guards had tracker dogs, then there would be no escape. The shed had no back door for her to flee through, which was contrary to everything she had been taught. The attack dogs that had chased her in the Palace grounds were not of a breed known for their tracking abilities, so Femke felt safe from them. However, she did not know what other assets the guards had at their command.

It was dark in the shed, but not overly so. A small amount of light leaked in through the edges of the shuttered window. After a few minutes Femke found her eyes beginning to adapt to the low light and she felt confident she could move around without accidentally bumping into anything. Making a noise now could prove disastrous.

From what little Femke could see, the shed was used both as a workshop and as a storage room for gardening equipment. Long-handled garden tools were neatly arranged in a rack to the right of the door, whilst a workbench boasted a plethora of woodworking tools, all neatly arrayed on various hooks and shelves below the shuttered window to the left. At the far end of the small shed a strange, hulking, shadowy shape lurked, like some great monster crouched ready to pounce. Femke froze for an instant before reason took hold. There was nothing to fear here other than discovery by the Royal Guards.

Wary of making any noise, Femke stepped gingerly towards the black shape. Exploring with her hands, she realised it was a soft dark cloth wrapped over something hard. Suddenly Femke froze again. The sound of someone knocking at the main house door was followed by the sound of approaching boots on the path outside.

'Hello, what can I do for you?' Femke faintly heard someone say.

'Good morning, my Lord, we're looking for a woman who was last seen heading in this direction. She's slim, dark-haired . . .'

Femke held her breath. As she listened to the guard speaking to the owner of the house, there was a rattle as someone tried the handle to the door of the workshop. A loud thump sounded as he decided to give the door a hard shove to check it was locked and not merely stiff, or barricaded from within.

Crouching down, Femke silently lifted the edge of the material in front of her and squinted into the darkness beneath. The cloth covered a stack of cut timber. To her delight there was just enough room at the left-hand edge for her to squeeze under the cover and sit hidden from casual inspection. Hardly daring to breathe, she twisted her body into the small space. Femke had barely settled when there was a loud cracking sound and a flood of light shone in through the side window. Whoever had tried the door was suspicious enough to wrench open the outer wooden shutters of the workshop window. If Femke had not hidden, the guard would have caught her like a snake in a pit.

'Hey! Be careful! There's no need to force those shutters, they've got catches top and bottom. I hope you haven't broken them.'

'Sorry, my Lord,' apologised a man's voice, though his tone did not reflect the apology. 'The outbuilding's clear, Sergeant,' the same voice stated. The sound of retreating footsteps caused Femke to expel a silent sigh of relief.

'Well, my Lord, if you do see the Ambassador, please alert the Royal Guards immediately. I strongly advise you not to approach her or restrain her, as she may be dangerous,' the Sergeant said respectfully.

'Yes, of course, Sergeant, I will be sure to do that. Good luck in your search.'

Femke smiled and quietly adjusted her position until she was as comfortable as she could be in the cramped space. Her bruised body ached in many places, but as the sounds of the search quickly faded, Femke did her best to ignore the pain, concentrating instead on planning her next move. Her initial instinct was to wait for dark. This would give the guards enough time to become discouraged by the fruitless search and start to get lax. As to where Femke should go next, she could not decide. Her mind flitted from one idea to the next as she turned over the possibilities.

Minutes passed silently and slowly, and Femke started to feel a sleepy lassitude overtake her. The stuffy air, combined with the darkness under the cloth, gradually worked its mind-numbing spell and her consciousness drifted until a sudden sound caused her to start with alarm. It was the sound of a key turning in the lock of the workshop door.

Femke kept perfectly still, praying fervently that whoever was coming into the workshop would not discover her. There was a slight creak as the door opened and more light entered the room. After a short pause the voice of the Lord who had talked to the guards spoke softly, but in clear tones.

'All right, Ambassador, you can come out now.'

CHAPTER FIVE

'I said, "You can come out now", Ambassador,' the voice repeated steadily. 'Don't try anything silly. I'm armed and I have no qualms about striking down a woman. Come out from under the cover and let's go into the house where we can speak in more comfort.'

Femke's mind raced, but there was little she could do except comply. The Lord had her trapped. It might be possible to disable or kill him and escape again, but that would pile on more trouble. Killing a Lord of Thrandor would do little to prove her innocence of the murder of Baron Anton. The man had known she was here, but had not alerted the Royal Guards. Why? It would be interesting to see what he was up to, she decided. Would he prove an unexpected ally? Experience told her this was unlikely. It was more probable that her intuition of danger when running from the Palace had been correct; rather than escape from it, she had leaped into its jaws.

'Very well, my Lord, you have me at a disadvantage,'

Femke said, also keeping her voice low. 'I accept your invitation. Would you happen to have any dahl brewing? I left the Palace in rather a hurry this morning and didn't get to finish my cup. It was most inconvenient.'

'I'm sure that a cup of dahl can be arranged,' the man drawled, his voice containing a hint of amusement at her cool request.

Femke drew back the cover and squinted at the dark silhouette in the doorway. The man was of medium height, but judging by his outline he was overweight. She could see that his hand was riding on the hilt of a sword, which was belted at his ample waist. Lords did not wear swords as a standard form of dress, so he must have donned it after the guards had left. Was he just wearing it to intimidate, or did he know how to use it? His bulk suggested the former, but Femke's intuition led her to believe the latter. He did not look agile at first glance, but who was to say he had not been a master swordsman in his youth?

As Femke eased out of the shadowy corner there was the faintest of crackling sounds, which she instantly recognised as the tearing of cobwebs. Spiders did not particularly bother Femke, but an involuntary shudder rippled through her body. Despite the pain it sparked, she brushed herself down vigorously. She ran her fingers through her hair several times, but could still feel a tingling sensation of movement over her scalp.

'The use of a bath would be welcome right now as well,' Femke said, trying to maintain a casual tone.

The Lord ignored her, taking a moment instead to look cautiously around outside whilst constantly monitoring

Femke for any sudden movements. Femke did nothing to promote any more unpleasantness. The pain emanating from her various bruises and cuts was making it difficult enough to stand properly. She had stiffened considerably in her cramped hiding place, and the last thing she felt like doing was to run again.

'Come quickly. Get in the house before anyone sees you.' He backed out of the doorway, beckoning to her with his free hand, his head constantly on the move as he watched for Royal Guards.

Femke complied as well as she could and staggered out into the daylight. Her best estimate told her she had hidden for less than an hour, yet it was enough for her eyes to have adjusted to the dark. Her right eye was still particularly sensitive. Whatever had lodged in it during her near miss with the crossbow bolt made it water in the bright light. Despite struggling to focus it was hard not to see all the blood on her hands and clothes.

'What the . . . ?' she exclaimed.

'No time for that now, Ambassador – get indoors. Quickly!'

Femke felt a firm shove between her shoulder blades and nearly fell as she stumbled along the short path around to a side door into the large house. The drips that Femke had assumed to be sweat as she had fought with the lock of the shed, and subsequently in the warmth beneath the timber cover, had largely been rivulets of blood from one or more head wounds. Although she could not remember any impact, Femke assumed that one or more of the stone chips sent flying by the crossbow bolt had cut her. Scalp wounds always bled profusely. Femke had seen enough to know that the slightest scratch could bleed spectacularly if it were in the right place.

'Damn!' she swore under her breath. It was going to be difficult to run anywhere looking like this. Her joking comment about a bath was more appropriate than she had known.

Femke staggered through the door and the Lord closed it softly behind them. They were in a kitchen area, though there were no signs of any kitchen staff. Femke turned and took her first proper look at her captor. The man looked familiar, though when Femke had seen him in the Palace, he had not worn the gloating smile he had now.

Femke had seen many Noblemen around the Palace during her short time there. There were always small groups of them wandering through the corridors. The King had briefly introduced her at a session of Court on her second day in the Palace, and she had used the opportunity to speak with several of them after the daily cases had concluded. Was this man one of those she had spoken to? She did not think so. Femke had a good mind for detail and would have remembered his name if she had spoken with him before.

'So, Ambassador Femke, I understand you've been having some adventures up in the Palace. You've stirred up the Royal Guards so that they're buzzing around like angry hornets. What have you done to upset them so much, I wonder? Are you disposed to telling me, or will I have to wait until I visit the Palace later?'

Femke considered the question for a moment. There was

something about this man she did not like. He was slimy. He reminded her of a bloated toad, with a hungry grin and greedy eyes. A picture of his tongue shooting out to capture her and draw her into his mouth flashed through her mind. A chill ran down her spine.

'I have been set up, Lord . . .'

'Count actually – Count Dreban,' the rotund Noble supplied, his face looking smug and more toad-like at her ignorance.

'*Count* Dreban,' Femke corrected with a nod to acknowledge the error. 'I've been framed on a charge of murder, when I'm here on a mission of peace. The whole situation is bizarre.'

The Count's eyebrows shot up at the mention of murder and his eyes narrowed with an unsavoury hunger. 'Murder?' he asked, his voice clearly relishing the taste of the word upon his tongue. 'Not the King?'

'No, my Lord, the King lives. It's Baron Anton who has been murdered, and someone cleverly made it look as though I was his killer.'

To Femke's surprise the Count began to laugh; a deep, slow laugh that was far from humorous. Another shiver ran down her spine as she watched the Count's mirth build. For a moment Femke considered attempting to escape there and then.

'Baron Anton! The Baron who would be King – murdered! Ho, ho, ho! Very funny, young lady, though you probably fail to appreciate the finer points of the situation.'

'I fail to see the humour in murder, Count Dreban. Particularly when I stand accused of it.'

The Count continued to chortle, pleased at Femke's news and unconcerned by her situation. At last he gathered his composure. Dreban smiled at her; the toad that had caught the juicy fly. His blue eyes glittered with malice.

'You're not Thrandorian, Ambassador,' he said cryptically. 'If you were, you would appreciate the beauty of the scenario. It is quite simple. Our glorious King, Malo, who to my mind is neither glorious, nor worthy to be King, has done nothing during his reign to lift Thrandor from the mire of obscurity. Indeed, he has failed so totally in his duties that he has neglected to sire an heir for when he finally performs a worthy service and departs this world. The lack of an heir has sparked a lot of interest as to who would gain the throne in the event of the King's death.'

'I can see how the lack of an heir apparent could cause excitement amongst those who are in a position to stake a claim,' Femke replied, choosing her words with care. 'We had a similar situation in Shandar recently. Was Baron Anton one of the stronger claimants?'

'Anton? Hardly!' Dreban snorted. 'He has ... *had* no Royal blood at all. It was Malo's idea to put Anton in the frame for the throne. It's been widely known in the King's Court for some years now that Malo intended to announce Anton as his successor. Once he had done so, the dynasty of the present bloodline would have ended for ever with Malo's death. Anton and his family would have founded a new dynasty and Malo would have been seen as a traitor to his kin for centuries.'

'What about the recent military victories? You can't dismiss those out of hand. Believe me, the Shandese Emperor takes King Malo very seriously. Given that before he took the Mantle, Emperor Surabar was a military general of the highest calibre, I would say King Malo has restored Thrandor's reputation as a strong country over this last year. I'm surprised he isn't universally seen as a hero.'

'The military victories!' Dreban spat derisively. 'I can dismiss them, and I will. On both occasions some commoner brat, who had no more Noble blood in his veins than a sewer rat, saved Malo. The King had no part in saving Thrandor. The truth is he was extraordinarily lucky on both occasions, and he knows it. The best thing Malo has done for Thrandor is to fail to produce an heir. It will give one of the more able branches of the family a chance to demonstrate what kingship is about.'

'I assume that if Baron Anton was the King's favourite to take the throne, this gained him a lot of enemies,' Femke said thoughtfully.

'I would say "rivals" rather than enemies, Ambassador,' Count Dreban countered, though his face contradicted his words. 'We do not conduct our politics by bloodshed here in Thrandor. Life in Mantor is not barbaric.'

'If you say so, Count Dreban, though to date my experience of your city would have me believe otherwise.'

'Oh, I doubt the murder of Baron Anton was politically motivated, Ambassador,' the Count responded.

'Really? How can you be so sure?' Femke asked, intrigued by the surety in his tone.

'I have the reputation in Court for being the most ruthless of the Nobles, yet even I would not stoop to such base levels. I do whatever underhand acts are necessary to undermine and discredit my rivals, but I would never resort to murder and there are none amongst our Nobility who would have the stomach for such bloody tactics. Mark my words, Ambassador, this is not a political killing.'

'But if it wasn't political, then who killed the Baron?' Femke asked, not convinced by the Count's argument. In Shandar there was always someone ready to kill in order to achieve his aims. It was an occupational hazard for those in power there and it was hard to imagine Thrandor was completely free of this sort of thinking too.

'I have no idea. I'm intrigued to find out, but as far as the rest of Thrandor is concerned, the answer to that question will be obvious. The visiting Ambassador is the random element involved. Of course you did it, and I will collect the glory for having captured you and brought you to justice. Who knows, it could give me an edge over the others in the new succession battle that is going to brew.'

The Count rubbed his hands together, his eyes distant for a moment as he revelled in his good fortune. Femke, meanwhile, was working hard on this latest turn of events. She did not want to make her position worse by injuring the Count, and she was not convinced she was in any fit state to disable him without doing so. But it seemed unlikely that the Count would take her straight to the King. If he had wanted to do that, then he could have handed Femke over to the guards when they had knocked at the door. No. If her assessment of the situation was correct, Count Dreban would lock her up and allow the King to sweat whilst the Royal Guards combed the city in vain. This meant she would have time to effect an escape. With luck she need not leave under such stressful circumstances as she had left the King's Palace.

Femke's deductions proved correct, though her hope that the Count would treat her with respect for her status proved ill founded. The Nobleman watched her with a hungry, lecherous expression as he forced her at sword point to strip to her underwear, though he made no move to touch her. His eyebrows had risen as the small arsenal of weapons secreted about her person came to light. By the time Femke was standing in her underwear, she was sure Dreban considered her much more likely to be an assassin. If he did, he made no comment. Instead he piled her things on the kitchen table next to her small knapsack. Without saying a word, he lit a torch from the kitchen fire and gestured for her to move through another door.

'May I have water to clean up my wounds, Count Dreban?' Femke asked as she was guided to a flight of cold stone steps to a cellar. The Count was taking no chances. He held his blade at her back the whole way down.

'I don't think that's necessary. It will make more of an impact if I present you looking like a fugitive, Ambassador,' he replied. 'Presentation is everything in politics.'

Femke reached the door at the bottom of the steps and stopped. It was dank and dark despite the flickering light of the Count's torch behind her. The lock and bolt were a simple arrangement and Femke silently gave a prayer of thanks as she noted the single bolt. Any more would have presented her with a severe challenge.

'Open the door, Ambassador. Your lodgings await you. I'm sorry my humble accommodation doesn't quite live up to the West Wing of the Royal Palace, but you'll have to make do for now,' he said.

Femke drew the bolt and pushed the door open. It creaked slightly about halfway open. As Femke stepped through the door she turned and gave the Count a look of disgust.

'Surely you're not going to leave me in this hole?' she asked. 'I'll freeze to death in no time.'

'I'll bring you a blanket later,' Dreban said with a grin that showed no sympathy. 'Judging by the items in your knapsack and the weapons you keep about your person, I find it difficult to believe you're a wilting flower who cannot endure a little discomfort. You're without doubt the most unusual Ambassador I've ever met. I almost believed you innocent for a while. You play the "I'm just an innocent victim" act well, but you bear the tools of a trained killer. There's no hiding from evidence like that. What I fail to understand is why the Emperor of Shandar would send you here now? It's strange timing. I'll want answers from you before I hand you to the King. Truthful answers.'

The Count stepped forward and forced Femke back further into the cellar with the point of his sword. There was barely time for her to glance around in the flickering light of the Count's torch before Dreban pulled the door closed with a resounding bang, plunging the room into inky darkness. There followed the sound of the bolt being driven home and the jangling of keys before the rattle and snick of the lock being secured. That one short moment of light was enough for Femke to allay her worst fear. The room was not bare. It was filled with a mishmash of old junk and out of vogue paraphernalia, but there were ample resources to enable her to escape.

Femke had already dealt with the most difficult part of opening the door. Dreban had made her take off her clothes, where the majority of her tools were hidden, but Femke had managed to secure one item in her mouth as she had lifted her dress over her head. She had always made a habit of tacking various oddments inside her clothes and this habit had paid off today. It had been easy to catch the little coil with her teeth as she removed her dress, biting it free and tucking it in her cheek with her tongue. Later, when Dreban divided his attention between watching her and lighting his torch, Femke palmed it from her mouth. It was then easy to manipulate the little piece of metal so that the coil of thin thread attached to it was free to unravel.

When Dreban had given his little speech at the doorway to the cellar, Femke had surreptitiously inserted the little piece of metal into the bolt socket with her thumb. Then, behind her back, she had partially unravelled the coil of thread and flicked the remaining cord inside the cellar to the left of the door. When she was ready to make her escape, all she had to do was to find the end of the cord and pull it gently. The cord would then pull on the attached piece of metal in the bolt socket, drawing the bolt out. It was a simple trick, but it did rely on the bolt not being stiff. The cord, whilst strong, was not unbreakable. Femke had no worries with this door, for the simple rectangular metal bolt had drawn easily at her touch. There was no reason to believe it would be stiffer when she came to draw it again.

The main problem was to find something with which to

pick the lock. With no light at all, Femke had to work solely by touch. It was difficult to keep track of time, but she estimated an hour had passed before she managed to extract a suitable nail from one of the shelves on the wall. At one point, a slight sound outside the door made Femke pause in her search and feel her way silently across the room. The Count could be bringing the blanket he had promised, or food and drink, she thought. Femke stood by the door and listened for several long minutes. There were no further sounds. Eventually, with a shrug, she returned to her work.

Once she had the nail it took less than two minutes for Femke to open the lock, but having done so, she relocked it again immediately. By her reckoning it was still late morning outside. The Royal Guards would still be out in force, looking for her. Femke was well hidden here and not in a hurry to jump back into the fray. Instead she located the cord leading from the bolt socket and tucked it down by the base of the door-frame to make it as inconspicuous as possible. Then she settled down to wait for night to fall.

Getting comfortable was difficult, but Femke found something that felt like an old wall-hanging or a thin rug and wrapped it around her body for warmth. Curling up in an old armchair she closed her eyes to rest, but despite the silent darkness, sleep did not come easily. The bruising across her body from her fall into the tree began to infiltrate her consciousness again. The pain crept over her like a vine. Growing. Squeezing. Invading. In comparison, the scrape on her leg where the dog had raked her with its teeth felt little more than a dull burning. Femke did not know where her scalp was cut, but the wounds there brought no pain so she left them alone for fear that poking around would restart the bleeding. Eventually, Femke drifted into a restless slumber.

Disturbing dreams troubled her throughout the lightless day. When Femke finally awoke with a start from a particularly disturbing nightmare, she could recall no specifics. One thing Femke knew with surety was that the Count had not come down to the cellar during the day. The spy felt sure she had never done more than skimmed the surface of sleep and was positive she would have shed her fragile slumber at the slightest of sounds.

There was no way of being certain of the time of day, but Femke knew instinctively that night had fallen outside. It was time for her to move and get down into lower Mantor before the Count handed her to the King.

It took a few moments to establish her orientation in the pitch blackness. Femke shivered as she shucked off her makeshift blanket. The stone floor felt freezing to her bare feet as she crept across to the door. For a moment she could not find the nail and cord. A surge of panic gripped her, but the dismay was fleeting as both came to hand seconds later. Femke sighed with relief and mentally berated her momentary loss of discipline.

With practised ease, Femke made no noise as she opened the lock. Adrenalin flowed as she took up the slack in the cord. There was always the danger that a sudden load on the cord would snap her link to freedom. With a silent prayer to any deity that chanced to be listening, Femke gritted her teeth and carefully increased the tension on the

111

cord. Her reward was the gentle scraping sound of metal against metal. Slowly – ever so slowly, Femke pulled until she felt the cord give as the thin metal plug pulled free from the socket. She winced as it swung, knocking against the escutcheon plate with a sharp tapping that sounded loud in the silence of Femke's dark prison. In reality the noise was not sufficient to carry far.

The door was open, but Femke knew that chance would now play a large part if she were to escape cleanly. Taking care not to open the door more than halfway, Femke slid silently out of the cellar. The stairwell proved as lightless as her prison, so she crept up the dark stairs on all fours, feeling ahead at every step for anything that could make a noise. The door at the top of the stairs opened into the passageway between the kitchen and what had appeared to be the main living area of the Count's residence. When she reached it no light spilled around the edges of the door, so it was reasonable to assume nobody would be in the unlit passageway.

Femke tried the handle and was pleased to find the door unlocked. The next few minutes would be crucial. Clothing was top of her priority list, but if she had to flee without it, she would. The last place she had seen her clothes was in the kitchen. Her knapsack was also last seen there, so the kitchen was the first place to look.

Faint light shone in through a small window in the passageway. It lit Femke's way as well as any torch. Before moving out into the passageway Femke paused to listen. The house was silent. Had Dreban dismissed his staff for the day to avoid one of them discovering her? It would not surprise her. It was also in character for him to renege on his promise of a blanket, and deny her food or drink.

The Count thought to parade me in front of the King's Court as a desperate fugitive, Femke thought grimly. When I've found out who did kill Baron Anton, I'll expose him for the slimy, underhand snake he is.

Again no light spilled around the edges of the kitchen door. She did not hesitate to open it. However, as she lightly turned the handle something pushed against the door, forcing it to open towards her. A dull thud echoed in the passageway as a large object impacted the floor by her feet.

Femke jumped back and jammed a hand into her mouth to stifle a scream, for as she looked down, a lifeless pair of eyes stared back. It was the Count. To Femke's horror, the greater ambient light filtering through the windows of the kitchen revealed that one of her knives was buried to the hilt in his throat.

Lord Danar rode back into Shandrim at a plodding pace ten days after he left on his quest to find Lady Alyssa. He was angry, frustrated and weary. Danar had left with high hopes that he would catch up with the young woman swiftly, and had ridden hard. However, Lady Alyssa's trail went cold within the first day. Beyond the first few hours of travel nobody had seen or heard of her, which seemed strange – Alyssa was hardly the sort of person one could readily forget.

Once or twice there had been those who, at the sight of money offered in reward for information, claimed to have seen her. But when Danar questioned them more closely, it became apparent that they were merely trying to take his gold. Alyssa had vanished without trace.

When he realised she had eluded him, Danar continued with his plan to press towards the nearest coastal city, and rode like the wind until he reached it. He rode hard until well after dark and then rose before dawn each day to continue with all haste. However, when he finally reached the port city of Channa, the young Lord found that the mystery of Lady Alyssa's disappearance deepened further.

Nobody amongst the nobility in Channa had heard of a Lady Alyssa matching the description that Danar gave. Apparently there was a Lady Alyssa, who was indeed the daughter of a rich Merchant Lord, but everyone to whom Danar spoke gave him the same story – Alyssa was neither attractive nor had she ever been to Shandrim. Danar found the stories difficult to believe. To make sure he took a trip to see this Alyssa in the hope that those he had spoken to were wrong. They were not.

The Merchant Lord was surprised to receive a gentleman visitor to see his daughter. None had ever called before. Danar noted the momentary hope that flashed in the Merchant's eyes when Danar announced his wish to see Alyssa. He also saw that hope die when he asked if Alyssa had recently been to Shandrim.

'No,' the Merchant Lord answered. 'She never goes anywhere these days.'

When his daughter emerged from a drawing room to greet them, Danar could see why. The poor girl was overweight and not blessed with a pretty face. Her hair was lank and thin, and where some girls could disguise much with nice clothing and make-up, it appeared this young woman was beyond caring.

Lord Danar had made his apologies for his mistake and left.

'It'll be just my luck to find that Alyssa has been in Shandrim all along,' Danar grumbled, as he steered his weary horse towards the city centre. 'I'll bet I've been flogging myself half to death hoofing it around the countryside whilst she's been partying with my friends here in the city. No doubt Sharyll and the others will laugh themselves hoarse at my expense. Well, let them! I'll pay my dues to Sharyll, but I'll be happy to have them laugh if I get to see Alyssa again.'

On arriving in the city centre, Danar went straight to Sharyll's house to see if his fears were well founded. Sharyll did laugh at Danar's fruitless efforts. He also took Danar's money, but the greatest insult was that Sharyll had heard nothing of Alyssa since the coronation ceremony.

Lord Danar was tired, dispirited and almost ready to give up on finding Alyssa altogether – almost, but not quite. There was one more avenue that he had not tried. The last time Danar had seen Alyssa she had been in conversation with Lord Kempten. Did the old Nobleman know where she had gone? It was worth a try, he reasoned.

If old Kempten doesn't know anything, then I'll give it up for now, Danar promised himself silently as he rode away from Sharyll's house. Alyssa is bound to surface again, so I'll make sure everyone is on the lookout for her. When she does, I'll make sure I'm around to find out more about her. If I could just put my finger on what it is about her that is so attractive . . .

The unfinished thought teased him. He could not identify what it was about Alyssa that made him willing to go to such lengths to see her. The young Lady was physically attractive, but no more so than many of the other young Ladies at Court. He had courted many women whose physical appearance had been more appealing. There was something – an indefinable quality about her that made him want to get to know her better. Was it that Alyssa was playing hard to get? Or was the young Lady really not bothered by his interest in her? It was hard to pinpoint. Both were new responses as far as Danar was concerned, and either held appeal for their freshness.

Danar was sure he wanted to see her again. He tried to convince himself that all he wanted was an opportunity to explore her character, but in his heart he acknowledged this was a deception to hide deeper motivations. Right now the motivation was irrelevant. He could not make progress unless he found her, and that was proving far more difficult than he had anticipated.

CHAPTER SIX

Lord Kempten's house was large and imposing. Shandese buildings were generally uninspiring to the eye, as the architects preferred practical designs. There were few even amongst the Nobility who wasted time and money with frivolously fancy façades that served no purpose. The exception, of course, was the Imperial Palace, but that was a matter of Imperial pride. The Empire could not be seen as being ruled from a soulless square brick building, no matter how practical it was. Therefore the Palace had been an ongoing project for generations of the best stonemasons in the land, and its presence and beauty dominated the central area of Shandrim.

Danar reached up and rang the brass handbell sitting in a recess in the wall to the right of the main door. He smiled as he placed the bell back and wondered how many bells Lord Kempten had been forced to commission during his lifetime. Most Noblemen these days had given up on the old tradition of handbells and had settled for having ornamental doorknockers fitted instead. This was due to several spates when collecting doorbells had become fashionable amongst the youth culture of both commoners and Nobles alike.

The daring involved in acquiring some of the more 'difficult' bells had made them all the more desirable. Danar remembered some of his own exploits. He particularly recalled the beating he had received from his father when he was caught attempting to relieve Lord Vittara of his brand new bell only minutes after the crotchety old fellow had placed it outside his door. The beating had been painful, but it had not stopped him from returning the following day and adding the bell to his collection.

The door to Lord Kempten's house opened. A maid in a plain brown dress with a starched white apron greeted Danar politely, inviting him to step inside out of the cold. Danar was happy to oblige, thanking her kindly as he moved quickly in over the threshold. More memories were triggered as Danar looked around the entrance hall at the pictures, hangings and old battle flags that decorated the walls. He had been here once before with his father some years ago. Nothing had changed – nothing at all. The entire hallway was identical to the way he remembered it.

'Ah, young Lord Danar, what an unexpected pleasure!' exclaimed Lord Kempten, as he strode into the hall from a side door. The old Lord extended his hand in the greeting of equals as he approached, which momentarily surprised Danar, for he was used to his father still treating him as an itinerant young boy. 'Come now, join me in some dahl. I've just had a fresh pot brewed and from the flush of your face

I'm guessing it's chilly outside. A drop of something warm inside you will no doubt be welcome.'

'Thank you, Lord Kempten, that would be most kind,' Danar responded, genuinely surprised by the old fellow's welcome. He remembered Kempten as a sour-faced old man who had no time for youngsters and rarely uttered a good word about anyone. At the coronation ceremony he had worn his usual dour expression. This warmth was suspiciously out of character.

Lord Kempten led the way into a drawing room where Lady Kempten was sitting in a comfortable chair with a needlework frame on her lap and an open box with a mass of thread reels on a small side table. A steaming pot of dahl on a tray with two empty cups and a small pot of sweetening were arrayed on a nearby table. As Danar bowed to Lady Kempten and began to apologise for interrupting their relaxation time, another maid with a third cup entered and began to pour out the dahl.

'Not at all, Danar, not at all,' Lady Kempten said graciously, placing her needlework to one side and gesturing for him to take a seat in one of the other soft chairs nearby. 'It is always a pleasure to have visitors. I'm afraid all of our youngsters are away from the house at the moment on one errand or another. Which of them was it you wanted to see?'

'Actually, my Lady, it was Lord Kempten I wanted a quick word with, but it will be my pleasure to join you for a cup of dahl first,' he replied with a slightly embarrassed smile.

'Ah, man's talk is it?' she said with a wink. 'I'll not

119

embarrass you. Would you like to be alone with my husband for a few minutes? I can easily find something to do if you'd rather I left.'

'Nonsense, darling, I'm sure there's nothing young Lord Danar here would have to talk about that would not be suitable for your ears,' Lord Kempten stated firmly. 'Isn't that right, young man?'

'Well . . .' Danar started hesitantly.

'Don't bully him, love. If he would feel more comfortable talking man to man then it's no problem for me to leave you for a minute or two.'

'Thank you, Lady Kempten. I appreciate your understanding. I promise that I'll only take a moment or two of your husband's time.'

Lady Kempten finished pouring the dahl before taking her cup and quietly exiting the room with a gentle smile on her face. Danar fervently hoped that Kempten was not involved in some form of extramarital relationship with Alyssa. Lady Kempten looked a wonderfully content wife and Danar could not bring himself to think of her hearing that Lord Kempten was having an affair.

'Now then, Danar, what is all this about? Are you courting one of our girls? If so, then my wife is more than able to cope with news of that . . .' Kempten began, a little annoyed by the departure of his wife.

'No, no, my Lord, it is nothing like that. I want to talk to you about the young Lady you were with at the coronation ceremony a couple of weeks ago,' Danar interrupted quickly, keeping his voice down at a conspiratorial level.

120

'Lady Alyssa?' Kempten asked, not lowering his voice in the slightest. 'What about her?'

'Well, my Lord,' Danar continued, embarrassed by the old man's boldness. 'Firstly I wanted to ask what . . . I mean . . . well, you were walking closely at the ceremony and I wondered . . .'

'Ha, ha, ha . . .' Lord Kempten roared loudly with laughter at Danar's awkward attempt to broach the subject of the older man's relationship with the young Lady. 'You think Alyssa and I . . . ha, ha, ha!'

'Well!' Danar sighed loudly, his face flushing bright red with embarrassment. 'That answers that question, I suppose. A more important question to me, though, is if you know where I can find Lady Alyssa? I've been searching for nearly two weeks and there's no sign of her anywhere.'

'Well, young Danar, I appreciate your trying to save me the embarrassment of talking of this in front of Lady Kempten,' the old Lord said, the sound of mirth still evident in his voice. 'I have no relationship with Lady Alyssa of the sort you were thinking, but I do owe her a debt, which I'll be sure to thank her for when I next see her in Court. Unfortunately, I don't know where she's likely to be found, and I wouldn't be surprised if Alyssa were to remain a mystery woman for a long time to come. I doubt there are many in the Empire who would know where she was at any one time, for I have my suspicions about her.'

'May I ask what sort of suspicions, my Lord?' Danar asked, curiosity bubbling inside him as his mind sought to consolidate his relief, frustration and interest with what

Lord Kempten was telling him. The idea that the old Lord was in Alyssa's debt was fascinating, but Danar knew enough to stay focused on his primary goal. If he allowed Lord Kempten to begin imparting long tales unrelated to Alyssa's whereabouts, Danar knew he might lose the opportunity to learn where she had gone. Any clues the old fellow had would be better than nothing.

'I cannot voice such things in any company at present, I'm afraid, but I'll make one suggestion for you to try if you're determined to find out where Alyssa is,' Lord Kempten replied, his voice lowering slightly as if he were about to reveal a secret.

'Anything,' Danar responded eagerly. 'Please, I'll listen to any suggestions.'

Lord Kempten looked at the young Lord with a curiously pleased expression and Danar began to feel a strangely uncomfortable itch between his shoulder blades. Why was the old Lord enjoying this so much? Did he have a positive lead, or was he just enjoying the power of having Danar in the palm of his hand?

'Well, if you want to know where the Lady Alyssa is, then I suggest that you book an audience with the Emperor and ask him,' Kempten said slowly.

Danar's jaw dropped.

'The Emperor? Are you serious, my Lord?' he spluttered. 'I know I have a reputation for practical jokes and retribution is ripe for the taking, but I would appreciate it if you would put that aside for a moment. I deserve reprisals. I deserve to have my leg pulled. However, this matter is of great consequence. I need a straight answer, my Lord. This is more important to me than anything that I have ever done in my life.'

'I am serious, Danar. Go and ask the Emperor. I have reason to believe he knows where Alyssa is. Of course, I have no idea if he'll disclose the information to you, but if you don't ask him, then you'll never know.'

'What in the name of all that's sacred . . . ?' Femke breathed, her mind reeling in horror as she stared down at the body of Count Dreban.

Being framed for one murder was bad enough, but now the young spy had another corpse to deal with. If she were found anywhere in the vicinity, it would look as if she had been caught red-handed. For a moment her shock held her motionless as her brain tried to come to terms with this latest turn of events. Someone, somewhere, was intent on making trouble for her, but Femke did not have the slightest clue as to whom or why.

It appeared these events were directed at her personally, but Femke could think of nobody she had alienated sufficiently in the short time that she had been in Thrandor to warrant this sort of reprisal. Was someone trying to make trouble for the diplomatic process that she had begun, or was someone using her as a convenient scapegoat for crimes planned before her arrival? If this last theory held true, then Femke had been incredibly unlucky to choose the house of Count Dreban as her initial hiding place.

'There's no chance in this,' she whispered quietly to herself. 'Dreban was the one in the wrong place at the wrong time. The killer must have followed me from the Palace, or somehow intercepted me during my escape.' Femke had been fairly desperate by the time she had dropped over the Palace wall. She was not overly surprised that she had not noticed anyone following her.

'Come on, Femke! Pull yourself together,' she muttered, taking a deep breath and forcing herself back into action.

Carefully avoiding the Count's body, Femke stepped into the kitchen and was delighted to find her pack and clothing was still there. The pack was open. Someone had rifled through it. But as she quickly emptied everything out onto the side it became apparent that nothing was missing other than the knife used to kill the Count. To her surprise, even the money was still there.

Speed was of the essence. Femke quickly dressed in dark coloured clothes from her pack and bundled the dress she had been wearing during her escape from the Palace in with her other recovered equipment.

Femke was not squeamish, but recovering the knife from the Count's body was not a pleasant task. As she pulled the blade from his throat, Femke noted the accuracy and force with which the blade had struck. Whoever had thrown it had known what he was doing, she thought grimly. There were not many who could throw a blade that hard and that accurately – a fact which narrowed her field of search.

Although it was tempting to sneak around the Count's house to look for more clues to the killer's identity, Femke knew that doing so could invite further trouble. She was unlikely to find anything even in daylight, but to risk lighting lamps would be foolhardy in the extreme. No, it was time to leave. There would be time enough to puzzle through the conundrum once she was safely tucked away in a quiet inn somewhere in the lower city.

Femke slipped out through a side door to the house. As she left, she heard sounds of multiple booted feet approaching the front of the house. The heavy thump of someone knocking at the front door with a clenched fist sounded loud in the stillness of the night air. Her decision not to search the house looked to be the best choice she had made all day. Silent as a shadow, the spy closed the door and slid around the rear of the house to seek another exit from the grounds. Fortunately there was plenty of shadow for her to use as cover. Femke's body was still extremely stiff and sore. It also occurred to her that with the shock of finding the Count, she had forgotten to clean up her face of the dried blood from her earlier escapades.

As an experienced spy, Femke knew that blaming the stress of the situation for mistakes was all very well, but it did not change the fact that she was still making crucial errors. So far she had managed to improvise around those mistakes by using hidden skills, desperate tactics and a lot of luck. This was no way to progress if Femke was to solve the mystery and prevent the potential diplomatic disaster that could easily ensue.

So much for Surabar's trust, she thought grimly. He should have sent a proper diplomat. All I've done is cause mayhem. Why did I have to run? If I'd stayed at the Palace and done what any normal diplomat would have done, then at least the situation wouldn't have worsened. I seem to be attracting disasters like moths to a lamp.

There was a wall to a neighbouring garden ahead under the shadows of a line of three mature trees. Femke gave silent thanks that the wall was not high. She had no problems scaling it noiselessly without provoking much additional pain to her battered body. Her mental hourglass was trickling down the time remaining until the soldiers found the Count's body. There was not much left, but Femke knew that in the dark her chances of escaping undetected from the Count's residence were much improved.

Crouching into the shadows close up against the wall, Femke moved at a silent run through the garden and up along the edge of the large neighbouring house. The curtains in the windows were all drawn, but experience and her recent run of bad fortune made her take no chances of being seen by those inside.

Cracks of light spilled out from where the curtains in some of the rooms were not fully closed, or did not quite sit flush against the inside wall. These shafts of light were brilliant in comparison with anything that she had seen since being locked in the Count's cellar. Because her eyes had now adapted to the dark Femke avoided the temptation to look at them for fear of losing her night vision. The starlight felt bright and she could see clearly without the aid of artificial light.

Femke moved quickly around to the other side of the house and was rounding the corner when she heard the commotion that signalled the discovery of the Count's body. There would be a few more minutes now whilst the soldiers searched the house and generally discussed what to do next, she decided. Then they would send for more men. It would depend on who led the party that had called at the house as to how quickly the inevitable chain of events would progress. Again logic told her the lowest ranking person likely to lead a party to a count's property would be a sergeant. If it were a sergeant, her luck would be running particularly badly. Officers tended to think they should do more themselves before calling for help. Sergeants often applied more common sense to situations and organised things more quickly. Silently, Femke sent up a prayer for someone with no common sense to be leading these men. Any edge now would help.

Femke raced along the side of the building to the front corner of the house, where she paused, still shrouded in shadow. Nobody was visible in the street, but the curtains would soon start twitching. The initial commotion Femke had heard from Count Dreban's house had sounded loud to her, but was unlikely to be heard inside other houses along the street. If she had been leading the patrol that had discovered the body, Femke would have been quick to send men to every neighbouring house to check for more surprises. She would also have warned people to lock their doors and be alert for possible intruders.

There was no choice. Cover from here to the corner of the street was sparse. The streetlamps were bright, lighting everything in a way that accentuated any sudden move-ment. She would have to run for it and hope for the best. So, not allowing time for nervous thoughts, Femke made a break for the nearest deep shadow at the end of the street.

The end of the street was further than it looked from the corner of the house. Femke expected to hear shouts and sounds of pursuit with every pounding step she took, but they never came. When she lunged gratefully into the shadow again, she paused for a moment. Her chest heaved painfully against the earlier scrapes and bruising, and her leg ached madly where the attack dog had raked her with its teeth.

Femke looked around. Something was not right. The hairs on the back of her neck were prickling as some sixth sense warned her that despite the lack of outcry and obvious pursuit, someone was watching her. It was a skin-crawling feeling, but no matter how hard she looked, Femke could see no sign that her senses were not overreacting to the extreme circumstances. If there were someone out there, then he was not doing anything to impede her escape. It remained, therefore, to ensure her watcher did not manage to follow her to wherever she decided to spend the night.

Judging by the position of the constellations, Femke assessed the time to be before midnight, so there would likely be a number of people still abroad in the lower city. As most professional villains went about their work at night – or at least they did in Shandrim, and there was no reason for Femke to believe Mantor was any different – care was needed if she were not to blunder blindly into more trouble.

If you're out there, you're going to have to work hard to follow me, Femke vowed silently to her imagined watcher, and with that she set off down the hill towards the lower city.

Femke took all precautions as she moved. The young spy

moved silently from shadow to shadow, taking a random selection of turnings to avoid falling into any pattern, but constantly seeking to work her way towards the lower city. On many occasions she stopped suddenly in deep shadow and paused, sometimes for several minutes, to see if she could detect anyone following her. Nothing appeared to move. Strangely, rather than relaxing, her tension increased. The feeling of being watched heightened until she became convinced that somehow, someone was following her. It was most unnerving.

Femke tried every trick she knew to catch her imagined shadow. Altering speed, hiding behind corners, doubling back on her tracks – but none yielded results.

As she descended to the lower streets of the city, more and more people were abroad. Catching her tail, therefore, became more difficult. Keeping to the shadows prevented most people from seeing what a state she was in, but she knew there would come a time shortly when someone would notice the dried blood on her face and in her matted hair. Questions would inevitably follow – questions that could lead to trouble.

Although the feeling that she was being shadowed had not abated, there was still no obvious pursuit by the Royal Guards. However, there were no guarantees that the guards were not closing in on her. The need to get cleaned up and into a disguise that would fool her pursuers grew stronger with every step. Once in disguise, Femke knew she would gain thinking time, which in turn would allow her to formulate her next series of steps.

From what Femke had learned of Mantor over the last

few days, there was a natural spring somewhere within the walls of the city that produced a supply of water in the event of a siege. Unfortunately, Femke only knew it was somewhere in the northwest quarter of the city, and she did not want to spend all night looking for it. Ideally she hoped to find either a dimly-lit tavern where she could use a washroom before anyone noticed anything wrong, or to break into an empty residence. The second option, although illegal, made more sense under the circumstances, as that way nobody would have a chance to witness her transformation.

Breaking in anywhere this early at night carried risks, but no more so than being seen as she was. Femke could not afford to spend all night staking out a house, so she decided to gamble.

The houses here were nothing like the Count's extensive residence. They were basic, terraced rows that belonged to the lesser merchants, the middle ranks of the military, or the better tradesmen. The trick was not to work out to whom the houses belonged, but rather to decide if anyone was at home. There were plenty of clues aside from the obvious ones of lights shining between the cracks of closed shutters, or wisps of smoke emanating from chimneys. The custom of most hereabouts was to leave their boots in the porch on entering the house. If there were no boots on the doorstep, then there was likely to be nobody at home.

Femke had also noticed that many in Mantor preferred to attach washed clothing to lines of cord strung across garden areas in order to let the clothes dry in the open air rather than hang clothes over wooden frames and place them in front of the fireplace to dry. This was supposed to make clothes smell fresher, but Femke doubted the practice would ever catch on with the Nobility. Because clothing was likely to become damp again if left out after dark, it stood to reason that people would bring their washing in from the garden area before night fell. Therefore, houses where there was still washing out on the line had a good chance of being empty.

Femke realised this would not always hold true, but it helped to build a picture of whether the house was empty and how long it would be before the occupants returned. There was little point in breaking into an empty house if the owner was going to return imminently. What Femke needed was a bit of breathing space and a chance to regroup.

It did not take her long to identify a likely property. It took even less time to break into it. Once inside, Femke decided to take a chance and light one small lamp. All the shutters were closed and there was little chance that anyone passing by on the street would consider it strange to see one steady light. What she knew to avoid was moving her light around, as it would look suspicious. The trick was to make it seem as if the occupant were involved in something in one room of the house, or as if a light had been left on as a deterrent to anyone considering breaking in.

Femke decided the best place to light the lamp would be in the kitchen. She wanted to get cleaned up, but also wanted to be able to spread her things out on the kitchen table and give time to changing her appearance sufficiently for her to roam Mantor without fear of discovery.

With the light on, it did not take Femke long to find the water butt outside the back door and a child's mirror that was fine for her purposes. Using a square of cloth she found in the kitchen, together with a bowl of cold water, Femke proceeded to wash her hair and clean up her face. The dried blood was difficult to shift at first and the cut on her head began to weep despite her care in washing around her scalp. With gritted teeth, Femke applied some table salt to the wound in an attempt to help close it. The pain was instant and sharp as the salt entered the cut, but it was short-lived, reducing to a throbbing ache within a minute or two.

Femke treated her leg as best she could. There was always the chance of infection from an animal bite and Femke took no chances. Most households in Shandar would have kept a jar of liquefied brimmel root, which was known for its disinfectant properties. If the owner of this house had anything like this, it did not turn up in Femke's search of the likely cupboards, so she was forced to concentrate on cleaning out the long line of torn flesh as thoroughly as she could with cold water.

As the young spy finished her first-aid efforts and was tying off a self-styled bandage made from a strip of material torn from her dress, a hand clamped over her mouth from behind and she felt the telltale prick of a knife point at her throat.

'Hello, Femke! Fancy meeting you here. Don't even think about shouting out or I'll cut the voice from your throat.'

The whispering tones of Shalidar were unmistakable. Femke's heart leaped with shock and then froze in her chest with the cold, paralysing fear that the assassin's voice brought. Her mind, wearied though it was from the traumas of the day, instantly raced through a welter of possible actions, as Femke realised she could be dead or dying within the next few seconds unless she did something spectacular. The knife-point did not waver at her throat as Shalidar removed the hand from her mouth to allow her to speak.

'Hello, Shalidar. Did you enjoy the evening stroll through Mantor? You should have joined me earlier and we could have enjoyed the sights together.'

It was impossible to keep the strain completely from her voice, but Femke was pleased that even to her own ears she remained calm and confident. If she could keep him talking for a while, Femke knew there was a small chance she could get Shalidar to relax enough to make a mistake.

'Ah, but then I may have been seen conspiring with a murderer. I wouldn't want to stain my reputation by being linked with a dangerous criminal,' Shalidar responded, almost gleeful. 'The authorities here are most keen to lay their hands on you, Femke. It's said you're here posing as some sort of bogus Ambassador for the Emperor of Shandar in order to get inside the Royal Palace and kill the King. Speculation is running wild that the Emperor sent you as an assassin to bring chaos to Mantor before sending his next wave of soldiers across the border into Thrandor.'

'What rubbish!' Femke spat scornfully. 'I doubt the King believes this pack of lies.'

'You would be surprised at what King Malo is willing to believe, Femke. He has recently come to terms with the fact that magic is real, making him the first Thrandorian monarch in several generations to do so. I agree that you're implausible as an assassin. A real professional would not have made anywhere near as many basic errors as you have, but then Malo doesn't have any assassins of his own, so he has nothing to compare you with. All he knows is two of his Noblemen are dead, including his best friend of many years. He's not thinking as rationally as he normally does.'

'Why this visit, Shalidar? Are you planning to kill me here after framing me so neatly? What's the point in that? Or are you worried I'll prove capable enough to get back to Shandar and escape the King's gallows?' Femke asked, deliberately goading her captor.

It had become clear to Femke that Shalidar was not about to use his knife, or he would have done so by now. Femke got the impression that the assassin was here to gloat. The Emperor had warned her that Shalidar would want revenge, but had assumed he would take it by attempting to kill her. Femke doubted that anyone could have predicted Shalidar would go to these lengths to exact a simple act of vengeance.

'Oh, no, my young spy friend. Nothing like that, I assure you. You see the gallows await you in Shandar as well. I've sent messengers to the Emperor with the tale of your treachery here. I'm sure they will find it easy enough to convince Surabar that the Thrandorians are preparing to launch a military strike in response to the murders you've committed. If you consider the Thrandorians have now seen both an invasion and an assassin sent by the Emperor, why should they not respond with force? If I read Surabar correctly, then he'll mass a defensive force at the border, which will be seen in turn by the Thrandorians as another invasion force. It should not take much of a spark to set off full-scale war from there.'

Femke was stunned. 'Why?' was all she could think to ask. 'Why break your own precious Assassins' Creed and force the two countries into another war?'

'Oh, I didn't break the Creed, Femke. Both kills were paid for. I'm always careful to obey the Creed to the letter. Besides – war is good for business. Why else?' Shalidar said, his whispery voice thick with repressed laughter. 'There are always people on both sides who want rid of key figures from the opposing force. Assassinations are far more popular during wartime. I'm simply making provision for my livelihood. After you destroyed my previous plan I had to devise something to keep me comfortable in my old age. Being able to gain my revenge on you at the same time added sweetening to the cake, of course, but was incidental to the plan.'

'So now I know,' Femke sighed. Her mind raced, battling with more than how to escape. Who had paid Shalidar to kill the exact people he wanted at just the right times? That was too convenient for words. 'What now?' she asked, stalling for time. 'Are you planning to kill me, or hand me over to the Royal Guards? I appreciate the chat, naturally. When you fall into a whole pile of dung, it's always nice to find out who pushed you. It puts everything in perspective and allows the hope that in time the tables will turn again.'

Shalidar laughed and his knife-point jiggled at Femke's

throat as he gave voice to his amusement. A trickle of blood ran slowly down her neck from the tiniest of cuts, tickling as it went. Yet another injury to add to the tally, even if this one's only a scratch, Femke seethed silently. There has to be a way out of this – there has to be.

'What am I going to do with you now? Why, let you go, of course!' Shalidar replied, still laughing, as he told Femke the last thing she expected to hear. 'Oh, you'll no doubt avoid the Royal Guards for a while, but you'll get caught in the end. You've got nowhere else to go, so I'm sure you'll do your best to prove your innocence. I'd be terribly disappointed if you didn't at least try. Nobody will believe you, of course, even if you do manage to tell the King or his close aides what is happening. The weight of evidence against you is overwhelming. Now, I suggest that as I take away this knife you remain very still. If you don't then I *will* be forced to kill you, which would be most disappointing after the effort I've spent setting up this little game. Stay where you are long enough for me to get clear of the house. Move too soon and I'll kill you as you leave. Move too slowly and you'll be swamped in Royal Guards. They're going to pick up your trail again within the next few minutes. Have fun, Femke.'

The knife was removed from her throat and Femke got the sense that Shalidar was moving, though she could hear nothing. A bead of sweat rolled down her forehead. How long should she wait? Was he really gone? Shalidar was too good at moving silently for Femke to tell. Seconds ticked by, but Femke was determined not to give in to the fear that the assassin had instilled in her. If he were still there, then

136

she was determined to make him earn his kill. If not, then she was not going to let him get a long head start.

Mind made up and heart pumping with anticipation, Femke threw her body sideways off the chair into a rolling dive.

'Phagen! Phagen! Have you heard?' Kalheen gasped, bursting into their room, his face red with excitement.

Phagen sighed at the intrusion. Kalheen did not appear to understand the meaning of peace and quiet. The big man was the most irritating roommate he had ever known. Phagen put aside the tunic he had been repairing and looked up at Kalheen, the patient expression on his face hiding the exasperation he felt. It was nearly lunchtime. He had hoped to finish the tunic by then, but that now looked unlikely.

'Ambassador Femke has been accused of murder!' Kalheen continued. 'Murder, Phagen! She's fled the Palace and is on the run in the city. I would have come and told you earlier, but the guards held me for questioning after I delayed them getting into the Ambassador's rooms.'

'Is she OK?' Phagen asked, his voice displaying quiet concern.

'I think so. I saw her escape over the wall. You should have seen it, Phagen. She was amazing! She jumped into a tree from the ledge outside her window. I swear I thought she would never make it . . .'

Kalheen rattled out a description of Femke's escape that was clearly exaggerated, but Phagen waited patiently until his story was complete.

'This murder happened last night, you say?' he asked when the big man finally paused for breath.

'Yes. Late last night.'

'You were out late last night. Did you see anything unusual?'

'No, nothing. I was . . . er . . . chatting with Neema, the maid we met in the servants' common room yesterday. We met again after dinner. She's a lovely girl,' Kalheen replied, his round face reddening further.

'Well, I think we should start our own investigation,' Phagen said thoughtfully. 'If we can help Ambassador Femke, we should.'

'Absolutely, Phagen. I totally agree. I'll go and get Sidis and Reynik. I'm sure they'll help.'

'Mind if I join you?'

After attempting to follow several sets of directions, Reynik had finally found the secluded weapons training area at the rear of the Palace. It had not been easy to find his way through the maze of corridors in the Palace, but now he knew where it was, Reynik decided he would walk around the buildings rather than through them on his next visit.

Several of the Royal Guards were engaged in sparring with blades. They all looked accomplished swordsmen. On hearing Reynik's polite enquiry, the nearest pair of soldiers paused their mock fight and saluted one another. They both eyed the young Shandese soldier with suspicion.

'Shandese?' asked one of the men quizzically.

'That's right. I'm here with the Ambassador on a diplomatic visit. My travelling companions, however, have not been very enthusiastic about sparring and I'd like to get some practice. Would you mind if I joined you?'

'Not at all,' said the taller of the two guards with a wicked looking grin. 'I didn't get a chance to cross swords with any of your countrymen at Kortag, so it'll be a pleasure to see if you Legionnaires are as good as the rumour-mongers whispered. I assume swords are OK, or do you have a preferred weapon?'

For a moment, Reynik's mind flashed back to his recent exploits with a staff, but he dismissed the thought. 'I don't really mind,' he said. 'I'll appreciate the workout whatever the weapon.'

The Royal Guard looked at him sharply, trying to determine whether the young Shandese soldier was being cocky, or whether he really was adept with all weapons. He looked too young to have been trained to any level with more than one, but there was something about him that belied his youth.

'Can I borrow a blade to practise with? I had to hand in my weapons when we arrived at the Palace. They've not been returned to me yet.'

'Here. Borrow mine,' said the shorter guard, passing his weapon to Reynik.

'Thanks.' Reynik took a couple of moments to swing the blade experimentally, feeling the weight and unfamiliar balance. It was different from his sword, but Reynik had fought with enough practice blades in the past that it would not make a significant difference in a sparring session. Lifting the sword in salute, Shandese style, Reynik settled into a defensive stance.

'Just like that? No warming up? Are you sure you're ready?' Reynik's opponent asked with a frown.

'I'll warm up as I go,' he answered with a grin.

The Royal Guard shrugged, gave a quick salute, and took up a similar pose to Reynik's. Without further warning, the Thrandorian attacked. His blade flashed at Reynik's body in a fierce slashing cut. Reynik deflected it easily, ignoring the instant opening for a counterattack. He swung again and Reynik blocked the blade a second time, slightly taken aback by the ferocity of the guard's blows. The metal ringing on metal was far louder than that of the other sparring pairs around the training area. The sudden vigorous clashing of blades drew attention to the pair. Many stopped to watch.

The guard launched into a rapid sequence of strokes, all dealt with far more force than was customary in a sparring contest. Any one of his strokes could easily have maimed, or even killed if they had landed. For a moment, Reynik wondered if coming here had been such a good idea after all.

It was obvious from the outset that the guard was looking to impress. Reynik, however, was up to the challenge. He blocked and parried the guard's strokes with a grace that could not be denied.

The guard lunged and Reynik deflected the blade so that it passed harmlessly to one side, drawing a slight gasp from the watching guards. The Thrandorian was quick, but not enough to worry Reynik unduly. He did begin to wish he had not been quite so casual about a lack of warm-up, though.

There were plenty of opportunities for counterattack, but Reynik ignored them all. Instead he concentrated totally on defence. He had no intentions of hurting anyone. He had come to build bridges, not destroy them. In his own way, he considered this his ambassadorial role for Shandar. He did not taunt. He did not rise to the baiting of the other soldiers. He did nothing provocative. He simply blocked and parried the guardsman's attacks, whilst making certain that those around could see that he was doing so deliberately. After a few minutes of fierce swordplay, his tactic paid dividends.

'Enough, Espen! He could have killed you a dozen times, or more.' The shorter of the two Royal Guards stepped forward between the two combatants, forcing them to part or risk hurting the unarmed guard.

'You are skilled indeed, Legionnaire. I am Faslen. What's your name?'

'Reynik,' he replied, shaking Faslen's proffered hand with a firm grip.

'Welcome, Reynik. I apologise for my companion's lack of friendliness in his sparring. You handled it well and your skill does your Legion credit. Tell me, how many weapons are you proficient with?'

'I'm good with a staff, reasonable with longbow and crossbow, and can use pike, axe and mace adequately. I'm told my best skills lie in my unarmed combat, though,' Reynik added modestly.

'Unless you're a lot older than you look, your instructors

have done an amazing job. I'm sure we could learn a lot from you. Come, let's do some more *friendly* sparring, shall we?' he asked, giving Espen a pointed look.

'Sorry, Reynik, I got carried away,' Espen apologised.

'No harm done, Espen. I'm sure that a Thrandorian visiting the Legions would have received a similar test. Why don't we try again before I take on Faslen? I've warmed up a bit now,' Reynik suggested with a grin.

CHAPTER SEVEN

'Enter,' the voice of Emperor Surabar ordered brusquely.

Lord Danar took a deep breath, opened the door and stepped smartly inside. There was something in the Emperor's voice that required one to stand straight and look smart, as if anyone entering the door was on parade. Long years of military leadership had honed Surabar's voice so that it instilled an instant feeling of inferiority in anyone listening. Danar appreciated this was a useful asset for an Emperor. The Emperor's voice had him on edge before he had even entered the room.

Stepping through the door did little to relieve the feelings of smallness and scrutiny. The room had minimalist furnishing and décor. The single large desk, behind which Emperor Surabar was sitting, faced the door across the room. The only adornments on the walls were some crossed weapons and a few depressing battle-scene paintings and wall-hangings. There was nowhere for Danar to sit, so he closed the door behind him and walked forward to stand before the desk.

The Emperor was studying some parchments intently as Danar approached the desk. The young Lord came to a silent standstill, feeling uncomfortably like a schoolboy called into his headmaster's office, not knowing if he is there to receive praise or a reprimand.

'So, Lord Danar, what can I do for you?' Surabar asked bluntly. 'I trust this is not a social call, as I'm led to believe you move in specific social circles.'

Danar clasped his hands behind his back to prevent them from betraying his nervousness any more than he knew his voice would. His palms were already slick with sweat and he knew he would fiddle with his fingers unconsciously if he did not do something positive to prevent it.

'Well, no, your Imperial Majesty, not social exactly,' he said quickly. 'I come seeking information actually – information about Lady Alyssa. Lord Kempten advised me to speak to you, as he indicated you might know where Alyssa is.'

Surabar looked up into Danar's eyes with a gaze that would have pierced rock.

'Lord Kempten said that, did he? And did Lord Kempten say anything else about Lady Alyssa, or why I might know anything of her whereabouts?' the Emperor asked, his voice pointed and his eyes flashing dangerously.

The young Lord had felt awkward to begin with, but now he felt that he was about to be grilled alive. Listening to Lord Kempten had not been such a good idea, he thought, as he struggled to give tongue to a coherent answer.

'No, your Majesty. Lord Kempten alluded to Alyssa as something of a mystery woman at Court. This was hardly new information to me. He refused to expand on this, but he did tell me he owed her a debt, the background of which he did not choose to reveal. In fact he said little about Alyssa at all, except to tell me you could help me find her, if you were so minded.'

'A debt? Kempten said he owed her a debt? Now that is interesting,' the Emperor said thoughtfully. 'You're sure those were his words?'

'Yes, your Majesty. Lord Kempten was clear about that. He indicated his intent to offer her his thanks when he next sees her in Court,' Danar replied, puzzled at the Emperor's interest in what he had considered a minor point in his conversation with the old Lord. It had obviously been of more significance than he had realised.

'And why exactly do you wish to find Lady Alyssa?' Emperor Surabar asked, and then shook his head as he finished the question. 'Forget I asked that. It's patently obvious why you seek her. Why else would Lord Danar seek any attractive young Lady of the Court?'

'Your Imperial Majesty, I assure you this is no passing infatuation. I respect and honour Lady Alyssa and wish to explore the possibility of a serious relationship with her,' Danar protested, his indignation making him bolder.

'A relationship between you and Lady Alyssa would be impossible on many grounds. I suggest you desist in your search for her and concentrate instead on the more serious aspects of Court life. Your father is no fan of mine, and I can empathise with his viewpoint. I'm an impostor on the throne in his eyes – a commoner who should never have taken the Mantle of Emperor. But he is treading dangerously with some of his liaisons. I suggest you take notice of his meetings and his plotting. Don't let him do anything stupid, or you may find yourself rising to lead your House earlier than you expected. I will not tolerate treason. Those guilty will be punished in the traditional fashion. Don't let your father be among those I make examples of, or you'll find your days of dallying with the ladies a thing of the past.'

Emperor Surabar lowered his eyes back to the sheets of parchment in front of him and Danar knew this was his dismissal. Anger rose in him like a well of fire brimming to the peak of a volcano.

'That's it?' he asked, his voice rising slightly as he failed to completely maintain his cool. 'Politics are important, your Majesty, I'll not deny that. I promise I'll do my utmost to convince my father to stop any traitorous activities, but please, I beg you, tell me something of Alyssa. Do you know where she is?'

The Emperor raised his eyes and there was a cool, calculating calm behind his gaze that chilled the heat in Danar's heart to ice.

'Yes, I know where Alyssa is. No, I will not tell you where. I'll watch carefully to see if you keep your promise and then, if I am impressed by your efforts, I might reconsider that decision. Now, go and do something worthwhile with your life.'

There was no denying that tone. It commanded with an absolute authority that Danar doubted anyone would dare gainsay. He could hardly believe he had found the gall to make his final plea to the Emperor, but was pleased that he had. At least this way Surabar would not consider him a complete worm. Danar had demonstrated spirit, even if Surabar felt it was misguided.

Danar bowed low, but if Surabar noted the formality he did not acknowledge it. The Emperor was already deep in his paperwork again. Danar left the room silently. Lost in thought, he considered Surabar's command as he trudged through the corridors of the Palace to the nearest exit. There appeared nothing for it but to do as the Emperor wished.

Danar's father was getting involved in schemes that could see him hanged. As the Emperor was clearly aware of this involvement and had supplied a timely warning, Danar could not ignore it. All of a sudden the responsibilities of age and family position crashed in on him. He needed to act quickly to save his family's reputation, but he was far from giving up on finding Lady Alyssa. If this was what it took to get the Emperor to help him find her, then so be it, he decided.

King Malo was awash with emotion. He found his mind swinging wildly between anger and grief, and was finding it hard to think rationally about anything.

'Why would the Emperor of Shandar send an assassin to kill Anton?' he asked the empty room again as he paced up and down. 'The Ambassador's disguise was so effective she could have struck me down with as much ease as Anton, so why him?'

147

The situation was confusing enough without the grief that had kept his eyes full of tears all day long. Killing Anton simply made no sense when the assassin could have struck at the King and thrown the country into new chaos. It was possible that the Emperor saw Anton as the real driving force behind Thrandor's recent military victories, but surely that was not enough to place him higher on an enemy's target list than the King.

Now there was the added confusion of Count Dreban's death. Was this killing another assassination, or was Dreban simply in the wrong place at the wrong time? There were no obvious links between Dreban's interests and those of Anton, and it was hard to think of two men at further extremes of the political and social spectrums. Malo would not mourn the death of the Count, but he would protest his murder in the strongest terms to the Shandese Emperor. Whatever the reason behind these killings, Ambassador Femke had a lot of questions to answer. King Malo was determined to have her found and brought to him so he could pose those questions personally.

'Krider!' he called loudly. 'Krider, get in here now, please.'

The door opened almost instantly and the old servant entered quietly. Krider's eyes too showed the puffy redness of recently shed tears, but his emotions were under control as he bowed stiffly before the King.

'Yes, your Majesty?'

'Summon the fastest message rider. I wish to send a letter to our neighbour, Emperor Surabar. There has not been an assassination in Thrandor for over a hundred years and I'm not about to stand by and let this go unanswered. Get the stables to prepare their best horse. I want my letter in the Emperor's hand in a week.'

'Yes, your Majesty, at once,' Krider said, bowing again.

Malo knew that to get to Shandrim in a week was impossible, but he was determined to speed the Royal Messenger on his way with all possible urgency. As soon as the old servant had closed the door, Malo went to his desk and began composing his letter of protest. He pulled no punches with his language, laying blame for this atrocity firmly at the Emperor's doorstep. As he signed it off, he hesitated for a moment. Was he being too hasty? This was a damning missive that could easily spark a war. 'No,' he resolved firmly. 'The time for rationalising things away has long since passed. These last few months have seen one act of violent madness follow another. Let Surabar see my anger and grief at this latest act of aggression. I'll not play the meek ruler of a minor kingdom any more.'

Femke hit the floor and rolled smoothly into a fighting crouch, a knife drawn and her arm ready to hurl it with all force. Scanning the room in an instant, Femke realised that Shalidar had gone. How far he had gone was not certain – her instincts told her he had left the building, but there was little point in taking unnecessary chances. Femke was not about to go through the house to the front, as it gave far too many opportunities for Shalidar to prove her wrong. Instead, she snatched up her pack, threw in her belongings and slung it over her shoulders.

Moments later, Femke left the house through the kitchen

window. Like a spider she climbed the rear face of the building, drawing her body up onto the shallow slope of the slate-covered roof. The aches and pains in various parts of her body were still present, but for the moment it was her professional pride that hurt more. The assassin's stealthy approach in the house had taken her by surprise, and now Femke was determined not to let Shalidar totally win the day. Stubborn perseverance drove the spy to push her body beyond weariness and pain.

With her senses heightened by the dangerous nature of the situation, Femke crept silently up to the peak of the roof and surveyed the road below. For a full minute her eyes probed the dark corners and shadows of the street, looking for the assassin. Surely Shalidar could not have gone far in the short time that she had waited, motionless, in the kitchen, she thought, unable to believe that the slippery character could lose her so easily. He could still be in the house below her, but again her gut instinct told her otherwise. He may also have anticipated her taking to the rooftops. If he had, he would hug the near side of the street to minimise his exposure to her aerial view.

'OK, Shalidar, which way have you gone?' Femke whispered to herself. 'If I were you, where would I go? I would go . . . left, I think.'

Mind made up, Femke pushed her body into a crouching run along the rooftop, keeping as low as possible and trying not to skyline herself against lights higher up the hill. It would not do to give Shalidar his wish by getting herself caught by Royal Guards within minutes of leaving the house.

At least Femke was now dressed more suitably for stealth in her dark clothes. Her clean face and hair were less likely to draw attention to her in a crowd, but she had not had time to change her appearance significantly. Anyone with a reasonable description of her would easily recognise her as the Shandese Ambassador.

Fortunately Shalidar had caught up with her before she had used the few disguise elements that resided in her pack. A couple of mouth inserts to change the shape of her cheeks, together with the wig of dark hair to replace the light coloured one that she was currently wearing, and Femke knew that she would look very different from the description given to the Royal Guards. As soon as it was safe to do so, she would effect the transformation.

Femke reached the end of the line of houses and crept back up to the peak of the roof. Sure enough, she located the assassin in the adjoining street. He had company. A patrol of Royal Guards was talking to him. Given his gestures, he was giving them directions to the house where he had left Femke.

'Damn you, Shalidar, but you're a smooth son of a—'

Femke did not complete her muttered curse, for she had to duck back down behind the peak of the rooftop to avoid being seen by the patrol. Sliding gently and completely under control down to the edge of the rear of the house, Femke started searching for a convenient route back down to ground level. The corner of the building proved suitable, with ample hand and footholds.

Within a few moments she had descended and slipped out into the street near to where she had seen Shalidar with the guard patrol. The guards had already moved into the cross-slope street in the direction Shalidar had pointed. Femke caught a fleeting glimpse of the assassin disappearing around a corner some way down the hill into a parallel street. She knew she would have to be extremely careful if she were to track Shalidar successfully. He would employ many of the tricks that Femke had tried to trap him with when she had been running from Count Dreban's house earlier. Her experience of the assassin told her that he was also likely to have a few novel tricks and traps of his own, so she would have to be doubly careful.

Shalidar would expect her to follow him, but a sudden thought crossed Femke's mind that made the whole dangerous chase scenario irrelevant. On the day that she had entered Mantor with her four companions she remembered seeing someone who had looked like Shalidar disappearing into one of the larger houses some distance up the hillside from here. Femke grinned as she recalled exactly where the house was.

'I'll bet my last copper sennut that's where you're staying, Shalidar,' she muttered gleefully. 'It's time to change the rules. We've been playing cat and mouse under *your* rules for too long. Now you can fiddle to my tune for a while.'

Taking care to avoid being seen for some distance, Femke worked her way along streets in a completely different direction from that in which Shalidar had headed. Then, deep in shadow, tucked down a quiet side alley, Femke removed her pack and extracted her limited items of disguise. The wig and mouth inserts would do the job well enough for this evening, Femke decided confidently. Tomorrow it should be easy enough to augment her supplies from the market stalls in the lower city streets. By lunchtime tomorrow, Femke knew she would be all but invisible.

An hour later, settled into a small room in one of the inns in the lowest level of Mantor, Femke eased herself into the narrow bed. Despite the aches and pains that riddled her body, she slipped instantly into a deep, dreamless sleep, confident that nobody would be able to trace her overnight.

The sun had been up for several hours when Femke awoke, and the smell of cooking food wafting in through her open window set her stomach knotting with hunger. It was then that Femke realised she had not eaten anything for a full day, which explained the ravenous emptiness that gripped her now.

With a groan of pain, Femke rolled out of bed and slowly straightened her body as she got to her feet. There was not an inch of her body that was not hurting, but after collecting the bowl of water and small bar of soap left out-side her door, Femke was pleased to discover that most of the aches and pains receded with movement. Many of her muscles were stiff from the abuse she had dealt them the previous day, but providing she did not attempt anything overly strenuous for the next day or two, the minor injuries she had sustained during her flight should heal quickly.

As Femke adjusted her wig in the mirror, it suddenly occurred to her that it was Shalidar who had been through her pack at Count Dreban's house, rather than the Count as she had first assumed. There was no point in taking any unnecessary risks, she decided. Therefore, Femke resolved that as soon as she had finished breakfast, the first task of the day would be to get a couple of completely new sets of clothes and a more comprehensive set of items with which to build disguises.

It transpired that the heavenly odours of food that had drifted into Femke's bedroom had not been coming from the kitchens of the inn, but from one of the stalls outside. All along the lowest street of Mantor, market stalls lined either side. As far as Femke could tell, the market was a semi-permanent one. Poorer merchants hawked their wares from ramshackle stalls in direct competition with the more permanent shops in the buildings on the road.

Several stalls were serving sandwiches. Thick slices of steaming-hot hog roast, dipped in rich gravy and placed between two slabs of freshly baked bread, made for fine eating. Each vendor claimed loudly that his or her sauce was the best in Mantor. Femke could quite appreciate them all telling the truth, depending on one's taste.

Femke gathered her knapsack of belongings and left the inn to join the lively bustle in the street. The innkeeper had insisted on being paid in full the night before, so there was no bill to settle. Femke doubted she would stay in the same place twice for the next few nights. It was better, she decided, to keep a random element to her whereabouts for the time being. In her heart, Femke hoped that with her experience in the field of intelligence gathering, she would be able to collate enough evidence to nail Shalidar quickly. That way she could repair any diplomatic harm done by this whole affair before it got out of control.

Femke would have been far more at home tackling the problem had she been in Shandar. Shalidar was more comfortable here than Femke. The assassin had clearly visited Mantor before.

With a huge, hot meat sandwich in her hand, Femke weaved through the great market street, looking for suitable clothing and other necessities. Everything she needed was available in abundance. Femke could have spent her money ten times over, but she was aware the small amount of gold she had grabbed during her escape from the Palace would need to last. Spending it all on the first day would not be wise. Stealing money was always an option, but it carried an element of risk.

It had been several years since Femke had survived in her home city of Shandrim by making free with the money of others, but she was more skilled at the art now than she had ever been in those bleak days. If Femke had not been the best young pickpocket in Shandrim, then she had been one of the best. For several years she had survived comfortably from her harvesting of purses and trinkets, which she had fenced on the black market. During that time she had never come close to getting caught. Then one day Femke had chosen the wrong target and her life had changed for ever.

In retrospect, attempting to pick the pocket of Lord Ferrand was actually a most happy mistake, for it was he who had turned her unusual collection of skills into something productive and legitimate. He had trained her in the art of being a spy.

The process had taken some time – particularly learning the etiquette of the Nobility and the finer arts of acting like a Lady of Court. However, Lord Ferrand had been patience personified throughout the training process and he had possessed a wonderful way of finding something good in even her most disastrous attempts at new skills.

Femke had lived at his house throughout the process, cut off from the outside world until her new Master was content she was ready. With constant encouragement and coaching, Femke had changed from a streetwise urchin girl into a sophisticated and highly skilled spy in under a year. Femke had never known such an enjoyable time during her earlier childhood years. Her family home had never been a happy place. Therefore, the restrictions that Lord Ferrand had placed on her freedom had not irked her much. They had also not stopped her from testing the Lord's limits and resources, but Femke quickly realised these were more than adequate to contain her. As he had caught her picking his pocket when they had first met, so the Lord had apprehended her in the act of trying to slip out on a sly visit into the city. Ferrand's seemingly all-seeing abilities, together with his warning that he would throw her back out on the street if she ever disobeyed him again, were sufficient to keep Femke contained.

Femke had high hopes that she would somehow resolve the situation here in Mantor before it came to stealing, but it was comforting to know she would not starve – whatever happened. She knew whom she was up against, which removed the uncertainties of yesterday. If Shalidar had not decided to gloat, then it could have taken her weeks to discover who was behind the sting. Shalidar was a known quantity. Therefore, it should be straightforward to work

156

out what precautions to take as she gathered information.

Patrols of Royal Guards were in evidence on the street, but none showed any interest in Femke. Given a couple more hours, the young spy knew she would be able to walk the streets without apprehension. Like a human chameleon, Femke would simply disappear into the background of life in the city.

Femke took her time choosing two new sets of clothing and made discreet enquiries as to who supplied the Palace with uniforms for the Royal house staff. She remembered overhearing a conversation between two of the servants whilst she was in the Palace. One of the senior maids was due to retire shortly. The snippet of information would be most useful.

As a spy, Femke had been taught that lies were always best when based around incontrovertible facts. This way, the vague hints that Femke dropped as to the nature of the maid's position she hoped to fill, when combined with the fact that there was a known upcoming vacancy, meant that, if questioned, the people whom she had talked with would piece fact and fiction together to fit the situation. In effect, the vacancy made Femke convincing and she quickly learned the name of the uniform supplier.

A short while later the spy acquired a maid's uniform for the Palace. This was purchased under the same premise. There were no questions asked and Femke did not volunteer any information, instead allowing the merchants to draw their own conclusions.

A visit to an alchemist provided an oil that, when rubbed onto her body, would darken her skin to a deep golden tan for up to a week at a time. Femke also bought bleach to lighten her real hair to a pale blonde and some make-up materials for colouring the lips and eyelids in the fashion popular amongst the ladies of all classes in Mantor at present. She purchased another wig of dark hair in a different style from her current one and was pleased with both its fit and quality. The wig makers here in Thrandor had progressed their techniques well beyond the expertise of the Shandese, and Femke vowed she would never buy another Shandese wig again.

Later that afternoon, having taken a room at a different inn, Femke emerged a different woman from the one who had booked in a short time earlier. Nobody paid her any attention in the inn or on the street outside. The new, non-uniform, clothes had been chosen specifically to deflect interest rather than attract it. It appeared she had chosen well.

'OK, Shalidar, let's see what you're up to, shall we?' Femke muttered to herself. 'Firstly, a visit to the house I saw you entering a few days ago, I think.'

Femke knew that establishing a link between Shalidar and Baron Anton was not going to be easy. Furthermore, proving Shalidar had murdered the Baron, when her brooch had been found in his dead hand, would be tricky, if not impossible. Comparison of the knife wounds would also demonstrate a match with her blades, but Femke knew that such evidence should be viewed as circumstantial unless her missing knife had been found at Anton's murder scene. The second murder may help. It meant Shalidar would need two alibis. That could tip the balance in Femke's favour a little, but it was too early to tell.

It took an hour to walk up through the city to the large house where Femke had seen Shalidar. For what felt like an age – but was barely more than a minute – Femke studied the large detached property, lost in thought.

'Are you all right, miss? Can I help you?'

The voice of a passing merchant caused Femke to start slightly. She had been aware of his presence, but the spy had dismissed him as being irrelevant and no threat. Alerts were now triggered throughout her brain and body. Anyone taking an interest in her spelled danger, so Femke answered with care, trying not to arouse any further undue interest.

'I'm fine, sir, though if I may be so bold as to ask, do you know to whom that beautiful house belongs? The design of the building and the gardens is enchanting.'

'Indeed, yes! That house belongs to one of the few regular Shandese merchants here in Thrandor. He has been trading in Thrandor for some years now and is well respected for his honesty and business acumen.'

'His name wouldn't be Shalidar, would it?' Femke asked, already knowing the answer.

'Shalidar, that's the one. Do you know him? A nice man by all accounts, though I wouldn't be surprised if he doesn't suffer a hard time over the coming weeks,' the merchant said, lowering his voice for the last sentence, as if sharing a secret.

'I know of him by reputation, sir. He's to have a hard time, you say? Why is that?' Femke asked curiously.

'Surely you've heard the news? Firstly, the Shandese Ambassador killed Baron Anton the night before last, and it's said she struck again last night. Count Dreban was the victim this time. Naturally the situation has sparked more bad feeling towards the Shandese, if that's possible.'

'I had heard something of the sort,' Femke replied, nodding knowingly. 'There are patrols out all over the city looking for her, I understand. Please, sir, indulge me for a second. Although I've heard of Merchant Shalidar before, I was not aware that he owned property here in Mantor. Has he had the house long?'

'Some years I believe, miss. He's been trading in Mantor for a long time, though I believe he has interests in many other places around the world – a wealthy man by all accounts. I believe he's in the city now, though he often travels. Before he arrived about a week ago, he'd not been seen in Mantor for some time, but in view of the recent troubles that's probably wise. I expect he's wishing he'd stayed away a bit longer, in light of this Ambassador affair.'

'Thank you for your time, sir; I don't want to hold you up any further. I'll be sure to compliment Merchant Shalidar on his taste in houses if I should meet him.'

Femke moved on down the street at a steady walk. Shalidar owning a substantial property in Mantor was an unexpected development that could easily prove problematical. If Shalidar owned a residence here and had a good reputation as a merchant, he was likely to have a good number of allies in the city. It would therefore be more difficult to convince the Thrandorians that they had been harbouring a snake in their midst for all this time. If

160

Shalidar had been trading here legitimately over a period spanning some years, then his word as a respected merchant was going to be held in a lot more esteem than that of an ambassador who had been here for only a few days and already was the prime suspect for two murders.

The game was getting more complex by the minute and it was going to be difficult to win if Shalidar continued to hold all the trump cards. 'Come on, Femke – think! What would Ferrand have done now?' she muttered, trying to focus on anything that would provide a ray of light in the black pit of darkness threatening to swallow her. Ferrand would not have lost his cool, she thought. And, above all, he would not have given up. That thought lightened her step.

CHAPTER EIGHT

'Ambassador? Is that you?'

Femke froze. For a split second her heart leaped in her chest and her right hand went automatically to the hilt of a knife. It took a moment for her brain to register the voice and complete the identification process.

'Kalheen! What are you doing wandering around the Palace at this time of night?' Femke asked, keeping her voice low as she turned to face her Shandese servant. How he had recognised her, Femke could not begin to guess, but the fact he had done so unsettled her. Was her disguise so poor that it could be seen through readily? No, surely not, she reasoned silently. The guards had not shown the slightest glimmer of recognition as she had entered through the staff gate.

'I could ask you the same question, Lady Femke,' Kalheen replied in a hoarse whisper, closing the distance between them and looking all around as if he was expecting trouble at any instant. 'Are you completely mad, returning here so soon? You've walked into a trap, my Lady. The

Royal Guards are expecting you. I overheard them being briefed to that effect yesterday, so I've been hanging around this part of the Palace all evening in the hope of finding you before the guards do. Fortunately, Shand has blessed me with success, but now you must leave and quickly. Get away from here and don't come back.'

Kalheen's tone was so urgent that Femke almost gave in to the temptation to run for the nearest exit, but curiosity and the need for information held her firm. The young spy could do nothing unless she learned more about what was happening. She was exceptionally keen to look around Baron Anton's quarters in the hope of finding something, anything, which tied his death to Shalidar. Without evidence to support what she knew to be the truth, Femke realised she had no hope of getting out of this situation with her future looking anything but bleak.

'Kalheen, before I go anywhere I need to know how you saw through my disguise?' Femke asked, also taking a quick look up and down the corridor. There was nobody in sight. 'I thought it was pretty good, but you saw through it straight away.'

'Lady, your disguise is fine, but I travelled with you for three weeks, remember? Also, I should confess that I knew your real profession before we left Shandar.'

'How?' Femke asked, genuinely shocked.

'I keep my eyes open, my Lady. There were always a fair number of spies around the Palace and after so many years of serving there, I suppose I got used to identifying them. You were one of the more difficult ones to spot, but I guess I got better with time.'

'Damn! If I'd known you were so observant, I'd have used you more effectively on this trip,' Femke swore, livid with herself for misjudging the talkative servant. 'Tell me, have you noticed anyone else from Shandrim here in the Palace?'

Kalheen smiled. 'If you're talking about Shalidar, why not say as much? It makes things much easier if you're plain honest. The thing is, my Lady, there isn't time for this. I'm serious – you need to get out of here now.'

'No, Kalheen, I need to know. Did you see Shalidar on the night of Anton's murder? I've got to start putting the pieces together as fast as I can. You know who Shalidar is, but are you aware what he does for a living?'

'I would guess he's a spy too, my Lady. I didn't see him around here the night of the murder, but he was in the Palace all the next day, I think. He had several meetings with the King and several of his senior Noblemen. I'm not quite sure whom he met with, or in what sequence, as I didn't exactly follow him around. Come to think of it, I think Shalidar hosted some sort of a dinner party on the night of the murder, because when I saw him here in the Palace the next day I remember him being thanked for his hospitality. A passing Nobleman commented that everyone had enjoyed the evening. Why? Are you not working together on whatever you're doing here?'

'No, Kalheen, we are not working together. Shalidar is not a spy. He's an assassin – one of the best Shandar has to offer. Unfortunately, our paths crossed professionally not long ago and I made a mess of some of his personal plans. I think he's set me up, but I've got nothing solid on which to base an accusation.'

'An assassin,' Kalheen breathed, clearly frightened just by the sound of the word. 'Shand alive, Lady! For goodness' sake get out of here now. If you've crossed an assassin, you're as good as dead unless you start running.'

'Pull yourself together!' Femke ordered, her voice low but firm. 'I haven't got time for panic. I need your help and I need it now. Where are Baron Anton's quarters? I need to look round them. There may be clues there – evidence I need to nail Shalidar with. I know it's a long shot, but I have to take a look.'

'It's a trap, Lady. Don't do it,' Kalheen pleaded. 'Royal Guards have been swarming around that part of the Palace all day. You'd be spotted for sure. Shalidar will have anticipated you trying this. If he's as good an assassin as you suggest, then there won't be any clues there. The top assassins never leave loose ends – you should know that.'

As he finished his sentence a slight sound from behind Femke drew her attention. A patrol of Royal Guards had appeared from a side corridor and was coming down the passageway towards them. The soldiers were still some distance away and Femke was about to tell Kalheen to bluff it when a strong hand grabbed her wrist and twisted her arm up behind her back with painful force.

'What are you doing, Kalheen?' she muttered in horror to him.

'Trust me, my Lady. I promise I'll do my utmost to get you released,' he whispered back. Then in a loud voice he called out down the corridor to the Royal Guards. 'Here she is. I've caught her. No need to hurry, gentlemen, she's not going anywhere.'

165

Femke groaned softly, she looked back to check the corridor in the other direction. Another group of Royal Guards had appeared there as well and was closing in on their position. Any thoughts of breaking Kalheen's grip and making a run for freedom were instantly abandoned. There was no point. The soldiers had her well and truly cornered. She should have listened to Kalheen from the beginning. He had tried to tell her to run, but she had thought she knew better. So far on this trip to Thrandor Femke had not exactly bathed herself in glory with either her skills or her judgement.

'Damn you, Shalidar!' she cursed through gritted teeth. 'How are you staying so far ahead of me?'

The guards were not overly rough, but neither were they gentle. The first thing they did was to manacle Femke's hands together behind her back in a pair of thick metal bracelets joined with a short chain and locked in place by a double lock. Even left alone with her favourite lock-pick Femke knew she would have trouble opening these bonds, as her hands could not manoeuvre sufficiently to be used effectively.

The senior guard thanked Kalheen for his assistance and then dismissed him to return to his work, or his quarters, whichever was appropriate. Femke was pleased they had not held him as well, for he had tried to warn her, but in her stubbornness she had refused to listen. There was no point in sulking over poor judgement – Ferrand had taught her that. The best thing Femke could do now was to roll with the punches and be prepared to take advantage of any slight mistake that her captors made.

With her hands securely locked together, Femke was manhandled along the corridor towards the King's central chambers. The audience chamber, the King's private study, his Royal Courtroom and many of the other day rooms he used for meetings and the hosting of guests were all centrally placed in the Palace. There was little talking aside from the occasional command for her to keep moving, which Femke saw as ridiculous. She was not likely to stop, given the number of hard pushes she was receiving between her shoulder blades.

They reached the corridor which led to the King's private study. The senior guard halted. 'Keep her here and don't relax your guard, men. Remember what we discussed. I don't want any of her collaborators to have the slightest chance of setting her free. I'll inform his Majesty the Ambassador has been apprehended. It won't take long.'

Femke was mildly amused. Collaborators! she thought with a wry smile. What I wouldn't give for a few collaborators right now!

Then she realised that in fact she did have a collaborator in Kalheen, but there was little point in dwelling on that thought. What could he do for her now? Nothing. Femke was on her own – she had been so from the start. All she could hope for was inspiration and a chance to use her skills to dig her way out of this increasingly dire situation.

Somehow, Femke doubted any of her tools would escape the inevitable body search that was bound to follow. It amazed her that the guards had not already divested her of the various knives secured around her person, but as she would have to be a contortionist to reach them with her arms secured as they were, there was little she could do with them.

The Royal Guards led her to the King's study and held her outside whilst the senior member of the party knocked on the door. A muffled order to enter sounded from inside, which Femke instantly recognised as the King's voice. The guard slipped inside and a quick exchange followed that was not audible to those waiting in the corridor.

Suddenly the door opened again and the guard signalled for Femke to be taken inside. When she stepped forward, she was shoved with considerable force between her shoulder blades, causing her to stumble in through the doorway. Femke looked back over her shoulder at the slightly amused face of the guard who had pushed her, then gave him a look that would have caused anyone who knew Femke to sleep lightly for at least a month.

When Femke looked forward again, she found the King was studying her intently. The expression on his face was not one she had ever thought to see, and it cut into her deeply.

'There, your Majesty, what did I tell you? Caught, exactly as I told you she would be. I wouldn't be in the slightest bit surprised if *you* were not her target tonight, but fortunately, as I said before, I know this young lady and how she operates. I suggest, your Majesty, that you deal with her swiftly and severely, for your Kingdom will not be safe until such vermin as she are exterminated.'

The instant the voice began speaking, Femke knew she had been outwitted yet again. Shalidar was in the room with the King and Femke was beginning to feel like a puppet dancing on strings that the assassin was pulling at will. Right now, he was making her dance a jig that could well be the death of her.

'Well, Merchant Shalidar, much as it pains me to say so, it appears you were correct all along,' King Malo admitted with a heavy sigh. 'I would not have believed it if I hadn't seen Ambassador Femke so with my own eyes. I cannot tell you, Ambassador, if that is indeed what you are, how disappointed I am that you've not proved true to the brave words you claimed to bring from your Emperor. I so hoped that all the unpleasantness of recent months was behind me, but now it seems the bad times are still in their infancy. Have you any explanation for your actions over the last two days? Why are you now dressed as a servant of my household, with your face disguised so that only those who knew what to look for would identify you?'

'Your Majesty,' Femke began, her voice heavily laced with humble apology. 'Believe me, nobody here in the Palace could be as disturbed by the events of the last two days as I've been. I know it was wrong to run when it was brought to my attention that someone had set me up as the murderer of Baron Anton. I should have stood my ground and tried to prove my innocence before the situation got any worse. I'm fairly certain I know who did kill your friend, but I can offer no firm proof to validate any accusation, so I must hold my tongue at this time.'

'You know who murdered Baron Anton, you say? But you won't name the killer – interesting! I wonder why? Could it be that you feel the murderer is here in the room with you?' the King asked pointedly, glancing across to Shalidar in a hint that could hardly be less subtle.

'I'd rather not say, your Majesty. I hope one day you'll understand. I know you have to lock me up and see justice done, but I beg you to stay vigilant. I promise you I'm not the killer you seek. The Emperor desires peace. Whoever's behind these murders is doing everything in his power to disrupt Emperor Surabar's overtures,' Femke said, unable to prevent herself from glancing at the smug face of Shalidar as she made her plea.

'You see, your Majesty?' Shalidar interjected, his whispering voice forceful. 'It's exactly as I told you. Femke is an assassin, yes, but not the brightest of killers. I know what she seeks. Her motives are revenge and nothing more. I've met this young woman before, and after I thwarted her plans at that particular encounter, I knew she would come looking for revenge. I can only apologise that it was your Noblemen Femke chose to use as her tools for this end. It was an easy guess that she would cook up some ridiculous story about me in order to shift the blame for her dirty work in my direction. Well, Femke, it won't work. You left far too many clues at the crime scenes for anyone to take your wild stories seriously this time, so there's little point in wasting your breath. You'll gain no vengeance here today, do you understand?'

'Not today, *Merchant* Shalidar, but one day soon you'll be discovered for what you really are,' Femke answered with as much disdain as she could put into her tone. 'I can see that there's little point in playing my hand whilst you hold all the trump cards, so I'll save my breath. I would beg you, your Majesty, allow me a proper trial, with unbiased representation from my own country. Would that be possible?'

The King looked thoughtful for a moment as he looked from one face to the other and back again. 'Given who has been murdered I thought I wouldn't consider it, but this is no simple case. I'll consider your request, Femke, but I promise nothing. Whatever I decide, I will not delay exacting justice for long. Anton was my best friend for many years. I will not allow his death to go unpunished and this alone . . .' Malo grated, his voice harsh with suppressed rage as he reached down to Femke's boot, drew one of her distinctively modelled knives and waved it in front of her face, '. . . this alone makes me want to see you hang for his murder. I don't care about your personal squabbles, but I know that in the cold light of day my conscience would nag at me if I hanged the wrong person. For now I want both of you out of my sight. I need to grieve in peace.'

'Of course, your Majesty,' Shalidar said smoothly, gliding towards the door with an instinctive grace of movement. 'I'm at your disposal should you require anything else of me. Goodnight, your Majesty.'

As Shalidar slid out of the room, the guards who had remained inside grabbed Femke again and drew her roughly to the door.

'Make sure the Ambassador is thoroughly searched, men, but have it done by a woman. I want no improper accusations made should she be found innocent at trial, am I understood? Judging by the skills she has displayed already, I don't want young Femke to surprise us any

171

further by managing to slip out from between our fingers,' Malo ordered firmly.

'Of course, your Majesty,' the senior guard answered instantly. 'It will be done straight away, your Majesty.'

The guards saluted before shoving Femke back out into the corridor. Then there was a welter of activity as men were sent off to find appropriate females to search her, along with prison garb for her to wear during her confinement. Femke could not help wondering where exactly that confinement would be, for she had never noticed any guarded areas of the Palace. There was a chance that the cells were not within the Palace grounds, of course, but Femke could not imagine the King allowing such an important prisoner to be held far away

Initially, Femke was taken to one of the Royal drawing rooms and forced to sit cross-legged on the floor with her head down until the women body searchers were found. When the women arrived and the men left, Femke discovered that these ladies knew what they were doing. To her dismay every last one of her hidden tools and implements was found. Although the young spy had half expected this, she had harboured the faint hope that they would miss at least one of the smaller items. It was not to be. A short while later, Femke was being led along the corridors towards the ground floor of the servants' wing. She was barefoot, wearing a long, plain tunic and a simple set of underwear.

A door, which looked much like all the other doors in the servants' wing, was opened to reveal a descending spiral staircase. This did not fill Femke with good feelings about the nature of the cell towards which she was being led. The staircase was narrow and dark. Despite the torches being carried by some of the guards it was not a pleasant descent.

At the base of the stairwell was a hall with four doors leading from it. The guards pushed her towards the door directly in front of them. One of the men drew a large bunch of keys from his waist belt, opened the lock and swung the door inwards to reveal a small, dark chamber. Femke was shoved forwards again and forced into the cell, where another guard unlocked her manacles.

Femke rubbed at her wrists as she took a quick look around the room. There was a small cot bed with a single blanket neatly folded on top, a hole in the floor in the corner of the room, which Femke assumed served as a toilet, and a small vent in the ceiling with a heavy metal grille over it. The guards said nothing as they left, closing the door firmly behind them and plunging the room into pitch darkness. The sounds of the bolts being driven home and the key turning the heavy metal lock caused a deep depression to settle in Femke's heart.

'Twice in two days!' she muttered, angrily. 'Caught and locked up twice in two days! This isn't funny any more.'

It took a few seconds for Femke to realise that the darkness in this cell was not as complete as it had been in Count Dreban's cellar. There was still noise outside at the base of the stairwell and a slight glow of torchlight lit the crack at the bottom of her door. Listening hard, Femke quickly realised the guards were arranging a constant watch on her cell. At least the hallway outside would be lit on a permanent basis, which would filter a little light into her cell, she reasoned, trying to make something positive out of this development. With a little light, her prison would not feel so claustrophobic.

The dull sound of talking outside faded to silence, but the light under the door remained. Femke sighed in resignation. There would be no easy way out of here, but there was a strong spark of determination within her that was not ready to be extinguished. Femke knew King Malo might decide to try her without independent representation, but, if she had read his body language correctly, the spy felt confident that the King would grant her request. Allowing such representation was unlikely to affect the outcome of any trial, but it would show willingness to Emperor Surabar to see that 'justice' was done.

Femke's primary interest in the request was to buy her some time – time that would allow her a greater chance of escaping and subsequently proving her innocence. At the moment her mind was still awash with irritation at having been outwitted again by Shalidar, so she decided to sleep on the problem.

The blanket on the cot bed smelled musty, but Femke was pleased to have something to wrap herself in. In comparison with her situation in the cellar of Count Dreban's house, she was actually quite comfortable. She eased down onto the narrow bed. Her cuts and bruises were not as painful as they had been the previous day. With a bed to sleep on, both clothing and a blanket to keep her warm, a small amount of light and the probability that the guards would bring her food on a regular basis, things could be a lot worse.

Strangely, despite all of the bad things that had dogged her over the last few days, Femke's last thoughts before she went to sleep were of Lord Danar. His roguish features and mischievous smile popped into her head from nowhere, as they had done several times during her journey to Mantor. Femke did not know why she kept thinking of the young Lord, but she did wonder vaguely how he had reacted to Lady Alyssa disappearing before he had managed to woo her with his legendary charm.

If any of the guards had chanced to look in on their prisoner at that moment, they would doubtless have been surprised to see that as sleep overcame her, a look of peaceful happiness formed on her face and stayed there for some considerable time.

'Ah, Lord Danar, come in. I've been expecting you.'

'Your Imperial Majesty,' Danar responded, pausing to bow low before moving fully into the Emperor's study. 'I came as quickly as I could.'

Surabar smiled, his face displaying the warmest expression Danar had yet seen from the recently crowned Emperor. For a moment it was hard to reconcile the expression with Danar's last encounter with him. The young Lord's first impression had been of a hardened leader of soldiers whose body and mind were taut with discipline. He had thought Surabar to be uncompromising, autocratic, cold and heartless; yet the silver-haired man smiling up at Danar from the desk now looked to be none of those things.

'Thank you for your swift response to my messenger,

Lord Danar. I am most pleased with both your prompt arrival and the reports I've been getting of your recent efforts at home.'

'How do you . . . ?' Danar began to ask without thinking things through properly.

'That's a question you don't want to know the answer to,' Surabar said, with a slight chuckle. 'Though I'm sure you will work it out quickly enough. My sources tell me you were both eloquent and forceful in your representations to your father. Time alone will tell whether this will be enough to turn him fully from the path down which he embarked, but I can assure you that you've won my respect for what you did after our last meeting. Because of your loyalty, both to me and your family, I've decided to tell you where Lady Alyssa has gone.'

'You have?' Danar exclaimed, his voice suddenly full of hope and joy.

'I have,' the Emperor repeated. 'However, my reason for this revelation is not to aid your love life. There are some things I'm going to tell you about Lady Alyssa that must never be spoken of outside this room. You will have noted already that I'm well informed about what is going on beyond the Palace walls. You may assume that I'll know if you break this part of the agreement. Do I make myself clear, Lord Danar?'

'Crystal clear, your Majesty,' the young Lord replied, a little taken aback by the tone change from convivial to threatening in a couple of sentences. This ex-military General was a many-faceted character who would take some fathoming out, but Danar was willing to forgive Surabar any

176

quirks if he released the information on Alyssa he had promised.

'Good, because what Alyssa is doing is most sensitive in nature and is highly confidential. If the slightest hint is dropped to the wrong person of her activities, then it could prove embarrassing to the Empire, and fatal to her,' Surabar said gravely. 'I'm sure you don't want anything bad to happen to the young lady, so I feel confident the knowledge that her life depends on your discretion will help keep you from making any foolish slips of the tongue.'

Lord Danar nodded mutely, his eyes registering shock at the strength of the Emperor's words. If he had thought Alyssa was an interesting character before, his opinion had now strengthened a hundredfold.

'Lady Alyssa is a member of the Imperial spy network. Indeed, Alyssa is not merely a member; she is a top agent who often operates undercover, playing any number of different roles. I should tell you before we go any further that Alyssa is not her real name, or at least I don't think it is.'

The Emperor paused for a moment, looking thoughtful.

'There again, it could be her real name, but I'm fairly certain Alyssa was not born into a Noble family, so her title at least is fictional.'

'That would tie in with what little I found out about her when I tried to track *Lady* Alyssa down,' Danar offered, trying to encourage the Emperor with his train of thought.

'Well, it should be enough to know that at present, Alyssa is going by the name of Femke. I was under the impression this was her real name, but now I think of it, I have nothing to substantiate that as a fact. Femke has gone as my Ambassador to Thrandor to extend a hand of reconciliation and peace to our southern neighbours – as well as to do some reconnaissance and general information gathering, of course. Unfortunately, it appears things have not gone as we planned.'

'In what way, your Majesty? Do the Thrandorians not want peace?' Danar asked. 'I would have thought that after their recent troubles, they would have leaped at the chance of a peaceful resolution.'

Surabar saw the expression and he knew he was doing the right thing. This young Lord was ripe for induction into Imperial service. Danar was committed to a goal, which at present tied in with Surabar's plans. If he twisted it with some family blackmail, then everyone should come out of this scenario happy.

'Oh, the Thrandorians want peace well enough, but something has gone wrong in Mantor. Someone has murdered two senior Thrandorian Noblemen whilst Femke has been a guest of the King. A messenger from King Malo arrived not more than an hour ago outlining the basic facts. They make for a depressing report. All the evidence suggests Femke was the killer. Items of hers were found at the scene of the murder and, to make matters worse, when the King's men went to Femke's quarters to find her and take her to the King so she could give her version of events, Femke ran away from them. There is such a huge weight of evidence against her that, if I were in King Malo's position, I'd find it difficult not to believe that she's the killer.'

'But why would Alys ... Femke want to kill Thrandorian Noblemen? It makes no sense,' Danar protested vehemently.

'You can see that, and I can see that, but it appears someone will have to convince the King of Thrandor of Femke's innocence. I believe you'll stand as good a chance as anyone else of persuading the King, which is why I'm sending you there right away,' Surabar said firmly, his face managing somehow to look serious whilst smiling at the same time.

'Me? Convince the King? But how?' Danar asked, suddenly not so sure of himself.

'I'm sure you'll think of something,' Surabar replied confidently. 'If you don't, I'll be hanging your father inside a month for his involvement in organising the fracas outside the Palace at my coronation. Besides, I'll be sending a member of the Imperial spy network along to help you. He'll be under orders to aid you in any way he can in order to settle this affair with the minimum amount of fuss and to limit the chances of the situation deteriorating into another war. The Empire needs some peace and stability if it's to prosper. Recent events have damaged our international relationships and the confidence of our own populace in Imperial rule. If we're to remain strong, we must have time to allow our wounds to heal.'

Danar's mind raced as he thought the situation through. He had never liked politics, but he was left with little choice. He would not stand by and allow the Emperor to hang his father if there were a chance of a pardon. Finally he had a chance to do something to win his father's respect.

It would also endear him to the Emperor, whilst allowing him to follow Alyssa, or Femke, or whatever her real name was. Everyone would win. Better than that, the trained spy assigned to go with him was likely to do most of the work, but he would get all the credit. The situation could not have worked out better if he had planned it.

'Very well, your Majesty, I'll leave at once. Where will I find my travelling companion?' the young Lord asked impulsively.

'You'll find him waiting for you at the Palace stableyard, Danar, but don't be too hasty. Have you any idea how you will find Femke when you get to Mantor? Femke may look nothing like the Lady Alyssa, so you'll need to have some sort of plan of action for when you arrive. What do you think the best approach to this situation will be?'

Danar thought for a moment, his right hand automatically going to his chin and his fingers stroking it slowly as if he were straightening hairs in a beard. His eyes flickered as he flashed ideas and plans through his consciousness in an attempt to identify something that had merit.

'Would it not be better if I went openly?' he suggested, his eyes dancing with enthusiasm. 'I could arrive, much as Femke did, carrying a response message from you to his Majesty, the King. The King will then know his message has been received, and that you are concerned enough to respond by sending a Nobleman to reply to the charges levelled against your Ambassador. At the same time, with me riding into the city openly, Femke is bound to hear word of more Shandese visitors and should endeavour to make contact with us. Once we have her side of the story,

180

your spy and I, together with Femke, of course, will have a chance to decide on how to proceed.'

Emperor Surabar considered his answer and then nodded thoughtfully.

'It sounds like a good starting point. Talk it over with your companion. I believe he wishes to be known as Ennas for this trip. Listen to him, Danar. He is experienced at espionage and will provide you with a lot of information and expert advice if you give him a chance. Safe journey and good luck.'

'Thank you, your Majesty. I won't let you down,' Danar promised fervently. He bowed and turned to leave, adding under his breath, 'And I won't let you down either, Alyssa. I'm coming.'

CHAPTER NINE

'Where have you been, Phagen? You've been gone ages.'

Phagen was surprised to find Kalheen in their room. He had not seen much of his roommate recently.

'I was trying to arrange a visit to see the Ambassador,' Phagen replied, his voice not much louder than a whisper.

'Really? Did you get to see her? I feel terribly bad about handing her over to the guards the way I did. Maybe I should have given her a chance to bluff her way out. It was a tricky situation. I didn't want to get locked up as well.'

Phagen did not answer. He pursed his lips and shook his head.

'No joy? I tried myself a few days ago, but the Royal Guards are a stubborn lot,' Kalheen continued, not noticing the undertones of Phagen's gesture. 'They're determined not to let anyone near her until the trial. I spoke to Sidis and Reynik earlier as well. They've not found out anything helpful about the murders. All the evidence still points at the Ambassador. Do you think she did do it?'

'I don't,' he replied. 'But I've not found anything either. Time is running out. If we don't find the true killer soon, it'll be too late.'

'Don't be long. Let's not invite trouble.'

'I won't. Thanks, Faslen,' Reynik replied in a grateful whisper.

The door to the cell opened. Ambassador Femke looked pale and slightly worried, though she brightened the instant she saw who was entering.

'Reynik! How did you convince them to let you down here? I didn't expect to see anyone until they called me for trial.'

'I've made a few friends amongst the Palace Guards. They're a good bunch once you get to know them,' Reynik replied with a grin. 'Listen, I only have a minute. I just wanted to know you were all right and to see if there's anything we can do to help. We – me, Sidis, Kalheen and Phagen that is – don't believe you committed those murders, but we haven't been able to find any clues as to who did.'

'It was a man named Shalidar,' Femke said quickly. 'He's a Shandese assassin. He has a house here in the upper quarter of Mantor. Apparently he's known here as a wealthy Shandese merchant and probably runs a perfectly legitimate business.'

'Shalidar. Right. I'll keep an eye out for him.'

'Kalheen knows who he is, but listen: Reynik, do the others know you're here?' Femke asked urgently.

'No. I've only just managed to persuade Faslen to bring me down.'

'Don't tell them you've seen me. I may be paranoid, but I think the less people involved, the better. If you can snoop around a bit, I'd appreciate it, but be careful. Shalidar is extremely dangerous. He'd kill you as soon as blink. I know he did it. He told me himself, but I have no proof. I get the feeling that evidence will not be easy to come by.'

'Don't worry, Ambassador. I'll be careful. I'll do my best and . . .' Reynik dropped his voice as low as he could, 'I'll see if there's any way I can get you out of here. Be ready when the time comes.'

'Please don't do anything silly, Reynik. This trip has been a disaster for international relations as it is. I don't want to make it worse.'

'Trust me, my Lady,' Reynik whispered with a grin that made him look positively boyish. 'I'd better go now. Chin up.'

'Excuse me, sir.'

'Yes, Hanri, what is it?' Shalidar asked, irritated by the disturbance.

'One of the watchers has reported a young man hanging around outside. They say this is the second day he's been seen watching the house. Would you like the men to bring him in?'

Shalidar thought about it for a moment. 'No,' he said with a dismissive wave of his hand. 'Have them "dissuade" him from loitering, would you? Tell them not to kill him. Just get them to rough him up. He'll soon get the message.'

'Very well, sir. I'll see to it right away.'

*

Femke drummed her fingers on the edge of the wooden cot bed. Has it been fourteen days now, or fifteen? she wondered dully. Five days had passed since Reynik's visit, but had there been nine, or ten days in prison before that? It was irrelevant really. In all that time she had come no closer to finding a way out.

Femke had long since decided that whoever had designed this cell had done a good job. The door was solid, with a double bolt and a sturdy lock. It had two small, sliding metal plates fitted. One was at head height, square, with a similar width to Femke's spread hand. The other was a small distance from the floor and was slot-like. This was where the guards would push through plates of food at obscure times of day and night. As far as Femke could tell, there was little rhyme or reason to the timings of her meals, but she knew a little about the psychology behind the treatment of prisoners. It was likely an attempt by the guards to disorientate her by playing with her concept of passing time. She ignored it.

The vent in the roof which, judging from the small amount of natural light that filtered through during the daytime, led up to clear air about thirty feet above the cell. It was too narrow to climb through and was blocked by securely fixed iron bars. The toilet drain hole was also narrow and barred. The vent, toilet hole and door comprised the only entry and exit points from the cell. Femke explored every potential avenue for exploiting them, but found nothing positive.

The small cot bed had been Femke's first thought for possible escape materials. Listening hard at the door to discern when the guard outside was taking a nap, Femke had waited until she felt safe to make some noise without raising suspicion, then she had tipped the bed on its side and traced every join of the wood. The maker of the bed had been extremely clever and had not used a single metal nail or screw in its construction. The entire bed had been put together using fitted joints with glue, so there were no stray bits of metal of any kind for her to work with.

The plates of food the guards pushed through the slot were no better. Femke had been delighted when she had seen the outlines of cutlery in the dim light of the cell. But the joy was short-lived for the knife and fork proved to be wooden. Nowhere within the confines of the small chamber was there anything that could be used to pry, pick or poke at the door locks effectively. Without some sort of outside aid, Femke had nothing that would enable her to make a break for freedom.

Once the young spy had established she could not escape, she bent her mind towards working out exactly how Shalidar had anticipated her moves so cleverly, and how to prove it had been he who had killed Anton and Dreban.

Thinking back to sequences of events and the timescales involved, Femke constructed scenarios in her mind. The spy set aside her own beliefs and used her objective expertise to study the facts as the King would see them.

Shalidar appeared to have cast-iron alibis for the time of both murders. From what Kalheen had said before Femke was caught, the assassin was hosting a dinner party at his house at the time of the first murder and had somehow managed to be in the Palace over the approximate time the second murder took place. If Femke took Kalheen's word as a reliable source, then it indicated that Shalidar could not have murdered either man. If Kalheen was not reliable, then lots of possibilities opened up.

What had Kalheen been doing out in the corridor in the middle of the night? Had he really been looking to help Femke, or was he in league with Shalidar? Kalheen had set her running from the Palace in the first place with his message that Anton had been killed. Had Kalheen been genuinely concerned for her, or was he simply looking to make her appear guilty of the crime? The more Femke thought about the servant's role in this affair, the more of an enigma he became. Was he really observant enough to identify her when she was in disguise, or had he been following her for some time beforehand?

Then there was Shalidar. So much of the information available about the assassin and his role here did not add up. It could be the case that having had his plans foiled in Shandar, the assassin had decided to come to Thrandor to pursue a legitimate trade as a Merchant here in Mantor. This, Femke decided, was most unlikely. Shalidar was at the height of his powers as an assassin. Why would the man give up something he was a master of, simply because one of his plans had been thwarted? Femke could think of no reason. Then again, if Shalidar had killed Anton and Dreban, then who had paid him for the hits? The Assassins' Creed did not allow them to kill for personal revenge or pleasure. Allowable kills (other than for money) were those that prevented their anonymity being breached.

It was possible, as Count Dreban had indicated, that the

jealousy of one of the other Noblemen had offered a motive for hiring an assassin to kill Baron Anton. It was also possible that Count Dreban had riled someone enough to warrant hiring an assassin. What was difficult to resolve were the chances of those killings being ordered for reasons unrelated to the framing of Femke. The probability of no link was very remote, particularly given the young spy had been in the perfect place to pick up the blame on both occasions. This meant either Shalidar was breaching the Assassins' Creed, or he had arranged to be paid to kill both Noblemen. He *might* have justified the kills on the grounds of maintaining his anonymity, but he had already told Femke the kills had been paid hits.

No matter how Femke jiggled the pieces of the jigsaw around, they did not fit. One thing was certain: Shalidar was not working alone here in Mantor. With hindsight, that should have been obvious from the beginning. Femke kicked herself for not realising sooner. That Shalidar had a house here showed he was no stranger to Mantor, and would therefore have associates and possibly a whole network of contacts around the city. This would explain how he had managed to continue tracking her after he had disappeared following their encounter in the lower city.

Shalidar had deceived Femke with a similar trick before in Shandrim, yet Femke had not considered the possibility of him doing it here. It was a simple enough ploy but, with the stress of the situation, Femke had failed to take precautions against it. The assassin must have organised someone to follow him discreetly, she realised, maintaining enough distance to see whether anyone else was trying to do so. He could even have had a tail on the tail if he was being particularly careful. The basic principle was simple: the assassin would set off on a random course to a pre-determined rendezvous point where, if his shadow had seen nothing, he would get a signal that all was clear. If Shalidar did not get the signal, then he would lead whoever was following him on a wild goose chase or into a trap.

Femke had decided not to follow Shalidar the night of Count Dreban's murder. However, given she had thought to have gained the initiative, she had neglected to check if she was being followed. Whoever Shalidar's arranged tail was had simply locked on to her and followed her right to the tavern where she had taken lodging for the night. Once her tail had decided she was staying the night, he would have reported her location to Shalidar, who would then have arranged to have the place watched for her to emerge.

Femke was particularly irritated to realise she must have been followed the following day as well. Shalidar knew everything, she decided grimly. He knew exactly what clothes she had bought, when, and from where. If he had, as she now suspected, arranged a small team of people to follow her every move, then he knew she had visited his street, asked questions about his house, and more importantly that she had entered the Palace in disguise late in the evening. In short, she had neglected one of the basic rules of spying: never focus on something without considering that others could be watching you.

'Oh, Shand!' Femke cursed suddenly. 'Reynik! I didn't warn him!' She swore again.

It was too late now to help the young soldier. He would

know nothing of Shalidar's network of operatives. All Femke could do was to pray that he stayed out of trouble.

Reynik was frustrated. He had surreptitiously observed Shalidar's house for a couple of days and seen nothing suspicious. It had not taken long to find out where the man lived, as many people appeared to know of him. However, catching sight of the supposed merchant was proving more problematic.

It had crossed Reynik's mind that Shalidar might be his uncle's killer. If that was the case, then Reynik had a particular interest in proving him guilty of the murders here at the Palace. Unless he could spot him, however, there seemed little likelihood of finding out.

Reynik sighed and moved away from the house again. He did not want his observation of the property to become obvious, so he restricted his viewings to short periods. He would just have to be patient, hope for a bit of luck and keep trying.

The young soldier had not gone far when he noticed he was being followed. A quick glance behind showed four men striding down the road after him. They did not look friendly. Reynik's heartbeat accelerated as he realised they were coming after him.

'Calm down,' he told himself silently. 'You don't know that for certain.'

Reynik took the next right turn into a little side street to see if they would follow. They did. More than that – they accelerated, running towards him. Should he run away? If he ran and they caught him, he would stand less chance in a fight than if he stood his ground here. Distance running had never been one of his strengths. He did not want to try to fight four of them. It was hardly good odds, but it was not yet certain they were looking for a fight. Reluctantly, Reynik decided to let them approach to see what they wanted.

When they saw Reynik turn to face them, the four men slowed slightly. The lead man's face twisted slightly into an ugly smile. His look did not bode well, Reynik decided. Not one of the men was blessed with good looks. They were all burly with tough-looking faces. As they approached, they spread out and encircled him.

'Good evening, gentlemen, what can I do for you?' Reynik asked politely, focusing his attention on the man who had grinned. He appeared to be the leader.

'You've been watching a certain 'ouse,' the man said in a gruff voice. 'The master don't like it. 'E says you're to stop.'

'Watching a house?' Reynik asked innocently. 'Which house might that be?'

'You know full well which 'ouse. We're 'ere to show you that watchin' the 'ouse is bad for yer 'ealth,' he answered, his grin becoming wider and uglier than ever.

'Very well then. I'll make sure I don't watch any more houses. Thanks for the warning.'

'It's too late for that.'

At the leader's nod, the four men attacked simultaneously. Reynik was ready. He spun, his right foot lifting into a high kick that sent one of the men behind him spinning to the floor. Almost at the same time, his left hand flashed out to strike a blow at another man's throat. The impact stopped him in his tracks as he clutched at his adam's apple in shock and pain. But fast as he was, Reynik could not stop all four of the men.

Even as he struck the second man, a third grabbed him in a great bear hug, forcing his arms to his sides. Before Reynik had a chance to think about trying to break free, the leader of the band of four drove a fist hard into his stomach. He tensed against the blow as best he could, but was still left winded. The grinning thug followed his first punch with a roundhouse to the side of Reynik's face that connected with such force he wondered for a moment if his jaw had broken. He knew in that instant if he did not break free in the next few seconds, he would be completely at the men's mercy.

The thought filled him with fear and an inner strength he did not know he possessed. Using the leverage of being held from behind to his advantage, Reynik drove his right foot up with all the force he could muster into the leader's groin. As the man doubled over with a look of sick shock, Reynik's left knee followed up the kick by smashing into the man's face. He went down like a pole-axed cow.

Having lifted both legs up, Reynik then forced them back down again, driving his heels down as hard as he could onto the feet of his captor. The man roared with pain and his grip loosened just enough for Reynik to take advantage. With a rolling twist, the young soldier flipped the fourth man over his shoulder so that he crashed into the man who Reynik had previously hit in the throat. Both of them went down.

Reynik quickly looked around. The man he had felled with his first kick was just recovering to his feet. The other three were all down. This was not a fight Reynik wanted to prolong, so he decided it would be best to leave before the odds switched back against him.

Still slightly winded, he staggered away at a jog. As he suspected would happen, the one man who had regained his feet made no move to follow. Reynik knew he had been lucky. If he met them again they would be more wary, and his chances of getting away with a couple of bruises would be slim.

Femke had tried on many occasions to engage the guards in conversation. For the most part this was unsuccessful, as fraternising with the prisoner was against their rules. However, one of the younger guards had eventually begun to open up and talk to her when he was on duty. Worn down by the boredom of the long shifts, he started by giving occasional one-word answers to Femke's questions, whilst listening to her jovial-sounding chatter. Although he never told Femke his name, he did talk openly about all sorts of subjects to pass the time.

The guard spoke extensively about his family and how they had always lived out in the countryside, never wanting to come anywhere near a city, much less the capital. She learned that the guard's mother had worried terribly about him joining the army, but was terribly proud when he had been chosen for the Royal Guards. His voice was warm when he spoke of spending his first wages on having a street artist draw a sketch of him in his uniform, which he had then sent home for his mother. It now sat in pride of place on her mantelpiece.

Femke heard all about the guard's new girlfriend, their dreams and aspirations for a nice house in the upper city before retiring, wealthy and happy, back to the country-side. He had great hopes of becoming a captain in the Royal Guards one day, which would provide him with the financial means to reach his domestic goals, and he bemoaned the fact he had missed a chance to gain rapid advancement during the recent conflicts. Instead of going where the action was, he had been set another guard duty, protecting the Royal Treasury.

As the guard spoke of his time guarding the Royal Treasury, a tiny seed germinated within Femke's mind. Ideas began to flow. The problem was, the seed could develop into anything from the tallest, most magnificent tree of a master plan to the smallest, most insignificant weed. All she could do was to nurture it in the hope it would prove to be a wonder when it was fully grown.

By Femke's count it was the afternoon of the fifteenth day of her confinement when the sound of multiple sets of feet descending the stairs set her heart pounding with apprehension. Were these the men who would take her to the King's Court for her trial? Had the King decided to progress the trial without allowing her any independent representation?

The young guard had recently gone off shift. Femke knew there was no use in asking the current guard for information. But she did not have to wait long for an answer.

'Open the door. Let the priests in,' ordered a voice to the current guard.

'Yes, sir,' he replied, and the sound of jangling keys and

bolts being drawn back heightened Femke's apprehension further.

Did the presence of priests mean she was to be blessed then executed? Had there been a trial in her absence? Her heart was pounding in her chest and she wrapped herself in her blanket, sitting back on the small cot bed to hide the nervous shaking in her arms and legs. The door was thrown wide open. Three figures dressed in dark brown robes entered the small cell with the guard.

'You may leave us alone with the prisoner,' one of the priests said, in a serene voice. 'I'm sure this one young girl will not harm us in the few minutes we'll be here.'

'Very well, Priest, but you know what charge she is being held on, don't you? Murder. The girl is a killer, Priest, so don't get too complacent.'

'We'll be careful, Captain. Thank you for your concern. Please allow us to keep one of the torches so we can see whom we're blessing. We'll then complete the task our goddess has called us to,' the priest intoned calmly. 'Now, child, we are priests of Ishell, and we're here to ...' the priest began, his voice lowering as he spoke until Femke found she had to strain to hear what he was saying to her.

The door thudded shut, but with one of the priests still holding a torch, the little cell was filled with more light than Femke's eyes could cope with. Holding her hands as shields against the brightness and squinting for all she was worth, Femke tried her hardest to focus on the man who was talking to her in a low voice.

As soon as the door had shut, the lead priest took a

glance at it to ensure that the viewing plate was definitely shut and then threw back his hood. Femke blinked in astonishment as she registered who was standing in front of her.

'Lor—'

He clamped a hand over her mouth and grinned. 'Surprise!' he whispered with a chuckle. 'Come on, let's get you out of here.'

As he whispered, the other two men started chanting prayerful-sounding incantations to mask their conversation. The sound filled the small chamber with solemn tones that were somehow both fitting and yet out of place.

'But how?' Femke whispered back, shivering slightly with excitement and the discomfort raised by the doleful sound of the chanting. 'If we overpower the guard, there'll be more to contend with around the Palace.'

'Don't worry, Ambassador, we've figured it all out,' whispered a familiar voice. Reynik pulled back his hood to reveal his boyish grin as he resumed his chanting. His lip was split and swollen on the right side of his mouth, but otherwise he looked fine. Femke was so pleased to see him alive that she gave him a spontaneous hug. Questions filled her mind, but she knew this was neither the time, nor the place for a discussion.

'There won't be any need for violence,' Danar assured her, a touch of jealousy in his tone at the show of affection to Reynik. 'Ennas here has agreed to take your place for a while. Hopefully he'll be able to keep the guards fooled for some time before they realise you're gone.'

'Ennas? Do you realise you'll then be an accessory to my

escape and will be held accountable for it?' Femke asked, not wanting to place him in danger.

'Don't worry, Femke, I'll be ready to leave when the time comes,' Ennas replied, removing his robe and tossing it over to her.

'You! I take it the Emperor sent you to fetch me?' Femke asked, recognising Ennas immediately as one of the better Imperial spies.

'Actually, the Emperor thought you'd still be on the loose. I'm surprised you were caught so quickly. You must be slipping,' Ennas commented softly, his face twisting into a teasing sort of grin.

'Don't! I've been well and truly stitched up from the moment I stepped through the city gates. I'll tell you about it some time,' Femke breathed, her voice full of suppressed anger at her ignominy. Moving swiftly, she divested herself of the tunic and threw it to Ennas. 'Sorry about the smell,' she said with a grin as he caught the unwashed garment. 'The Thrandorians don't believe in allowing their prisoners much in the way of personal hygiene.'

Ennas wrinkled his nose, shrugged, and then drew the long tunic over his head. Femke was dressed in the priest's robe equally quickly. With a flush of pleasure she pulled the hood up, allowing the cowl to droop down low over her face. Grabbing the blanket, Ennas wrapped it around himself and lay down on the cot bed with his face away from the door.

'Ready?' asked Danar.

Everyone nodded, so Danar thumped on the cell door with the side of his hand. 'Open up, please,' he called to the guard. There was a slight pause, followed by the sounds of the key being turned in the lock and the bolts being drawn back. The door opened and the captain and the guard were both waiting outside with interested expressions.

'Is everything all right?' the captain asked suspiciously. 'You weren't in there for long.'

'It appears the Ambassador does not believe in our "pagan worship" of Ishell. The lady told us she would only accept blessings from priests of Shand, so there is little cause for us to remain any longer. We have offered our prayers, but there's no more we can do without her co-operation,' Danar replied sadly.

The captain looked past the priests. In the semi-darkness of the cell he saw the figure of the Ambassador settling down under the blanket on the small cot. Her back was towards the door in what looked like a deliberate snub. 'Each to their own,' he said with a shrug, the suspicion dropping from his tone. 'Follow me then. I'll show you back out to the gate.'

'Thank you, Captain. Your help in facilitating this visit is much appreciated. I'll be sure to offer prayers for you and your family when I get down to the temple.'

Femke smiled quietly under the shadow of her hood. If Danar lays the oil on any thicker, we'll struggle to follow the captain up the stairs without slipping, she thought with a mental giggle. Then the cold fingers of doubt slid around her heart as Femke considered Danar's inexperience at this sort of deception. Don't go over the top, she willed silently, hoping with all her heart that the young Lord did not do anything silly. He had done so well until now. It would be a terrible waste for it to fall apart at the last moment.

Femke need not have worried. The walk through the Palace went without incident. Before long they were outside the Palace and walking down through the city towards the temple of Ishell. Once they had moved down out of the immediate vicinity of the Palace, Danar turned to talk to Femke. She rebuked him quietly.

'Stay in character until we are out of the robes,' she told him sternly. 'There'll be plenty of time for talk later. Are we really going to the temple?'

'Yes,' Danar replied. 'There's a dressing room at the back where we can leave the robes. There are some suitable clothes for you stored in one of the lockers there along with ours.'

'Good,' Femke replied shortly and then resumed her head-down shuffling walk.

Nobody took the slightest notice of three priests walking slowly through the streets. It was almost as if they were invisible, Femke thought wryly. People paid more attention to priests in Shandar, as the senior priests of Shand tended to dabble in politics. Here, the priesthood almost exclusively served the poor and the afflicted. The rich, together with those who felt they were upwardly mobile in society, did not associate themselves with the churches at all. When one wanted to avoid the gaze of the Nobility, what better disguise than as a person they would ignore on principle? It was a nugget of information that Femke stored jealously in her mind, wishing it had been her idea.

When they reached the temple, Femke was also surprised to find that it was not the grand affair she had been expecting. It was large but practical, with none of the trimmings of the great temple of Shand. The three of them shuffled, heads down, around to the rear of the building and entered into the changing room Danar had mentioned. A row of wooden lockers lined one wall and a long coat rail with regularly spaced hooks sported a smattering of robes along the middle of the room. The place was conveniently empty of people, so Danar retrieved keys from inside his robe and opened some lockers.

'Here's your clothing,' he said to Femke, with a tenderness in his voice that rang warning bells in her head.

All the way down from the Palace Femke had been playing over in her mind the question of what had brought Lord Danar the many leagues to Mantor and into her cell. The obvious answer was one that the young spy did not want to face. The moment when he had removed his hood in her cell had nearly caused her to scream in fright. She had dreamed about him a few times during her imprisonment, fondly thinking of how she might have fostered a relationship with him had her life been different. It was as if one of her dreams had come to life in front of her eyes. For an instant, Femke had wondered if she was hallucinating, but as soon as Danar had spoken, she had known he was real.

But what was he doing here? Lord Danar was a playboy – a young man out of control amongst the lovelier Ladies in the Shandese Court. Could he truly be serious about a relationship with her? Particularly now that Danar had to be aware that she was not Lady Alyssa, but a spy for the Emperor? Femke was almost too frightened by the prospect

200

to want to follow that line of thought. The best thing to do, she concluded, was to be cold and uncaring towards him. If Femke could convince him to lose interest quickly, then she would be able to continue her life as if nothing had happened. There was no future in a relationship between a Lord and a spy. Someone would get hurt. And Femke knew that in all likelihood, that someone would be her.

They all changed quickly, hanging their robes randomly on unused hooks and throwing on the garments in the lockers with all haste. Danar left the keys in the locks of the empty lockers and proceeded to take the lead out of the door through which they had entered. Femke and Reynik said nothing. She wondered for a moment whether Reynik knew why Danar was really here. Did the young soldier know what he was dealing with? Did he even realise yet that Femke was a spy? It might be better not to involve him more than was necessary, she thought.

Danar had assumed the leadership role as if it were his rightful place. He would not keep the lead for long, Femke vowed silently. There would be an enlightening of the young Lord's mind in the near future that would place his position in the larger scheme of things clearly in perspective – and it would be Femke who would do the enlightening.

Once they were back out on the streets, Femke moved alongside Danar and started to try to find out what sort of hand they held for the renewal of the game. Danar smiled warmly at her, but if he expected to get an equally warm response, he was disappointed.

'Where are we staying?' Femke asked, keeping any

intimacy from her voice and not allowing the mixed emotions that surged inside her to show in any way.

'We have rooms booked at the Old Wagoneer,' Danar replied, his enthusiasm not dampened by her flat question. 'It's not exactly salubrious, but Ennas convinced me that we didn't want to draw attention to ourselves by staying somewhere too plush. The problem is that people remember those with money, particularly if they're willing to spend it.'

'I understand the reasons, Lord Danar. Do you think I know nothing? The Old Wagoneer will be fine to begin with, but we will need to move shortly – preferably today.'

'Why would we want to do that?' Danar asked curiously. 'Ennas was all for staying at this inn. Reynik agreed too, didn't you, Reynik?'

'True – I did,' Reynik acknowledged, rubbing his hands together nervously. 'However, Femke is right, we need to move from there quickly. As soon as the Royal Guards realise they're no longer holding the Ambassador of Shandar but an apparent dimwit who they'll think was paid to take her place, they will start to follow our tracks. The guards are not stupid. I know several of them. It won't take them long to work out we were not real priests, which will bring them to the temple. From there to the Old Wagoneer should take a little longer, but I suspect someone will point them in the right direction quickly enough.'

'So should we leave for Shandar straight away then?' the young Lord asked, sounding less certain. 'Surely it's too dangerous for you to remain here now?'

'I'm afraid things have gone too far for me to run away,'

Femke replied grimly. 'Unless I can prove to the King that Emperor Surabar did not send me here as an assassin, it's possible another war will start. Neither country wants that. Also, I'm not going back to Shandar until I know Ennas is out of that dungeon safely and Shalidar has been exposed. It would be a good idea for us to get out of the city for a while though. Too many people have seen me in different guises. I'm going to need a radical new one, for which we will need certain materials. They can be obtained easily enough.'

Lord Danar did not look happy, but Reynik nodded thoughtfully. 'I'll get what you need,' he offered. 'I've walked the markets and know where to find most things. Give me a list. I can judge your size well enough. Do you have a plan in mind?'

Femke grinned. 'Oh, yes!' she replied with a wicked little laugh. 'I have a plan, and it's a real dancer!'

'You know, Lady Ambassador, when I was given this assignment, I thought it would be boring. If I'd known it would be this much fun, I'd have been a lot more enthusiastic,' Reynik said, his face beaming.

Lord Danar looked from one smiling face to the other and he began to feel a strange apprehension. This whole trip to Thrandor had been an adventure. Posing as a priest with the risks involved in penetrating to the heart of the Royal Palace and rescuing Femke had reminded him of his pranks back in Shandrim. He suddenly realised that he had been viewing this whole mission like one of the stories his father had told him as a boy. He had seen himself as the dashing hero setting out to rescue his imprisoned princess and then sweeping her off her feet to live happily ever after.

The realities of the situation were beginning to sink in. Femke, although as attractive as any woman in the Shandese Court, was no swooning young Lady to be swept off her feet. Instead she was a tough spy with an indomitable will and a determination to see her mission through to the end.

Lord Danar still found himself attracted to Femke, but now that the rose-tinted glasses had come off, he began to wonder what he had got himself into.

King Malo sat in his study and drummed his fingers on the large oval table. The funerals for Baron Anton and Count Dreban had been very different affairs, but a common atrocity linked them such that the ageing monarch could not get the occasions out of his mind. Murder: simply thinking about the word brought a chill of cold anger and outrage to his heart. Both men were killed by knife wound – one struck in the heart and one in the throat. The medics' report suggested a knife of exactly the same dimensions as the one found protruding from Anton's chest had killed the Count. The same knife had been identified by one of the Ambassador's servants as belonging to her.

All the evidence clearly indicated that Ambassador Femke had committed the two crimes. No ambassador that Malo had ever met had possessed the skills required to escape from the Palace in the spectacular fashion Femke had demonstrated. The merchant, Shalidar, had corroborated this evidence by confirming that the woman was an assassin. So why was something niggling in the King's mind that refuted all the evidence?

Something about his short interview with Femke bothered him. There was an air of innocence about the Ambassador that haunted him. He knew he would have to interview her again, but he had been putting it off for days. The messengers he had sent to the Shandese Emperor should both have long since arrived in Shandar. Another Shandese delegation would doubtless arrive shortly. The question in the King's mind was when to interview the Ambassador again. Should he wait for the Shandese representative to be present, or should he question her now? It was a difficult decision.

The King had interviewed each of the other members of the Ambassador's party with varying degrees of success. The two soldiers had said little. They had kept to the military code of 'the less said, the less trouble it will cause'. It did not help the King.

What little the two men had said was illuminating. They had both told how the Ambassador had asked them to gather information on recent events, but that they had not had a chance to report their findings. Why would an assassin be interested in such information? That was more general information gathering, which was in line with an Ambassador's role or at least an espionage operation – not that of an assassin. The King did get a strong feeling that if the Ambassador was the murderer, the two soldiers had no prior knowledge of any assassination plot.

The two servants had been more difficult to read. One had been so unforthcoming that the interview had proved a waste of time. Whether this was through shyness, secretiveness, or whether it was reluctance to say anything that would incriminate the Ambassador, was hard to determine. The other servant, however, could not have been more different. Trying to halt the flow of words that poured from him was akin to attempting to stop the tide from coming in with your bare hands. Unfortunately, the information he did provide was completely useless, for he was fiercely loyal to the Ambassador and would not say the slightest word against her.

Malo was glad he had conceded to Femke's request for representation from Shandar. It had given him time to think through the whole bizarre series of events several times and there were a lot of minor things that did not make sense. It had also given him time to calm down enough to be more objective about the charges Femke faced. This would be good when the trial came to court. He now felt sure he could give the Ambassador a fair hearing, which he would not have been able to do had he held the trial immediately.

There was also something strange about the merchant's information. Shalidar had appeared to take pleasure in condemning the Shandese Ambassador, and his story of having thwarted a previous plot of hers did not ring true. If his story about her wanting revenge were true, then it did offer a valid motive. But the King was sure there was more to all this than met the eye.

'Oh, Anton!' he sighed out loud. 'Why did it have to be you? It's times like these that I need your calm head and clear judgement. What should I do, old friend?'

Silence fell again in the room as the King's voice died away. Malo knew there would be no answers from the stillness unless they came from his own heart. He would wait. The Ambassador was not going anywhere. He could afford to await the Emperor's response to Malo's messengers before he brought the matter to the Court, he decided. Surely Surabar would not delay in responding to such urgent messages.

Malo decided to give the Emperor three more days. If nobody arrived in Mantor within that time, then the Court would convene regardless and the trial would begin.

'Three more days,' he vowed. 'Three more days, then I'll put this to rest.'

CHAPTER TEN

'Is that everything?'

'Oh, yes, and a pair of scissors – I'm going to need a hair cut,' Femke replied, finishing the list. 'Thanks, Reynik. When you get back we'll work on the details of the plan and think about where Danar and I are going to move to tonight. Try not to be too long. You'd better be back up at the Palace before it gets too late, or questions might be asked.'

Reynik nodded and raised his hand in a quick gesture of farewell before slipping out of the door. Femke gave him a grateful smile before reluctantly turning her attention to Lord Danar, whom she sensed was looking at her with his puppy-dog eyes. It was a novelty to be pursued romantically, and flattering that it was by a handsome, young Nobleman. However, it was also most inconvenient and inappropriate given the current situation. She could not consider allowing a relationship to develop, no matter how attractive and dashing he was.

Femke could not deny her attraction to Danar, though she would die rather than let him know how his charm had affected her. She had seen it catch the hearts of many other young Ladies of Court and had scoffed at their foolishness. If anyone had told her Danar would travel to Thrandor in order to pursue a relationship with a Lady before she had left Shandar, Femke would have laughed it off as ridiculous. He had plenty of attractive women at his beck and call right there in Shandrim.

He'll have to wait, she thought ruthlessly. He's come this far, so he'll not give up easily. I wonder if my new disguise will put him off?

'So, Lord Danar, I haven't had the chance to ask why you came to Mantor with one of the Emperor's best spies,' Femke said aloud, determined to clear the air between them.

'Please call me Danar. There's no need for formality.'

'Very well, Danar. So what did bring you here?'

'Well, it was a bit strange,' Danar answered, his lips twisting into his characteristic mischievous smile. 'I was looking to finish a conversation with an attractive young woman who I met at the recent coronation ceremony of the new Emperor of Shandar. For some reason the young woman, who is known to the Shandese Court as Lady Alyssa, felt disinclined to meet with me after the ceremony, and proceeded to leave the city before I had a chance to persuade her to change her mind. I made some enquiries after her that eventually led me to have a conversation with Emperor Surabar. He kindly furnished me with a competent travelling companion and sent me here to Mantor.'

Femke sighed and looked Danar straight in the eyes. 'Then you have made a wasted journey, Lor . . . Danar. The woman you seek does not exist. Lady Alyssa is a figment of your . . . no, of *my* imagination, created for a specific purpose. That purpose is not, and never will be, diverted towards a frivolous relationship.'

'I know,' Danar replied softly, his face still smiling. 'I realised Alyssa was not real some time ago, but that doesn't matter. I'm sure the creator of Alyssa will be equally, if not more, interesting. My problem is how to learn who that person is and, when I do discover more about her, how she will view my interest?'

Femke could not help but smile slightly at his phrasing. This man was a born charmer and she did not possess the immunity she would dearly love at this moment to ignore his charisma.

'To be perfectly honest, I'm not totally sure,' she said. 'You should know my background is about as far from yours as it is possible to get. If you're insistent on chasing the illusion, then let me dispel it now. I was born the third child of six to a poor family in the eastern quarter of Shandrim. My father is a failure in every respect. The last I heard, he'd been sacked from his menial job in the cloth makers for being persistently late for work. My memories of him are not pretty. He was nearly always drunk and he used to beat my mother, who was either too stupid or too stubborn to leave him. He beat us children as well, when he was sober enough to catch us. I became an habitual thief by the age of nine and was notorious by the age of twelve. If you have any romantic notions about me being a bored rich girl who turned to spying for a bit of excitement, then forget them now. My family had no idea where I disappeared to eight years ago, nor did they appear to care. From what I could tell, my disappearance simply meant one less mouth to feed.'

'Your family history doesn't matter to me. It's *you* who I want to know – the woman whom the girl has grown into. What of that person? Can I hope to discover more about the creator of Lady Alyssa and all the other characters?'

'I'm not sure, Danar. Until the current situation here in Mantor is resolved, neither of us is likely to find out. The events here over the next few days will determine matters far more important than any personal relationship. I have dangerous work to complete. If I survive, then I'll consider exploring your questions more fully.'

Danar nodded. 'I understand,' he said. 'I believe you're wrong, but I do understand. Much is forged by personal relationships and the way people interact can have a profound effect on the world around them. I'll be the first to admit that I'm not completely in the picture as to what's been happening here. However, I'm sure that one or two good personal relationships between key people would smooth those problems away.'

Femke laughed and instantly regretted it as she saw the hurt that her laughter inflicted. Danar was right – he did not understand. How could personal relationships heal the hurts caused by murder, deception and war? This situation was so complicated now that little short of a miracle was going to mend the growing rift between the two countries. Femke had a plan with the potential to go some way

211

towards that goal, but it was fraught with danger and there were no guarantees it would work.

'Please don't take this the wrong way, Danar, as in some ways you're right. If Surabar and Malo were best friends, then yes, I can see that things would be different. However, this is unlikely to ever become a reality unless I repair the damage Shalidar has done over the last few weeks. Shalidar must be exposed and that won't be easy.'

'Well, I don't have your expertise, but if I can be of any help . . .'

'It's a kind offer, but I don't think it would be appropriate to place you in that sort of danger, or to involve you in some of the less . . .' Femke coughed and looked slightly embarrassed, 'er . . . less *legal* activities we'll have to undertake to make my plan work. It would be better if you don't know what I'm planning. If you don't know about it, then you can't be accused of failing to stop it,' she finished with an apologetic grin.

It was Danar's turn to laugh this time.

'My dear Femke,' he chuckled. 'It is Femke, isn't it? Or is that another assumed name?'

Femke shook her head with a grin. 'Femke is my real name,' she confirmed.

'Well, my dear Femke, you must know from your times in Court that I've lived my life permanently in trouble since I was about six years old. I've more of a reputation for breaking rules than any other Lord in Court ever had. Do you think you're going to put me off because I'll have to break a few rules here and there? I'm already involved in this up to my neck. I helped break you out of the Royal

Prison, didn't I? I doubt the local authorities would look too kindly on that if they were to find out.'

'I suppose not,' Femke agreed reluctantly. 'But if you're going to get involved any further, then you must agree to do exactly what you're told. No improvising – understand? If you step out of line once, then I'll have Reynik tie you up and stash you away in a hole somewhere until we're ready to head back to Shandar. If you want to make yourself useful, go and get some food. The stuff I've been eating for the last couple of weeks has been nutritious enough, but it couldn't be described as appetising. Anything tasty would be appreciated right now.'

Danar got to his feet and bowed. 'Yes, my Lady. Is there anything else my Lady would like? A light wine? Or a jar of fragranced oil for her parlour?' he asked, humour dancing in his eyes.

'"My Lady" would like to see the back of Lord Danar disappearing rapidly to fetch me some food,' Femke growled with mock anger. 'Now!'

Danar laughed again, but did as he was bid. Femke sighed with relief as the door closed behind him. Maintaining her focus over the next few days would not be easy, she decided.

Much to Femke's relief, it was Reynik who arrived back first about half an hour later with a largish bundle under his arm. By the smile on the young soldier's face, she took it that his short shopping trip had been successful.

'That didn't take long. I take it you had no great difficulties?' Femke asked, eyeing the bundle with anticipation.

'Nothing drastic,' Reynik replied casually. 'The hardest

item to come by was the scissors. For some reason, nobody had any they were willing to part with. Not to worry, I obtained some in the end.'

Reynik deposited the bundle on the bed and Femke began unwrapping it within seconds. She did not raise the question of where the scissors had come from, but hoped he had used discretion. Tunics, hose, boots, a belt, gloves, bandages, make-up – all the things that Femke had asked for were spread across the bed. Femke held the plain tunics up to her body in turn and nodded with pleasure at Reynik's eye for style and size.

'Perfect!' she muttered and then thanked Reynik for his efforts. 'You don't mess about, do you?' she added. 'It would have taken me hours to get that lot.'

'That's why you will always find men in the tavern early,' Reynik laughed. 'My father taught me not to linger in the marketplaces looking for the ultimate bargain. It's in, out, and into the bar. We spend a senna or two more, but look at the drinking time we save!'

Femke joined with his laughter, for she knew he was not a great drinker. It was all part of the military bravado that the young man had been soaking up in the Legion.

'Tell me, Reynik, can you cut hair as fast?'

'Sure, if you want to look like a man,' he said with a snort.

'That's the general idea,' Femke replied. 'Why do you think I wanted the tunics and hose rather than dresses?'

'Well, I've seen quite a lot of women here in Thrandor dressed in tunic and hose,' Reynik said thoughtfully. 'I thought you were simply going for a different style. So the bandages are for . . .'

'Flattening my chest – yes,' Femke said with a grin. 'Not that it needs a lot of flattening.'

'I'm glad it was you who said that,' laughed Reynik. 'Yes, I'll cut your hair for you. I think you'll make quite a good-looking young fellow. No doubt you'll have young maidens flocking into your arms in no time.'

Femke gave him a mock warning look and he laughed all the more. What a difference from a few hours ago, Femke thought with a small sigh of pleasure. From sitting in the darkness of her cell in the Palace, wondering when her trial would begin, to laughing and joking in the room of an inn. Life had been full of surprises recently. Not many had been pleasant. But then, when one lived the sort of life that Femke did, the tough turns of fate were common occurrences.

'Tell me, Reynik, did you manage to find out anything about Shalidar's activities? You look as though you've been busy,' she noted, pointing at his lip.

Reynik's hand went involuntarily to his face. He nodded, gesturing for Femke to sit on a chair in front of the small dressing mirror before setting about her hair with the scissors.

'I discovered nothing, I'm afraid. I never saw Shalidar, though I did meet a few of his men. They're not exactly a friendly bunch.'

'You did well to walk away,' Femke noted. 'Thanks for trying. Did Shalidar see you?'

'Well, someone did. I've no idea if it was Shalidar though. I thought I was pretty discreet. It seems I have a lot to learn about spying on someone.'

True to his word, Reynik did not take long cutting her hair. He was making the final few snips to tidy up the back when Danar returned.

Danar stopped abruptly, halfway through the door, as he saw what Reynik had done to Femke's hair. To say he looked shocked was putting it mildly. Femke turned and had to fight hard to keep from laughing aloud at the look that bordered between pure shock and outright horror at the change Reynik had wrought with a simple pair of scissors.

'Well!' he exclaimed as he recovered his composure. 'You're constantly full of surprises, aren't you? I wouldn't have recognised you if I hadn't known you were waiting for me here.'

'That is the general idea,' Femke said with a grin. 'I'll not be wearing a ball gown for a while – unless I have a wig to hand, of course – but then my role is not glamorous on this occasion.'

'So I see,' Danar said, looking regretfully at the locks of hair scattered on the floor around her chair. 'Here, I've got us all some food. Let's eat.'

Danar had bought a good spread of food and Femke was quick to tuck in. The two men ate heartily, but without the single-minded dedication that Femke was devoting to demolishing everything in sight. Once Femke's initial hunger pangs were sated and she had slowed to a more regular eating pace, Danar broke the silence that had descended whilst they were eating.

'So, Femke, are you going to tell us your plan? I'm intrigued to know what you intend to do now, but I'd like to know the background first. The Emperor told us you'd been accused of murder, but he also said you were on the run somewhere in Mantor. How did you get caught, and how were you set up in the first place?'

Femke took a deep breath and then, between mouthfuls, proceeded to relate her story of the disastrous visit to the Thrandorian capital. It took a while, for there was a lot to tell. Reynik nodded grimly, touching his bruised face once more when Femke told of her realisation that Shalidar had an entire network of people here in Mantor.

'Then you kind gentlemen turned up, so now the game begins again.'

'Game?' Danar said incredulously. 'Is that how you view all this – as a game?'

'Well, it's as good an outlook as any,' Femke answered. 'I'm sure your father would have you believe that Empire politics is deadly serious and never to be joked about, but I doubt you support that view. How is this situation any different? In the end it's all about getting the results you want. Whether it's viewed as a game to be taken seriously, or a hostile diplomatic incident with potentially deadly implications, doesn't matter. I am a professional and I do what is needed to see the will of the Emperor is done.'

'And what do you see as the will of the Emperor?' asked Danar cautiously. 'I told the Emperor I would try to convince the King of Thrandor you were not the murderer of Baron Anton or Count Dreban. I also told him we would be arriving in Mantor openly. So far I have done neither of those things. It would be good to think we're doing *something* in line with what the Emperor wishes.'

'Ah,' Femke sighed, wincing slightly as she considered that. 'Well, you'll want to think twice before you agree to what I'm about to propose then.'

Danar groaned and put his head in his hands in mock despair. Reynik laughed.

'Come on – tell me the worst. What do you have in mind?' Danar asked, his tone resigned.

'Well, before I say anything I need to know how much money you brought with you.'

'Money?' Danar asked, in genuine surprise. 'More than enough to live comfortably for a while, I suppose. Why do you ask?'

'Would you have enough money to hire an assassin?' Femke asked, knowing what the answer would be.

'Hire an assassin? Certainly not! At least, I doubt it. I assume they don't come cheaply. What are you up to, Femke?' Danar asked, shaking his head.

'In that case we're going to need a lot more money,' Femke said, ignoring Danar's question.

'And of course you know just the place to get it from,' Reynik suggested with a grin.

'Absolutely,' Femke replied. 'The Royal Treasury – where else?'

'Your Imperial Majesty, another messenger has arrived from Thrandor. He says that he bears grave news for your immediate attention.'

'Another one? You'd better bring him in immediately. Let's see what disaster has occurred this time,' Surabar said with a sigh that spoke of fatigue and stress.

218

'Right away, your Majesty.'

The servant scurried off after the briefest of bows, and Surabar watched him go with a degree of tired amusement. Sitting patiently behind his desk, he stared at the latest pile of reports without attempting to read them. There was so much information to sift through every day, but he was gradually learning which reports needed careful attention and which he could skim through. The intelligence received from the borders with Thrandor had not mentioned anything unusual. If King Malo were considering military action then he had made no significant moves yet.

There was another knock at the door and Surabar called out for the person to enter. It was the same servant again, his face slightly flushed but his breathing controlled and his voice steady as he introduced King Malo's messenger.

'Welcome,' Surabar announced warmly. 'Please, do come in. I understand you bring urgent news from King Malo. I would be glad to hear it. Our last tidings from the King of Thrandor were grave. I hope your tidings are of a happier nature.'

The messenger looked uncomfortable and shifted his shoulders slightly in an unconscious gesture before he replied.

'Well, your Imperial Majesty, King Malo wanted to inform you that Ambassador Femke has been found and detained. Further evidence of her guilt in the deaths of Baron Anton and Count Dreban has also surfaced. There are character witnesses present who have named her an assassin, which has placed grave doubts over future international relations between Thrandor and Shandar.

Ambassador Femke has requested an advocate from the Empire to represent her interests at the trial, which is to be held in the Royal Court at Mantor. The King asks that you reply with all haste. He is keen to commence the trial and see justice done.'

Surabar was genuinely shocked by the news. From all that he knew of Femke, she was quick-witted, clever and excellent at blending in so well with her surroundings that he would have wagered half the treasury on her not being caught by the Thrandorians. The situation in Mantor was dire indeed.

'A representative? Did the King specify what sort of representative?' he asked.

'No, your Majesty. King Malo said that Ambassador Femke had requested a representative to be present at the trial to view the evidence and make a defence. The King did not specify any particular rank or profession.'

Emperor Surabar got slowly to his feet, his right hand rubbing thoughtfully at his chin. For a moment he looked lost in thought, then he looked straight at the messenger with a piercing gaze.

'Very well,' he said firmly. 'Ambassador Femke shall have her representative. I had not planned to make a visit to Thrandor yet, but the outcome of this trial is of such importance to the future of our two countries that I believe it would be best if I come in person to see her interests are properly represented.'

The messenger gulped and much of the colour drained from his face.

'I trust you will not come alone, your Majesty,' he

croaked, his voice cracking as he voiced his immediate concern.

'No, that would not be wise,' Surabar replied thoughtfully. 'But equally I should not arrive at the head of a small army. I don't want to cause alarm. Would a troop of about twenty to thirty guards cause any problems, do you think?'

'I think twenty to thirty would be fine, your Majesty. I cannot imagine such a small contingent causing major consternation. I will bear the news of your impending visit as quickly as I can to the King.'

'Thank you, I would appreciate that. Do take time to rest and enjoy some refreshments before you get underway. I'll not be able to set out any earlier than tomorrow. It will take a short time for me to get my affairs here in order, and my party will travel slower than a message rider. Go and get some sleep. You have earned it.'

The messenger bowed deeply and turned to leave the room. The servant, who had remained standing inside the door during the brief exchange, opened it again to allow the messenger to go. He too bowed and prepared to leave, but Surabar called to him before he left. 'Once you've seen King Malo's messenger to his quarters, could you send for Lord Kempten please? I need to talk to him urgently.'

The servant bowed again and closed the door behind him as he left. Surabar looked distantly at the door and wondered if he were doing the right thing. He had hardly had a chance to establish himself as Emperor. There had been visible opposition to his rule in the attack on the day of the coronation. There was still no firm evidence as to which of the Nobles were responsible for that, but he had a good idea who the key players were. Should he dash off on an errand to Mantor? He could easily send someone else. Femke was ostensibly an ambassador. Ambassadors were as expendable as soldiers or spies. True, it was not good to lose ambassadors – particularly under circumstances such as those presently being faced – but it was not for the Emperor to take a close personal interest in such things.

'It's a good job that I see being Emperor as a temporary inconvenience,' Surabar said aloud to himself. 'Let's see what old Kempten is made of, shall we? Who knows – maybe he'll prove to make a good successor to the Mantle. At least by leaving him in charge I won't have to worry about one of the old-school Lords trying to seize control.'

There were never any guarantees in high-level politics and power mongering. Surabar knew that as well as anyone, but the General felt he could do far worse than leave Kempten as Regent in his absence. Time alone would tell.

'The Royal Treasury! Are you completely out of your mind?' Danar exploded.

'Shhh! Do you want everyone to know? Keep your hair on – I know what I'm doing,' Femke replied, her voice calm and placating.

Danar lowered his voice to a harsh whisper, but it kept cracking into normal speech. 'Aren't two murder charges enough to be going on with? Now you want to add grand theft and conspiracy to murder to the list. What in Shand's name do you want to hire an assassin for? Surely there's been enough killing here, and if you intend to have Shalidar killed, then you are wasting your time and money.

Assassins will not take out contracts on one another. Surely you know that?'

Femke raised an eyebrow at Danar and gave him a look that spoke volumes. 'Hold your judgement for a moment, *Lord* Danar, and give me a chance to explain fully. All will become clear. We're not going to empty the Royal Treasury, just borrow a bit of it. A couple of thousand gold Thrandorian crowns should prove enough of a temptation for Shalidar to take on a contract. Professional assassins like Shalidar have their own code of honour, known as the Assassins' Creed, which they swear to uphold when they accept membership into their secret Guild. Once he's taken the down payment, then he'll be bound by the Creed to make the kill or die trying. The sting is that we'll be ready for his attempt, and we'll ensure it's public enough for Shalidar to be exposed. If he does manage the hit without being seen, I've got a back-up plan that will trap him anyway. Then, with the cooperation of the King and the Royal Guards, it should be possible to recover the gold from the down payment and it will be much easier to prove that Shalidar killed Anton and Dreban.'

Reynik and Danar sat silently for a moment, both looking thoughtful. Neither of them were particularly happy.

'It could work,' Reynik said slowly, as he thought through the line of Femke's logic. 'It's awfully risky though, particularly for whomever is going to be Shalidar's target. I take it you have someone in mind?'

'Well, yes, actually I do,' Femke said, reddening slightly with embarrassment. 'Before you two came along, I was going to set myself up as the target. There are obvious problems with that, but now we have a new Ambassador from Shandar.'

Reynik and Femke both turned their eyes towards Lord Danar.

'Why do I get the feeling I'm not going to like this?' he asked with a small groan.

'You said you came here to help me,' Femke suggested, with a lopsided little smile.

'I didn't exactly anticipate setting myself up as a target to be peppered full of arrows for your amusement, Femke,' Danar hissed angrily.

'Well, if we plan this properly, it shouldn't come to that.'

Femke added silently to herself that she would not let it, because she was already developing feelings for him that she didn't want to admit. What she was doing was abhorrent. She was using him. Using him in the worst possible way, because she knew he would do just about anything to win her heart at the moment. It was the worst form of abuse, but she could see no other option. She justified it by telling herself it was for the good of the Empire. 'Let's get the first phase of the plan over with and then we can discuss it again,' she said firmly, clamping down hard on her thoughts. 'Our first hurdle is to rob the Royal Treasury.'

'Surabar is not likely to approve of that—' Danar started, his voice still angry.

'Danar! Stop it! I suggest you listen carefully. There is risk involved in everything we do from here on, so let's try not to make silly mistakes. Hear out my full plan. Then, if

224

you have any better ideas, I will listen to them. If you don't want to help, go home. I'll find another way around the problem. I think it fair to say we all need to keep open minds throughout the next few days. Remember that Shalidar is no fool. Despite thinking I'm safely tucked away in the Royal Prison, he's unlikely to drop his guard. We need to outwit, out-plan and out-think him at every turn, or this is not going to work. We must succeed totally. If we fail . . . well, let's not fail. I don't want to live with that sort failure on my conscience.'

CHAPTER ELEVEN

'Have you heard the news?' Reynik asked excitedly.

'Yes, it's all over the city. Surabar is coming here. I hear he's expected in about four or five days from now,' Femke replied. 'It doesn't give us much time.'

'No, but it makes my job easy tonight,' Reynik bubbled enthusiastically. 'It's the perfect trigger for a demonstration in front of the Palace. I should be able to pull most of the Royal Guard to the front gate for you and keep them there for some time. I've already found a suitably enraged local who'll make a great front man. It won't take much to wind him up. Then I'll slide into the background and watch the fireworks. Once I'm sure the distraction will give you enough time to get in and out, I'll come to the servants' exit and wait nearby in case you need any last minute help.'

'That sounds great.'

'How did you get on with the other things we needed?'

'No problems,' Femke answered with a pleased smile

at her success. 'Danar and I will be kitted out by mid-afternoon. The uniforms are all but ready and the armourer has promised I can pick up the weapons after lunch. We'll be ready to go any time after then, so don't worry if your diversion blows up a little early. We should be flexible enough by then to be able to initiate the plan at any time.'

'What about the more exotic requirements?' Reynik asked, curious to see how far Femke's success stretched.

'Also sorted,' Femke replied with a grin. 'The alchemist knew exactly what I wanted and supplied everything without question, despite the quantities I required. It's nice to find there's one trade left that doesn't ask awkward questions at strange requests.'

'I wouldn't be surprised if he doesn't report it to someone though,' Reynik said seriously.

'It doesn't matter if he does. It's unlikely that Shalidar will be monitoring alchemists – why would he want to? If the King is informed, well, it'll make little difference to the plan, so let's not worry about what we can't fix.'

'Where's Lord Danar? I haven't seen him this morning.'

'I sent him out for food again,' Femke replied with a grin. 'He's happy to be useful and he does have a knack of finding tasty snacks.'

'I thought the stomach was the way to a *man's* heart,' Reynik jibed.

'As I am a man at the moment, he could be on the right track,' Femke replied pompously, in an exaggeratedly deep voice. She failed to keep a straight face for more than a few seconds and laughter followed.

Later that afternoon, Femke gave silent thanks for the

talkative young guard who had inadvertently given her so much information during her time in the Royal Prison. It had not proved difficult to intercept a requisition order from the Royal Quartermaster and alter it slightly to include two extra uniforms. Knowing the routine was half the battle of getting hold of materials by deception. After her long chats with the guard, Femke felt she understood the Thrandorian military system well. A simple note at the bottom of the requisition order had arranged for the two uniforms to be collected direct from the tailor's. It would be some days before the Quartermaster noted the extra cost on the order, if he ever did.

Danar collected the two uniforms. Each came packed inside a medium-sized rucksack. The tailor's shop was the collection point, but the boots, belts and various other accoutrements had all been gathered and included inside the rucksacks. The only parts of the uniform not included were the weapons. These had to be picked up separately from a smithy. Femke went to collect these.

The smith gave Femke a penetrating look when she told him why she was there. 'So you're to become a Royal Guard, are you?' he asked, taking in the slim, boyish figure dressed in tunic and hose.

'Yes, sir,' Femke replied, nodding enthusiastically.

'I'll be honest – I'm surprised that you passed the strength test with arms like those. You've no muscle on your bones at all, lad.'

'I'm stronger than I look, sir,' Femke said with a perfectly straight face, taking in the smith's tree-trunk-like arms and legs with apparent unconcern.

'I suppose you must be. I understand you're collecting for two?'

'That's right, sir.'

'Well, good luck with the training, son. If you've any sense you'll eat more and exercise some meat onto those arms of yours. You'll never be taken seriously in a fight with biceps like those.'

Femke thanked the smith for his advice and promised him she would try. Then, with the swords and knives tucked under her arms, she left the smithy and walked quickly back to the arranged meeting place.

When Femke saw the rucksacks that Danar was carrying, she was delighted. With the rucksacks effectively being an extension of the uniform, there would not be many questions asked if a Royal Guard were to wear one into the Palace. It would be the perfect way to carry the loot from their raid, together with some of her purchases from the alchemist's shop.

'Looks like we're all set,' Femke commented as she approached Danar at the rendezvous point.

'Apparently so.'

'OK, let's nip back to the Baker's Arms and get changed. We need to get to the Palace soon in case Reynik gets ahead of himself. Rabble-rousing is an inexact science. We wouldn't want to miss our opportunity.'

The Baker's Arms was another mediocre inn that offered acceptable, if basic, accommodation at low prices. Femke had chosen the inn because there was a back exit. The back door was kept locked, but the landlord had conveniently supplied them with a key each for the duration of their

229

stay. The arrangement was not the safest, as it was ripe for abuse by thieves. However, as they had little that was worth stealing and were carrying those things they valued with them, Femke cared little.

The back door of the inn opened onto a quiet alleyway. This led to one of the small side streets, which in turn led to one of the major thoroughfares up through the levels of Mantor. Danar and Femke elected to slip in through the back door, change, and slide out again before anyone noticed their presence.

Danar carried his rucksack, in which Femke had carefully placed several glass vials of different-coloured powders wrapped in cloth. Half a dozen vials of blue powder on one side of the bag were separated from a similar number of vials filled with green powder by lots more layers of soft cloth.

'What are those for?' Danar asked, as Femke took great pains to protect the integrity of the vials.

'Let's just say that if we need to use them, things will not be going to plan,' Femke replied, her tone implying 'And that's that, so don't ask any more'.

'I thought I'd ask in case I need to use them,' Danar muttered grumpily.

'You won't be using them,' Femke stated firmly. 'If in some insane moment I decide to let you use the vials, you can be sure I'll give you specific directions. Try to forget they're there, and don't mess with them unless I tell you. Is that clear?'

'Perfectly,' Danar muttered.

'Here – take this,' Femke added, passing him a strange-looking circle of cloth. It was about three inches wide and laced with a stretchy material top and bottom. 'If I get the vials out, pull the cloth over your face and wear it like a mask across your mouth and nose. Keep it where you can get at it quickly at all times.'

'Great!' Danar said sourly, fingering the strange material and wondering what on earth it was made of. 'Remind me why I'm coming on this trip again?'

'Because you volunteered. Because you didn't want to be left out. Because you can't get your stubborn head around the fact that I could do this perfectly well on my own,' Femke answered, counting off the reasons on her fingers. 'And also because this way I don't have to lug the spoils all the way back down through Mantor,' she added with a grin meant to soften the harshness of her previous comments. There was little point in taking him if he was going to sulk all the way. Silently, she had to admit to herself that one of the main reasons for taking him along was because she loved looking at his roguish, little-boy smile.

Shand, but he's cute, Femke thought, her heart leaping at the thought that this handsome young Lord was actively pursuing her affections. It was amazing to her that he still appeared willing to leap into notoriety on her behalf, despite her dressing as a man and treating him as if he were an inconvenience. If this jaunt goes well, I'll ease up on him a little, she promised herself.

It was later in the afternoon than Femke had intended by the time they took up position close to the main gate to the Royal Palace. There they waited, keeping a low profile until

231

the first sounds of a rapidly approaching, angry mob reached their ears.

'Sounds like Reynik's on his way,' Danar commented with a grin.

'About time! At least he's bringing plenty of friends with him. Come on, let's go,' Femke said, relieved to be moving again. The worst bit about a mission like this was always the waiting. Once events were in motion and the adrenalin was pumping, Femke was in her element. Today was no different.

Together they marched around the Palace wall to the servants' gate where they were admitted without question. Femke had never worried that her uniform would give her away, for she knew her appearance was convincing. The one element of the disguise that worried her was her walk. Despite much observation and practice, Femke had never truly mastered the art of walking like a man. There was something about the movements that were so alien she could not mimic them with authenticity.

Both Danar and Reynik had assured her they felt her approximation was passable, but for Femke nothing less than perfection was acceptable. The knowledge that it was something she could not totally master had left her feeling irritable.

Because Femke knew precisely where she was going, there was no hesitation as she led Danar from the gate to the nearest door into the main Palace building complex. Servants and courtiers alike passed them by within the crisscrossing maze of corridors with no more than the usual courtesy nods of acknowledgement, so they progressed quickly and without incident into the heart of the Palace.

Exactly as the young guard had said, there was a plain door a little way down the corridor from the entrance to the main chamber of the King's Court. Femke paused at the door and looked Danar straight in the eye.

'Remember – don't say anything. Let me do the talking,' she said firmly.

'Whatever you say, sir,' Danar replied with a wry smile and a cheeky wink.

Femke groaned silently and hoped he would not do or say anything stupid. All was going smoothly, but the next few seconds were crucial. Taking a deep breath, Femke opened the door and they stepped through into the short corridor on the other side, closing the door behind them. Four torches lit the corridor, casting a flickering light from where they were mounted in brackets on the wall.

The two guards at the far end of the corridor saw them instantly and their hands moved to their sword hilts instinctively. On seeing the uniforms they stopped short of drawing their weapons and their stances relaxed a little. Femke and Danar walked confidently down the corridor towards the two guards until they were ordered to halt and state their purpose.

'One of the captains sent us,' Femke answered. 'I'm sorry, but I don't know his name. We haven't long since started our training, but the captain ordered us here to relieve you. He wants you at the front gate. It sounds like there's a riot going on down there – a protest about the Emperor of Shandar coming. The captain's words were quite colourful. "Get your arses down to the Treasury door and send the two numb-knuckles you find there to the main gate. Even you should be able to stand in front of a locked door without looking like a complete pile of horse—"'

'Captain Mikkals,' the two guards chorused together, grinning at one another with a knowing look. 'Any other instructions?'

'No. Get down to the main gate and help was all he said,' Femke replied with a shrug. 'If you could go quickly we'd appreciate it, because . . . well we didn't exactly know where the Treasury was and it's taken us a while to find you. You know what the Captain's like. He'll skin us alive on the next training session if he thinks we've been slack.'

'Oh, he'll give you a hard time anyway,' one of the guards replied, still grinning broadly. 'That's Mikkals. I'm convinced he's a sadist. Come on Wils, we'd better get down there and see what's up.'

'I don't know. Shouldn't one of us go and confirm the order? It's highly unusual to be relieved mid-shift,' Wils answered uncertainly.

'How many riots have you seen at the Palace gates?' the first guard asked impatiently, clearly wanting to get in on the action. 'None! And neither have I. Come on. We've been given a chance to do something interesting and you're worried about leaving the most boring duty there is.'

'Well, I just think . . .'

'You think too much. Come on, let's go.'

The two guards started to move down the corridor. 'Hey, what's with the rucksack?' asked Wils suspiciously as Danar passed him.

Danar opened his mouth to reply, but Femke jumped in quickly.

'We were on our way to the training quarters when the Captain collared us. Sodan here trashed some of his kit so badly during the last training session that we had to go and buy him a replacement set before the next inspection.'

'There goes the training pay, huh?' the other guard said with a tone that held a mixture of sympathy and amusement.

Danar nodded glumly.

'Bad luck, Sodan. Still, look on the bright side – it's only a couple of months until you start getting more than a couple of silvers a week.' The two guards laughed and continued down the corridor at pace. 'We'll try not to be long. Have fun,' they called back as they disappeared out of the door.

The door closed behind them and Femke remained motionless for two or three seconds before whirling around and peering with an expert eye into the lower of the two locks on the solid metal door behind them.

'That went well,' Danar commented as Femke drew a lock pick from her pocket and carefully inserted it into the lock.

'Hmm,' Femke replied, already engrossed in her work.

'Anything I can do to help?'

'Yes, actually,' Femke replied absently as she manipulated the metal tool within the lock mechanism. 'You can empty the vials out of the rucksack to make room for the gold. Be careful how you handle them. Keep them wrapped in the cloths, keeping the two different types well apart.

Oh, and put them somewhere you're not going to tread on them. When you're done, you can watch the far door for anyone entering. I don't need to tell you what will happen if someone comes into the corridor and catches me picking these locks. Now, shut up and let me concentrate.'

Danar did as he was told, handling the glass vials with extreme care as he took them out of the rucksack. He made two separate nests of cloth, one on either side of the corridor. Then he took up a guard position a little way down the corridor towards the exit, and listened for anyone coming. He knew there was little chance of hearing anything unless they happened to be talking as they approached. The plush carpeted floors of the main corridor outside silenced the steps of even steel-capped boots.

Seconds ticked by into minutes and Danar found himself looking over his shoulder nervously at Femke. She was still concentrating all her attention on the lower lock.

'What's the matter?' Danar asked in a hoarse whisper. 'I thought you were good at this stuff?'

'The matter? Nothing's the matter. I'm staring down the barrel of one of the best locks I've seen in years, that's all,' Femke replied. 'Short of magic, the King couldn't have put a better safeguard system on this door.'

'Magic! That's a thought. Are you sure that the Treasury isn't guarded by some form of magic?' Danar asked in a worried voice.

Femke paused for a second and looked over her shoulder at Danar. Exasperated scorn was clear in her features.

'Don't be stupid, Danar – this is Thrandor, remember? They haven't allowed magic here for two hundred years.

236

The King is the least likely person in Thrandor to use magical protection. Doing so would undermine the laws by which the kingdom has been ruled for centuries. Now, have a little faith, give me a little space and . . .'

Femke turned back to the lock and gave a twist of her lock pick. There was a satisfying 'snick' as the lock opened and Femke gave a smug glance over her shoulder at Danar.

'. . . your patience will be rewarded,' she finished. 'One down, one to go.'

'Look, I don't want to rush you, Femke, but we're rather vulnerable here. We could get caught red-handed at any second,' Danar pleaded.

'Yes, yes, I know,' Femke replied absently. 'Fortunately, whoever installed the lock system used virtually identical locks top and bottom. Good they might be, but when you know how to open them . . .' There was another loud snick. '. . . they drop like flies,' she said, with a purr of satisfaction in her voice that spoke of pure pleasure.

'Great work!' Danar congratulated. 'Come on, let's get what we came for and get out of here.'

'Yes, let's,' Femke said with a grin and opened the door, gesturing for him to enter first.

Danar dashed back up the corridor, grabbed a fresh torch from a small stack on a shelf by the door and lit it from one of the burning torches. With the flaming torch held ahead of him, Danar entered through the open Treasury door. He had gone no more than a pace or two inside before he stopped and stared in utter amazement. Of all the things he had expected to find, he had not expected this.

'There's nothing here!' he exclaimed in amazement. 'The whole Treasury set-up is a hoax!'

'It does rather look that way, doesn't it?' Femke replied, calmly stepping through the door behind him. 'Would you mind moving forward a little further so that I can get inside as well? Thanks.'

Femke swung the door closed gently behind them. It shut with a dull thud against the frame. Then she started feeling around the doorframe, obviously looking for something.

'What are you doing?' Danar asked, a tinge of panic starting to set into his voice. 'We need to get out of here. Have you gone mad?'

'No, Danar, I'm simply finishing the job we started. Ah, here it is!'

Suddenly a slight grating sound came from the far wall of the empty room and a section of it rotated through ninety degrees to reveal a second room beyond. The room was filled with treasures of all kinds. There were stacks of gold and silver bars, together with bags of gold pieces and precious gems, but there were also works of art, sets of rare pottery, beautiful dresses mounted on special manikins and much more. It was breathtaking.

'Clever, isn't it?' Femke said with a grin. 'The outer door must be closed and the concealed button pressed in order for the real Treasury door to open. What thief would step into an empty room with no obvious route onwards and then close the door behind him? None that I know.'

'But how did you know what to do?'

'Let's say I had a bit of "inside" help,' Femke replied with a chuckle. 'Come on, don't stand there gawping. Less than a minute ago it was you urging me to hurry up. Bring the rucksack and let's pack what we came for. Don't take anything we don't need. A couple of thousand gold pieces will do nicely. If we take them from the right places, they'll be unlikely to notice it missing.'

It was a bold statement, and Femke quickly realised that it was also wrong. Two thousand gold crowns was a lot of coins. They were never going to be able to conceal the fact it had gone. As soon as they realised the futility of attempting to conceal the theft they began simply scooping coins into the bag until Femke estimated that they had enough.

'OK, that should do it. Let's get out of here while the going's good,' Femke ordered.

Danar did not question her this time. He swung the now heavy pack up onto his shoulders and raced back out into the empty room. Femke found the secret button again to close the hidden door and then reopened the metal door back out into the guard corridor.

To their relief, the corridor was still empty, aside from the two cloth piles containing the small glass vials. Femke swung the metal door closed and paused for a moment, torn by indecision. Personal pride made her want to lock the door. For a moment, pride and practicality warred within her. Practicality won the day. They did not have an infinite amount of time to play with, so she put aside her desire for neatness and concentrated on getting them out of the Palace safely.

'Danar, stand still whilst I repack the vials,' she ordered. 'I'm not leaving them behind.'

Danar quickly jammed the burning torch he was carrying

into a spare wall bracket and then held as still as he could, barely daring to breathe as Femke picked up the glass vials from where he had stacked them a little earlier.

Femke put first the blue vials and then the green vials back into the rucksack, taking care to place plenty of cloth over the gold coins and a thick barrier of cloth between the two types of vials. However, rather than put all the vials inside, Femke kept back one vial of each colour, which she held, one per hand.

'An insurance policy,' she said with a slight shrug, as Danar noted what she had done. 'I've also left the top of the rucksack unfastened, so don't fall over. Falling could prove messy. Come on, time to go.'

They moved swiftly to the end of the corridor. Femke pressed her ear to the door to see if she could hear anything outside. Nothing was discernible so she cautiously opened the door a crack and peered out. The corridor was empty as far as she could see. With gritted teeth, Femke opened the door a little further and checked the other direction. Again, all was clear.

'Looks like Reynik's diversion is working well,' Femke murmured softly to Danar as she stepped out into the corridor.

Danar had barely stepped through the doorway when a group of Royal Guards emerged from a side corridor some distance towards the front of the Palace. One glance told Femke that two of them were the guards she and Danar had replaced.

'That's them, Captain. Hey, you! Stop where you are!' one of the guards shouted.

'I thought this was too good to be true,' muttered Femke through clenched teeth. 'Got your mask handy like I told you? Get it on. Things are going to get messy. Don't watch me – go that way. Now!'

Danar fumbled in his pocket for his mask and started off along the corridor. Femke did not wait to see if he had done as he was told. Instead, she took a couple of deep breaths and marched purposefully towards the oncoming guards, who were now approaching at a run with their weapons drawn. Holding the second breath, Femke raised her hands high above her head and threw the two glass vials to the floor in front of the oncoming soldiers. Hurled with such force, the glass vials smashed instantly, despite the thick pile of the carpet. The coloured powders mixed.

Femke turned her head away and grabbed her own mask from where she had tucked it into a pocket. There was a short hiss, followed by a loud whooshing noise as the corridor filled instantly with billowing clouds of acrid blue smoke. Femke whirled and ran down the corridor after Danar, putting her mask on as she ran. Twice she ricocheted off walls as she blindly sprinted forward until she burst out of the edge of the cloud. As Femke found clear air she discovered that Danar was not far ahead of her. Behind her, muffled by the still expanding cloud of thick smoke, the sound of men retching told her there would be little pursuit from that direction for a while.

'Danar!' Femke called through her mask. 'Danar, stop. Let me grab another couple of vials.'

'Shand alive, Femke! What in the name of all that's holy is that stuff?'

'Trust me, you don't want to know,' she replied. 'Got 'em. Come on, we need to stay ahead of the cloud. Take off your mask, but keep it in your hand. Be ready to put it back on again if I tell you. If we meet anyone on the way out, it would be better if we bluff. I don't want to use any more of this stuff than I have to.'

Femke took off her own mask. With a quick glance back at the swirling mass of smoke still expanding along the corridor, she set off through the Palace at a steady run in the direction of the servants' exit. They encountered a couple of servants along the way, whom Femke advised against heading towards the middle of the Palace.

'I think someone has tried to assassinate the King with poisoned gas,' she gasped. 'Alert everyone to look out for intruders. We're going to secure the servants' exit.'

Danar simply followed in Femke's wake, watching with an ever-growing respect as she manipulated people with bold, directive orders and statements. Servants, courtiers, and other Royal Guards all followed her orders, simply because they could not resist her powerful, authoritative supervision. With Femke's bold bluffing, they raced through the Palace with ease until they were within sight of the servants' gate.

Femke saw the crowd of guards at the gate and instantly recognised trouble. Someone with sense had reasoned that with insurrection at the main gate, there was the possibility of further trouble at the secondary gate. As a result, a whole section of men had come to augment the regular guards.

Femke's initial estimate placed the head count around twenty. Worse than that, there was a sergeant amongst the guards. His eyes narrowed with suspicion the moment he saw the two of them running towards him. Femke did not slow down, but continued to lead Danar at a run towards the gate until they were almost on top of the main group of guards.

As she got to within about ten paces of the front guards, Femke simply yelled 'MASK!' at the top of her voice and hurled the two vials in her hands at the feet of the soldiers. The tinkling smash of the glass was followed by the same hiss and whoosh that Danar had experienced in the corridor earlier. This time, however, he did not react fast enough. Before he had a chance to get his mask on, he was engulfed in thick, blue smoke.

Danar did not inhale much of the noxious gas, but even a little was enough to incapacitate him instantly. Nausea gripped him and before he knew it, the young Lord was doubled over and vomiting helplessly. Any thought of getting the mask into place dissipated instantly as the gas entered his system and overthrew his control of bodily functions. Danar struggled in vain to regain a measure of control over his stomach, as more and more of the smoke entered his lungs.

It took a few moments for Femke to realise Danar was no longer following her. As she threw the vials down, Femke had taken a deep breath and held it for the second or two required to get her own mask in place. Then, with the cloud growing rapidly, Femke bowled into the guards and scattered them like a runaway cart hitting a fruit seller's stall. The combination of the smoke's incapacitating effect and Femke's lightning fast fists, elbows, knees and feet cracking into the guards was devastating. The entire party of Royal Guards were rendered helpless within a matter of seconds.

Because the powders had mixed in open air this time, rather than in the confined space of the Palace corridor, the cloud dispersed quickly, rising into the evening air in a great billowing plume. So as soon as Femke realised that Danar was not following, she turned and saw him through the thinning blue smoke, doubled over and firmly in the grip of the smoke's pernicious effects.

'Damn!' she swore, her expletive muffled by the cloth mask.

There was not a moment to lose. More guards could arrive at any time. It was obvious that they could no longer make a slick getaway with Danar unable to stand straight, let alone run. All she could do was to help him out through the gate and hope to drag him away before more guards appeared.

Femke ran back and grabbed one of Danar's arms, wrapping it around her neck. Then, with strength born of desperation and a flood of adrenalin, Femke all but carried the young Lord out through the servants' gate and into the street. Reynik suddenly appeared as if from nowhere, taking up position on the other side of Danar. Between them, they whisked him away from the Palace and into the increasing gloom of the approaching night.

In the distance, Femke could hear chanting and a babble of angry voices, which she assumed was the demonstration in front of the main Palace gates. As soon as she could, Femke ripped off her mask with her spare hand and cast it aside.

'Can I assume you got what we needed?' Reynik grunted, as they pulled Danar into a quiet side street.

'You can assume away,' Femke replied in a voice that brimmed with success. 'We're all set for the next phase.'

CHAPTER TWELVE

The Emperor had hardly left Shandrim before Lord Kempten started to get trouble from the more senior of the old-school Lords. The first delegation came to see him before the day was out. Lord Veryan led the party of five in through the study door and made it quite clear he was their spokesman.

'So, Kempten, old man, why did Surabar leave *you* in control? I thought you were opposed to his ascension to the Mantle.'

'That I was, Veryan. In fact I'm still not totally convinced by him, though my respect for the General is rising. What's your point?' Kempten replied, instantly roiled to the core by the snide tone of his fellow Lord.

'We're here to organise the takeover of Shandar. With Surabar away and power transferred to you, the Legions are no longer on his leash. It will be easy enough to install a true Emperor before the pretender returns from Thrandor.'

'Treason, Veryan, is treason. If you want to hang for it,

then go ahead, but I'll not stand for any such nonsense whilst *Emperor* Surabar is away. He made me Regent in his absence. I intend to see his Empire is waiting for him when he returns.'

'Really, Kempten? *Emperor* Surabar, is it? Come; do tell us. How did he buy you? Did the offer of power as his right-hand man win you round? Was the promise of being Regent enough to win your soul? Or were you always a secret radical, desiring to give power to the common people?'

Kempten looked at Veryan with contempt. As he scanned the faces of the other Lords, he recognised the same blinkered mentality in each of them. There was little point in trying to negotiate with them. They were as open to change as a rich merchant was to opening his purse for a beggar. Talk would get him nowhere. He needed to show them the door swiftly, before they prompted actions everyone would regret.

'Emperor Surabar didn't bribe me, Veryan. Nobody was more surprised than I when he made me Regent. I don't know why he chose me. I do know he's aware of *my* flirting with treason against him, but I'll not stain my Noble birth-name further by breaking the trust he's shown. He has honoured my house. He *is* Emperor. He made *me* Regent. Those are the facts. Now, gentlemen, if you don't have any further business, then I suggest you leave.'

A nod to the guards who had remained in the room was enough. They stepped forward and placed their hands upon their sword hilts. This was more dramatic than Kempten had wanted, but it was effective.

For a moment, Lord Veryan and his companions did not move. They simply stared at Lord Kempten with a mixture of fury, disbelief and disgust in their eyes. Then, after a moment that appeared to hang in the air for ever, Veryan turned and led the others out of the Emperor's study.

'Shand alive!' Kempten breathed as the door closed behind them. 'If Surabar has to cope with that sort of attitude every day, it's no wonder he's not interested in keeping the Mantle. I sure as hell wouldn't.'

'Psst! Ambassador Femke? Are you awake?'

Ennas was lying on the narrow bunk with his back to the door and his solitary blanket drawn around him as he always did when he heard the guards change over. The oncoming guard always opened the little window at the door to check on the prisoner. It was part of the handover procedure.

The last thing he wanted to do was to talk to the guards. He knew he could never convincingly imitate Femke's voice. All he could do was remain still and pretend to be asleep, he decided.

'Ambassador?' the insistent voice asked again, slightly louder this time. 'Ambassador, you'll never guess what happened yesterday.'

Ennas groaned inwardly. Femke would have to gain a verbal rapport with one of the guards, wouldn't she? he thought ruefully, hoping his lack of answer would put the guard off. Gaining interaction with a prison guard was normally impossible because prison authorities invariably prohibited exchanges between guards and prisoners.

However, Femke had seemingly managed to achieve a relationship with this member of the Royal Guard, so it would be difficult to maintain his silence indefinitely without raising the guard's suspicions. Judging by the guard's voice he was young and inexperienced, and he was excited about something, which meant he would not be put off easily.

'Ambassador?' the guard asked again, much louder this time, as if to prove the spy's point. 'Ambassador, you're not going to believe what happened yesterday.'

Ennas knew he could no longer remain silent, so he gave a little moan as if he were stirring. It was enough.

'Hey, Ambassador, it was amazing! Would you believe that thieves managed to penetrate the Palace defences . . .'

Not difficult, thought Ennas smugly.

'. . . and they managed to raid the Royal Treasury. What do you think of that?' The guard paused for a moment for a response, but when he did not get one, he carried on undeterred. 'Not only did they manage to get past the guards and the locks on the outer door, but somehow they knew about the secret inner door as well. The sergeant believes it was an inside job, and both the captains and the NCOs have been grilling everyone with an outside chance of being involved. They even interviewed me! Can you believe it? I've never stolen anything in my life, but they quizzed me for a whole hour. Of course I haven't told a soul – except you, of course. Telling them about our chats would hardly have been relevant to the investigation. Besides it would have landed you with a harsher regime, which wouldn't be fair.'

Ennas grinned silently. Oh you naughty girl, Femke! he thought, his lips twisting up into a smile. Why would you want to raid the Treasury, I wonder? I wish we'd taken time to talk before Danar and Reynik whisked you away. It would be a lot easier if I knew what harebrained schemes you'd cooked up during your confinement.

The big question was whether he should use Femke's relationship with the guard to effect an escape, which Ennas deemed possible but risky, or whether he should stay quiet to conceal Femke's disappearance for as long as possible. It was a close decision, but he elected to remain quiet. There was no knowing what Femke, Danar and Reynik would be up to, but anonymity always helped a spy's work. If everyone knew categorically that Femke was being held in the Royal Dungeon then, as the young guard had done, everyone would assume she was not involved in outside events. It was the perfect alibi, so Ennas decided to maintain the fiction.

'Are you asleep, or aren't you?'

'Mmm,' Ennas breathed in his best approximation of Femke's pitch.

There was silence for a moment and Ennas held his breath whilst he waited to see if the guard had seen through his impersonation.

'Well, if you can't be bothered to answer me, then I won't bother you with any more news,' the young guard said, his voice sounding sulky. 'If you're not well then speak up. The Royal Medics will surely attend you if you're ill. With the Shandese Emperor on his way to Mantor, I doubt the King will want you to die in his cells before you've had the chance of a trial. If you want them, say the word and I'll ring for someone to come down and give you medical treatment.'

Ennas held his tongue. He was desperate to ask when Surabar was expected to arrive, but he had to hope that the guard would tell him of his own volition. Unfortunately, this was not to be. The young guard had obviously had enough. The shutter to the small window slid shut with a decisive thud. Ennas had learned a lot. He could try to make guesses about what the others were up to. What they appeared to be doing did not make any sense, but he was pleased to gain some information about the outside world.

Hurry up and get things sorted out, Ennas prayed. Shand allow the guards remain fooled for long enough. I don't think you have long, Femke.

Danar felt queasy as they rode through the gates of Mantor and up towards the Palace. Some of the churning in his stomach was due to the after-effects of inhaling the noxious gas the previous day. However, Danar was enough of a realist to accept that much of it was due to nerves.

What if the King or someone else in the Palace recognised Femke as the Ambassador, or indeed either of them as those who had raided the Royal Treasury the night before? Had the Thrandorians discovered that the person in the Royal Dungeons was not the Ambassador? Had Shalidar realised what they were up to? If so, what nasty surprises did he have prepared for them? Danar could think of many unpleasant things that could be waiting for them at the Palace.

251

True, they were both in different guises from their previous personas, and Danar had to admit they looked different. He was constantly amazed at how simple little changes to a few basic areas could radically change their appearances. This revelation made him wonder if he would spot some of the spies at work in the Imperial Palace in Shandrim when he got home. He silently resolved to become more alert for such things on his return to Shandar.

Femke looked very different, she had not done much to change her physical appearance. She had applied a dye to her hair, already cut in a short, manly style, together with a gel-like substance to slick it back. In conjunction with the bandaging that flattened her chest to that of a young man's, Femke's semblance had altered significantly. Some different clothes, darkened eyebrows, a pigment applied to her skin to darken her complexion, and Femke was no longer recognisable as the person whom Danar had first met as the beautiful and haughty Lady Alyssa.

What am I doing here? he asked himself silently. I know so little about this woman, yet I'm captivated by her and willing to risk my life to win her approval. He looked across at Femke in her new guise as his young manservant and he shook his head almost imperceptibly. At the moment, Femke appears more like a young man than a beautiful woman, yet still I'm drawn to her. What would Sharyll and the others say to that? How they would laugh! Sharyll would think I'd totally lost my mind, Danar thought morosely. Privately he was beginning to wonder if he had.

Danar had always had a reputation for being particular

about the looks and physical attributes of his female friends. Only the most beautiful were considered, and Danar had cut a wide swathe through the fairer sex of the Shandese Court, breaking many a fair Lady's heart with his 'love them and leave them' attitude, but it had not stopped them from falling for him. Therefore, the fact that a young woman was now toying with his affections instead of swooning at his feet was intensely irritating.

The Emperor was only three or four days away from Mantor. Despite having gone along with Femke's plans, Danar could not shake the feeling that the Emperor would not approve of his spy's method for gathering evidence against Shalidar. Somehow, Danar doubted that raiding the Thrandorian Royal Treasury to create a sting with which to trap the assassin would feature highly in Emperor Surabar's list of proud moments from the Shandese history of international relations. However, he could not help himself. Danar was too deeply involved to back out now. He had allowed himself to become the lure to draw Shalidar out from his cover, and had become entangled in the complex web of deceit Femke was spinning – despite knowing he would be placed in a position of extreme danger.

The thought of having Shalidar planning to kill him sent a chill down Danar's spine, but this was instantly offset by memories of Femke's sympathetic ministrations the previous evening. Having Femke mop his brow with a cool cloth had made the debilitating nausea and the risk of a knife worthwhile. It had given him the chance to look deeply into her eyes and bring every ounce of his charm to bear. Even in his sick state, Danar knew the power he had over women. Happily, Femke's attitude to him had softened considerably during the evening.

Femke chose that moment to look across at him. She gave him a warm smile that caused his heart to leap. Suddenly all feelings of nausea were banished to the back of his mind. The danger from Shalidar, or from being recognised as a participant in the Treasury heist, receded.

'How's your stomach?' Femke asked quietly as they made their way up towards the Palace.

'Much better, thanks, but still a bit sensitive,' Danar replied truthfully. 'When do you think Reynik will arrange the next phase? Will he be all right? What if Shalidar recognises him?'

'He'll be fine. Money talks. Shalidar will probably think he made a mistake in ordering his men to attack Reynik. After all, it's not unreasonable for a person who is plotting murder to take precautions. Reynik could easily have been assessing Shalidar prior to proposing the contract. I expect him to make contact later this afternoon,' Femke replied, automatically looking around to make sure nobody was in earshot before she answered. 'We didn't set a fixed time, but I expect him to allow word of our arrival to spread before he starts the ball rolling. The contract should be placed by this evening. Reynik is aware of the time constraints; he knows we have to resolve this swiftly. The good thing is that Shalidar will be forced to act quickly. Reynik will use the Emperor's arrival as the timescale for the contract. Shalidar is very proficient, but with such a short timescale to work with he won't have time to organise anything elaborate. He'll try for the simple hit and we'll be ready for him. We must nail him first time. I'd like to lose my fugitive status before Surabar arrives.'

'That's understandable. Surabar gives me the impression he doesn't suffer fools gladly. Rightly or not, I doubt the Emperor will be impressed with either of us unless we can demonstrate a breakthrough in our relationships with the Thrandorian King before he arrives.'

'Right! Are you happy with what to say to the King when we get there?'

'Yes, I'm sure,' Danar replied with a grin. 'You worry too much. I know my lines. Don't fret, I won't let you down.'

'I'm sure you don't intend to, but I want to be sure you remember, that's all. I haven't survived all these years as a spy without being meticulous in my preparation for role-play.'

Danar smiled at her phrasing. '"All these years?" You can't be more than twenty years old!' he said with a laugh. 'You make yourself sound like a grandmother lecturing her little grandson on how to be a good boy.'

'With you, that's not far off how I feel sometimes,' Femke replied with an exaggerated huff of mock irritation. 'Come along now, Danar, do as you're told and eat up your greens,' she added, in a convincing old woman's high-pitched, querulous voice. Danar looked around in surprise.

Femke laughed at his expression and raised an eyebrow at him. 'It's not all in how you dress, you know. You have to fit your voice into the role as well. Come on, let's get up the hill and treat the King to your impression of a Shandese

Lord. It should be interesting to see how you cope with trying to fit yourself into the role.'

'Why you cheeky . . . ! If you're not careful, I'll start my stay at the Palace by seeing to it that my servant boy is given a good flogging before he's given any quarters. It would be a fitting punishment for impertinence. In fact I think I'll ask for the rod so that I can administer it myself. Oh, and water rations for the duration of the stay.'

'You wouldn't dare,' Femke said with a confident grin, but as she looked at his face her smile faded, for he looked deadly serious.

'Try me,' Danar said firmly, his face hard and his tone self-righteous. 'Members of the Nobility don't allow commoners to ridicule and undermine their birthrights. Culprits always face appropriate punishments. It would be fitting that I give you a good thrashing in order to help you remember your place. More so as you've misrepresented yourself as one of the Nobility on many occasions. In fact I think the beating should be particularly severe to reflect your complete disregard for the status of the people you repeatedly mock.'

Femke was suddenly less sure of herself as she tried to decide if Danar was messing around, or if he was genuinely considering giving her a flogging.

'You see, I can play the part as well as the next spoilt Lordling,' he said, his face suddenly resuming its normal, mischievous smile.

'Point taken,' Femke said with a rueful grin. 'I accept this is one role you know well. Don't get carried away though. Try to remember there's a point to your role. This is not about having fun. There's a lot of danger in this situation. We need to pin Shalidar to the wall – fast. If we don't, then we'll not only have King Malo breathing down our necks, but Emperor Surabar as well. That is, of course, assuming Shalidar doesn't nail us first.'

'My, aren't we the optimist today?' Danar replied, his voice heavy with sarcasm. 'It's your plan, remember? I'm counting on you to keep me alive, so don't let me down, OK?'

'I'll do my best, your Lordship,' Femke said, tugging at her fringe and bowing her head slightly in a mocking gesture.

'Careful, Femke, or I might reconsider that flogging!'

They both chuckled quietly for a few moments. Then someone rounded a corner a short distance ahead from a side street and turned up the hill to follow the same road towards the Palace. All laughter was instantly banished and the ride up to the Royal Palace was continued in silence.

When they reached the Palace gates Danar announced himself both a Lord of the Shandese Court and Ambassador to the Emperor of Shandar, and requested an audience with the King of Thrandor. A hurried exchange of whispered conversation between the two guards followed, then one went running off at double time to fetch the Captain. An escort was arranged to accompany them to the Palace. This time, however, there was triple the ratio of guards to visitors that there had been when Femke had arrived with her original party. With all the recent excitement, the Royal Guards were taking no chances.

Again the Palace staff offered the visitors a chance to

freshen up before meeting with the King, but unlike Femke's first official visit as Ambassador, Danar declined the offer.

'I was charged by the Emperor to meet King Malo with all possible speed, and that is what I intend to do,' he intoned pompously. 'Please advise his Majesty that I request an audience with him at his earliest convenience to discuss the recent tragic and unfortunate events that have occurred here in Mantor. I place myself at his immediate disposal, and am happy to forego refreshments in order to fulfil my duties.'

Krider had bowed deeply at Danar's little speech and bustled off to inform the King at once of the visitors and their intentions. When he returned, Krider looked embarrassed as he asked if Lord Danar and his servant would mind being subjected to a weapons search before entering the presence of the King.

'Not at all, not at all,' Danar assured him graciously, raising his arms above his head and turning to the nearest Royal Guard to allow him to begin checking him for weapons. 'Search away. We handed our weapons over at the main Palace gates, so we have nothing to hide. My servant will not be coming with me to see the King. If possible, I'd like him taken to my quarters to unpack my things, and to arrange for my bath to be ready for me when I complete my conference with the King. Would that be all right? If you need to search him, then go ahead. It makes no difference to me.'

'No, no!' Krider replied instantly. 'The order was to search any going into the King's presence. If your servant is going to your quarters, then I need not doubt your word, my Lord. Thank you for your cooperation. This is all most unfortunate and terribly embarrassing, but . . . well I'm sure you understand the reasons.'

'Absolutely. Think nothing of it,' Danar purred, oozing with the charm he normally reserved for the ladies. 'After the occurrences of the last month, it is gratifying that the King will see me at all.'

Don't overdo it, Danar, Femke willed him silently. You've got Krider where you want him. Don't lose it by getting carried away.

But to Femke's surprise, Danar's charm won Krider around as effectively as it had so many female members of the Shandese Court. The old fellow could not do enough for Danar. He apologised with every other breath for any conceivably perceived insult taken from the actions of either the Royal Guards or the house staff during the arrival process.

Before she knew it, Femke was being led away through the Palace towards the West Wing, having avoided being searched – much to her relief. It was not that Femke feared the guards finding weapons on her, for she wasn't carrying any. She was worried they would feel the ridges of the bandages around her chest and start to question her about them. If they discovered she was not the young man she appeared to be, then it would not take them long to deduce her real identity.

To Femke's amusement, the Royal staff led her to the room next to the one she had occupied a few weeks before. The door to her old room had several wax seals along the line where the door met the door-frame to prevent anyone entering without alerting the guards that the room had been tampered with. Femke had ways of circumventing wax seals, but she had no intention of using those skills. The key to this whole affair was revealing Shalidar's true identity to the King. If they failed to do this, then it would be all but impossible to prove her innocence.

Once inside Danar's room, Femke took his saddlebags through to the bedroom and proceeded to unpack his clothing. Femke smiled at the things that he had packed, for they were so typical of the Shandese Lord. Beautiful silk shirts with ruffed fronts, fancy collars and ruffed sleeves had clearly been cut to show off his narrow waist and broad chest. Also, there were jackets that would accentuate his shoulders and trews that looked like they should cut him in half. Just looking through them made Femke giggle. She found it hard to believe anyone would travel great distances with no sign of anything practical in their packs. However, these were Lord Danar's packs, and she could imagine Ennas being forced to lend him practical clothes during the journey to avoid being laughed off the road.

When Femke had finished unpacking the clothing into the cupboards she returned the saddlebags to the doorway, where she called for one of the Royal servants to help her. There were two house staff members in the corridor outside the room. The man and woman were poised, waiting for such a call.

'Excuse me, but would it be possible to get Lord Danar's saddlebags cleaned and waxed?' she asked politely. 'If not, then I'll happily do it myself – all I need is the appropriate cleaning materials. I used the last of our supplies yesterday and we didn't have time to stop in the city for more.'

'Don't worry your head about it, lad,' the matronly lady replied kindly. 'Give them to me and I'll have the stable boys clean them up like new. It's good to give them something useful to do, other than mucking out the stables and polishing tack that doesn't need it.'

'Thank you, that's most kind,' Femke said gratefully. 'My master also asked me to prepare a bath for him. Can you show me where I can get hot water? It will take a lot of trips to fill the tub in the bathing room and I'd like to get started.'

The two Royal house staff members smiled at one another with smugly superior grins.

'Oh, you don't need to worry about carrying pails of water around this Palace, lad,' the man said, his tone mirroring his smug grin. 'Hot water can be pumped into the tub through a special system of piping. Here, let me show you.'

Femke already knew about the piped hot water, but it was important to build her character with those who would see her most. Once established as a young male servant who knew nothing and followed orders blindly, then the house staff would see nothing else.

'Pipe system? I've never heard of such a thing!' Femke exclaimed, allowing her eyes to go wide with feigned amazement. 'I confess I wasn't looking forward to filling that mammoth tub. I'd have been back and forth all night!'

The man and woman laughed warmly and the woman patted Femke gently on the arm.

'Don't you worry,' the woman assured her. 'Regis here

will show you how it works and you can amaze your master by leading him to the biggest, hottest bathtub he's seen in many a year.'

Femke chuckled appreciatively, keeping her voice from slipping out of the deeper notes into its normal register.

'That would be great,' she enthused. 'It's always good to keep one step ahead of the old man.'

'I would like to place a contract,' Reynik said quietly, looking around to ensure that nobody was within earshot. 'A *final* contract, if you get my meaning?'

'I'm not sure I do, sir,' the butler replied, looking blankly at Reynik. 'My master has asked me to ensure he's not disturbed this afternoon. He conducts most of his business transactions in the morning. Would you like me to book you an appointment to meet with him? I should be able to fit you into his schedule sometime early next week.'

Reynik gave the butler a withering look. 'Tell your master there's someone at his door who is willing to pay two thousand gold Thrandorian crowns for a *final* contract. I'd heard he was in business to supply the sort of results I require, but if my information is incorrect then I'll go elsewhere.'

'I'll deal with this thank you, Hanri.'

Shalidar appeared out of a side door into the hallway behind the butler and waved the pristinely dressed old fellow aside. Reynik's heart skipped a beat. It was *him*! Shalidar was the assassin who had killed his uncle. There was no doubt. That face had been imprinted on his mind. Anger flashed through him, threatening to take over. A burning desire for revenge swelled inside him, but he fought

262

the inner battle well, keeping his exterior cool. He met the assassin's eyes with a calm veneer as Shalidar surveyed Reynik, looking him up and down as if searching for something.

Reynik's mind raced. Did he know? Had Shalidar recognised him? Was his inner anger transmitting?

'I think you'd better come inside for a chat,' he said finally, standing to one side and gesturing for Reynik to enter. 'However, before you enter I should warn you of something.'

'Yes?' Reynik asked, his voice calm, but his mind apprehensive.

'If I get the slightest inkling you're not telling the truth, I will not hesitate to kill you.'

'I take it my information about your second profession is correct. You do deal in *final* contracts?'

'Come inside,' Shalidar ordered in a tone that brooked no disobedience.

Reynik complied. As the door swung shut behind him, he tasted fear in the back of his throat. There was no place for fear here. He ruthlessly drove the emotion back down into the depths of his heart. Shalidar must not suspect anything was amiss.

'Go through to my drawing room,' Shalidar said, his voice again commanding. 'It's the second door on the left. Hanri, bring us some wine in about two minutes, would you?'

The butler bowed and disappeared off down the long entrance hall with a steady stride. Reynik entered the drawing room as he had been directed and looked around with

263

what he hoped was a casually interested air as he walked straight into the heart of the room. The room held plenty of interest to look at. There were bookcases on every wall, together with delightful pictures of a high quality – all skilfully mounted and framed. Two were superb depictions of dragons, which Reynik quickly discovered was a theme that ran through the room. There was a dragon ornament, exquisitely made in intricate detail, placed tastefully in what looked like a purpose made alcove. A small decorative table in the centre of the room had carved dragons for legs and a dragon motif embroidered on the tablecloth. Also, in pride of place on the mantelpiece, a beautiful silver bowl was displayed. Reynik marvelled at the skill of the silversmith who had made it, for there was a beautifully crafted circle of dragons and firedrakes chasing one another around the outer edge.

There had been no expense spared in this room, Reynik observed, rapidly totting up his estimation of the value of some of the items in his head. If all the other rooms held objects of similar value, the house was worth a fortune.

'So, what is your business with me and why have you approached me in such a fashion?' Shalidar asked bluntly, his eyes narrowed slightly as he watched Reynik's response minutely.

'My master wants a termination service performed. He instructed me to make contact with you to determine if his information about your other career in Shandar was correct. If it is, then he's willing to pay two thousand gold crowns for your services.'

Shalidar looked at Reynik thoughtfully for a moment or two and his eyes narrowed further.

'Assuming that I were in the business you describe, two thousand in gold is a *very* large sum of money. Exactly *who* are we talking about terminating here? If it's Royalty, you can leave the house now. I'm not getting involved in anything which could result in treason charges.'

'No, no, it's nothing like that,' Reynik said smoothly. 'My master has reason to want rid of the new Shandese Ambassador who arrived in Mantor this afternoon. I'm told his name is Lord Danar of the Imperial Court of Shandar. Does the name mean anything to you?'

'I know the name,' Shalidar admitted, relaxing slightly, but still maintaining a high level of alertness. 'May I ask the reason for the termination?'

'My master did not confide that information.'

Shalidar looked deeply into Reynik's eyes for several seconds. Reynik stared back with what he hoped was a suitable degree of calm. As the seconds ticked by, Reynik could feel his cool façade being eroded by Shalidar's gaze. The urge to leave became steadily stronger. Finally, Shalidar spoke again.

'Why were you watching my house the other day? My men have confirmed it was you, so there's no point in denying it. They led me to believe they had given you enough of a beating that I wouldn't be seeing you again. It appears that they were frugal with the truth.'

Reynik smiled slightly, though he was now feeling the fringes of panic touch his gut. 'I was watching the house for signs that there was more to you than your merchant persona. Your men gave no reason for their unfriendly behaviour, so I assumed they were common hoodlums. I'm sorry if they were a little the worse for wear afterwards, but they didn't stop to introduce themselves.'

'There's nothing to apologise for. If the four of them could not best you, then they're not worth the money I've been paying them. They will be looking for alternative employment tomorrow.' Shalidar paused for a moment, looking thoughtful again. 'Very well, I'll accept the contract – on the following terms. The fee is two thousand five hundred gold pieces. One thousand five hundred will be delivered in advance; the other thousand will be due on confirmation that the job is complete. There will be no further negotiation. Your master either accepts, or he goes elsewhere.'

Reynik bowed in response.

'My master anticipated your raising the price, sir. Your terms are acceptable. I will deliver the gold in one hour, but there is one final thing.'

'What is that?'

'The job must be done quickly. It's said the Shandese Emperor will arrive in a few days. My master wants rid of the Ambassador before the Emperor arrives,' Reynik said.

'That won't be a problem.'

Shalidar put forward his hand to shake on the deal. As Reynik clasped the assassin's hand in the accepted fashion of accepting a deal, the killer's sleeve rode up his arm a little, revealing a tight-fitting silver wristband that sported a dragon as its central feature. Apparently, Shalidar had something of a fascination with the mythical creatures.

266

'So when will the job be completed?' he asked, being careful not to allow his eyes to linger on the wristband.

'Before your master's deadline. That's all you need to know. Ah, Hanri – the wine. Thank you. Now, shall we drink a toast?'

'A pleasure,' Reynik answered. 'What shall we drink to?'

Shalidar poured two glasses of deep red wine and handed one to Reynik.

'To a swift and successful conclusion to our business,' Shalidar offered, raising his glass slightly.

Reynik raised his glass in response and took a slow sip. I'll drink to that, he thought silently.

CHAPTER THIRTEEN

'Thank you very much ... No, nothing else, thanks. I'll send my servant boy out if I require anything.'

Danar closed the door with a sigh and leaned against it briefly before turning around to look at the room.

'Is my Lord ready for his bath now?' Femke asked casually from a large sofa. She was sitting with her feet up, drinking a glass of water.

'Make yourself comfortable. Don't mind me,' Danar said sarcastically. 'A bath would be wonderful right now. I don't suppose you'd like to start drawing the water for me? I mean, I wouldn't want to distract you from your other duties or anything.'

'Consider it done, my Lord,' Femke replied, her voice heavy with subservience. 'If my Lord would like to take a look in the bathing room, my Lord will find his heart's desire.'

'I doubt that,' Danar replied with a tired grin. 'Unless you're clever enough to be in two places at once.'

'Very droll, Danar, though actually, if you think about it, I am! I'm here with you, yet I'm also in the King's dungeons,' she replied. 'The bathing room is through that door. I think you'll find the water temperature to your liking.'

'There's no chance of you scrubbing my back, I suppose?' Danar asked wistfully.

'As much chance as there is of Lady Alyssa walking in from the hallway right now,' Femke replied airily. 'Everything you need is in there. Here, take a drink with you. We can talk about your conversation with the King when you've cleaned and changed. I've laid out a change of clothes.'

'Thanks,' Danar said. 'I won't be long.'

'Take your time. There's no rush. I doubt we'll see Shalidar tonight, but I've rigged the windows just in case. When you're ready for bed, I'll rig the door as well. If Shalidar comes, we'll get plenty of warning.'

'*We?* So you're going to stay here tonight?'

'Don't get any ideas, Danar. This is serious.'

'So am I,' he muttered under his breath as he went into the bathroom. 'But you think I'm toying with you.'

A little while later Danar emerged from the bathroom wearing the silk shirt and hose that Femke had placed in the bathing room for him. His eyes were sparkling with renewed energy and his dimpled cheeks were glowing with the aftereffects of the bath. His dark hair was still wet, but was combed back neatly over his head with a wave at the front that accentuated his roguish looks. Femke eyed him up and down with a cool objectiveness.

'Feeling better?' she asked.

'Much, thank you.'

'Good, now come and tell me what the King had to say.'

Danar walked across the room towards Femke, but changed his mind halfway, choosing a chair on the other side of the low rectangular dahl table in the centre of the room. He sank into the chair with a gentle sigh, then reached for the jug of cold water on the table and poured some into a crystal glass.

'The King is not happy—' Danar started, taking a sip of water.

'You don't say,' Femke muttered.

'If you'll let me finish – the King is not happy because he's having second thoughts about whether Ambassador Femke killed Baron Anton and Count Dreban,' Danar said firmly, his eyes sterner than Femke had ever seen them before. In this more masterful guise she could imagine Danar being an effective Lord. After all his impulsive gestures and his boyish romanticism, this came as a genuine surprise.

'Really? Now that is news,' Femke replied.

'Yes . . . and no,' Danar said thoughtfully. 'King Malo is obviously a thinker. He's clearly reviewed the facts and drawn his own conclusions about the two murders, but he was reticent about sharing his theories with me about who did kill Anton and Dreban. He mentioned you looked convincing in your servant's uniform when they caught and imprisoned you and commented that you were nobody's fool. I don't think you're totally off the hook in his mind. He told me his new advisor on matters magical had

270

cautioned him to be careful in negotiations with you, because he considered you to be particularly sharp-witted. Therefore, King Malo could not make sense of why you would kill both Anton and Dreban with weapons which were clearly your own. That isn't to say he's ruled out the possibility altogether.'

'Good logic,' Femke commented.

'Good for you too, when it comes to your trial,' Danar said positively. 'The way he spoke about you initially made me think he was halfway to believing you innocent. However, he may have said it for diplomacy's sake. The King stressed to me that I wasn't to feel unwelcome because of the "unfortunate events" that occurred during your short stay. He suggested I remain here in the West Wing unless I was going to and from pre-arranged meetings with him, to minimise the chances of any repeat embarrassments. I said I would comply with his wishes whilst in the Palace, but I didn't like being cooped up all day every day. The King was gracious. He suggested I take walks in the Palace grounds where the guards could monitor me, or us, if you wished to join me. He said it was for our own safety. He cited the demonstration at the gate the other day as a clear sign that the general populace here in the city are in a volatile mood.'

'Huh!' Femke huffed. 'So we're rats in a trap. What other restrictions did he place on us?'

'We're not to leave the West Wing without an escort and we're not allowed to visit Ambassador Femke,' Danar said, his voice and facial expression showing no humour in the strangeness of that statement.

Femke nodded, a small smile flickering across her face. 'It's for the best. We would be exposed as untrustworthy if we tried.'

'I was thinking the same,' Danar said. 'Our discredit would be a diplomatic disaster on a scale that even Emperor Surabar would have problems fixing. It's fortunate for us that the possibility of a visit to the prison has been removed.'

'OK, so you're effectively confined to quarters. I'll be able to move a bit more freely around the Palace, as I can always "get lost" whilst running errands for you. I never did have a good head for direction. No matter how hard I try, I always seem to end up in places that I'm not meant to be,' Femke said with a grin. 'Overall, the situation has worked out well. It limits the number of avenues for Shalidar to attempt his hit. It will make it far easier to watch for him and to protect you whilst you're confined to such a limited field of movement.'

Femke looked thoughtful for a moment or two and then smiled across at Danar. 'Things are beginning to swing in our favour. Let's hope we can give the final proof to the King that I'm innocent of the murders before the Emperor arrives, shall we?'

'Sounds good to me.'

'OK, I'll rig the door now – unless you have anything else you require from outside?'

'Food would be good at some point,' he replied, rubbing his stomach slightly to emphasise his requirement. 'How long will it take to disable whatever it is you're about to set up?'

'A few seconds,' Femke assured him. 'If someone knocks at the door it won't be a problem. The alarm will be rigged to alert us when someone is entering who hasn't knocked. The problem then is that Shalidar will come armed to the teeth and we haven't got a single regular weapon between us. I'll try to rectify that tonight if I can. If it proves impossible, I'll get us something to improvise with.'

Femke got to her feet and started to move towards the door. Danar rose as well, intercepting her before she had gone more than a few paces. Before Femke realised what was happening Danar had put an arm around her waist and pulled her body close up against his. The kiss started as a one-sided affair, but after a couple of seconds Femke found herself kissing him back with a passion she had not realised she possessed. They finally parted and Danar breathed a deep sigh of satisfaction.

'Thank you,' he breathed, his mouth close to her ear as he continued to hold her tightly.

'For what?' Femke replied. 'For the kiss, the bath, or for trying to keep you alive?'

'For everything,' he whispered. 'For being the most amazing, most daring, most devastatingly attractive, surprising, remarkable woman I've ever met – and yes, for the kiss too. I've waited a long time for it.'

'I hardly merit "devastatingly attractive" at the moment, or if I do, then I'm a bit worried about you! Didn't it feel strange, kissing me when I look like this?' Femke asked, pulling back slightly from him and grinning as she indicated her boyish looks.

'Well, if I'm honest, then yes – a little,' Danar admitted

273

with a lopsided smile. 'But it didn't make any difference, because I know what's hiding under that disguise. I have a reputation for dallying with attractive women, Femke, but looking at you now, I see the beauty that *is* you. You can be as attractive as any woman if you choose to, but you're far more than just a pretty girl, Femke – you are special, unlike anyone I've ever met before.'

'I can't help but wonder how many other pretty girls have heard similar sincere-sounding speeches,' she noted sceptically. 'Your reputation is coloured, Lord Danar. Don't forget I'm no Lady of Court. I'm a commoner. And I'm not some air-headed fool who sees you as my chance of marrying into a title. I'm not proud of my heritage, but I am realistic about my future. Please, try to be realistic about yours. This is not a good idea.'

'I don't care if it's a good idea or not. I didn't travel the length and breadth of Shandar and then all the way here to Mantor on a whim. I felt that if I didn't do it, I would have missed out on getting to know you. Getting to know you has been at the forefront of my mind since I first met you. Surprisingly, it's been the single most consuming drive I've ever known. Common sense never came into it.'

Femke gently pulled herself from Danar's arms and stepped back, not sure whether to be flattered, or frightened by his intensity. She knew that moving this relationship forward now was a bad idea. It would distract her from her goal, which could prove disastrous.

For the briefest moment, Femke wished she could forget her responsibilities and run away with him back to Shandar. Common sense told her that any relationship she had with

274

Danar was doomed to fail. Lord Tremarle would never stand for his only son to marry a commoner. He would see it as dilution of the bloodline. The best Femke could hope for would be a romantic interlude. That was not practicable now, whilst she was a fugitive. This situation had to be resolved before she could return to her life as a spy. And then what? Giving up her profession was not an option. She enjoyed the life too much to relinquish it in exchange for a dead-end romance. The whole situation was very confusing.

'All right, Danar, let's imagine for a moment I accepted your sincerity and I was interested in exploring the possibility of a relationship with you. I still couldn't do it right now,' Femke stated, trying desperately to keep the angst from her voice.

'Why not?' Danar asked, his eyes giving that sad, puppy-dog look which silently accuses its owner of being cruel and heartless for not returning its selflessly offered devotion.

'Shalidar is now working on a way to kill you. Regardless of feelings, I must keep you alive. You're distracting enough without making things more complicated. No. You've waited this long, you'll have to wait a little longer. Please, Danar, don't touch me again until this is over – I beg you.'

Danar looked at her with his sad eyes and nodded. Feelings of guilt and frustration swamped Femke until she almost gave in to them. The temptation to throw aside common sense was overwhelming, but she steeled her heart. Having regained some fragile self-control, Femke turned away and set about rigging the door. Being busy would help, if only for a short while. Much of the next few days would be time spent waiting, and Femke sensed the temptation would worsen. It would taunt her at every opportunity, playing with her mind until it distracted her as much as if she had gone ahead and flung herself at the handsome young Lord.

'Oh, Shand!' she groaned quietly. 'Why me?'

As soon as the guard changeover was complete Ennas knew he was in trouble. It was the young guard again and he sounded determined Femke should not ignore him this time. Ennas remained silent while the young guard rattled the door and called in through the window at him.

'You're ill, aren't you, Ambassador? That must be it,' he said eventually. 'Speak to me, Ambassador. If you're ill, the medics should see you. I'm sure the King doesn't want you to die in there. And even if he does, I'm not going to let that happen.'

Don't come in. Please, don't come in! Ennas prayed silently, fervently hoping the young guard would just leave him alone.

'Right, I'm coming in,' the guard announced. 'Don't try anything foolish. I don't want to have to hurt you.'

Oh you poor young fool! Ennas thought sadly. Please, no. Do your job. Guard the door. Don't try to be a hero.

The metallic ring of a sword being drawn from its scabbard was followed by the rattling sound of a key turning in the lock. Ennas tensed. He knew what he had to do. He had to escape. Surprise would be crucial, but the guard was alert as he entered the cell, which would make it difficult to achieve.

Unfortunately for the guard, the occupant of the bed he was approaching was neither ill, nor a female ambassador. The prisoner was an experienced spy in prime physical condition and not afraid to kill.

'Ambassador?' the guard said hesitantly as he approached the bed. He held his sword ready, but not aggressively forward.

Ennas let the guard get as close as he dared. He reasoned that the guard's eyes would not be adjusted to the dark and would not realise his mistake until it was too late. Ennas was correct. The guard moved within range and Ennas's hand shot out with the speed of a striking snake, grabbing the wrist of the guard's sword arm.

'You're not—'

The guard did not get to finish his exclamation, for the straightened fingers of Ennas's other hand struck him hard in the throat. With an almost casual shift of position, Ennas flipped the guard head over heels to land half on the bunk. Without pause he cut the young man's throat with his own sword before the guard had a chance to realise what was happening. Ennas instantly wished he could have just knocked the man unconscious, but he knew how difficult that was to do with any certainty. Some men snuffed out like a light with a decent knock to the head, whilst others just refused to go under no matter how many times you hit them. It was a terrible waste of life, but he could not afford to risk a fight.

Ennas looked sadly down into the young man's

panic-filled eyes and a deep feeling of guilt overtook him. He watched as the terror gradually gave way to resignation and then finally to peace.

'I'm so sorry,' he said softly, as life left the guard's eyes. 'So, so sorry.' Had it really been necessary to kill him? Should he have at least tried to knock the young guard out and leave him locked in the cell? With hindsight, Ennas could not help feeling that killing the young guard would stain his soul for ever.

Aside from the moral issues, cutting the guard's throat had made an awful mess and left Ennas with a tough choice. The guard was slim. He could get into the guard's uniform, he decided, but it would be a tight squeeze. Also, it was covered in blood, which reduced its effectiveness as a disguise. If he used the uniform, then he could not walk out of the Palace without inventing a good cover story. A visible wound of his own would explain the blood, but that would make leaving the Palace more difficult to explain. The other guards would want to direct him to the Palace infirmary. He knew he had to solve the dilemma quickly. Ennas had not planned to escape. His intention had been to stay in the cell undetected for as long as possible. By escaping he would set the Royal Guards looking for Femke again. Worse, she would now be accused of a third murder.

Murder. The word reverberated in his mind. I am a murderer. It was not a thought Ennas had ever dreamed would enter his thinking. It was distracting and he could not afford to lose focus. He had to put it aside and concentrate. There would be time for remorse later.

What are my alternatives? he thought, bringing his attention back to the immediate problem. There should be time to think things through. The guards had changed over a few minutes before, so it was likely to be hours before the next person came down to the dungeon. There was always a small chance of a visit from one of the guard captains. There had been a few such visits before and Ennas did not want to take chances. If he were caught before he left the dungeon area, the Thrandorians would show him no mercy. The Royal Guards were no fools. If he were caught here, they would not take long to work out what had happened. On the other hand, if he could get out of the dungeon and into the Palace before being caught, the picture would be more confused.

I could make a run for it dressed like this – not a good option. I could try to steal more clothes from somewhere within the Palace and then get out – possible. I could try to hide somewhere in the Palace for a while and wait for more alternatives to become viable – dangerous. The sooner I get out on the streets, the sooner I can disappear into obscurity.

Ennas did not like it, but he stripped the guard of his uniform and squeezed into it. The hose didn't fit too badly, but the tunic was far too small across the shoulders. It felt tight and stretched. Fortunately the belts had plenty of adjustment in them, which allowed him to make them look reasonable. The boots were much too tight, but Ennas gritted his teeth and forced his feet into them. Running would be difficult, but with luck he should not have to do more than walk out of the Palace.

As soon as he was fully dressed in the uniform, with the sword safely sheathed in the scabbard at his side, Ennas moved the young guard onto the narrow bed and covered him with the blanket so that he appeared to be sleeping. Then he exited the cell and locked the door behind him. As an afterthought, he posted the keys through the little window into the cell. With any luck, whoever came down here next would think it was the guard who was missing rather than the prisoner. Time would then be wasted looking for the wrong person. If he did suspect something was wrong, not having the keys to check inside the cell would build in a further short delay.

It occurred to Ennas that he had no idea what time of day or night it was. It made no difference. He had to escape now, while he had the chance.

Creeping up to the door at the top of the stairs, Ennas peeped out into the corridor. All was silent. Judging by the lack of movement and the number of torches alight, it was late night, he thought, pleased with his luck so far. Not all the torches were lit, making the corridor a dim, flickering place of constantly moving shadows. Exactly the sort of place for a spy to feel at home, he thought wryly. Stealthy as a stalking cat, he padded out into the corridor and began to look for a way out of the Palace.

Ennas realised that wandering aimlessly was incredibly risky, but when he had been led to the Royal Dungeon disguised as a priest of Ishell, he had entered the Palace through the main gates and had been brought via a tortuous route. He could not remember the way, nor would he try to backtrack it, as he had no intention of trying to leave the

Palace through the main gate. There had to be a less obvious way out: a servants' entrance, or a suitable point to scale the outer wall. The first trick was to get out of the main building.

At the end of the corridor Ennas turned right, as there were fewer torches lit that way. All was deserted and Ennas had no problems moving stealthily along the passageway, despite the boots crushing every portion of his feet. There were no obvious exits. When he reached the far end of the passageway, the T-junction offered him the choice of well-lit passages in both directions.

'Damn!' he muttered. 'Oh well, I suppose it was asking a bit much to be able to walk unseen to the nearest exit and disappear. Here goes nothing.'

Ennas turned left this time in an effort to try to work away from the area of the Palace around the Royal Dungeon. The further he got from it, the less likely it was that people would associate him with it if he were to be rumbled as an intruder. He knew the guards would be wary of anything strange in the aftermath of the Treasury raid. He just hoped he was not inadvertently walking towards the Treasury.

This corridor quickly proved to be one of the major arteries of movement within the Palace. Before Ennas had taken twenty paces he could see several passageways ahead on either side. Adrenalin pumped around his body as he saw two people in Royal house staff livery cross the corridor some distance ahead of him. His relief when they failed to look in his direction was overwhelming, but short-lived.

'Hey, you! What are you doing here at this time of night?'

Ennas jumped involuntarily and his heart started pounding loudly in his chest. He stopped walking the moment the challenge rang out from behind him and silently cursed that automatic reaction. By stopping, Ennas had left no room for ignoring the call and continuing casually on his way. The choice was now to run, or turn and face the questioner. Neither choice offered an easy way out.

He elected to turn and face his questioner. There were two guards moving down the corridor towards him and both of them were armed. Ennas cursed silently. He would have considered disabling one, but he did not want to fight two. The uniform he was wearing was too restrictive. He would have to bluff, he decided.

'I'm on my way to the infirmary to get fixed up,' Ennas said, deliberately mumbling his words as if he were having problems forming sounds properly.

'The infirmary? That's nowhere near here and you're heading in the wrong direction. I don't recognise you. Who are you?'

'Jared. Private Jared of the Royal Guard. Who're you?' Ennas replied, deliberately focusing and unfocusing his eyes on the approaching soldiers, whilst swaying slightly on his feet.

'Hey, Pakka, that's blood on his tunic. Tarmin's teeth, there's loads of it and he doesn't look stable. Do you think he's hurt badly?'

The guards stopped a good distance from Ennas and looked at him with open suspicion.

'That's not our problem. I don't recognise him,' Pakka replied, his voice flat and uncaring. 'He's walking where he shouldn't be on his own. The Captain's orders are clear. We're to restrain anyone who's acting strangely. Let's take him to the Captain and let him decide if the medics are needed.'

'Why don't we swing past delta post? It's on the way. We can send one of them to fetch a medic while we take Jared to the Captain. It looks like he's lost a lot of blood already. It wouldn't look good if he died without us having made an effort to help him.'

'That makes sense. If we must then.'

Ennas's tactic had failed. The guards stepped towards him. He needed to act fast if he was to avoid going back in a cell. Ennas did not want to hurt anyone else, but he could not see another way. The element of surprise would give him a momentary advantage. It was a small edge, but it would have to be enough. Despite his restrictive clothing, he decided his best remaining chance was to tackle the two guards head on. Stumbling along the corridor towards them, Ennas continued his injured soldier act. The tight boots made it easy to simulate.

The guards were wary as Ennas approached them, but not wary enough. They allowed him to get far too close before ordering him to stop. When Pakka finally did tell Ennas to stop, it was within a couple of paces of striking distance.

Ennas stumbled the last few steps forward with his expression blank and his eyes completely out of focus, as if he were about to collapse at any second. Then, at the last instant, he sprang into action. In one slick movement, Ennas drove a fearsome punch into one man's solar plexus, and spun a high kick that caught the other man across the face. Both men went down. The first was wheezing and unable to speak as he crumpled, and the second went spinning to the floor in spectacular fashion. The spy could have followed either strike up with a killing blow, but he did not relish adding more lives to his conscience this evening. Instead, he turned and ran.

Now the race was on. The men behind him would raise pursuit within a couple of minutes. Ennas had to get out of the Palace quickly. He ran around a corner that took him out of the direct line of sight of the two soldiers, and then started trying every door along the corridor to find an open one. Several were locked, but eventually Ennas found one that opened and he slipped inside, closing the door softly behind him.

The room he entered was dark and for a moment Ennas could see nothing. As his eyes gradually began to adjust to the light, he picked out the lines of curtains on the far wall. There was not enough light to see what sort of room he was in, but he could see the line of the curtains and for the moment that was enough. Behind the curtains would be windows, and a window was as good as a door.

Outside the door Ennas could hear multiple pairs of booted feet running down the corridor. They were approaching fast, spurring Ennas into setting out across the inky darkness of the room without allowing his eyes to adjust properly. The pale light from the cracks in the imperfectly drawn curtains was not enough for Ennas to see a clear path to the window. He had hardly moved before he barked his shins on something hard. The collision did not make much noise and he bit his tongue against crying out from the pain of the impact.

Ennas heard the booted feet reach the door. He held his breath, preparing to leap towards the window. He resolved that the instant they burst into the room, he would throw his body through the curtains. With luck he would smash through the glass cleanly. He did not want to think about hitting the frame. However, the stomping feet did not pause. They passed by and the sound of them faded as quickly as it had built.

When he felt around, Ennas realised the object he had walked into was a low-level table. He had entered a drawing room. He needed to be careful not to bump into chairs or smaller tables supporting ornamental pots. Palace drawing rooms were always filled with such things. The immediate danger of pursuit had passed, but Ennas was determined not to draw attention to his presence by inadvertently knocking something over. Silence was his friend. If maintaining that friendship cost time, it was a small price to pay.

Feeling his way, he moved painstakingly over to the curtains. There were no further collisions. On drawing the curtains, he sighted his goal. The outer Palace wall was about fifty yards away.

'Jackpot!' he breathed.

He sprung the latches on either side of the window and gently eased it open, praying hard that the hinges had been well oiled. The window opened noiselessly. Within a few seconds, he had climbed up onto the windowsill, out through the window, and eased himself down to the ground. Once there, he turned and made sure the curtains were fully closed. It was not easy from outside, but he managed to arrange them to his satisfaction. When he had finished, he pushed the window to as well. He could not secure the window because the latches were on the inside, but there did not appear to be any wind to speak of, so he felt it unlikely that the window would move much. He had concealed his exit point as best he could.

The wall did not look far, but the moon was bright, washing everything in silvery light. The ground between his position and the wall was open with no shadow to hide his movement. Ennas scanned the sky for clouds. Even a fleeting reduction of the moonlight would help. There were none. The weather would not help him tonight. He scouted around the edge of the building briefly to see if there were any less exposed routes across. None were obvious. There was no choice but to run for it. Taking a couple of deep breaths, Ennas gathered his courage and with gritted teeth he launched himself away from the side of the building in a full-out sprint for the wall.

To his surprise, the spy had not covered ten paces before a shout went up somewhere to his right ordering him to stop. He ignored it, focusing instead on the wall ahead. A surge of adrenalin gave him strength to accelerate further. There were more shouts and the barking of dogs, but Ennas did not hear anything. All that mattered was reaching and scaling the wall.

The fizz of a crossbow bolt zipping past the spy reinforced

the urgency of the situation, but broke his concentration for an instant. He stumbled, pitching forward onto the grassy lawn. The landing was not pretty. Ennas skidded and rolled some distance before he could leap back to his feet to cover the final short distance to the high perimeter wall.

For a moment he could not find a first handhold. His panting breath became more laboured as he felt frantically across the surface of the wall for a place to begin climbing. Finding suitable purchase he pulled hard, hoisting his body the first few feet off the ground. His feet scrambled for a moment against the wall before finding a tiny ridge on which to rest. He reached up again, his fingers searching for another hold. It was taking too long. The guards were closing on him. Suddenly, there was a sickening thud and pain exploded in his back. Ennas fell and the ground rushed up the short distance to meet his body with a terrific smash. Blood roared in his ears and he vomited before he could think about regaining his feet. With a determined effort, Ennas tried desperately to stand, but all strength had drained from his limbs and he had a sudden involuntary urge to cough as his mouth filled with blood.

The realisation dawned on him. He had been hit square in the back with a crossbow bolt. He was dying. The dull thudding of approaching booted feet, the clamour of voices and the barking of dogs wavered in his ears as a dreamy lassitude overtook him.

Ennas relaxed. It was over. There was nothing he could do now.

If ever justice guided an arrow . . . he thought as his mind slipped gently into the long sleep of death. I wish I hadn't killed the guard.

As the first Royal Guard reached him, Ennas gave a cough and died.

CHAPTER FOURTEEN

'Hello, Izzie, what are you doing here?' Lord Kempten asked, surprised to find his wife walking into the Emperor's office unannounced.

Lady Kempten looked at him with an expression of mild disapproval.

'Do you know what time it is, dear?' she replied, looking around the bleakly spartan office, notably unimpressed by her husband's working environment.

'Time? No. Should I?'

'It's the early hours of the morning again. You're working too hard, dear. Come to bed.'

'I've got a hard act to follow, Izzie. Surabar is a devilishly clever man, you know. I think the Noblemen here would do better to learn from him, rather than plot against him. Here, look at this.'

Lady Kempten smiled indulgently at him and walked around to his side. 'Two minutes, dear, then you're coming to bed if I have to drag you there.'

Kempten smiled at her and nodded his acceptance. There were mountains of parchment arranged in neat piles all over the desk. Most were scribed in the same neat hand. Lady Kempten put an arm around her husband and looked over his shoulder at the parchment immediately in front of him.

'Look, the man thinks of everything. He's been in office a few weeks and he's already assessed more elements of life in Shandrim and in wider Shandar than I'd ever considered. This is a report on the state of the military and the local militia – a subject clearly close to his heart, but look at this. Here's a report on education and another on the state of the treasury and detail of the tax collection process. Here's one on the situation of the roads, irrigation, sanitation, the list goes on and on. Somehow he's collated preliminary reports on a whole host of subjects – collated, assessed and drafted his initial thoughts. He has plans on how to improve every area of life in Shandar.'

'Well? That's good, isn't it?'

'Good? It's amazing! Shandar hasn't had an Emperor with a genuine interest in the people for longer than I care to imagine. The problem is the Nobility will never stand for it. They'll overthrow him regardless. To them, all that matters is to have one of their own wearing the Mantle. The worst thing is that until recently, I was the same,' he admitted. 'I would have given my life to stop him reaching power. Now I'd give it to keep him there.'

Lady Kempten smiled to hear him speak so passionately.

'It sounds like your priorities have changed for the better then,' she said, gently stroking his back. 'It takes a brave man to admit he's wrong about something, particularly when he's passionate about his initial belief.'

'Yes, but shifting *my* priorities isn't enough, Izzie. Somehow I've got to change the thinking of the other Noblemen. Surabar could prove to be the best Emperor in Shandar's history, but if they're not stopped, the old-school Lords will dispose of him before he has a chance to demonstrate his ability.'

'You need to talk to them. Convene the Court, dear, and tell them what you've told me. Your passion will win converts. Rally those around you and Surabar will have the support he needs. You're a good man, and you have the respect of many. You'll do it if you put your mind to it. I know you will. But you won't convince anyone if you look like death warmed up. Now, come to bed.'

The knock at the door startled Femke from sleep. It was light outside, but it felt early. The air held an early morning stillness that spoke of a sleepy world reluctant to rise.

Slipping from the sofa, Femke brushed the worst of the wrinkles from her tunic and ran her fingers through her short hair. Thank goodness for men's hairstyles, she thought, throwing herself a quick grin as she surveyed her appearance in the wall mirror.

The knock sounded again at the door – a little louder and more insistent this time. Femke walked to the door and unhooked the string she had tied across the top corner from the little bell she had rigged. Composing her face into a mask of quiet servitude, Femke partially opened the door to find two Royal Guards outside, one with his fist poised to knock again.

'Good morning, sirs, what can I do for you?' Femke asked politely, nodding to the nearest soldier.

'Is his Lordship awake yet?' the nearest guard asked, keeping his voice low.

'Not yet, sir. It's still early. Lord Danar had a busy day yesterday.'

'I'm sure he did, but the King requests his presence immediately,' the guard said earnestly. 'Please ask his Lordship to come at once.'

'Of course, sir. Would you mind waiting out here until Lord Danar is dressed? I'm sure he won't be long,' Femke said smoothly. She did not want to risk the guards noticing the security measures she had installed around the suite. If they thought the Shandese Lord did not trust Palace security, it would do little to endear Danar to them.

'Not at all, but please hurry. The King does not like to be kept waiting.'

Femke nodded and closed the door. Her curiosity itched. What was important enough to get the King up at this time in the morning, and require Danar's presence? Had they discovered Shalidar's profession on their own? Had there been another murder? What if Shalidar had now set Danar up as well? She quickly ruled that out. The pattern would be too obvious; Shalidar possessed more subtlety. One Ambassador accused of a serious crime was unlikely, but two would simply be unbelievable. Besides, the King was no fool. He would see through such an obvious ploy and Shalidar would not make things that easy.

This was something new. Femke hoped it was good. Until now, bad news had dogged her path in Mantor. Surely it was time for her luck to change.

Striding across the living area, Femke threw open the door to Danar's bedroom and marched across to the bed. Grabbing Danar by the shoulder, she gave him a solid shake and then moved on to throw open the curtains with a flourish.

'Come on, sleepy head. Get up! The King wants to talk with you and he doesn't want to wait all day,' she said loudly, grinning at the groans Danar made as he shielded his eyes against the bright morning sunlight.

'What does he want?' he asked through a long yawn. 'Can't it wait until later?'

'No it can't wait until later. When the King asks you to jump, you don't ask "Why?" you ask "How high?" Now get out of bed and make yourself presentable. You have two minutes before I tell the Royal Guards outside that they can come and drag you there in whatever state you emerge in."

'You wouldn't!' Danar laughed, making no move to climb out of bed.

'Try me,' Femke said haughtily and swept out of the bedroom. 'Time's running, my Lord. Don't dally,' she called over her shoulder, for both his benefit and also for the guards, who were sure to be listening at the door.

Lord Danar did not believe Femke would make good her threat, but there was enough doubt in his mind to make him dress swiftly. He would not let the Royal Guards see him doing less than his utmost to meet the King's wishes.

He was here in the guise of an Ambassador, so Ambassador he would play.

Danar chose a silk shirt from the wardrobe and pulled it over his head in one unbroken movement. For the briefest of moments he luxuriated in the feel of the silk against his skin before moving on to find underwear and clean trews, and then to slip his boots on. He made a quick dash to the bathing room where he drew water with the ingenious pumping mechanism over the bath. He then splashed it over his face and hair until it was totally soaked. A quick rub with a towel, followed by a few sweeps with a hairbrush and he glanced at his reflection in the mirror.

'Dashing as ever, you devil,' he muttered with a grin, and then strolled through to the living area where Femke was waiting for him impatiently. I definitely look more civilised and prepared to meet a King than you do, he thought, but then he realised this was how it should be. He was the Lord and Ambassador. Femke was the servant boy. The contrast was fitting.

'Ready?' Femke asked.

'Yes, I'm set. Any idea what this summons is all about?' Danar asked quizzically.

'None at all. Stay on your toes this morning, my Lord. There are many things that could harm us here – and not just physically,' Femke answered in a normal voice. Then she lowered her volume so that nobody outside the room could hear. 'The King is an astute man, as I'm sure you've noticed. See what he wants, but be careful. Think before you speak and above all, keep your eyes open for

Shalidar. I'll be watching your back, but you must stay alert at all times.'

'Very well, let's go.'

Femke opened the door. In true servant style she gestured for Lord Danar to precede her. The two Royal Guards immediately came to attention and bowed.

'Please follow us, my Lord,' one of them asked politely. He turned on his heel to lead the way down the corridor. The other guard fell into step beside him.

Danar did as he was bid, maintaining a gap of a few paces to gain some visibility ahead. Femke followed along at the rear, her head constantly moving as if she were looking in awe at the pictures and décor along the corridors, but actually scanning for the slightest hint of danger.

The Palace was not so much one large building as a complex of buildings all linked by stone built corridors that gave the impression of one huge construction. It had gradually expanded over the centuries. Different kings had added new sections, nominally to increase the magnificence of the place, but in reality to leave their personal mark. Thrandor had historically been a peaceful country, so without the national drive to expand and conquer that many nations felt, Kings were left with little to do but try to keep taxes low enough to content the populace and to build something that future generations would associate with their reign.

Femke had walked through some of the Palace and the grounds during the short period of her visit before Baron Anton was murdered, but the two Royal Guards quickly led them into an area she had never explored. The unfamiliarity made her doubly nervous. She kept her movements as calm and untroubled as she could, though her eyes were darting around like flies, unable to settle.

Eventually, the two Royal Guards reached a door and knocked firmly on it twice.

'Enter,' a voice ordered.

The moment she entered the room, Femke's nervousness climbed to a new height. It was a morgue; and that meant one thing – another death.

The King was there, his face grave and lined with a mixture of sadness and anger. A cloth covered a body lying on a long table behind him. The room held a strange odour, but Femke did not want to think about the mixture of things that caused it.

The Royal Guards saluted the King. Danar and Femke bowed.

'Thank you,' King Malo acknowledged, waving the guards to leave and beckoning for Lord Danar to come closer. 'I'm sorry to call for you so early, but a series of events occurred last night that concern you closely. I felt I had to put comfort aside and try to get to the bottom of this matter as swiftly as I could.'

'What's happened, your Majesty?' Danar asked curiously. 'Has there been another murder? If so, how does this involve me? Am I implicated in some way?'

'Yes, there has been another murder, but the motive for this one was far clearer than the previous ones. At the moment you are not directly implicated. However, given that you arrived yesterday, the timing of this is rather unfortunate. Ambassador Femke escaped last night.'

'She did?' Danar gasped. His shocked voice sounded convincing to Femke. She was impressed, as she had not thought Danar would dissemble well. 'Is Femke now accused of yet another murder? Who was the victim this time?'

'There's no proof that Ambassador Femke killed anyone this time,' the King answered carefully. 'In fact, I find it unlikely. The person killed was a young prison guard who was on duty outside her cell last night, but Femke did not necessarily kill him. The Ambassador had outside help with her escape. We believe this man aided her,' he said, pulling back the sheet that was covering the body on the table. 'Do you know him?'

'Alas, yes I do,' Danar replied sadly, causing the King's eyes to narrow and Femke to look at him sharply. 'His name is Ennas and he worked in the Palace in Shandar. I've seen him there, though I'm not entirely sure what his role in the Palace was.'

Femke was stunned on two counts. Seeing the body of a man who had given his life for her freedom was shock enough, but hearing Danar confess to knowing him froze her to the core. What was he thinking of? Had the sight of her fellow spy, Ennas, his face drained of life and drawn with the pain of his demise, completely unhinged Danar's common sense?

'Did you know he was here in Mantor?' the King asked quietly, continuing to watch Danar's face closely.

'No, I didn't. I don't remember him being a member of Ambassador Femke's party. If I remember correctly, she took two servants and two guards with her. I'm sure

Ennas wasn't among them,' Danar answered thoughtfully.

Femke was impressed. When Danar had first admitted to knowing Ennas, she thought he had been about to blurt out everything, but instead he was lying with true skill. He was blending the perfect amount of truth with his fabrications to make the whole believable. She had underestimated him, she realised, her mind still in shock from the sight of Ennas on the table.

'And what of you, young man? Do you know this Ennas?' the King asked Femke gently.

'I'm not sure, your Majesty. His face does look familiar. So many people work at the Imperial Palace that it's hard to be sure. I haven't had a chance to meet all of them yet. I've not worked there long.'

The King's eyes narrowed slightly again as he watched Femke give her answer. Her heart leaped for an instant as she thought the King had seen through her disguise. A flicker that bordered on recognition dawned in his eyes, then the moment of clarity passed and he nodded his acceptance of her answer.

'I understand. This Palace is much the same. It takes years to get to know all the house staff, never mind all those who come and go. I still don't know everyone by name and I make a positive effort to do so. Don't fret over it. Ambassador Femke will not be able to run for ever. Sooner or later she'll face the charges levelled against her. I'll discuss it further with your Emperor when he arrives. In the meantime, I suggest you both stay in your rooms as much as possible in case anything else untoward happens.'

'Of course, your Majesty – whatever you desire. If possible I'd like to discuss things with you further before his Imperial Majesty arrives, but I'll understand if events prevent it,' Danar said graciously.

'Thank you, Lord Danar. There is much going on here that I don't understand. I'll call for you again later. Thank you for coming so promptly. Please, do go now. I need to think on this turn of events, for there's much that does not fit together as it should. I'm trying to comprehend what Ambassador Femke hoped to achieve by her actions, but nothing is adding up. A stroll in the gardens should bring some clarity to my thoughts.'

Danar and Femke bowed and left the room. The two guards were waiting outside and immediately stiffened to attention as the door opened.

'Do you need us to lead you back to your quarters?' one of the guards asked Danar.

'No, there's no need, thank you,' Danar answered with a friendly smile. 'I think I noted the way accurately, and I can always ask someone if I become unsure. The King spoke of going for a stroll in the grounds. Given the troubled events of the last few weeks, might I suggest it would be more appropriate if you accompanied him on his walk? The Palace has proved a dangerous place recently. I don't like to think of his Majesty walking the grounds alone at the moment. Enough damage has been done to relationships between our two countries. Let's not run the risk of a total catastrophe, shall we?'

The two guards looked at one another and then back at Lord Danar. They nodded and bowed.

'We'll do as you suggest, my Lord,' said the spokesman of the two. 'Thank you.'

Danar nodded back and set off down the corridor with Femke once again following a few paces behind. He did not turn to see if she were there, or speak to her at all. He simply walked silently along the reverse of their route from the visitors' suite.

Femke understood his silence, for she was deep in thought as well. Part of her mind was mourning Ennas, whilst another was trying to imagine a sequence of events that would lead to his killing a guard and trying to escape. The image of Ennas on the table in the morgue filled her thoughts. Unfortunately, this lack of focus on her surroundings could not have come at a worse time.

It was the slightest flicker of a movement, but it was enough to break through Femke's reverie and register in her mind as danger. Without thinking she launched forward into a dive and shunted Danar to the left. A blade flashed through the air, passing just over Femke and directly through the path Danar had been walking. Someone had leaned around a corner ahead and hurled the blade with deadly accuracy. Femke landed heavily, her mind leaping to the conclusion that the 'someone' had to be Shalidar. The spy was on her feet again in a flash.

'Get back to the suite,' she ordered Danar, who had crashed into the wall and fallen to the floor. 'Don't open the door without Royal Guards present. I'll get there as quickly as I can.'

With that she sprinted off down the corridor and around the corner in pursuit of the assassin. What she was going to do when she caught up with him, Femke was not sure. Shalidar was bound to be carrying more weapons and she was unarmed, but Femke desperately wanted to catch him. It was now a matter of principle. He had taken the bait. The rest was up to her.

As she turned the corner, Femke caught a glimpse of a running figure disappearing into another side corridor a little way down on the right. Powering forward as fast as she could, Femke raced after the fleeing figure. As she turned the corner into the side corridor, he was already out of sight again, having made another turn into the small maze of passages that made up this part of the Palace.

Damn, he's fast! she thought, zipping ahead to the next intersection where she paused to listen. The thick carpet muffled the sound of the assassin's footfalls, but it did not silence them completely. Femke could hear enough to tell that he had turned right again. He's circling around, she realised with a surge of panic. If Shalidar gets to Danar before he's moved, the crafty fox will get a second chance.

The thought that Shalidar would get to Danar before she caught up with him injected even more pace into her legs and she all but flew down the corridor in pursuit. When she reached the next intersection, the assassin had turned right again and once more she caught a fleeting glimpse of him disappearing around a curve in the corridor ahead.

As Femke passed the place where she had left Danar a minute or so before, she was pleased to find he was no longer there. With luck the assassin would not follow the same path through the Palace as Danar, she thought. Femke had not noticed the assassin's knife anywhere along the corridor, so either Shalidar or Danar must have picked it up.

Please let it be Danar, she prayed as she pelted along the corridor, her jaw set with fierce determination.

Suddenly, Femke reached a four-way junction and she skidded to a halt. To her astonishment there was no sign of the assassin anywhere, yet she could see a significant distance in all directions. Nobody could run that fast.

Trying hard to control her panting breath, Femke strained to listen for signs of the assassin's footfalls. At first, she thought the blood pounding in her ears was masking his escape, but as she calmed her breathing still further, Femke realised there was no sound to listen for. Shalidar had disappeared.

'Damn you, Shalidar!' she shouted in frustration, punching one fist into her other hand in extreme annoyance. 'Damn you to hell!'

The assassin must have somehow slipped through one of the many doors along the corridors, but whether she had passed his hiding place, or whether it was further on from the junction, Femke had no way of knowing. It struck her that although she had not caught the assassin, neither had she come across Lord Danar. This was good, in that Shalidar was also unlikely to have seen him; but confusing, as she would have expected Danar to return to his room this way. Danar had disappeared as well.

What in Shand's name is going on? she wondered. What should she do next? Searching the rooms nearby would be dangerous, as Shalidar would lay traps for her. The logical thing to do now was to return to Danar's suite.

If she was honest, Femke had not expected to catch Shalidar. Allowing him a chance at a hit without Danar being surrounded by an army of guards had been the riskiest part of the plan. She was cautiously pleased that it appeared Danar had not been hurt. Shalidar would not get another easy chance. The next phase of the plan was to go to the King and arrange for the Shandese Ambassador to be surrounded by the most intense security cordon possible. With the tight timescale left for Shalidar to complete his contract, Femke felt sure he would try something risky rather than lose such a large amount of gold. That was when they would nail him. By displaying Shalidar's true colours to the King, Femke felt sure she could clear her name and restore some trust to the peace negotiations she had begun. Failing this, she had a fall-back option that was equally as convincing.

There was a niggle in Femke's mind about the attempted hit that bothered her. The fleeting glimpses she had gained of her enemy teased her that she had missed something vital. Femke could not define it and this was not the time to be distracted. The spy knew she was vulnerable standing exposed at the junction of the corridors. The need to move away from the place forced her to make a decision.

Torn briefly between retracing her steps, and going back to the suite, Femke decided on the latter to see if Danar had made his way there by a different route. If Danar was there, then they could swing straight into the next phase of the plan. If not, then Femke would have to search for him and hope Shalidar did not get to him again.

*

Danar was not sure if he should be insulted at Femke treating him like some little boy needing protection. True, she had saved his life by pushing him out of the way of the knife, but then to send him to his room while she ran unarmed after the assassin did little for his ego.

Femke had disappeared around the corner by the time Danar got to his feet. In a gesture of irritation he brushed at his tunic and hose. Before Danar had finished the gesture a hand suddenly grabbed him across the mouth from behind and he felt the cold line of a blade resting on his throat.

'Come this way, Lord Danar. I want to have a little chat before I kill you,' the sibilant whisper of Shalidar ordered in his right ear.

Danar was stunned, but left with little choice. If he did not cooperate he could be dead in seconds. If he went with the assassin, there was a small chance Shalidar could make a mistake. How had the assassin gone from being in front of him a few seconds before to behind him? Was he a magician that he could transport himself from place to place? If not, then who was Femke chasing?

Shalidar manoeuvred Danar back up the corridor a short way and through a door into a storage room. The assassin closed the door silently behind them and then remained still, as if waiting for something. Before long, Danar heard the sound of someone running past at high speed. There was a pause of several seconds and then another person raced past the door and on down the corridor.

'Now then,' Shalidar whispered gleefully. 'We shouldn't be disturbed for a while. If you try to call out, you'll not finish the attempt. This knife is *very* sharp and will slice through your windpipe in an instant if you don't do exactly as I tell you. Do you understand?'

Danar moved his head in the subtlest of nods.

'Good,' Shalidar approved, removing the hand from Danar's mouth. The blade at the young Lord's throat did not waver. 'Now that we understand each other, you can start by filling in a few gaps. What has Femke been cooking up for me?'

'Femke? How would I know? I've only just arrived—'

'Don't play innocent with me, Danar,' interrupted Shalidar with an angry snarl in his voice. 'I know you sprang her from prison. I know that was her outside in the corridor a moment ago. What did she hope to gain by having me kill you?'

'Kill me? What do you mean? Femke likes me. I'm sure she does. Why would she want me killed?' Danar spluttered, determined to string Shalidar along.

'If you expect me to believe you're not in on this, *Ambassador* Danar,' he said, sneering the title as if it were the lowest form of filth, 'then you must take me for Shandar's greatest fool. I'm no fool, Danar. Your acting is not gaining you anything. Femke either thinks she's good enough to catch me, or she wants you out of the way for some reason. The sad thing for you is that either way, you get to die. You see, Femke will never be good enough to catch me, and if she wants you dead, then she has the good grace to pay well.'

'I . . . I . . .'

'I can see I'm going to get little of use out of you, am I? Aside, that is, from one and a half thousand gold sovereigns I've already been paid. Rest assured I'll put your bounty money to good use, Danar. Your head isn't worth such a price. You're pathetic. Surely you realise that Femke is a spy through and through. I've watched you, Danar. I've seen the look in your eyes. You must know she doesn't share your love and never will. Femke has used you from the moment you arrived in Mantor. She has used you like she uses everyone – as a means to an end, a pawn in her grand game of cat and mouse. Well, Danar, you and Femke alike are the mice here, and I'm the cat. And I'm afraid the predator must kill its prey.'

'Wait! No! I'll tell you everything,' Danar offered frantically. 'You don't have to kill me, Shalidar.'

'Ah, then you know my name at least. Good! Now, what is the little minx up to this time?'

Danar took a deep breath and tried desperately to think of a plausible story. The blade pressing uncomfortably against his throat tightened a fraction. Any thoughts he had of lying left him then and he lost his cool altogether. In a panicked babble, Danar blurted out the basic plan. It was irrelevant now, he thought. The primary plan had not worked. The idea had hinged on Femke preventing Shalidar from getting to Danar on his first attempt. The assassin had outwitted them.

Shalidar listened silently until Danar had finished outlining how they had planned to get the King to order such heavy security around Danar over the next couple of days that it would be impossible for Shalidar to get close to him without exposing his identity. The guards would then be ordered to stop Shalidar and search him for weapons at every opportunity. When the Emperor arrived, Femke was going to use her influence with him to have Shalidar exposed as an assassin. Femke would then be reinstated to her position as Ambassador, and her reputation restored.

'Having Femke as a respectable Ambassador would fit nicely into your plans as well,' Shalidar noted casually. 'Having a relationship with an Ambassador would bring less disgrace to the family name, wouldn't it? Whereas I'm sure the more traditional members of your family would not look on your dallying with a spy so favourably. It would all have been so neat. Unfortunately, however, I've never seen the value in lovers, or in love itself for that matter. I'm not the romantic type.'

Shalidar paused and Danar squeezed his eyes shut, expecting to feel the knife slice across his throat at any second. The assassin had what he wanted. Danar could not think of any way out of this situation. Death seemed inevitable.

He could have volunteered Femke's back-up plan, but telling the assassin about this would achieve little. Exposing the rest would buy him a few seconds, but Shalidar already appeared content with the information he'd been given. Danar knew more. Lots more. But holding back that knowledge gave him a small source of inner triumph.

He tried not to think about what it would feel like for the blade to cut though his windpipe, but his mind was filled with pictures of a slow, gory death. Then, to his complete astonishment, Shalidar gave him a glimmer of hope.

'Femke has been a complete nuisance ever since I first met her. Tell her if she wishes to live to see another year, she must give herself up to the King and take responsibility for the murders of Baron Anton and Count Dreban. If she does this, I'll not interfere with the decision of the Royal Court, nor bother her if she escapes jail again. However, she must further promise not to meddle in any of my affairs again. If I discover she has done so, then I'll hunt her to the ends of the earth to see her dead. Is that clear?'

'Absolutely, Shalidar, I'll take your message to her immediately.'

'Yes, you will, because if you don't go straight away, then you'll die before you have another chance,' the assassin rasped, and then he jabbed something sharp into the back of Danar's leg. Danar flinched and felt the knife blade at his throat cut the skin slightly. A trickle of blood ran slowly down his neck and Danar wondered what on earth the assassin was doing.

Shalidar pushed Danar towards the door, but did not open it straight away. A pulsing sensation began in Danar's leg where he had been jabbed and suddenly a sick feeling rose from within the pit of his stomach.

'If you want to live, then you'd better get to Femke quickly. Tell her that I've blessed you with a wound filled with nepthis. It's a rare poison, but I know Femke has used it before. If you're lucky she'll give you the antidote. Don't waste time, Danar. Nepthis does not take long to do its work. Good luck and don't forget my message.'

With that, Shalidar opened the door, removed the knife from Danar's throat, and shoved him hard in the middle of the back, propelling him out into the corridor. The door slammed shut behind him. The snick of a key turning in a lock sounded before he could regain his balance.

Whirling in outraged fury, the young Lord turned back to the door and banged on it hard with a clenched fist. It was a futile gesture for he was still unarmed, but Danar felt better for his small act of defiance.

The young Lord had no knowledge of the action of poisons, so he made no effort to curb his boiling anger as set off towards the guest suite at a run. All he knew was the faster he reached Femke, the faster she would be able to give him the antidote. His logic was flawed, for by staying angry and running rather than maintaining his cool and walking gently, Danar began pumping the deadly toxin rapidly around his body.

CHAPTER FIFTEEN

King Malo strolled through the Palace grounds, his head filled with theories. Anger gripped him whenever he thought of the murder of his dear friend, Anton, but his mind was consumed now with solving the recent riddles. Never had Malo known such a time of intrigue in the Palace.

As a boy, Malo had loved solving puzzles. His tutors had marvelled at his powers of reasoning and his dedication to following a problem through. It was a skill that had been most useful during his reign, but the current maze of conundrums appeared impossible to solve.

Thrandor had enjoyed forty years or more of peace with its neighbours. King Malo had faced many diplomatic issues, but none had degenerated to the point of taking up arms until the invasion last year by the Terachite nomads from the desert lands south of the border. Since then the world had gone mad, Malo reflected sadly. Bloodshed had abounded, magicians had appeared to spring from nowhere to duel in front of his city gates and now, after years of predictable Court life in the Royal Palace, suddenly came a deluge of murder, theft and deception.

Why? he asked himself silently. Why now and why here? What did Ambassador Femke have to gain by killing Anton and Dreban? Did she kill them? What was the link between the two men and the Ambassador?

Malo had not known Anton and Dreban to have any dealings together. Anton had appeared to dislike the Count intensely, blocking Dreban's moves to gain power within the Royal Court. Dreban had enjoyed an unsavoury reputation. Malo was aware of the Count's manipulative nature, though he had never seen evidence of illegal or treasonous activities. If the Count had been plotting for power, his secret remained intact.

As far as the King knew, Ambassador Femke and Baron Anton had met only once, when Femke had brought the gifts from Emperor Surabar into the Royal Court. Count Dreban had not been present at the time. To the King's knowledge, Femke and Dreban had never met before he had been murdered, though it was possible that they had seen one another during the open Court session Femke had attended.

Now the Ambassador had escaped the Palace Dungeon, a feat King Malo had thought impossible. Had this Ennas fellow, whom Lord Danar had identified as being from the Shandese Court, had a hand in the robbery of the Royal Treasury as well as in Femke's escape? When had he arrived in Mantor? Why had the robbers taken so little? They could easily have carried away more. There were a myriad of questions Malo would love answers to before the Shandese Emperor arrived, but unless inspiration sparked, or Femke was found, the King knew he was unlikely to discover the truth.

Malo regretted not having visited Femke whilst she was in custody. He had squandered the opportunity to question the Ambassador in depth about the murders, thinking he should wait until the trial, to avoid biasing the result. Now he was faced with an unholy mess: the Emperor of Shandar would be here in a couple of days; Malo still had no idea what had motivated the killings; Ambassador Femke was loose in the city again; the guards had killed a Shandese man in the Palace grounds because he had not stopped running when ordered; and to top it all, Malo now had disgruntled Thrandorian Merchants complaining that his order to cease trading with the Shandese Empire was killing their businesses. Thrandor was beginning to return to normal after the two recent battles. Malo did not want to provoke further conflict – particularly not with such a powerful neighbour. Life had never been simple, but Malo was beginning to wonder if he were getting too old to deal with these sorts of situations.

Will the arrival of the Shandese Emperor bring clarification, or more confusion? he wondered dolefully.

The new Ambassador, Lord Danar, was an amiable enough young fellow, but Malo had sensed he had not told the entire truth this morning. The young man had spoken smoothly, admitting to knowing the dead intruder, which was a confession Malo had not expected. But for all his calm veneer and honest-looking face, the Ambassador had been

312

hiding something. The King was also sure the Shandese Ambassador's servant boy had known more than he was admitting. If pushed, the young lad could be a good source of information, Malo mused. The trick would be to separate him from the Ambassador for long enough to question him more closely. That might not be easy, but it was worth consideration.

Yes, he decided. The servant boy could be the key to unravelling this whole mystery. If I get the guards to intercept him the next time he's sent out on an errand, I'll have them bring him to me. Without the shield of his master's presence the boy might reveal more.

The King smiled sadly. He would not harm the lad, but he would use intimidation if it became necessary. A servant boy faced with direct questions from a King would find it hard not to give answers. Malo was not a naturally devious man, but strange situations demanded radical solutions.

Femke reached the West Wing guest rooms. She called to Danar, but there was no answer. She was not surprised. Her first impulse was to retrace her steps in the hope of intercepting him, but on reflection she decided this would not be wise. Danar could be returning to the suite by a number of different routes. No. Femke had returned to the apartment to meet him, and here she would stay.

Instinct took Femke's eyes to the alarms she had set at the windows and she realised instantly that at least one had been tampered with. Femke was immediately on her guard. There was a chance whoever had disturbed her alarm mechanism was still here.

The hair on the back of the spy's neck rose as she entered the apartment. She acted casually, but her senses were straining to locate the intruder. All was silent. There were not many places a person could conceal himself effectively. Her mind raced. If I'd broken in here, where would I hide? she asked herself.

The bedroom, she decided. Anyone entering their sleeping room would naturally be at their least wary. She would most likely find any intruder there.

Rather than reveal information by her movements, Femke decided to leap straight in and brave the bedroom first. As she had already announced her presence by calling out for Danar when she had first entered the living room, there was nothing to be gained by trying to be stealthy. Instead, arming herself with a handy, metal-based oil lamp, Femke pushed the door fully open on the way in, to ensure there was nobody standing behind it. The door swung freely open until it met the wall. There was nobody there.

Femke crouched down and checked underneath the large central bed. That was clear as well. It was obvious nobody was hiding behind the curtains and the wardrobe doors were fully shut – difficult to achieve from the inside – but Femke approached the large upright wooden wardrobe with caution nevertheless.

Grabbing the handles, Femke flung the wardrobe doors open, simultaneously jumping backwards. Aside from the clothes, the wardrobe was empty. The room was clear. Femke sighed with relief and walked back into the living area.

As she re-entered the room and turned to check the

bathing room, Femke sensed a movement behind her. There was no hesitation. With no warning, Femke spun on her left heel, her right foot lifting up into a vicious kick. The foot was stopped from striking home by the intruder's lightning fast wrist block, but before she could focus on the man's face she followed up her attack by throwing her body into a back flip, cracking the man under the chin with her rising left foot and sending him staggering backwards.

'Ow! Enough!' came a familiar voice.

As she flipped, Femke cast the oil lamp aside and sprang off her hands to land nimbly on her feet. Her hands snapped up automatically into a defensive posture. A sheepish-looking Reynik faced her with one hand clutching at his chin and the other raised in a signal to stop.

'Reynik!' Femke hissed angrily. 'What do you think you're doing here? You're supposed to be watching Shalidar.'

'I was trying to. I tailed him from his house, but Shalidar's one slippery customer. He had one of his own men watching him. I'm glad you warned me of the possibility, or I would have been caught. He led me a merry dance around the upper city, before coming to the Palace. This damned place is like a maze. I thought I knew it quite well after all my exploring over the last few weeks, but I lost him. I thought it best to come here and warn you.'

'You're a bit late,' Femke muttered, the anger not quite dissipated from her voice. 'He made his move not ten minutes ago.'

'Danar?' Reynik asked, his voice immediately anxious.

'I don't know,' Femke sighed, shaking her head. 'I managed to shove him out of the path of Shalidar's knife. Then I told Danar to come here whilst I went after Shalidar. I never caught up with him, and Danar has disappeared. I don't know what's happened, but I fear the worst.'

'Oh, Shand!' Reynik exclaimed, a note of horror in his tone.

'What? What is it, Reynik?'

'Before I lost him, Shalidar met with someone here in the Palace. I don't know who it was, because I couldn't see the person he was talking to. I'm sorry, Femke. I'm a soldier, not a spy. Shalidar was giving him instructions. I can't be a hundred per cent positive, but my guess is that Shalidar isn't working alone in the Palace.'

A sick feeling spread through Femke's stomach. A lot of things clicked into place like the final pieces of a jigsaw. The picture it made was not a pretty one. What if Shalidar's associate here in the Palace was not simply another of his minions? What if that associate was another assassin? A whole lot of things could then be easily explained. When Femke had chased the person who had thrown the knife at Danar, something had gnawed at her mind about the chase. Because she had assumed that Shalidar was the knife thrower, it had been impossible to resolve the feeling. Now it made perfect sense. The knife thrower had not been Shalidar. Which meant that . . .

'Shand's teeth!' Femke spat, turning and running to the door.

'What?' Reynik asked, automatically following her across the room. 'What's wrong?'

'The knife thrower earlier wasn't Shalidar. Danar is in more trouble than I imagined.'

Femke wrenched the door open and ran out into the corridor where she skidded to a halt. Reynik followed and was momentarily confused by the expression on her face. It was flickering between pleasure, horror, fear and uncertainty. He followed her gaze down the corridor to see Lord Danar, staggering in a drunken fashion along the passageway towards them.

Femke appeared rooted to the spot, but Reynik was quick to help the young Nobleman, who collapsed into his arms with a groan of pain. Reynik staggered as Danar lost control of his limbs and went completely limp, leaving the young soldier to bear his full weight.

'Quick! Help me get him into the room. He must be injured. Grab his other arm and we'll carry him together. Ready?' Reynik ordered Femke. His firm tone and specific directions were exactly what Femke needed to spur her back into action. They hoisted Danar up between them, carried him into the living area and laid him on the sofa.

'Where are the house staff when you need them?' Femke muttered angrily, as she knelt down next to the young Lord and began tending him.

'We're lucky they're *not* here,' Reynik objected. 'My presence would be difficult to explain. Let's keep them out of it, shall we? We don't want to invite more trouble.'

'Get me a cloth, would you? I need to clean this blood away to see what we're up against,' Femke replied, ignoring him.

There was a lot of blood around Danar's neck, but as

317

soon as Femke wiped the surface blood aside, she could see that the cut to his throat was superficial. There had to be something more, Femke decided.

'Danar? Can you hear me? It's me, Femke. You're safe now. You made it back to the guest suite. What happened? What's wrong?'

Femke rattled out the questions, but she managed to keep her voice panic-free. Danar did respond slightly. His eyes, which were still wide open, focused on her briefly and he smiled as he recognised her.

'Femke. Thank Shand,' he slurred, his voice weak and indistinct. 'Shalidar ... poison ... nepthis ... need antidote ...'

'Nepthis!' Femke exclaimed in horror. 'How long ago? How much?'

'Don't know,' Danar mumbled, his eyes making a long blink. 'Ran as fast as I could ...'

'Blast it, Danar! Don't you know anything?' Femke cried, her voice anguished. 'Running forces the body to pump blood around faster, so the poison spreads more quickly. Reynik, we have to get the antidote quickly. Nepthis is a deadly poison. Danar doesn't have long.'

'Where are we going to get an antidote for nepthis?' Reynik asked with desperation in his voice. 'I can hardly go to the infirmary and ask for it. Besides, I've never heard of it before. Is the Palace infirmary likely to hold the antidote? I could try to steal it if they do, but I'm no thief. I'd be caught for sure.'

'I've got antidote,' Femke said defiantly. 'It's in my little hand case.'

'Well, don't just sit there. Where's the case and I'll get it?'

'It's with the rest of the things that could be tied to Ambassador Femke – the things I left at the tavern.'

Reynik looked at Femke with horror in his eyes.

'But that's in the lower city. I'll never get there and back in time.'

'It's his one chance, Reynik. It's either that, or we sit here and watch him die.'

Femke's face looked haunted by an inner torment that Reynik could not begin to imagine. The guilt within her eyes touched Reynik's heart. He nodded, gritting his teeth in determination.

'I'll get there and back with all possible speed,' he promised.

'Reynik.'

'Yes?'

'Be careful. The guards shot Ennas in the grounds last night. He's dead,' Femke told him, her voice flat as she fought to keep her emotions under control.

Reynik did not reply, but Femke knew the news had hit him hard. Everything was going wrong and there seemed little they could do. Reynik looked down at Lord Danar, taking in his shallow breathing and his pale face. He was young and his body was strong, but Reynik could see that the nepthis was already well established in his system. Reynik was not familiar with the poison, but he did not have to be. Femke's face had told him all he needed to know. He knew there was little hope. He did not want to leave Femke to face the inevitable alone, but he had no choice.

He pulled Femke into a quick, tight hug. 'Be strong,' he said simply.

'Be quick,' she replied gratefully.

Reynik ran to the door, looked briefly around outside and then disappeared at a run. Danar groaned in pain. His face was drenched in sweat and so pale he almost looked green.

'Easy, Danar,' she crooned, gently stroking his brow with her fingers. 'It's going to be OK. Here, have a sip of water. It will help.'

'I'm going to die, aren't I?' Danar asked, his voice barely more than a whisper.

'No, you're not going to die. Reynik has gone for the antidote. You'll be fine,' she responded, pouring a glass of water from the jug on the table. Her words were brave, but her voice lacked conviction. Danar recognised it instantly.

'Good,' he said, his lips twisting into an ironic smile. 'Because I'd hate to have come all this way simply to die before I'd finished winning you over.'

Femke lifted Danar's head forward and held the glass of water to his lips so that he could drink. Tears welled in her eyes, despite her efforts to hold them back.

'That's impossible,' she choked, her voice thick with emotion. 'You're Lord Danar – fiendishly handsome and irresistible to women. You won me over a while ago, Danar. I've simply been too stubborn and preoccupied with nailing Shalidar to admit it.'

As she said the words, Femke realised that although she had spoken them to make him feel better, they were true. Danar had won her heart. Romance had never had a place in her life; yet here was a man who had drawn her under his spell. Danar had shown a level of commitment to winning her that she had never known, nor expected from anyone. He was a man whom she now realised she could have come to love, and he was dying before her eyes. Her hard life had never been so cruel.

'You're just saying that, but I thank you for it,' Danar replied, his face lifting with a pained smile.

'No, Danar, I'm not just saying it. I mean it,' Femke sobbed, finally losing control of her tears as they streamed down her cheeks in rivers. Placing the glass of water back on the table, Femke bent over him and kissed him with gentle passion. The kiss lasted some time. When their lips finally parted, Femke laid her head lightly on his chest, unable to look at his face any more.

'Fiendishly handsome and irresistible, eh? I like the sound of that, but I think you missed out charming, witty, stylish . . .' he joked, his voice wheezing out the words.

Femke could not reply. Her throat felt swollen and her stomach felt sick. Tears would not stop running from her eyes and she simply held her cheek against his chest and listened, hoping desperately that he could hold on long enough for the antidote.

'Femke, listen,' Danar said suddenly, his voice a little stronger and his tone changing from jovial to serious. 'Shalidar gave me a message for you and it's not one you're going to like.'

'What did he say?' Femke eventually croaked, not moving position at all.

'He said to tell you to go to the King. He wants you to

take responsibility for the deaths of Anton and Dreban. If you comply and don't meddle in his affairs any more, he promises not to interfere with the decision of the Royal Court.'

'Anything else?' Femke asked softly.

'He said he would hunt you to the ends of the earth and kill you if you didn't do as he asked.'

'Oh, that's all right then.'

'Femke!' Danar protested. 'He's serious. He'll kill you and I—'

'Shhh! Hush, Danar. Be calm. Be still. I know he's serious. I didn't mean to agitate you. Sarcasm has become a bad habit of mine recently. We'll deal with Shalidar once you've recovered. Now concentrate on calmness. Calmness will stave off the effects of the poison. You have to hold on until Reynik returns.'

'I didn't tell him, Femke.'

'Didn't tell him what, love?' she asked gently.

'About the plan – the whole plan. He doesn't realise . . .'

'Shh! That's wonderful. Forget the plan for now. Concentrate on calmness. Please do as I say. I don't want to lose you.'

Femke felt Danar slowly relax his muscles into the sofa again. His breathing slowed to a shallow, regular rhythm. Femke's tears gradually dried as she concentrated on the rise and fall of his chest and she found herself praying to any deity that was listening for Reynik to get the antidote and return swiftly. Religion had never paid any part in Femke's life as she had always considered it a crutch for the weak, but at this moment she was so desperate that she was willing to try anything in the hope of a miracle.

Time trudged forwards with the dreadful lethargy of a death march. Minutes silently dragged their way from one to the next as if reluctant to pass into history. Femke's mind wandered in the stillness. The warmth of Danar's chest against her face took her to happier places – the peaceful quiet of a simple home in the countryside and no worries of spying, dangerous missions, or assassins.

After a while, she tried to picture where Reynik might be. Would he have run down through the streets to the tavern? she wondered. Or would he have tried to find a horse nearby that he could use? Would his contacts amongst the Thrandorian Royal Guards supply him with a horse? No. Why should they? Reynik would not waste time with such things. He's young and fit. His practical, military training will lead him to make with all possible speed on foot.

The thoughts gradually shifted to different questions again. What if he couldn't find the hand case? It wasn't very big. Would he bring the case, or would he take it apart to get at the antidote. There were a number of vials in the case. What if he gets the wrong one?

Femke's mental torment continued for some time. Her one solace was that Danar's breathing remained settled and quiet throughout. Not wanting to move for fear of disturbing his peaceful state, Femke decided that he must have slipped into sleep, as he was so quiet. Suddenly, his breathing started to speed up again as a new wave of panic gripped him.

'Femke?' he called, his voice full of fear.

'It's OK, Danar. I'm still here. What is it? What's wrong?' she soothed.

'I can't see anything. I'm blind. It's all gone dark,' his voice rose in panic.

Tears leaped back into Femke's eyes. This was it – the beginning of the end. If the poison had spread sufficiently to rob Danar of his sight, there was little time left. Reynik had to arrive soon, or the antidote would not be able to act quickly enough to save Danar.

'Don't worry. Reynik won't be long now. It will all be fine. Relax. Try to stay calm.'

Femke sat up, taking her head off Danar's chest. Though it caused her extreme anguish to look at him, she began stroking his face and hair with her hands to let him feel that she was still there. He looked so bewildered now, like a lost little boy in a strange world.

'I love you,' he said plaintively. 'Even if I can't see you, I still love you.'

'Shh. I'm still here. I love you too.'

Femke's voice cracked as she said the words. As she spoke, Danar's body began to spasm and shake. There was nothing she could do but stroke him soothingly and wait for the end. Thankfully, she did not have to wait much longer. One moment Danar was shaking violently, the next he was still and lifeless. He was gone.

Silently weeping, Femke closed Danar's eyelids and continued to gently stroke his hair for a while. When Reynik returned a little while later, he found her still kneeling on the floor at Danar's side with her head on his tear-soaked chest. Reynik was not prone to deep emotional reactions, but when he saw them, he found he had to fight to hold back tears. The scene was one that Reynik would never forget. He felt helpless. The best he could do was to place a consoling hand upon Femke's shoulder and squeeze gently.

Femke placed her hand on his and squeezed back.

'This is my fault,' she said quietly. 'I should never have let Danar be the target. My arrogance allowed me to believe I was good enough to keep him alive despite his lack of training.'

'Laying blame and feeling guilty will help no one now, Femke. Shalidar is one of the best assassins around. He must be to have worked within the Imperial Palace the way he has. There are never guarantees when you mess with killers like him. You did your best for Danar and I'm sure he didn't blame you for what happened. He was given the choice. He didn't have to stand in the line of fire. He knew what he was doing.'

'Yes, but he was doing it to impress me. He didn't need to do it. He wasn't trained as a spy or a killer. He was a stupid, damned romantic.'

'A romantic, yes, but stupid? No, I don't think Danar was stupid. He was brave and tenacious, but not a fool. He was a good man, Femke. Don't colour your memories of him with such thoughts. It isn't right.'

After a few moments Femke lifted her head and got to her feet. To Reynik's surprise, though her face was tear-stained and ravaged by grief, there were no fresh tears brewing. Instead, there was a fire deep within her eyes that he would have defied any man to see and not feel fear.

'Shalidar has killed for the last time,' she said simply.

Reynik nodded. There was little point in arguing, or trying to talk her out of anything. All he could hope was to try to prevent her from doing anything rash.

'What are you thinking? Are we going to continue with the original plan?' he asked. 'There's no reason not to, you know.'

'Actually, we are going to need to change our thinking,' Femke replied. 'The plan will need to be adjusted, but the amendments will be minor. The basic principles can remain the same.'

'What's changed?'

'Not what, but who,' Femke said, her voice grim. 'Shalidar's not our killer.'

'What! But Danar—'

'Was killed by Shalidar, yes,' Femke interrupted. 'However, Shalidar did not kill Anton or Dreban.'

'But everything pointed at him! If it wasn't Shalidar, then who was it?'

Femke told him and Reynik's eyes went wide with shock.

'You're sure?' he asked incredulously. 'The Emperor is due here any time in the next couple of days. If you're wrong, or the plan doesn't work, there'll be no way out for you.'

'As sure as I can be. There's only one way to find out . . .'

'And that relies both on King Malo being willing to cooperate and the killer falling into the trap. There are still a lot of variables and a lot of things could go wrong, Femke. How are we going to cover both of them? I assume we're still going after Shalidar?'

'Oh, yes! Nothing will please me more than to nail him

to the Courtroom wall. Let someone try to stop me . . .'

'Let's run through the plan again,' Reynik suggested. 'I don't mean any disrespect to Danar, but we need to go over this carefully before his death becomes public knowledge. The King may wish to talk with him again at any time. We need to be prepared.'

'I know,' Femke sighed sadly. 'From the top then . . .'

King Malo returned to his study from his walk in the Palace grounds and immediately called for Krider. When the old man arrived, Malo asked him to bring Lord Danar's servant boy to see him at the first opportunity.

'Try to bring him without Lord Danar's knowledge if you can. I'm sure the Shandese Ambassador will not be impressed to find I've questioned his young servant alone without advising him, but that's my problem. I think the boy may hold the key to these murders. I'll need some uninterrupted time with him to see if my hunch is correct.'

'Very well, your Majesty, I'll see to it,' Krider replied. 'Will there be anything else, your Majesty?'

'No thank you, Krider. I trust your discretion in this matter. Please pass word around the house staff that if anyone has seen anything unusual over the last few weeks, I want to hear of it. The murders of Anton and Dreban, together with the other unusual events, must be linked to some common goal. The Emperor of Shandar is due to arrive imminently. I must piece this together, or Thrandor's future relationship with Shandar could be irreparably harmed.'

'I understand, your Majesty. Leave it to me.'

The old man bowed stiffly before withdrawing. Malo smiled fondly as the door closed behind the head of the Royal house staff. Krider had been serving in the Palace since long before Malo had ascended to the throne. Between them, Krider and Veldan, the Chief Butler, had ensured the smooth running of the Palace for decades. Malo reflected that the two old men were likely to be feeling the strain of the last few weeks almost as much as he was, but to their credit, there was no sign of stress in their appearance. They were as steady and dependable as ever.

Malo did not want to think what the Palace would be like if they retired, but he suspected they never would. The two men had always been competitive about the amount of service they and their families had given the Royal Family. Malo suspected neither of them would bow out before the other, so they were likely to continue to work until they could no longer stand.

Efficient though Krider was, Malo was surprised when there was a knock on the door only twenty minutes later and the young Shandese servant boy was ushered inside. To Malo's further surprise, the lad did not look nervous in the slightest at being left alone in the presence of the King. Either the young man had spent a lot of time in the company of Royalty, or there was more to him than met the eye.

King Malo studied the young man's face for a moment before speaking. There was something unusual about him. Unfortunately, as with so many things recently, a fog clouded the King's perception so that he failed to distinguish what it was.

'Welcome, young man,' he started, putting as much warmth into his voice as he could. 'Please take a seat. I'm sorry to bring you here on your own like this, but I need to ask you some important questions.'

'I understand, your Majesty,' Femke replied, bowing reverentially and then moving over to sit in one of the comfortable seats at the side of the room. 'There have been a lot of dark deeds done in your Palace over the last few weeks and I'm sure you want to know who did them and why.'

'Exactly! I couldn't have put it more succinctly myself. You're a perceptive young fellow. Forgive me, but Krider neglected to announce you and I don't know your name.'

Femke looked at the King and smiled. 'Actually, your Majesty, you know my name better than you think. It is I who should apologise to you, not the other way around.'

Malo's eyes narrowed as he studied the young man's face suspiciously. It took a moment, but then it was as if scales fell from the King's eyes and he gasped as he realised the true identity of the servant.

'Ambassador Femke! But that's impossible!'

CHAPTER SIXTEEN

Lord Kempten faced the packed Imperial Court, took a deep breath and began to speak.

'Lords and Ladies of Shandrim, as Regent I feel it's my duty to make a report to you on the initial activities of our new Emperor and other matters which gravely effect the future of the Empire. This report will shock and dismay some of you today, but what I have discovered cannot remain hidden . . .'

Several of the older Lords began to smile smugly, and none more so than Veryan. Kempten had bowed to pressure. A public condemnation of the new Emperor in the Imperial Court was precisely what was needed to spark the revolution Veryan felt was inevitable. With the Lords united against Surabar, the pretender would be forced to lay down the Mantle. Control of Shandar would then return to the Noble Houses and normality would be restored.

And not before time, Veryan mused. Surabar should never have had the chance to snatch the Mantle in the first place. If it hadn't been for the presence of the Legions, the other Lords would have shown more backbone and driven the General out of the Palace on the day Vallaine was exposed. It's taken Kempten long enough to realise where his loyalties lie.

Two minutes later, Veryan's smile was gone. Soldiers marched in through the doors of the Court to arrest Veryan, along with the other four rebel Lords, and hold them on charges of treason pending the Emperor's return. Veryan did not go quietly. He hurled abuse and threats at Kempten all the way to the door, but holding his proud stance in the speaker's podium, Lord Kempten did not rise to any of it. With his initial point made, Kempten relaxed. The Court had not exploded into chaos at the sight of the arrests, so he felt confident they would give audience to what he had to tell them.

From a balcony high on the wall of the huge Courtroom, Lady Kempten watched with pride as her husband began his address.

'Ladies and gentlemen, let me tell you what I've learned of Emperor Surabar . . .'

'Mantor, Imperial Majesty. Quite something, isn't it?'

Surabar looked across the valley at the city upon the hill and could not help but be impressed. Whoever had chosen the site had possessed a keen appreciation of beauty. The tiered capital with its golden-yellow walls gleaming in the sunlight made a picturesque sight, though its designer had clearly considered the defensive qualities of the position as well. For centuries Mantor had stood untouched by assault. Intelligence on recent conflicts suggested that those shimmering walls had withstood an assault by an overwhelming force of Terachite nomads. Looking across the valley, the Emperor did not find that difficult to believe.

As a general, Surabar could well appreciate the defensive advantages of such a hilltop city. Shandar's capital, Shandrim, had no such advantages. It was no more than a few months ago that Surabar had considered in detail what sort of force it would take to sack his home city. It was an interesting exercise in military planning and strategy, and Surabar had always possessed a keen interest in such things. Thinking back on his conclusions was depressing. If he were faced with a choice of cities to defend, he would take Mantor over Shandrim without hesitation.

Rumour and conjecture also abounded about the Shandese invasion force that had entered Thrandor. This force was also sent with a view to taking Mantor, but it was said the Legions never came close to the Thrandorian capital. The rumours Surabar had heard from Shandar's troops spoke of a Sorcerer's deception. It was said they were fooled into attacking a city named Kortag many leagues to the south. Surabar had hoped Femke would discover the true fate of that army, but unless she was cleared of her involvement in the murders at the Palace he would be forced to look to other sources. He hoped to discover the truth soon.

'It's an impressive sight,' Surabar agreed. 'Come, let's go and meet the ruler of this land and see if I can restore a neighbourly relationship with him.'

The ride down into the valley and back up to the gates of Mantor did not take long. Surabar rode in silence the whole way, soaking up the detail, his head in constant motion as he assessed and reassessed how he would mount a campaign against such a place. Not all of his thoughts were on military strategy. He also noted the huge amount of effort being expended in rebuilding a large settlement in the base of the valley. Many buildings had been destroyed by fire, presumably torched by the Terachite nomads during their assault the previous year.

A huge amount of rebuilding had been completed during the intervening months, but Surabar wondered why there appeared no effort to make the new buildings more defendable than the previous ones. The King of Thrandor obviously did not expect any more ravening armies at his door in the immediate future, though he would have done better to look further ahead and build less vulnerable houses for the next generations.

But who am I to mock the wisdom of the King of Thrandor? Surabar thought wryly as he considered his observations. I've been Emperor little more than a month and here I am questioning the actions of someone who has been King of his country for decades. Then again, I've been Commander of a Legion for as long as Malo has ruled here. I don't know much about diplomacy, or the welfare of a nation, but I do know about defences and about military matters in general. If I were King of this country, I would not bow to public pressure on this issue. He's wasting resources for the sake of sentimentality by rebuilding there.

As Surabar's party approached, the huge city gates split

open and a substantial number of mounted Thrandorian soldiers rode out to meet them. The Thrandorian cavalry wheeled with impressive speed and within a minute were lined up in a defensive formation in front of the gates. Emperor Surabar raised his hand and his group of two-dozen riders halted, deliberately maintaining their travelling column formation to avoid unnecessary confrontation.

A single rider dressed in the black and silver uniform of the Thrandorian Royal Guard rode out to meet the column. The guard's horse pranced forwards with proud steps to halt a few yards in front of the Emperor. The soldier wore the knots of a captain on his shoulder. Surabar smiled as he noted the Captain's wary expression.

'His Majesty, the King of Thrandor, sends greetings to Surabar, Emperor of Shandar. Your Imperial Majesty, you and your men are welcome to ascend to the Palace, but due to recent events the King insists that you are escorted through the city. A certain amount of racial hostility has built within Mantor. King Malo does not want to allow matters between our nations to worsen through lack of simple precautions against potential troublemakers.'

'Your King is most wise,' Surabar replied. 'We will be honoured by your escort, Captain. Lead on.'

The Captain bowed in his saddle and turned to lead the way into the city. Surabar gave the signal to the Shandese party to follow. Once again the Thrandorian cavalry reacted to the approaching column with precision and discipline, first forming a front guard and then falling in alongside and behind the visitors in a fine display of organised riding.

If they fight as well as they drill, then it is no wonder the

Legions found them a formidable enemy, Surabar reflected as he passed under the arch of the gateway and into Mantor. The big questions that remain are: what sort of reception awaits at the Palace; and what has happened to Femke, Danar and the others?

As he passed into the city, the Emperor could not help feeling like a rabbit walking into a fox's den.

Reynik, together with Kalheen, Phagen and Sidis arrived at the Royal Court under escort and were taken to seats on the front row. The guards who accompanied them in took up post nearby. Whether this was to guard them as hostiles or to protect them was not obvious. Either way the King's personal protection force was adopting a vigilant stance. Reynik was tense. So many things could go wrong here. The plan Femke had concocted was risky in the extreme, but they had been left with few options.

The Royal Court was a large rectangular hall with tiered seating, which had been built in a three-quarter oval shape. The King's throne was flat to the back wall facing the main entrance, giving a focal point for the seating, which had been constructed to curve around the corners of the room. This gave the room a feeling of roundness at odds with the actual shape of the walls. The amphitheatre-style seating was built so that the top levels of seating were about two-thirds of the way up the high walls and a line of half a dozen windows on either side allowed natural light to supplement the three great torchlight chandeliers hanging from the central beam of the roof.

The King's throne had been shifted sideways today, and a

second throne, equally as magnificent, if slightly less raised, had been erected to the right of King Malo's. This was a sight that had not been seen in Thrandor in living memory.

As people filed in and shuffled to their seats, Reynik scanned the faces carefully. The Courtroom had been half full before he arrived, so Shalidar could be anywhere. At the same time, he made an assessment of the disposition of the guards and the various avenues of escape from the Royal Court. There were more potential exit points than he cared for. He could not cover them all – particularly as the escort guards were likely to delay him if he tried to move. However, the positioning of the guards brought some comfort.

Reynik and Femke had already checked the windows on both sides of the Court. The ones to the left-hand side opened above a clear drop of some twenty feet or more. The windows to the right, however, opened above the lower rooftops of another part of the Palace and provided a potential escape route for anyone trying to leave the Court in a hurry.

Reynik was pleased to see several Royal Guards positioned by the windows on the right-hand side, but was not overly confident in their abilities. It was unfortunate that unseasonably warm weather necessitated all of the upper windows to be kept wide open. He knew what Shalidar was capable of and he knew the skill levels of the average guards. If pressed, the assassin would cut through them like a scythe on harvest day. Guards were better than no guards, but Reynik would have given much to have a few Imperial Legionnaires, or spies, in strategic positions.

If only Ennas had managed to escape, he thought wistfully. One more really capable ally would have made a huge difference.

When Shalidar entered, he glanced casually across at Reynik and his companions. At first, Reynik thought the assassin was looking specifically at him, but then it became apparent that he was looking at someone else. Glancing around, Reynik noted the recognition in Kalheen's expression with interest, as the servant locked eyes briefly with the assassin. Shalidar did not let the glance linger. The assassin chose to climb high up the tiered seating on the right-hand side of the Courtroom. True to his nature, he was maintaining a valid escape route.

Reynik had felt from the beginning that the window escape route was their plan's greatest weakness. Femke had insisted the main door would be Shalidar's preferred exit point. The corridor system outside was a maze, which would help generate confusion amongst searchers. Femke had felt he would prefer this to the open rooftops. Reynik had deferred, as this was her area of expertise and her plan. Once again, though, the assassin had proved he was not easy to second guess. Reynik's fear had been realised.

Nothing could be done now. As far as the Courtroom could see, Reynik was being guarded. He would not move until the critical moment.

As Femke would most likely be chained, it would be down to Reynik to see that Shalidar did not leave the Courtroom once the action started. Not an easy task from here, he decided grimly.

The Royal Court soon filled to bursting point and the

temperature in the room soared. Everyone had pulled strings to get a seat at today's trial. Excited voices around the tiered seating crackled with anticipation. Today's events would be written into the annals of history. There were no records of the rulers of Thrandor and Shandar holding Court together. The fact they did so today to hear the case against the Ambassador of Shandar made the occasion all the more tantalising to the spectators.

Shandar was the larger and more powerful nation. In theory, this made Surabar, ruler of the Shandese Empire, eligible to assume the position of Judge. However, by all accounts Emperor Surabar had waived this option. General consensus held this as a sound political move. This was Mantor, capital of Thrandor. It was two Thrandorian Noblemen who had been murdered. Therefore, in the minds of the Thrandorian people present it was right that today was to be a Thrandorian trial. Everyone agreed that despite Emperor Surabar's magnanimous gesture, it would be fascinating to see how King Malo handled the delicate politics of the situation.

The conversations going on around Reynik were easily overheard. He kept his eyes firmly fixed on Shalidar, but his ears filtered through nearby chat with great interest.

'Malo'll bow and scrape to Surabar. I'd bet my last copper sennuts on it,' said one voice from behind him.

'He can hardly give the death sentence to the Ambassador with the Shandese Emperor sitting a couple of feet away, can he?' asked another.

'Oh, I wouldn't be so sure,' countered a third. 'Malo is quiet, but he can be pretty determined when he puts his mind to it. If he orders the death sentence, there'll be little Surabar can do about it, short of declaring war.'

'Who's to say he won't?' said the first voice.

'There's not much danger of any more wars for a while after the way we destroyed their Legions down at Kortag.'

'We, Merris? I didn't know you were there!'

'Well, I wasn't there, but . . .'

The conversation rattled on. Everyone claimed to have some sort of inside knowledge about what would happen today, but few had any real information. Speculation ran rife. The one thing everyone was able to agree on was that, aside from the battle against the nomads, the trial was the most interesting thing to happen in Mantor for years.

Reynik felt beads of sweat begin to trickle down his brow. The temperature in the Courtroom was rising, but his perspiration was generated as much by his intense concentration as by the heat. All the seats in the Courtroom were full now. Shalidar had not made any last-minute seat changes and Reynik was racking his brain for ideas on how to get within striking distance quickly.

Suddenly a double line of trumpeters filed into the Courtroom right in front of Reynik. With precision worthy of any elite military unit they formed a line, raised their trumpets and blasted out a fanfare that momentarily increased the buzz of expectation before washing it away to silence. All got to their feet and fell silent for the entrance of the King and the Emperor.

King Malo and Emperor Surabar stepped in side by side. Again the trumpeters moved with admirable precision to form an honour guard formation. The two rulers moved between them at a stately pace. As they passed between each pair of trumpeters, the men turned smartly through ninety degrees and marched out of the door.

Emperor Surabar climbed up onto the dais and sat down on his throne, arranging his heavy Mantle as he did so. Reynik could not help wondering how Surabar could stand wearing it in such oppressive heat, but he knew that the former General would never sidestep a duty.

King Malo reached his throne a moment later and turned to face the Royal Court. He took his seat and, with a rumbling that lasted several seconds, everyone else around the Courtroom sat down in turn. Once the last person was seated a breathless silence settled over the hall. The King took a few seconds to look around at the sea of faces waiting expectantly for him to speak before drawing a deep breath.

'Lords and Ladies of the Royal Court, it is my privilege today to welcome his Imperial Majesty, Surabar, Emperor of Shandar, to my Courtroom. I consider it an honour to have him sit next to me here in Mantor. I expect members of my Court to offer both Emperor Surabar, and his men, every respect due them during their stay here in Mantor. The Emperor was not in power during the recent violation of Thrandorian borders by the Legions and none of the men with him here in Mantor were involved with the events surrounding that unfortunate episode. Let us therefore use the opportunity afforded to us by this visit to welcome the newly invested Emperor and work to mend relationships between our two peoples.'

The King paused for a moment to allow his words a

chance to be digested. It was a predictable opening, but now came the difficult part.

'Emperor Surabar and I have found much common ground already in our brief conference together earlier today. We are both saddened that it has taken the violence of two brutal murders to bring about today's meeting. The further discovery of a third murder, two days ago, this time of the new Shandese Ambassador, Lord Danar, has made Emperor Surabar and I of one accord in wanting to see the killer brought to justice. Today's trial will allow the Court to hear the evidence brought against the original Shandese Ambassador, Lady Femke, and when the hearing is complete I will make a judgement based upon that evidence.' Suddenly, King Malo's voice turned harder and more determined. 'I will make it quite clear to you, as I have already done to Emperor Surabar – justice *will* be done today.'

A few spontaneous cheers sounded from various parts of the Courtroom along with a smatter of clapping. Mostly, however, there was an aura of shocked surprise; the Court had not expected King Malo to express his feelings so firmly in the presence of the Emperor. Malo held up his right hand for quiet and all voices fell silent.

'Let it not be said that my Court does not hear a fair trial. We will hear all the evidence from both the prosecution, brought by Lord Brenden, and from the defence, brought by Commander Sateris of the Shandese Elite Legion who has accompanied the Emperor here specifically for this purpose. Bring in the accused.'

At the order, the main doors were swung open again

and four Royal Guards marched into the Courtroom with the dispirited figure of Femke shuffling along between them. Many present were surprised at her appearance. The Ambassador was dressed in clothes befitting a female Ambassador, but her hair had been cut as short as that of the soldiers around her. Femke's hands and feet were manacled. Her head was down and her shoulders were slumped. There was little of the fire in her that had been widely rumoured. She certainly did not look like a vicious killer.

The guards marched Femke forward to a point about five paces in front of King Malo's throne. There they stopped and held their relative positions.

'Thank you, men. You may remove the prisoner's manacles. I don't believe Ambassador Femke poses a threat with so many guards present.'

Femke raised her eyes to the King for a moment and gave him a look that expressed gratitude for an un-expected favour. The guards looked less than impressed by the order. Reluctantly they complied. The manacles were removed from Femke's limbs and she rubbed at her wrists gently. Red weals were clearly evident where the metal had rubbed and Reynik noticed several people in the audience unconsciously rubbing their own wrists in sympathy.

'Good. That's better. Now, I think we're ready to begin,' Malo stated with a positive edge to his voice. 'Ambassador Femke, you have been brought before the Royal Court of Thrandor to answer the accusations that you did murder first, Baron Anton, and second, Count Dreban. How do you plead?'

There was a pause. Reynik concentrated hard on the expression upon Shalidar's face as he waited to hear her response.

'Not guilty on both counts, your Majesty,' Femke said loudly and clearly.

A look of anger and disappointment flashed across Shalidar's face. Despite sitting some distance away, Reynik saw the emotions quite clearly. Once the initial wave of anger had passed, though, the assassin raised his eyebrows slightly in a fashion that spoke of resignation and curiosity. Then the moment passed. Shalidar returned to concentrating on what was happening in the centre of the Courtroom.

'Very well. The Court shall take note Ambassador Femke denies the charges levelled against her. Lord Brenden, you may begin your opening statement for the prosecution.'

The King settled back in his throne and tried to clear his mind of all prejudice. Regardless of what he had agreed with Femke about today's trial, he was determined to listen to the presentation of evidence, for the young woman's life would be lived or lost through his interpretation of the information he was about to hear. If ever he needed clear powers of reasoning, it was now. There were a lot of unanswered questions that continued to nag him. When Femke had volunteered to be tried for the murders, she had insisted all his questions would be answered today. He hoped she was right.

Lord Brenden got to his feet and approached the dais. He bowed first to Malo, then to Surabar, before unrolling a sheaf of parchments and turning to read it to the Court.

Brenden had been well chosen. He had a clear,

penetrating voice filled with colour and passion. He made the words on the parchment, which detailed the events of several weeks before, when Baron Anton and Count Dreban had both lost their lives, come alive with his wide variety of pitch and intonation. Lord Brenden was a born storyteller. He had that rare talent which allowed him to transport the listeners' minds to wherever and whenever he wished to take them with his oration. So skilled was he in the art that even Reynik found he was picturing Femke creeping through the corridors of the Royal Palace to kill the Baron.

Everyone was swept into the vision of her struggling with Anton and plunging her knife deep into his heart, whilst the Baron, with his dying breath, tore her brooch unnoticed from her dress. Then came an account of her spectacular escape from the Palace, displaying skills no true Ambassador would possess as she traversed narrow ledges, made a death-defying leap into a tree and scaled the sheer Palace wall. Lord Brenden paused for a moment and swept his gaze around the Courtroom, as if to confirm his hypnotic story had gained a full hold.

'Then,' he said, pausing again to heighten the drama, 'then, the Ambassador used her assassin's skills to elude a huge force of Royal Guards sent to comb the city for her. Initially, it was thought she was simply hiding. She was not. Instead, she used her murderous talents to cause more mayhem. Ambassador Femke killed Count Dreban at his home that very afternoon, showing such contempt for our investigative skills that she committed the crime with an identical knife to the one with which she killed Baron

Anton. The knife was not recovered from the scene, but medical witnesses will swear the mortal wounds dealt to both Anton and Dreban were made with weapons of *precisely* the same shape and size.'

Reynik almost had to pinch his arm at the end of Lord Brenden's opening speech to ensure he was not having a bad dream.

Then it was the turn of Commander Sateris to give the opening statement for the defence. The contrast between the two advocates was stark. Where Brenden was melodious and hypnotic, Sateris was clear, crisp and to the point. He was the epitome of military precision with his short, sharp statements and his concise, calculated response to the prosecution's dramatic accusations. He spoke with authority, but without passion. He pointed out that the vast majority of what the Court had heard from the prosecutor was conjecture and reconstruction based on a thin line of material evidence, which would not hold up to intense scrutiny. He promised to raise questions in the minds of those who believed in the fairytale approach of the prosecution and to prove there was, in fact, little doubt Ambassador Femke was an innocent victim of someone determined to frame her.

Once the opening speeches were complete, the serious business of presenting evidence and calling witnesses began. Lord Brenden began for the prosecution by questioning Femke in broad terms about the circumstances surrounding each of the murders.

'Lady Femke, can you tell the Court where you were on the night that Baron Anton was murdered?'

'Yes,' Femke replied softly. 'I was here in the Palace. Asleep in my bed.'

'Here in the Palace, asleep in your bed,' Brenden repeated at a much louder volume, ensuring those at the back of the hall could hear. 'And where were you when Count Dreban was murdered?'

'I was locked in his cellar.'

'Locked in Baron Dreban's cellar?'

'Yes.'

'Very well, what about two days ago, at the time of Lord Danar's death? Where were you then?' Lord Brenden asked, his voice giving the impression he already knew the answer.

'I was here in the Palace, disguised as a servant,' Femke admitted, bringing a gasp from some around the Courtroom. Not many knew Femke had broken free from the Royal Dungeon, much less that she had been found again here in the Palace.

'So you were here in the Palace on the night of Baron Anton's death with no alibi. You maintain you were locked in Count Dreban's cellar at the time of his death, presumably alone, and therefore again with no alibi. Also, you happened to be in the Palace at the time of Lord Danar's death. Would I be too far from the mark if I were to assume that once again you have no alibi?'

Femke did not answer aloud. Instead she simply shook her head slightly.

'That is an unfortunate coincidence, Lady Femke. You happen to be in the vicinity of three murders with no alibi for any of them. Don't you think this a little unlikely?'

346

Femke shrugged and did her best to look disinterested.

'It appears not. Well, Lady Femke, I wonder if you can identify this knife for me?'

Lord Brenden reached down into a cloth bag at his feet and pulled out one of her set of knives: blades which she knew had been used for two of the murders.

'Yes, my Lord, it is mine.'

'Let the Court record Lady Femke identified the weapon used to murder Baron Anton as her own,' Brenden stated loudly, his voice almost purring at having gained the admission. It was a damning fact. 'Does it surprise you, Lady Femke, that a blade of identical dimensions to this one was used to kill Count Dreban?'

'Not at all, Lord Brenden. I saw the blade. It was also one of mine.'

'You saw the blade? It was yours?' This time, Brenden's voice was verging on incredulous as the admission came out. He had clearly not expected her to confess to this. A pleased smile flashed across his face for a moment as he realised she had strengthened his case further.

'Yes, my Lord,' Femke confirmed. 'The weapon was not found because I saw it, and removed it. I realised how damning it would be for someone to find a second one of my knives buried in a dead Nobleman. It made good sense for me to take it.'

Lord Brenden took a breath and paused for a moment to allow what Femke had said to sink in.

'If you removed it to hide the evidence, then why admit to it now? Nobody could have categorically proved Dreban's wound had come specifically from one of your knives.'

Femke looked Lord Brenden straight in the eye as she answered that question.

'I admit it because the fact will make little difference to the outcome of this trial, my Lord. I've been framed with these murders. I am aware of the weight of evidence against me. It is huge. Indeed, the evidence is so great that I must be the most incompetent killer in history to have left such a mass of clues behind me. It is clear to me that if I cannot prove someone set me up, then I am as good as dead. You see, Lord Brenden, I am not a bumbling idiot of a criminal. I did not come to Thrandor to kill, and I have not done so. However, someone wishes you and the rest of those present today to believe this is the case, so go ahead and present the rest of the evidence. I'm sure it will be damning in the extreme.'

Commander Sateris smiled wryly at Femke's answer. She knew the line his defence would take and had set up the criteria for his reply to the prosecution with perfect timing. There were few in the Court now who would see her as anything but a sharp-witted young woman, given the eloquence of her answer.

Lord Brenden continued his presentation of evidence, offering up the brooch found in Baron Anton's hand. Again, Femke clearly identified it as hers. He then brought witnesses who had been involved in chasing her when she had fled the Palace. His final witness was one that Femke did not expect.

'Prosecution calls Kalheen, servant of Ambassador Femke,' Brenden announced.

Judging by his expression, Kalheen had not expected the

call either. He rose and was escorted forward to take position in front of the throne.

'Kalheen, did you see the Ambassador on the morning after the death of Baron Anton?'

'Yes, my Lord.'

'And was the Ambassador different in any way when you saw her?'

'Well, no my Lord, but . . .'

'But? But what, Kalheen?' Brenden asked pointedly.

Kalheen looked first at Femke and then up at Emperor Surabar. 'I'm sorry, your Majesty,' he said nervously. 'I can't lie here.'

'Lie about what, Kalheen? Has someone asked you to lie?' Brenden asked, pouncing on the word like a cat on its unsuspecting prey.

There was a hushed expectancy as everyone leaned forward to hear Kalheen's answer.

'No, my Lord, no one has asked me to lie about anything. It's just . . . well . . . Ambassador Femke is not a normal Ambassador, my Lord. I don't know for certain, but the more I've thought about it since the murders, the more I've found myself wondering exactly what she does do. I've worked in the Imperial Palace a long time and I've noticed her there before, my Lord, but she is not always dressed as an Ambassador.'

A wave of gasps swept the Courtroom. Reynik looked up at Shalidar. The assassin was making no effort to conceal his smile.

'What then, in your opinion, is Femke's other profession, Kalheen? A spy – or an assassin?'

349

'Objection, your Majesty,' Sateris interrupted. 'Prosecution is leading the witness.'

'Overruled. I want to hear the answer, Commander,' King Malo replied firmly.

Kalheen looked at the Emperor apologetically as he answered. 'Either is possible, my Lord,' he said.

Lord Brenden dismissed Kalheen, all but preening as he continued. The servant's information had opened the floodgates. With the line open, Brenden piled suspicion on accusation over the question of Femke's character and raised questions about the nature of her true purpose here in Mantor. He posed the rhetorical question 'Why would an innocent person run?' which he then answered by stating his belief that they would not.

There was more and it went on for some time. Reynik was amazed Emperor Surabar was looking so calm. He did not know Femke's plan and the prosecution had in all but clear statement accused him of sending Femke to cause this diplomatic mess. Maybe he was going to allow her to take the fall and deny all knowledge of her mission here. If so, then taking the Mantle had changed the General. The Surabar that Reynik had heard about from his father and uncle would never have sacrificed one of his troops in such a way.

Commander Sateris, when he finally got a chance to speak, did so clearly and succinctly. His first move was to call Phagen as a witness.

'Phagen, if you had to describe Kalheen as a person, would you say he was an honest person?' Sateris asked.

'Yes,' Phagen replied quietly.

'Louder, please, so that everyone can hear you.'

'Yes. Kalheen is honest.'

Reynik gritted his teeth at both the question and the answer. Where is Sateris going with this? he wondered.

'So, you would not say Kalheen is prone to making things up?'

'No.'

'That's interesting,' Sateris observed. 'My information about Kalheen leads me to believe that he likes storytelling nearly as much as Lord Brenden here.'

Sniggers sounded around the galleries. Brenden looked irritated, but said nothing.

'Kalheen likes to tell stories, but he doesn't lie,' Phagen said, reddening with embarrassment.

'So he never exaggerates? He never stretches the truth to improve his stories?' Sateris fired the questions like crossbow bolts.

'Well, yes, he embellishes his stories, but . . .'

'I think I get the idea. Thank you, Phagen. You're dismissed.'

Reynik felt like applauding. By the expression on Emperor Surabar's face, Reynik guessed he did too.

He had destroyed Kalheen's credibility as a witness in just a few sentences. Having done so, Sateris did not play on emotion. He used simple logic. He presented Femke as an intelligent and highly capable young woman who had risen quickly to the position of Ambassador through ability, personality and trustworthiness. He questioned the lack of motive for the killings and pointed out that many people were present in the Palace during the times of the

351

murder of both Baron Anton and Lord Danar. Lady Femke's presence did not mean she had wielded the knife to kill Anton, nor the poison that killed Danar. He stated that because Femke had been placed at the scenes of all the murders actually lent more weight to the conspiracy theory. Finally, he told of the budding relationship between Femke and Danar and questioned her closely about it.

Femke answered as honestly as she could. Tears flowed freely from her eyes as she spoke of him, though she did not volunteer information about his involvement in breaking her out of prison, nor of the raiding of the Treasury. There were some around the Courtroom who muttered about staged theatrics, but a few were touched by the apparent honesty of her answers and her outward distress at the death of her fellow Ambassador.

When Commander Sateris moved to sit back in his seat, the King asked him if he had any witnesses to call. The Commander started to shake his head when Femke stopped him by interrupting in a loud voice.

'Yes, your Majesty. Defence calls Alchemist Pennold.'

CHAPTER SEVENTEEN

Lord Brenden frowned and shot a disapproving look across at Commander Sateris for introducing an unexpected witness for the defence at the last second. If Sateris knew anything about this announcement by Femke, then he was doing a good job of not letting it show. At present, the defence advocate looked about as much in the dark about what was going on as the prosecutor did. He was drilling a furious look into Femke.

'Your Majesty, I know it is unusual for the defendant to call a witness, but I beg your indulgence,' Femke added, hoping the King would keep his part of their secret bargain. He did.

'Very well, Femke, you shall have your witness. Bring in Alchemist Pennold.'

The doors opened and a curiously dressed old man with wild, silver hair entered with a tottering gait. His hair was sticking up in random clumps around his scalp and although he was clean-shaven, his face had an air of scruffiness about it. Mismatched colours competed with stains and burn marks on his clothing. Pennold had either not thought to dress smartly for his visit to the Palace, or he had no presentable clothes to wear. Either way, seeing the old man was like a breath of fresh air to Femke. His entrance brought a fond smile to her face. He wandered forward, obviously awestruck by his surroundings and shouldering a cloth sack with something heavy inside its folds.

'Master Pennold, did you bring the rock as I requested?' Femke enquired of the old man as he approached.

'What? Oh, the rock! Yes, yes, naturally, my dear,' he answered absently. 'Hardly would have been much point in my coming along otherwise, would there?'

'Excellent! Now, Master Pennold, if you could put the rock over there in the middle of the Courtroom please. Thank you so much. Your Majesty, I'm afraid that before you make your final judgement as to my guilt with regard to the three murders, I must first ask that another crime be taken into consideration.'

Mutterings swept around the hall. What was she about to confess to? Another murder? The King raised his right hand and silence fell.

'Go ahead, Femke. What is this crime, and what was your part in it? I'm sure I'm not alone in being fascinated to hear your answer.'

Femke had seen Reynik as she had entered the hall and had caught his signal as to the location of Shalidar within the Courtroom. Reynik had placed his right hand on his right shoulder as she had entered, telling her that the

354

assassin was high up on the right side of the Courtroom –
the last place that Femke had wanted him to be. He was a
long way from where Pennold was placing the rock. Despite
the alchemist's assurances that the rock's properties would
manifest perfectly well anywhere in a room of this size,
she felt nervous. If this did not work, then she was going
to look the fool in front of the entire Thrandorian
Royal Court, together with her own Emperor. If her
strategy failed she would be convicted of three murders.
Whilst Commander Sateris had done an admirable job of
presenting her defence, he was fighting an uphill battle
against a damning tide of evidence. If she were in King
Malo's position, Femke knew what her verdict would be.

'Your Majesty, I'm not sure if the raid on your Royal
Treasury is common knowledge amongst the members of
your Royal Court, but it was I, together with Lord Danar,
who carried out that raid.'

There were a few gasps from around the Court. A low
hum of angry muttering swelled briefly.

'I kept the incident quiet to give my security people a
chance to investigate,' the King answered, his voice stern
with disapproval. 'However, as the investigation appears
no longer necessary, I shall be most interested to hear why
you chose to do me the disservice of stealing my gold.'

'Well, your Majesty, I'd hate you to think we stole your
money for personal gain. Unfortunately, in order to prove
my innocence I needed to lay my hands on rather a lot of
money. Far more money than I, or any normal person, was
likely to have at my disposal. As most Royal Treasuries
contain lots of gold, and it was to you I needed to prove my

innocence, I decided it was not unreasonable to borrow some for a while.'

Most of the audience was silently shocked by Femke's impertinence, but a few, including Lord Brenden, who suddenly started coughing into his hands to hide his smile, saw the funny side of it. There was a twisted sort of logic to Femke's reasoning so far, but she was doing her case few favours with the manner of her presentation.

'And for what possible reason could you want all that gold, Ambassador Femke? Most good alibis would settle for a lot less.'

Femke smiled and nodded her head in acknowledgement of the King's riposte.

'True, your Majesty, but we did not need the money for an alibi – quite the opposite. We needed the money to hire the best assassin I know. His services have never been cheap, but I wanted enough money to entice him into attempting a hit at short notice. I knew from early on during this sad series of events that this particular assassin was behind the killings. He told me as much in person on the night after Count Dreban's murder. That confession would never hold up in this Court, for there were no witnesses present and it would be my word against his. His alibis for the times of the two murders were watertight, with eminent Thrandorians willing to testify to his whereabouts at the approximate times of both deaths. Also, he claimed both kills had been paid for. I did not realise how he had managed this until it was too late. I thought to prove to you he was a killer by catching him red-handed. Therefore, Danar and I set up what we thought was the perfect sting.'

'Your Majesty . . .' Lord Brenden protested, trying to stop the flow of Femke's story, as he recognised the looks from around the Court. Femke had everyone's absolute attention and people were beginning to get involved in her story. This was dangerous to his case. He knew the power of a well-told story better than most.

'Silence, Brenden, you had your chance. Let the Lady speak. Please, Femke, do continue. I assume, as Lord Danar died, something went wrong.'

'What went wrong, your Majesty, was that I didn't bargain on getting two assassins for the price of one. I had wrongly assumed all along that my adversary was personally responsible for killing the Baron and the Count. He was responsible all right, but he did not wield the knife on either occasion. He *commissioned* the kills. My miscalculation cost Lord Danar his life. I felt certain I could protect Danar from one, known assassin, but it never crossed my mind that the killer I was looking for would work in tandem with another.'

'So, you failed to protect Lord Danar from these killers, he was killed by them, and you failed in your attempt to catch them?' King Malo prompted.

'Not quite, your Majesty. My goal was to catch a killer red-handed and that is what I've done – in fact, I've caught two of them.'

'I'm sorry, Lady Femke. Your story is most interesting, but there's not a shred of it that has substantive evidence to back it up. Why should anyone believe you?'

'Well, your Majesty, you've not seen the *true* evidence yet. I will show you a link between the two killers that is undeniable. Whilst one's alibis are watertight, the other was not able to be so careful. I can demonstrate to the Court that the second man was perfectly placed, both to kill Baron Anton, and to frame me. Count Dreban's murder is more difficult to prove, but having established the first two links, I believe the rest of the story will fall into place quickly. Would you mind asking everyone in the Courtroom to hold their hands up with their palms forward at shoulder height, your Majesty, and you'll see what I mean.'

There was shuffling and murmuring around the hall as many people instinctively looked at their palms. Reynik noticed that Kalheen was particularly pale-faced and his palms were sweating. With a quick check to see that Shalidar was still in his seat, he prepared to move the instant he was required. It would happen soon and he did not want to let Femke down. If Kalheen made a move, he would not get more than a few feet.

King Malo saw no reason to deny Femke's request, so he ordered the Courtroom to comply. Reynik smiled as he noted the smug expression on Shalidar's face. That's one expression which won't last long, he thought with a tight grin.

When everyone had their palms up, the King looked around the room with a puzzled expression. 'I fail to see the meaning of this, Lady Femke. What relevance does it have to your story?'

'It is simply explained, your Majesty. The chances of my catching one assassin with bloodied knife in hand, so to speak, were remote. Even had I known there were two of them, for me to catch both would have been impossible. However, that was never my intention. The money was the key to my evidence, your Majesty. The gold held the answer. Alchemist Pennold here will testify that he provided me with a special substance with which I coated the gold – all of it. The rock in the middle of the Courtroom is emitting some sort of invisible rays that I don't pretend to understand, but they cause the substance to react when in direct line of sight. Anyone who has handled your gold will be affected, for it stains the skin with a coating that is virtually impossible to remove. Look now, your Majesty, and you will see the two killers, caught, as promised – red-handed.'

'Look – his hands are glowing red,' someone yelled. 'Stop him!'

Shalidar was already on the move. He had been sitting one row from the top of the tiered Courtroom. As soon as he realised his hands were beginning to announce him, he sprang to his feet and vaulted over the people behind to get to the windows. Reynik was poised to grab Kalheen, so he missed Shalidar's initial move. To his surprise it was not Kalheen's hands that began to glow, but Phagen's. Femke had confided her suspicion that it was one of their three companions who had to be the second killer, but she had not been able to determine whom. Reynik had been sure the other killer would prove to be Kalheen.

Phagen made his move a second or two after Shalidar. When he did, the assassin was incredibly quick. Reynik leaped to his feet to follow, but he had been caught off guard and Phagen managed to fell the two guards who had escorted the four Shandese men into the Courtroom before Reynik had a chance to react. Phagen's chances of escaping were slim. There were lots of guards between him and the door, but Reynik did not allow them their chance.

Diving forward, Reynik grabbed the slim man from behind, slamming into the assassin's legs in a spectacular tackle. Despite hitting the floor hard, Phagen twisted quickly and began to rain blows onto Reynik in rapid succession. Reynik reacted well, blocking the assassin's fists with lightning-fast reflexes of his own. The fight lasted but a moment. The four guards who had escorted Femke in swarmed over Phagen a couple of seconds later, pinning him to the floor. Once down against such odds, there was little chance of him getting up again until the guards had him bound and firmly under their control.

Kalheen was shocked to see Phagen run. He imagined what his mother would say when he told her he had unknowingly shared a room with a killer. The stout little seamstress with her flashing eyes and her stubborn manner had always berated him for his lack of attention to detail. She never appeared to miss anything. But then, he had always known that Rikala was an extraordinary woman.

With Phagen down, Femke looked up to the right-hand side of the Courtroom in time to see Shalidar despatch the second of the two guards posted to guard the windows. Silver flashed at his right wrist as he struck the final blow. He was getting away. There was no obvious path up to him through the sea of panicking people on the bench-style seats. Femke looked across to Reynik, who was still struggling to his feet. They were equally powerless to stop the assassin's escape. Scanning around the Courtroom for something to block Shalidar's getaway, Femke's eyes settled on the rope holding up the great central chandelier structure.

The thick rope stretched up from where it was secured to strong metal mountings on the wall next to the main door through pulleys on the ceiling to the right of the hall and across the ceiling to another pulley directly above the centre of the room. The huge metal structure looked enormously heavy. Femke saw instantly what she had to do and broke into a sprint towards the wall to the right of the main door.

'The rope, Reynik! Cut the rope!' she yelled, covering the ground quickly.

Reynik grasped her plan immediately and ran the couple of paces to the nearest guard. Before the guard knew what was happening, Reynik snatched the hilt of the guard's knife and drew it from its sheath.

'Hey!' the guard exclaimed. 'What do you think you're doing?'

'Just borrowing your knife for a moment,' Reynik called back, already in motion towards the mounting where the rope was fastened to the wall.

Femke leaped up from some distance away and her fingers grabbed for the rope. It was a great jump and her fingers connected with their target, gripping the rope firmly as her lower body swung through and collided heavily with the wall. Despite hitting it hard, Femke clung on to the rope and began to climb upwards, swinging hand over hand up the steep incline.

Reynik sprinted across the Courtroom, ignoring the uproar around him. Within seconds he was sawing at the rope with his newly acquired blade. Femke could feel every strand sever as Reynik sliced at the rope with gusto.

'Nearly there,' he warned. Femke stopped climbing and concentrated on hanging on. As the final few strands parted with a snap, the huge metal chandelier structure started to fall, drawing the rope up through the pulley system with a vicious lurch that threatened to yank her arms from their sockets. Femke's light frame hardly slowed the chandelier's descent at all. It accelerated rapidly to the ground, while she sailed through the air above the heads of the astonished courtiers and up towards the roof.

At the last possible moment, Femke let go of the rope. Her forward momentum carried her the last couple of yards over the top level of seating, but her landing was not so pretty. She crashed into the wall hard, partially winding herself. Shalidar was already disappearing through one of the windows, so there was no time to lose. With a discipline that few possess, Femke forced her chest to stop heaving and drove her shaken body to follow him.

The Courtroom was in turmoil at the spectacular turn of events, but Femke ignored it. Her focus was on stopping Shalidar. As she climbed nimbly through the window to give chase, she muttered, 'He must not get away. He must not get away,' repeatedly under her breath.

Shalidar, however, was no fool. He had lived life as an assassin too long not to have an escape route planned. No matter how angry he was with Femke, the killer was controlled enough not to be confused by anger. Shalidar concentrated on escape, bottling his rage with a savage professionalism.

He raced across the gently sloping roof, heading for the corner lowest to the ground. For once, luck was not with him. A patrol of Royal Guards out walking the Palace grounds spotted him as he approached the corner and called out.

'Hey! You up on the roof! Stop where you are. Don't move a muscle, or we'll have to shoot,' warned one of them in a loud voice.

Shalidar turned and ran back up the shallow slope, dodging and weaving to make it more difficult for the archers to pick him off. His twisting, stop-start run was effective. The patrol fired several bolts at him from their crossbows, but none of them marked him.

It was then that Shalidar noticed Femke closing in on him from the direction of the Courtroom. This was not the place to deal with her. The archers could get lucky and he did not want to give Femke the satisfaction of seeing him caught or killed. No. There were much better options. He had a split second to decide, but his choice fell with running to higher ground. Shalidar did not know how Femke felt about heights, but by leading her across the rooftops to higher surfaces, it would get him clear of the archers. Then, with a single push, he could dispose of Femke for ever.

Femke saw Shalidar register her approach and redoubled her efforts to close the gap between them. The next thing she knew crossbow bolts were ripping through the air around her. She instinctively broke the pattern of her stride and pace to disrupt the Royal Guards' aim, ducking and weaving as she ran. The patrol was also yelling at her to stand still now, but Femke was as unwilling to stop as Shalidar. The spy had no intention of letting the Royal Guards prevent her from avenging Danar. His death was too fresh in her heart. Shalidar had demonstrated a truly diabolical nature by his method of killing the young Shandese Lord, to say nothing of his cold-hearted co-ordination of the killings of Baron Anton and Count Dreban. He could not get away. Femke would not allow it. She did not want him to die because death offered too swift a resolution. She wanted him to suffer for his deeds. He had to be caught and she desperately wanted to be the one to catch him.

Shalidar scrambled up onto the adjoining rooftop and ran up the shallow slope to the peak. Femke chased after him. The assassin leaped fearlessly across gaps between rooftops. Femke did not hesitate to follow. The scrambling, running and jumping chase was spectacular but short, as Shalidar led Femke around the rooftops only to halt suddenly on the roof of the Great Hall at the front of the Palace. At the edge of the roof, overlooking the main gates, he stopped and turned. There was nowhere to run.

Femke slid to a stop a short way in front of him and looked at the assassin through narrowed eyes. It was not clear whether Shalidar had any weapons hidden about his person, but Femke was not about to take chances. The assassin was renowned to be as deadly with his hands as he was with weapons.

'End of the road, Shalidar. There's nowhere left to go.

Accept it. Give yourself up now,' Femke panted, glad to see Shalidar breathing as heavily as she was.

'Don't be a fool, Femke! The road never ends. Most people simply can't see well enough to interpret its twists and turns,' Shalidar replied, his voice rasping and scornful, his eyes filled with deadly intent. She could see Shalidar did not intend to go without a fight, and that suited Femke fine.

Padding forward lightly on the balls of her feet, Femke approached the assassin with her hands raised, ready to fight. Femke had hoped to face Shalidar with Reynik. The young soldier was an excellent fist fighter and without him at her side she could end up as dead as if the King had ordered her hanged for murder. But this way it was her choice. If Shalidar killed her, she would die in pursuit of justice and vengeance.

Femke circled warily. When Shalidar attacked it would be with every ounce of deadly strength and speed that he possessed. He knew no other way to fight. Femke felt ready. She was fast, agile and brimming with anger. She had never known a time when she had been so keyed up to fight.

'Finally we get to dance,' Femke said, calming her breathing and focusing on Shalidar's centre of balance. 'It's been a while coming. You've had the advantage over me ever since I arrived in Mantor. Getting Phagen into my little party was a masterstroke. It took me a long time to work out that one of them had to be involved. When I did, he was never top of my list of suspects. I can see it now, of course: the last minute addition to the mission due to a sudden illness, his quiet manner and his ability to fade into the background.

He's the perfect character to be an assassin, but why did you not have him kill me? Why the elaborate set-up here in Mantor? You said you wanted to start a war in order to increase business, but that doesn't ring true.'

All the time she was talking, Femke studied Shalidar's slow movements, looking for a weakness – any slight thing that could give her an edge.

'The "why" is simple,' Shalidar hissed. 'I wanted you to pay for your intervention in Shandrim. Everything was progressing nicely. Vallaine was infuriating, it's true. He was not the most stable of characters to work for, but I had allowed for that and was working towards replacing him with a suitably malleable successor – when you stepped in. I could have killed you at any stage, but that would not have been good enough. I didn't want to kill you. I wanted to destroy you. I wanted to strip you of everything you held dear. I had worked very hard over the previous year to set up my retirement plan. You ruined it. Now you've managed to threaten my legitimate business as well. In hindsight, I should have had you killed. But that is rectified easily enough.'

Shalidar sprang forward and struck at the middle of Femke's body with a vicious punch. Femke responded with a solid blocking manoeuvre that deflected his blow. With a twisting leap, she landed a stinging kick to the side of his face that sent him reeling. Femke moved to follow her kick with a series of punches and kicks, only to find each of them blocked, with some stunning counter punches flying back. Suddenly, Shalidar switched tactics. From nowhere he swept her feet out from under her and dealt her a kick that sent her rolling down the roof towards the edge.

It took a few rolls before Femke could stop her forward momentum. As she did so, she saw Shalidar closing in for the kill. Without hesitation and with a speed that took Shalidar completely by surprise, Femke managed to use his tactic against him. She twisted and swept the assassin's feet from under him as he approached. He landed heavily with a grunt. Using her supple agility to its limit, Femke twisted again and clamped her legs around Shalidar's neck and began to squeeze.

Where most would panic, Shalidar did not. He did not attempt to prise Femke's legs from their chokehold. He simply felt for the pressure points at the back of her knees and dug in his thumbs, with a force that caused Femke to cry out with pain and roll away.

Femke rolled into a crouched position a few feet from the edge of the roof and gently massaged the backs of her knees for a moment to lessen the pain. Shalidar in turn sat up and rubbed at his throat briefly before climbing to his feet. His face was set with an expression of cold fury.

Shalidar had the advantage over Femke in height, weight and reach. It was arguable who was the faster. The one area where Femke could claim an advantage was in her supple agility, but as she was already discovering, one slight advantage was not enough to make up for the areas where she was the weaker. Unless she could surprise him somehow, Shalidar would kill her.

The assassin was convinced now that he was the better fighter and he began to press home his advantage. He closed in on Femke. Another flurry of rapid punches and kicks followed, with Femke being forced to retreat, struggling hard to swing the fight away from the edge of the high rooftop.

A pedestrian passing by the main Palace Gates noticed the two fighting on the roof of the Great Hall and pointed it out to the guards on the gate. They called the Guard Captain, who sent runners to pass word to the King. The runners told everyone they passed, and before long there was a small crowd of Royal house staff running out in front of the Palace to see the spectacle.

Femke managed to spin under one of Shalidar's punches. She powered an elbow into his stomach, driving the hard point of bone as deep as she could, but she had no chance to follow up the slight success as the assassin whirled around and slammed his right foot into her side, once again sending her flying from her feet. Pain lanced through her chest as Femke rolled upright again. She coughed and instantly tasted blood in her mouth. Shalidar had broken at least one of her ribs.

As Femke looked up at him approaching her again, she noted the slightly smug expression. He knew the damage his last kick had done. By the look in his eyes, he was ready to finish the fight. Frantically looking around for anything that might help, Femke realised too late that Shalidar had closed the gap between them. He attacked again with a series of blindingly fast and powerful punches. Her blocks became progressively less effective. Shalidar landed several more blows in quick succession, driving Femke down onto her knees.

'Time to die,' he announced coldly, his breathy, whispering voice holding no emotion.

Femke had expected to hear triumph, or pleasure, but there was none of it. Her face felt swollen where he had landed several punches and was bleeding in a few places. Shalidar was also bloodied, but he looked fresh. Femke knew she had no chance of getting the better of him. He was simply too good and too strong.

Femke did not see the final kick coming. She did not roll with it at all. Her face suddenly snapped around, exploding with pain. Then she was rolling down the roof towards the edge. All coordination deserted her for a moment. As her body turned over and over, she could do nothing to reduce her momentum. Pain flooded her brain from every part of her body and a voice inside her willed her to go over the edge and end the agony. However, as her body approached the edge, Femke remembered Danar's final hour. He had not given up. He had trusted her and she had failed him. This was her one chance to redeem herself. She knew in that instant she could not give up.

Slapping her arms wide apart, Femke managed at the last moment to stop the rolling motion, but did so too late. Her body continued to slide, face-down over the edge of the roof. Somehow, with a desperate flailing, Femke grabbed one of the horizontal flagpoles from which the Royal Banners hung, and clung on to it with her right hand. She dangled precariously, hanging high above the great sweeping stone staircase that ran up to the front of the Palace. The stretching pain in her chest was unbearable, but she held on with every ounce of her will. With a supreme effort she managed to improve the situation by getting a hold with her left hand as well.

'Aren't you dead yet?' Shalidar's voice rasped from above her. Femke looked up and saw his cold eyes as he began to lift his foot to tread on her fingers and send her falling to her death. 'Goodbye, Femke, and good riddance,' he added flatly.

'Stop, Shalidar! Do it and you die too.'

Reynik's shout caused Shalidar to turn to assess the new threat. A young soldier was racing across the rooftop towards him, knife in hand. From the way he was holding the blade, Shalidar judged that his new opponent knew how to use it. He did not hesitate. The assassin knew when to fight and when to run. Without pause, he turned and ran along the edge of the rooftop, away from Reynik.

The young soldier's voice was heavenly to Femke and she realised that if he was quick, she might just be able to hang on long enough for him to help her. Her fingers were slipping over the smooth wood of the flagpole, but with a supreme effort, she hung on with all the strength she had left.

'Reynik!' she croaked, her voice weak from the pain in her chest.

Reynik was changing his course to follow the assassin when he heard the faint call for help. He did not hesitate. Although he desperately wanted to follow Shalidar, he knew instantly that he could not do it at the expense of Femke's life.

'Quickly,' she gurgled, her fingers slipping even further.

Spotting Femke's hands holding on to the flagpole, her fingers slipping, Reynik realised there was no time for a controlled rescue. With no care for his own safety, he cast aside his knife and launched into a dive towards the edge of the rooftop. Reynik's body landed hard, belly down, and he slid headfirst with alarming momentum towards the edge of the rooftop. For a moment he thought he had misjudged it and that they would both plummet to their deaths, but as his head and shoulders went over the edge of the roof, Reynik grabbed the pole to arrest his slide. His left hand and arm absorbed his momentum, whilst his right hand grabbed at Femke's wrist, just catching hold as her fingertips lost all purchase. The sudden weight lurching onto his right arm yanked so hard it threatened to pull his arm from its shoulder socket. He growled at the pain, but clung to her with iron resolve.

Looking down at the stone steps below, Reynik knew no one could survive a fall from this height. He could not speak. He was stretched to the limit, but one look at Femke told him words were unnecessary. She had passed out.

Inch by inch, he wormed his way back onto the roof until his right arm was holding Femke hard up against the wall. Then in a tremendous effort, he forced his body into a position where he could draw Femke up onto the rooftop without overbalancing. Her body was scraped as he pulled her over the edge, but it could not be helped. She was alive. That was enough.

Reynik did not have to look around to know Shalidar was long gone. It was over. He could only hope the Royal Guards had caught the assassin, but he knew that was a lot to wish for. Sitting on the rooftop with Femke lying back against him, Reynik felt exhausted.

Suddenly Femke coughed, regaining partial consciousness. A terrible spasm of pain tore at her side, bringing a fresh wash of blood to her mouth. It would be a shame to die now, she thought, feeling herself slipping back into the abyss. I would like to tell the Emperor the true story.

'Don't worry, Femke,' she heard Reynik saying softly in her ear. 'You'll be all right. Lie still. We'll get the medics up here soon. Hang in there, do you hear me? You can't leave me now. How am I going to explain this to the Emperor on my own? I'm a soldier for goodness' sake! You're the one with all the answers.'

Femke roused slightly at that.

'Naturally – I'm a woman,' she croaked.

Reynik laughed.

'That you are, Femke. Come on now. Concentrate on staying alive. Don't leave me, Femke. Stay. The Empire needs you. I need you. Stay.'

'Shalidar?' she whispered.

'Gone,' Reynik replied softly.

'Damn!' she breathed.

Reynik felt Femke's head relax and he realised she had lost consciousness again, but her breathing was steady and given her injuries she was better off that way. At least whilst she was unconscious she would not be aware of the pain. He cradled her head softly against his chest and rocked her gently.

Feelings of guilt and happiness washed through him. Guilt, because a secret little flame of joy had kindled in his heart that Femke was now free of any romantic entanglement. He had been attracted to her from the time they had left Shandrim, but at first he had judged her significantly older than he was and unattainable through status. Now he knew she was no more than two years his senior, which was not an insurmountable age gap. Also, she was a spy, rather than an Ambassador.

These truths had not surfaced until after the arrival of Lord Danar, so he had buried his feelings deep in deference to the Lord, who had seemed a vastly more appropriate suitor. Reynik had never been good at displaying his emotions. Maybe now he would get the chance to make his feelings known to her.

Sounds of feet approaching from behind caused him to smile. Royal Guards were coming. They would get Femke to the infirmary and he was sure she would be all right. The diplomatic mess would be sorted out. It was over – at least for now.

One fear remained. Shalidar. Reynik knew he had made an enemy of the assassin today. Shalidar was not one to forgive and forget.

'Well, Shalidar,' Reynik muttered under his breath. 'Neither am I.'

IMPERIAL ASSASSIN

by
Mark Robson

Declared outlaws by the Emperor, the Guild of
Assassins strikes back hard.

The Emperor must act fast. He needs someone to
infiltrate the Guild. All attempts to locate the assassins'
headquarters have failed. Femke is already known to
the assassins. So Reynik, the young legionnaire, must
penetrate their inner circle to discover the
Guild's secrets.

But secrets kept hidden for over five centuries
command a high price. Reynik is ready to risk his life,
but this mission may demand more – this could cost
him his soul.